Pasta Al Dente

Pasta Al Dente

A Novel

Mark Hartley

Ordering Information:
Quantity sales. Special discounts are available on quantity purchases by corporations, associations, and others. For details, contact the publisher at the address below.

Bratcher Publishing
P.O. Box 66
Chattaroy, WA 99003
www.bratcherpublishing.com
info@bratcherpublishing.com

Cover Copyright © 2017 Mark Hartley
Cover photo by: Custom CT Designs
Book cover design and production by: Gray Dog Press, Spokane, WA

Publisher's Cataloging-in-Publication data

ISBN-13: 978-1-946882-02-8
ISBN-10: 1-946882-02-X
Library of Congress Control Number: 2017941777

Printed in the United States of America

Dedication

To Shari who got it started. Tawana and the Liberty
Lake Writers Group who helped me finish it. Tina who
discovered it. And my wonderful wife, Roberta, who helped
me keep the whiole thing going.

San Jose, California 1955

"Momma, can I have—"

"No."

"Please," Matt whimpered.

"I said no."

"They're only a penny."

"Only a penny. Your dad works hard for every penny and I'm not wasting one cent on candy."

Together they moved in line to the counter. Mr. Acevedo, mustached and bald, greeted them.

"Yolanda, good to see you." He began ringing up the groceries. Matt watched as Acevedo pushed buttons and the numbers popped up in the cash register window. Half a gallon of milk – twenty-four cents. Tomato sauce – three cans for fifteen cents. Jiffy cake mix – ten cents. Numbers popped up and a bell rang for each of them.

"That'll be three dollars and twenty-four cents, Mrs. Connors." The grocer packed the items into two large paper bags. Carefully he placed the eggs on top.

"Out of five." He pressed a button and the cash register drawer popped out. Mr. Acevedo counted out the change. "And one makes five." Acevedo smiled, eyes twinkling, "And a Black Jack taffy for the boy."

"Goodie!" Matt's fingers stretched forth eagerly. "Taffy!" Acevedo leaned over the counter, the taffy tantalizingly close. "My favorite!"

Acevedo smiled.

"No thank you, Mr. Acevedo."

"Momma!"

"It's free, Mrs. Connors. I give some to all the kids."

"No thank you. I don't want him to have any candy."

"Just one, Momma?"

"I said no." That ended it.

"Sorry, kiddo." Acevedo straightened, sliding the two bags of groceries across the counter. "There you go, Yolanda. Say hello to your mother for me."

"Thank you, I will." She hefted the two bags. A grapefruit fell out. Matt picked it up and lifted it to his mother. She leaned over, spilling more grapefruit. Matt scurried after them, retrieving them where they lay.

"Here, Momma."

Yolanda stood up, replacing the bags on the counter. "I shouldn't buy so many grapefruit."

"Six for twenty-four cents. It's a good deal."

"I know—it's a good price." Hands on hips, she examined the bag, then she pulled out the carton of eggs. Taking the grapefruit from Matt, she repacked the bags. Satisfied, she picked them up and started to the door. Matt followed.

"Mrs. Connors," called Acevedo. Mom paused. "The eggs?"

She saw the eggs on the counter. After looking at both sacks, she glanced at her son. "Matt, carry the eggs."

He toddled to the counter. Mr. Acevedo handed Matt the eggs, and he clutched them to his chest. Conspiratorially, Acevedo slipped the boy a taffy. He waited.

Matt slipped the candy into his pocket.

"Matt, hurry up."

"Thanks, Mr. Acevedo."

"Anytime, kiddo. You're a good boy."

A good boy. Matt smiled.

"Get the door, Matt, and careful with those eggs."

He ran toward the door, using his full momentum and body weight to push open the door onto Willow Street.

Acevedo watched them go, unconsciously unwrapping a taffy and popping it in his mouth. Chewing, he shook his head. Cute kid, he thought. But the mom—beautiful but . . . what was the word he was looking for? Cold, maybe. Cold. Her smile never reached her eyes. Cold would do. He turned, slamming the cash register closed.

Aunt Rose's apartment was only one block from Acevedo's Grocery. Mother and son stopped at the stoplight. Yolanda shifted the two bags. Matt shifted the eggs he clutched to his chest. They slipped, catching on his vest. A grapefruit plopped down next to him.

"Get that, Matt."

He put the eggs down and grabbed the grapefruit. Mom bent forward and he put the grapefruit into the bag once again. Stepping back his heel hit the eggs, toppling them off the curb. As the light changed he picked them up and hurried after his mother.

They passed Sacred Heart School. Beyond the chain link fence uniformed children played kickball and hopscotch under the vigilant eyes of the black clad sisters. Matt watched them play wistfully.

"Come on, Matt."

He hurried to catch up, the egg carton slapping against the chain link fence as he went, past the granite steps of Sacred Heart Church. Gray-blue pigeons pecked at grains of rice from a recent wedding. He caught up with Mom at the next street corner, tapping shoes signaling impatience.

They crossed.

Matt stared up at the giant Midas Muffler Man on the corner, his smile as frozen as the gold muffler in his outstretched hands. On past the Italian restaurant, full of hanging glass bottles wrapped in baskets and cheeses wreathed in wax. Beyond the restaurant was the door to Aunt Rose's apartment. Juggling the bags carefully, Mom opened the door, they stepped in and the door slammed behind them.

Aunt Rose stepped out on the upstairs landing, wiping her hands on a dishtowel. "You remember the eggs?"

"Yes, Rose."

"Come on up. All I need is the egg for the cannoli." She disappeared back into the apartment. Mom began to climb.

Twenty-four steps. Twenty-four wooden steps, covered with a brown, threadbare runner. One hand on the rail, the other holding the eggs, Matt pulled the eggs up behind him. Step. Drag. Thump. Twenty-four stairs.

By the time he reached the top, Mom was in the apartment and Aunt Rose was pawing through the bags.

"Where are the eggs? You said you got the eggs."

"Matt has them, Rose."

Rose turned toward the boy. "Bring them here, Matty."

Proudly he climbed the last few steps, the gray carton held tight to his vest. Rose took the eggs, set them on the counter, and wiped her hands. "I think you broke one."

Matt looked crestfallen.

"You shouldn't have given him the eggs, Yolan."

Rose opened the carton. Eleven eggs were cracked and broken.

"I told you to be careful!" Yolanda slapped Matt full across the face, knocking him down.

"But, Momma—"

"Don't 'But, Momma' me. You broke all the eggs. All of them. Now I need to get more."

She exploded, grabbed a wooden spoon and began swinging.

"I told you,"—smack—"I told you to be careful."—smack—"You"—smack—"Broke all the eggs!"

"Yolanda!" Rose yelled. Mom composed herself, flicking back a stray lock of hair.

"I need more eggs," Rose said.

Mom slammed down the wooden spoon and stalked out.

Rose turned to the dish counter and began chopping almonds. After a few moments she looked down at the crying boy. "Skipper is on the back porch," she said, still chopping. "Why don't you go play with him?"

To the sound of more chopping, Matt got up. Slowly he pushed against the screen door.

"Don't let in flies," Rose yelled.

On the porch waited Skipper, a two-year-old cocker spaniel. Matt sagged against the door, sliding to a sitting position, welcoming Skipper. The dog pushed, squirmed and began licking Matt's face.

Matt reached into his pocket and slowly unwrapped the Black Jack Taffy. Biting it in two he shared it with the dog, then buried his face in her fur.

Chapter One

The lizard basked in the sunlight. Rising up on four legs, it bobbed up and down on the broken concrete slab, black eyes intently following the movement of a sow bug. Mouth gaping, it rocked back and forth anticipating an easy meal. Matt's movements were as measured and sure as those of the little lizard. Holding his breath, Matt's hand flashed out and grasped the thrashing lizard firmly and gently. His prey's body jackknifed back and forth, tail lashing, open mouth seeking something to bite.

"There you go," Matt whispered. "Look at you."

Holding up his prize, Matt examined the chocolate-brown lizard. Turning it upside down, Matt stroked the lizard's belly where pale white blended into a soft powder blue. He held the reptile to the sky comparing the colors. Identical. Matt smiled. The lizard's mouth yawned open aggressively.

A small avalanche of gravel and dirt announced the arrival of Fred, Matt's best friend. "Whatcha got?" Fred asked.

"A blue belly. Neatest lizard you can find."

"You like them better than alligator lizards?"

"Yeah. When alligator lizards bite, you can feel it," Matt said. "Besides, even though they are small, blue bellies have a kind of—I don't know—nobility about them. Alligator lizards are just big fat slugs."

"My brother thinks they look like dog turds." Both boys broke out laughing.

"They do. They really do. Big, fat, mean dog turds."

"Whatcha gonna do with him?" Fred asked.

"Bring it to school. I'm making a terrarium for science. I'll put him in with those tree frogs I caught yesterday. Sister Angelica wanted several examples of what we can find in our backyard in the terrarium."

"You should throw in a crawdad," Fred suggested.

"Nope. They would eat the minnows."

"Minnows?"

"Yeah, I'm going to put a cottage cheese container in the terrarium for a pond. Already got the minnows," he said.

"That ought to impress those ol' nuns of yours." Fred reached into his pocket. "Look what I got!" He pulled out a brand-new slingshot.

"Wow!" Matt said. Fred handed him the slingshot. "Where did you get this? It's a beaut."

"My dad bought it. At Sears, I think. It's a hunting slingshot," Fred said. "Look. It even has a sight."

Matt examined it longingly. The bright metal holder and rubber tubing was a far cry from the one he had built from a tree branch and strips of inner tube. "You got yours?" Fred asked.

"Sure."

Matt returned the new slingshot to his friend. Picking up the milk carton with the blue belly in it, he scrambled up and over the broken concrete to where a slab had fallen creating a large shelf. Next to a dog-eared copy of Arthur Conan Doyle's *Lost World* were three ripe apricots and Matt's hand-made slingshot. He picked up an apricot and tore it in half, tossing half into his mouth. He pulped it with his teeth, savoring the sweet juices trickling down his throat. Then he threw in the second half. Matt pocketed the black pit and picked up his slingshot, regarding it ruefully. It had none of the beauty or symmetry of the Sears hunting model.

"What do you want to shoot at, Fred?"

"There's always a lot of stuff dumped behind the Ruhlman's yard."

"Okay. Let's go see." Matt scrambled down to Fred and side by side the two boys walked along the gently flowing creek. Past whispering stands of dried bamboo and giant scabbing eucalyptus trees they walked, kicking stones. A leopard frog scrambled awkwardly, plopping into the creek's water and dove for the silty bottom. Above the broken sidewalk forests of poison ivy burned red and orange.

High in a walnut tree a lone mourning dove called plaintively for its mate. Brilliant blue dragonflies hummed by.

"Think you could hit a dragonfly?" Fred asked.

"I did once with a bb gun, but it was sitting on a twig. I don't think you could hit one in flight."

"Why not?"

"They're way too fast, Fred," Matt said. "Besides, they're kind of cool."

"They're just bugs."

"Yeah, but they don't hurt anything. I don't see the point of trying to kill one. I'd rather watch them." Both boys stopped.

Before them loomed a forty-foot pile of household and yard debris. Over the years, the Ruhlmans had tossed tons of cans and bundled newspapers, jars, old clothes, lawn clippings and autumn leaves. A broken aluminum chaise lounge lay tangled with dried tree branches. The pile had created an avalanche that reached almost to the top of the canyon walls that imprisoned the creek.

Matt turned to Fred. "Let's see what we can find."

"The more breakable the better."

The boys combed through paper garbage bags. Something slithered away in a rush as they overturned paper cartons and old car tires.

"Found a coffee can," Fred said.

"A Mrs. Butterworth's bottle," Matt replied.

"Here's a cracked dinner plate," Fred yelled, dislodging a pile of yellowing newspapers.

"Eureka!" Matt exclaimed.

"What did you find?"

"Light bulbs. A whole box of light bulbs." Fred hurried over.

"Oh, man," he said, peering into the box. "There must be six, seven of 'em. One of them's a car headlight."

"This is gonna be good shooting."

"Bet I hit every one," Fred bragged.

"With that fancy thing you should," agreed Matt. "Come on. Let's set this stuff on the stump." They ran over to the jagged broken base of an old black walnut tree, its base haloed with fragments of broken glass and porcelain, evidence of past shooting sprees. Matt set out their targets in a line, then waded across the creek to where Fred was standing. "You should go first, Fred. You got the new one."

"Okay." Fred took his stance, one foot behind the other and sideways to his target, the shaft of the slingshot grasped in his left hand. He brought it up to eye level, grabbed the leather pocket and put in a pebble. Carefully, evenly, he pulled back the rubber tubes. Squinting, he sighted and—fired. The pebble zinged through the air. Dust puffed up on the dirt bank behind the targets.

"Missed!" Fred cried.

"Try again," Matt said.

The tubes twanged. Another cloud of dust.

"Maybe you're not using the sight right," Matt suggested.

Raising his weapon, Fred carefully lined up the crosshairs with the head of Mrs. Butterworth. Slowly he released his breath and his hold on the pouch. The pebble flew straight and true–three feet behind the closest target. "Damn," he exclaimed. "Maybe we're too far away."

"Then you'd be kicking up dust in front of the target, not behind it," Matt said.

"You try!" Fred said.

Matt hefted his own sling. He dug in his pocket and pulled out the apricot pit. Placing it on the inner tube band he squeezed it, holding it in place, sighted across the top of the slingshot and let fly. The middle of the cracked dinner plate exploded outward leaving a half moon of chaos.

"Lucky," Fred said.

Matt stooped and picked up a rounded pebble. Fitting it in the strap, he casually aimed. "Mrs. Butterworth's head," he said.

"No way."

Zing. Mrs. Butterworth's head disintegrated.

Matt reached for another pebble.

"I'm tired of this," said Fred.

"There's a bunch of targets left."

"For you."

"You'll get better. Maybe the rubber tubing is a little stiff. That could throw off your aim."

"Maybe."

Both boys shoved their slingshots into their respective pockets, leaving the targets set up.

"You go to a Catholic school, right? You got a lot of nuns, right?"

"Yeah," warily, knowing that Fred was leading up to something.

"You ever think about nuns much?" Fred asked.

"Yeah, all the time."

"Really?"

"Yeah, they're like a flock of evil penguins always watching us and yelling at us. They even come into the bathroom when we are in there trying to take a leak."

"Really?"

"Some idiot wadded up wet paper towels and threw them at the roof of the bathroom. These surprise inspections are supposed to stop that."

"That's gross."

"You're supposed to stand at attention when a nun enters the room, but it you're pissing when that happens you pee all over your foot."

"Gross!" Fred laughed.

"Why?"

"Why what?"

"Why do you want to know about nuns?"

"I just wondered . . . do they have hair?"

"What!"

"Do nuns have hair?" Fred pushed on. "I mean they wear that thing—"

"A habit."

"A habit and I've never seen one with hair. Have you?"

"No." Matt hedged.

"My brother says that they have to cut it all off and burn it on an altar to become a nun."

"They don't do that!"

"How do you know? They live all secret in those converts."

"Convents."

"Who knows what they do."

"That's idiotic," Matt said uncertainly.

"And boobs."

"Boobs?"

"Boobs. Do nuns have boobs?"

"What the heck are you talking about?"

"Nuns! Do nuns have boobs?"

"I've never seen them."

"Exactly. That white thing they wear. They hang straight down. How can it do that if they have boobs?"

"I don't know, Fred."

"Look at this." Fred dug into his pocket and pulled out a piece of paper and handed it to Matt. Matt unfolded it and stared at it a minute.

"Wow!"

"See?"

"Who is she?"

"It says Jayne Mansfield."

"Wow."

"See the way her sweater fits?"

"She looks like the front end of my dad's Buick."

"If she was wearing a habit—"

"It'll stick out at a 45 degree angle."

"At least," Fred agreed. "So, do nuns have boobs?"

"Is she normal?" asked Matt. Fred just shrugged.

Matt shook his head in silent wonder.

"My brother said they cut them off."

"Oh, shut up!"

"Well, look at her!"

"Maybe," Matt grasped for an answer, "maybe they bind themselves."

"Like those Chinese women who shove their feet into wooden boxes so their feet never grow longer than six inches. And how would that work, exactly?"

"I don't know," Matt admitted.

"So?"

"Yeah?"

"So, do nuns have boobs?"

"Not like she does, that's for sure."

"And what about—"

"No! We are not talking about nuns or parts of nuns. Until today, I never used the word nun and boob in the same sentence. So shut up about nuns."

A voice floated in from the distance: "Matt!"

"Your mom's calling."

"And she's using the voice."

"Matthew!" came the tones, echoing down to them.

Matt winced.

"You'd better hurry. She's using *that* voice," said Fred.

"Yeah, I know. If she gets to three, I'm doomed."

The boys hurried to the back of Matt's house. Along the way he scooped up the milk carton with the blue belly in it. A quick glance indicated that the lizard was okay. Defiantly the little reptile stared up at him. Matt closed the carton.

"He going to be able to breathe in there?"

"Sure, Fred. There's tons of air in there for him."

"Matthew!" The voice was sharper this time.

"You better answer."

"Coming," Matt yelled.

"Get up here right now!"

"Sounds like you are in trouble."

"I wouldn't be surprised. I always seem to be in trouble for something."

"Did you hear me?"

"Yes, Mom. I've got to climb up. It takes a minute."

"I'm waiting."

"You could go up through the poison oak," Fred suggested.

"Nah. Last time I did that she broke out all over."

"That's the point."

"She *is* my mom."

"She is a witch."

"No argument."

"Hurry up down there."

"Coming!" Matt headed toward his backyard. "See you, Fred."

"Tomorrow."

"Bring the slingshot."

"Okay."

Matt climbed the three steps that led to the gate of the neighbor's property, then veered toward several crude steps dug into the dirt. He grabbed the roots of a giant elderberry tree and pulled himself up, then he swung up and walked across a thick branch. Balancing carefully, he stepped from the elderberry to a smaller scrub oak. From the oak he jumped down to the roof of his fort. A hinged door in the fort's roof revealed a ladder. Down he climbed, carefully nestling the milk carton with the blue belly in his free arm. He set the carton down on a broken dresser with only one drawer that served as a shelf for his museum—a collection of bee hives, birds' nests, dried frogs and other stuff collected from the depths of the creek. All his treasures were guaranteed to do one thing: they kept his mother out of his fort. He emerged, dusty and panting.

"What kept you?" His mother stood there, a five-foot-two-inch boiling volcano of anger. Her thin frame quivered and deep brown eyes flashed.

"It's a forty-fifty foot climb, Mom. Dad said he'd help me make the steps, but he—"

"Don't talk to me like that!"

"Like what?"

"You know what I'm talking about."

"No, Mom, I don't."

"You had chores to do."

"I know. I did them."

"You emptied the dishwasher?"

"Yes."

"And brought your laundry to the laundry room?"

"Yeah, and I divided it into colors and whites like you said."

"And you picked up the dog doos."

"Yes!"

"Oh?" She pointed with a finely manicured hand, her red fingernails flashing sunlight. "What's that?"

He looked. A pained expression flashed across his face. "That's a new one, Mom. I can't help it if the dog went when I was in the creek."

"How do you know it's fresh?"

"Look at the color. They get dark brown when they get older."

"Why were you in the creek anyway? You know I don't like it when you go down there."

"I was collecting specimens for my terrarium."

"Your what?"

"My terrarium. You know. I told you about it last week. Sister Angelica assigned us to create a terrarium reflecting one of the habitats found around town. I put it on the laundry table."

"Oh, that. I threw it out."

"What!"

"It was full of bugs and things."

"It's a terrarium. It's *supposed* to be full of bugs and things."

"How was I to know it was your science project?"

"It had aluminum foil on the top of it and I taped on the side a paper with 'Matt's science project' on it," Matt cried. "How could you not know?"

"It was full of bugs."

"You took me to Sears to buy the terrarium. You had to know."

"Well, I threw it out."

"Why?" he screamed in frustration. "It's due tomorrow!"

"I didn't know."

"I asked you this morning if you'd drive me to school tomorrow so I wouldn't have to carry it to the bus stop."

"Make another one."

He stared at her in silent frustration.

"Just make another one. How hard can it be?"

"Just make another one? Really? I spent three days in the creek collecting the insects and frogs and minnows and stuff for that project." He turned toward the fort. "I'm going back into the creek. I've got to catch more animals."

"No."

"What?"

"I said no."

"Why?"

"We're supposed to be at my mother's for dinner in—" she glanced at the gold watch on her wrist. "Fifteen minutes. We don't have time to waste."

"But my project—"

"I said no. And bring in the garbage."

She turned and headed for the house.

Seething with helpless anger Matt walked along the side of the house to the front yard. He savagely kicked one of the empty garbage cans, hauled it to the side yard and slammed it down. Turning, he grabbed the other can.

"Matt."

Matt slapped the garbage can lid down on the offending can.

"Matt."

Matt looked up, seeing Mr. Giannini, a trim man of about 40 with a perpetual smile and over-combed bald spot.

"Oh, hi, Mr. Giannini."

"I heard your mother."

"The whole neighborhood heard my mother," Matt said.

"Don't worry. I saved your terrarium."

"You did? Great! Where is it?"

"In my garage. I remembered last week when you were helping me with the retaining wall you talked about your terrarium, so when I saw it on top of the garbage I had a hunch."

"Great! Thank you, Mr. Giannini. You are a life saver."

"Your mom spilled most of the water in the pond you built. The minnows died."

"I can get more minnows."

"You don't have to. My guppies had babies. I dipped some into your pond."

"Thank you, Mr. Giannini," Matt said. "If you need more help with your wall or anything I owe you."

"Hello, Mr. Giannini," Matt's mom said.

"Why, hello, Mrs. Connors. How are you today?"

"Fine." She chilled the air with one word. If Giannini noticed, he didn't react.

"I was just telling Matt here that his terrarium is safe. I saw it when I took out my garbage and remembered him talking about it. So I got to it before the garbage men did."

Matt watched his mother's smile tighten as the man talked, "How nice." Her eyes betrayed no sign of nice.

"Thanks again, Mr. Giannini. Can I pick it up after dinner?"

"Sure." He smiled. "I'll leave it out on the table on the porch. Whenever you get home it'll be there."

Matt watched Giannini turn toward his home. As he did, a young man in Bermuda shorts and a Hawaiian shirt came out the front door with a set of keys in his hand.

"Hey, Unc," he called. "I'm going to head back to the dorms."

"Okay, Bob. I'll see you when I see you."

"Maybe next week. I got exams for the next few days." Bob waved, getting into his VW van. "See ya, Unc."

"Who was that?" Yolanda asked.

"Don't you remember? My nephew, Robert, from Seattle. He's attending San Jose State, studying to be an orthodontist. Two weeks ago you commented on the Spanish guitar he played for us. You thought it was lovely."

"That's right. I remember. It *was* lovely." A true smile slowly emerged on her face. "He has a lot of talent. He could be the next Jose Greco."

"I'll tell him the next time I see him."

"Come on, Matt. Let's go."

Goodbyes were said all around. As they walked off, Matt asked his mother, "So, can you drive me to school tomorrow?"

"Why?"

"The terrarium. I didn't want to carry it to the bus stop."

"It's only a block."

"Can't you drive me?"

"No. I'm playing golf tomorrow."

"The school's on the way to the golf course."

"I said no."

"Yolanda," a cheery voice cried out. Mrs. Morgan was tall, blond, beautiful and turned the heads of every man in the neighborhood. She led two Dalmatians on red leashes.

"Helene, we on for golf tomorrow?"

"Sure. I don't have anything planned."

"Early. I'll call you in the morning."

"Hi, Matty. How are you?"

"My name is Matt."

"He's fine, Helene, if you don't count his dandruff. He has the greasiest hair and the dandruff just sticks in there."

"I see."

"Mom!" Matt blanched.

"Now, Yolanda. He's a fine looking boy. Almost handsome." Mrs. Morgan's sympathetic smile tried to counter Matt's embarrassment. It failed.

"You know, I've tried everything for his hair. I heard of a new beer and egg shampoo I'll try next."

"He'll grow up to be a fine man."

Matt's ears perked up. He looked at Mrs. Morgan appreciatively, his eyes fixed on her kind smile.

"Well, Helene, we've got to be going. You know how my sister is about serving dinner exactly at five o'clock."

Helene laughed, a musical sound. "See you tomorrow then for golf." Commanding the two Dalmatians to heel she took off. Matt watched the sensuous tidal sway of her hips as she left.

"Jayne Mansfield," he whispered.

"What did you say?"

Matt watched as Mrs. Morgan strode toward the corner. "You never had a golf date," he said.

"I just made one."

"But you said—"

"I said I was going golfing and I am."

"Do you even have a tee time?"

She looked at her son. "My sister owns the course. I always have a tee time."

"What's she wearing?"

"What?"

"What's she wearing?" he asked. "They're not shorts and they're not long pants. What are they called?"

"Capris. Some of the actresses on TV are wearing them and they have become *the* thing. At the dress shop we can't keep up with the orders. Why? Do you like them?"

Matt just shrugged. "I don't know. They're different." He watched the retreating figure of Mrs. Morgan. "You have a sweater like hers, don't you?"

"You mean the cut or the fabric?"

"The fuzzy fabric. What is that called?"

"Angora. I have a brown sweater like that. It matches my skin tone better. Blue looks better on blondes. Though," Mom paused reflectively, "a darker blue might look better on her."

Matt followed behind his mother, still watching the retreating figure. "Jayne Mansfield," he whispered.

Aunt Rose was waiting at the front door, her pale complexion and graying hair washed out by the threadbare flowered housecoat she always wore over a simple pink shift. Thin and aristocratic. Her eyes were sharp and impatient.

"You're late," she stated as she opened the door. The smells of spaghetti sauce, roasting garlic and fresh bread poured out around her.

"It took me forever to get Matt out of the creek."

"Why do you let him go down there? It's dangerous."

"Actually, Aunt Rose," Matt said, "Mom stopped and was talking to Mrs. Morgan to set up a golf date."

"Oh, that woman."

"She's just a golf partner, Rose," Yolanda said.

"Dinner's on the table." Silently they followed Rose. A red and white checked tablecloth covered the small kitchen table. In the center was a pot of spaghetti, steam swirling in rising clouds. A bowl of plump meatballs, a platter of aromatic garlic bread brushed with Parmesan and a gallon of Ernest and Julio burgundy complemented it. Smaller bowls of shaved Parmesan, olives and salami filled any open spaces. Each dinner plate was bedecked with a white cloth napkin.

Grandma was already seated. Her plate full, she enthusiastically twirled spaghetti onto her fork. She looked up, fixing her blurry eyes on Matt and smiled. "Matty," she cried. "Sit down. *Mangia! Mangia!*"

"I am. I am, Grandma." He kissed her on the head and sat beside her. "Good to see you, Grandma. Everything looks great Aunt Rose. It sure smells good."

A faint smile graced Rose's face. "Hurry up and eat before it gets cold, Matty."

Matt picked up his plate and dug into the spaghetti, dishing up a large glob of noodles. "Where's the sauce?"

"On the stove," Rose said.

The clatter of pot lids indicated Matt had found it. He ladled out a large spoonful of the rich meat sauce and poured it over the mountain of spaghetti. Picking out a bay leaf, he returned to the table.

"Where is your husband?" Rose asked archly.

"He's still out of town, Rose."

"Oh."

Silence.

Matt reached for a slice of garlic bread as his mother dished up. "One at a time, Matt."

"Yolanda! Let him have as many as he wants. He's a growing boy," Rose said.

Silence.

"One's fine, Aunt Rose. I can get more."

"Eat!" said Grandma. "You're too skinny, like your mother."

"Momma!"

Silence.

Grandma looked myopically around the table. "Your husband's not here?"

"No, Momma," Yolanda answered patiently. "He's up in Idaho, at the hotel."

"You should have married an Italian. Italian men never miss a meal."

"He's busy, Momma. Running a hotel takes a lot of time."

Silence.

"You like your papa being away, Matty?" his grandmother asked.

Matt swallowed. "No, but I love Idaho. It's a great place. Maybe someday we can move there and be with him."

Silence. Longer this time.

"Matty, *mangia.* Have some more."

Matt forked another meatball, plopped it in his mouth then chewed, savoring the flavor. He reached for his glass.

"What are you drinking, Matty?"

"Uh, milk, Grandma."

"Milk! Nah! That's a drink for bambinos. Here." She lifted the jug of burgundy with a trembling arm, pushed an empty glass toward him and began pouring.

"Grandma, that's enough. I'm not old enough to drink wine."

"Italians are born old enough to drink wine."

He gently took the jug of wine from his grandmother and set it down. "I have some now, Grandma. Okay."

"Drink it up like a man. Not milk or the white wine"—she made the word "white" a curse—"like your father drinks." Turning to her youngest daughter she said to Yolanda, "You should have married an Italian. Drink, Matt."

Matt looked to his mother for help and found none. Slowly he lifted the glass. Swirling the dark red liquid he sipped it, trying not to gag. His throat burned as he managed a smile. "Good," he coughed.

"Bravo!" Grandma picked up her glass. "*Salute!*" She and Matt clinked glasses. She watched as he forced down another sip.

Silence.

Hastily Matt tore a bite out of a slice of garlic bread, blunting the taste of the wine.

"What are you doing in school these days, Matt?" his aunt asked.

"Just the usual. In science we are studying different habitats. I made a terrarium showing a desert habitat with a couple of lizards and—"

"How nice. Desert. Yolanda, that reminds me. Vicki is coming to town next week."

"Is she? Really? When?" Mom lit up.

"She said she thinks Monday. You know her. She'll be up at six o'clock telling Silvio to hurry up. Then she'll drive like a bat out of hell."

"Yeah, Mom. She'll make that eight-hour drive from Palm Springs in, what, five hours?" Matt asked.

"Great. There's a tournament Wednesday. Maybe she can play a round," his mother said.

"You two and your golf. I don't understand it," Rose said.

"It's fun, Rose. You should try it."

Rose turned sharply to Yolanda. "And who would take care of your mother? You? Your sister, Vicki? She's never in town. Rita? No. I'll just stay here and cook and clean."

"Rose! Vicki, Rita and I have all volunteered to help take care of Momma."

"Last time Vicki did, she got bored after two days and left. I had to come back from Reno early. You did nothing. Rita is less than worthless when it comes to taking care of Mother. I would come home and find that the house had burned down."

Silence.

"Why does anyone have to look after Grandma? She gets around okay," Matt asked, slicing his meatball with a fork.

No one answered him.

"What are you doing in school, Matty?" Grandma asked.

"Nothing much."

"When do report cards come out, *vita mia*?"

"I think they come out in two weeks, Grandma."

Grandma wiped her face with the white napkin, leaving a trail of red sauce across it. "Are you getting A's? You only get ahead in this country if you get A's."

"Yes, Grandma, I'm getting A's."

"Good." She took a slurp of wine. "Tell you what. I'll give you a quarter for every A you get. How's that?"

"Thank you, Grandma. That's great."

"Put it toward college. You need money for college."

"Thanks, Grandma."

"Who wants biscotti?" his aunt asked, rising.

"I do," Matt said. "Did you put almonds in them?"

"Of course, I always do," Rose replied, smiling.

"You make the best cookies—and spaghetti," he added.

"What about mine?" his mother asked coolly.

Matt paused.

"Yours is the best in the world, too."

Rose laughed and handed him a plate of biscotti. "I tell you what, Matty. If you get all A's, I'll bake your own plate of biscotti and even dip some in chocolate for you."

"And some of those little sesame cookies?"

Rose laughed again. "You drive a hard bargain, Matty. Okay, some of the sesame cookies, too."

"What about you, Mom?"

"What!"

"Well, Grandma's giving a quarter per A and Aunt Rose is baking me cookies. What'll you do?"

"You haven't earned the A's yet."

"But if I do—"

This time the silence was focused—at his mother.

"If? If you get straight A's, I'll give you a quarter each."

"Yola! You're his mother. Give him a dollar."

She looked bemusedly at her mother. "Each, Momma?"

"Of course each. Don't be cheap."

"All right, Momma. I'll give him a dollar." She paused, looking directly at Matt, "Each. If he gets straight A's."

Matt leaned back smiling, taking a bite of the fresh biscotti and washing it down with a slug of milk. His mother grabbed a biscotti and dipped it into burgundy. Slowly she placed it in her mouth and loudly sucked the wine out of the softening cookie. Suddenly her even white teeth snapped together with a click—cutting the cookie in half.

Chapter Two

Matt trudged out of the school building and headed for a sagging wooden bench, a crumpled paper bag in his hand. Careful to avoid nail heads, he sat down heavily. Leaning against the chain link fence, the warm sun washing over him, he let out a long slow breath. Closing his eyes he ignored the sounds of other students walking by and talking.

"Man, that history test was tough, wasn't it?" David asked. David sat down beside Matt. A frown marred his thin eager face. "Who would have thought the history of India was so hard?"

"I think I did okay," Matt said. "Gandhi was an interesting guy and I know I maxed the part on India's wildlife."

"You and animals. Is there anything you don't know about them?"

"There's a lot I don't know. But I can go through the alphabet five times naming an animal for each letter, including x, z and q."

"Q?"

"Yeah. Quagga, quetzal bird—"

"You got anything good to eat?"

"I'm afraid to look. My mom never puts in anything good."

"You remember when she gave you the spaghetti sandwich?"

"Actually, that was one of her better lunches." Both boys laughed, digging into their lunch bags.

"I got Twinkies!" Dave yelled triumphantly.

"I got—" Matt pulled out a limp sandwich wrapped in wax paper. "I got—" He peeled off the wax paper, tearing off patches of green soggy Wonder Bread. "I got a peanut butter and avocado sandwich. Again." He glanced at his friend's Twinkies.

"Ugh! That sounds awful."

"It doesn't taste that awful," Matt replied. "It's just that the bread gets soggy and the avocado turns black."

"It looks ugly. You ought to complain."

Matt threw the sandwich back in the bag. "When I complain, my mother screams at my dad about my ingratitude. Then Dad lectures me about how when he was a kid all he got for a year was a cold fried egg sandwich, sometimes with no bread. And how I should be glad to get an avocado sandwich. Then he usually slips me a Hershey bar or something later."

"Has your old man ever eaten an avocado sandwich?"

The phrase "old man" caused Matt to wince. "No. He not only says he never has, he has sworn, when Mom is not around, that he never will. He can't stand avocados. He says as soon as things get better he'll give me money for hot lunch more often." Matt dug deeper in his lunch bag. "At least there's an apple."

"Here," Dave said, "have a Twinkie."

"Thanks." Matt bit into the cream-filled pastry, then into the apple. Alternating bites, he polished them off quickly. Slowly he licked his fingers, savoring every morsel. He tossed the core of the apple over the fence.

"Why does your mother even make avocado sandwiches?" Dave asked.

"They're cheap. So's Mom."

"But your family has money."

"My aunts do. Mom doesn't. She pockets every cent she can, so I get avocado and peanut butter."

"Did you get milk?" David asked, opening his carton.

"No. It's always lukewarm. I can't stand warm milk."

Dave chugged his down.

David and Matt wadded up their lunch bags and shot for a nearby garbage can. Dave's hit the rim and bounced out. Matt's went in dead center.

"Good shot! You should try out for the basketball team. Coach wants you to."

"I know. I'm just not much of a team player."

"How tall are you?"

"About five-nine."

"You're one of the tallest guys in the school. You should try."

"No."

"Why not?"

"Remember baseball in eighth grade? We went into extra innings. My mother threw a fit. She screamed at the coach that we had to be at her mother's house for dinner at five o'clock. In front of everybody she pulled me out of the batter's box by the butt of my pants." He paused, shaking his head. "I never got to bat and the team lost."

"Oh, yeah." Dave tried not to laugh. "I felt sorry for you."

"I don't want people to feel sorry for me."

"Looks like the guys are starting a football game. Wanna play?"

"Nah."

"Susan Agnoletti and Marsha Puchinelli are watching. And Stacy Moore."

"Stacey." Matt hesitated.

Matt looked over at the knot of girls watching the boys play flag football on the hot blacktop and sighed. There seemed to be two types of girls at St. John Bosco High School. One group consisted of stout bodied, mean faced girls who seemed to live for the day when their future spouse died so they could shroud themselves in black, put their hair in a bun with a knitting needle through it and spend the rest of their lives scolding other people's children. The other group was the Annette Funicello wannabes. Slim girls with open faces and warm smiles whose doey brown eyes held hints of restrained laughter and promises to come.

Then there was Stacey.

Stacey Moore.

Her peaches and cream completion made her stand out from the herd of olive-skinned brunettes that populated the school. Sparkling blue eyes twinkled and beckoned. She was always smiling. Not the furtive shy smiles of the other girls. Her smiles—freely given— embraced the world—and the world smiled back. Shimmering long blond hair cascaded to her shoulders. Long legged, she moved with gracefulness and confidence. She was beautiful.

Matt's eyes found her. He sighed. "Nah. I'll just go to the library," he replied.

"Why? She's watching the game. You could make a great play and she'll notice you."

"Or I could fall flat on my face. No, I got stuff to do."

"You ride on her bus don't you?'

"Yeah. She lives down my block."

"Have you talked to her?" Dave asked.

"No. Not really."

"What an idiot. The most beautiful girl in the whole school rides on the bus with you and lives down the street from you, and you haven't talked to her. I don't get you."

"Look at her." Matt pointed. "I wouldn't know what to say."

"Well," Dave said in his most suggestive voice, "you just do what comes naturally."

"That's the problem," Matt said. "Nothing comes naturally. No, that's not true. What comes naturally when I'm around her is sweat and trembling and fear. Words stick in my throat. And when something finally croaks out it's just plain stupid." He shook his head. "No, I'll just sit here and read."

"Maybe you need to read a book on how to be human."

"I'll talk to her."

"Now?"

"No!" Matt paused. "But I will talk to her. I promise."

"Don't promise me, man. I'm the competition. Promise yourself."

"If you're my only competition, I don't have anything to be afraid of."

"Thanks, Matt."

"I'll talk to her."

"Soon?"

"Soon."

With a shout, Dave took off and disappeared into the group of kids playing ball. Matt pulled a thick paperback out of his back pocket, opened it and read. He'd read about three pages when—

"What are you reading?" A rich creamy voice poured over him.

"It's *Stranger in a Strange*—" He looked up and froze. Stacey.

She laughed, a musical sound. "I think the title is *Stranger in a Strange Land*."

"Yeah, by . . . uh . . . Robert . . . Rober," he croaked.

"Robert Heinlein."

"So." She sat down next to him and looked him in the eye. "Do you grok?"

"Grok?" he asked, confused.

"Yes. In the novel, they grok a lot."

"I haven't gotten that far yet. I just started. But I've read a lot of his other science fiction and thought I'd give this a shot."

"I'm not done with it either," she said. "But there's nobody in this school who reads much so I have nobody to discuss books with."

"I read," Matt exclaimed, a bit too loudly.

"I know. I've watched you."

"You have?"

She nodded.

"How come I've never seen you at the library? I practically live there," Matt asked.

"My dad does book reviews for newspapers all over the country—the *Mercury News*, *San Francisco Chronicle*, *Sacramento Bee*, *New York Times*—all over. Authors and publishers are always sending him books. So I read those." She looked at him. "You know that book gets kind of naughty in parts."

"It does?" He gulped, looking down at the book.

"Yes. But it's science fiction. So most adults don't pay any attention to what we read."

"Oh."

"Heinlein lives in Santa Cruz. Dad knows him." She got up. "You should meet my dad. He says kids today don't read enough. He even believes that one day we'll stop printing books altogether."

"Really?"

"He likes to talk to people who read. And so do I." She sashayed away.

Matt stared.

Dave ran up. "You dirty dog," he exclaimed.

"What?"

"You dog. 'I'll just sit here and read.' You sly devil."

"What are you talking about?"

"Stacey."

"You saw her."

"The whole school saw."

"Wow," Matt said softly.

"Wow is right. What did you do?"

"Nothing, man. I was just reading."

"What did you talk about?"

"This book." Matt held up the paperback.

"Books! Is that all?"

"She's a reader—"

"Beauty and brains, man you scored."

"And she said I should come over and meet her father, he writes—"

"Stacey Moore. *The* Stacey Moore wants you to come over. You absolute dirty hairy dog."

"I don't want to meet her dad."

Dave stared at him.

"You are an idiot."

"What?"

"She lives in the same house as her father."

"And?"

"She's inviting you over."

"Really?"

"Most definitely."

"Wow." Matt smiled for the first time that day. "Wow."

❧ ❧ ❧

The classroom was stark, hot and uncomfortable. Drab gray walls were decorated with faded posters and outdated maps. Slashes of blazing sunlight cut across the classroom, cooking anyone unfortunate enough to be caught in them. The only spot of color was the vase of red roses sitting before the statue of the Virgin Mary on the file cabinet next to the teacher's desk. With ruby lips and wrapped in a blue robe, Mary serenely gazed down on the sweltering students, indifferent to the heat. The windows gaped open but not a breath of air stirred. At the front of the room almost blending into the blackboard stood Sister Maria Tomas, a stick of white chalk in her right hand.

"So class, Gandhi. Considered by many to be one of the greatest men on earth." She turned to the chalkboard and began writing. "The Salt March and Martin Luther King's March on Washington. What did these two great leaders have in common?" She placed a period at the end of the last line she wrote and dropped the chalk into the chalk tray. Turning to the class, she brushed the chalk dust from her fingers. "Come on now, surely someone can draw some parallels."

Matt squirmed in the one-piece desk he was wedged into. Around him other uniformed students shuffled their notes trying to find an answer.

"Tony?" Sister Tomas asked. "Do you have any ideas?"

"Ah—they—they were both killed?"

"That's correct. They were both assassinated, Gandhi by his own bodyguards. Why?" She scanned the room. "What did they both do that would cause someone to fear them enough to shoot them?"

"They tried to change things?" a girl's voice ventured.

"Correct. What things?" Sister was a master of letting silence grow and drawing out answers.

"The status quo," the girl tried again.

"Excellent," Sister replied. "What common methods did they use to change the status quo?"

Sister waited.

Matt squirmed and a frown crossed his face.

"Matthew? Do you have something to say?"

"They both relied on numbers."

"Numbers?"

"Yeah. Look, both Gandhi and King relied on numbers. One policeman beating up one guy is unfortunate. A group of cops beating on a group of peoples is controlling a riot. But a bunch of cops beating on masses of people who are doing nothing to provoke them, that is obviously so wrong that no government can explain it away." Matt was on a roll. "Numbers insured both men's success. No prison could hold the number of peoples that had to be arrested. They overwhelmed the system."

"Excellent, Matthew." Sister Tomas nodded in approval. "And what was the name of the system they used?"

"Satyagraha. That's what Gandhi called it. King called it passive resistance."

"Very good." She beamed. "How can we use passive resistance today?"

"If we all refuse to do our homework, maybe teachers will stop assigning it?" a football player in the back row offered.

Sister laughed. "Don't expect that to happen."

"We can use it to stand up for what we believe in," Matt said.

"And what do you believe in, Matt, to the extent that you would take a beating for it?"

"I—I don't know," he admitted.

There was a knock at the door and Sister turned and went to it. Matt underlined "believe in" within his notes and circled it twice. Sister Tomas returned to her place at the front of the class. Hands folded, she waited as all of the students focused on her.

"In a moment, I will have you put your history books into your desk. Steve, I said in a moment."

Steve straightened up sheepishly.

"There will be a change in schedule today." She looked to make sure everyone was paying attention.

"Coach Harris will be talking to the boys in this classroom about personal hygiene and sex education." She paused, daring anyone with a look to giggle at the word sex. "Girls will meet in the Home Ec room and Mrs. Giotti will be talking to them. Needless to say, I expect you all to be on your best behavior."

She walked to the door and opened it. Then she returned to the blackboard and picked up a piece of chalk. The coach, a short, plump, balding man came in carrying an easel.

"Coach Harris, any problems—I want names on the board." She pointedly handed him the chalk. "Class, quietly put away your books. Girls, when you are done line up in the hall. I will take you to Mrs. Giotti's classroom."

She waited until all of the girls were gone. "Coach, do they need to take notes?"

"No. I think I'll just have them listen."

"Very well, then." She gave the room of boys a piercing look. "Be good." With that she left, shutting the door behind her.

The coach looked bemusedly at the chalk. He tossed it into the chalk tray where it landed with a metallic clunk. Fumbling for a few moments with his easel, he flipped back the blank cover revealing a simple line drawing of a man and a woman—naked. Some of the boys sat up a little straighter.

"Well, guys." The coach ran his fingers through his comb-over. "As Sister said this is the continuation of our class on personal hygiene and sex ed. We already covered the hygiene part. Most of you are well aware of the wonderful world of soap." He laughed, alone. "And last month we pretty much covered the plumbing of the human reproductive system. So—ah—today, I thought we would review the parts of the male reproductive system and then open it up to questions and answers."

The football player in the back of the room raised his hand.

"Yes, Carlotti?"

"Coach, do we really have to be able to know the vast deferens and seminal vacuoles to have sex?"

"Vas deferens, Carlotti. And no, but for the purposes of the class, yes, you got to know them."

A hand went up.

"Don, do you have a question?"

"Yeah. In the Bible it talks about man leaving his parents and clinging to his wife. Is that sex? Clinging? I mean I asked my dad what clinging mean and he said hugging. I've hugged my mom and sister a million times. Is that sex?"

"Hey, Donny!" Carlotti called out.

"Yes?" Don turned to face the football player, pushing his thick rimmed glasses back up on his nose.

"Didn't you say you wanted to be a priest?"

"Yes."

"Then what do you need to know about sex? Priests are sexless."

"So that when idiots like you come to me for counselling, I will know what I'm talking about."

"Hey, you—"

"Carlotti, put a sock in it," Coach Harris said. "Any more comments like that and you will be running laps for me for the whole practice."

"But—"

"Don't 'but' me, Carlotti." The coach and player locked eyes. "You understand?"

"Yes, Coach." Carlotti slumped in his seat.

"So, Don, what was your question?"

"Is clinging sex?"

"Well, hugging isn't sex, though it could lead to sex."

"What does that mean? Are there steps?"

"In a manner of speaking, yes," the coach said.

"Is it true that we can't have sex until we grow another hole in our penis?"

"Where'd you hear that, Tony?"

"My cousin is a year older than me and he said he read it somewhere. And it makes sense; otherwise the sperm would come out of the same hole we, ah, pee through."

"It's not true," said the flustered coach.

"Then they both come out the same hole. That's gross!"

"Well, they don't come out at the same time," the coach explained.

Matt raised his hand.

"Matt?"

"How does the body know which one to do, you know, during sex?" he asked. Matt could see beads of sweat beginning to form on the coach's forehead.

"The body gets messages telling it what to do when—"

"Messages? Where do these messages come from?" someone asked.

"Now, I need you to raise your hands, one at a time," Coach Harris said, getting flustered.

"Why do girls have breasts?"

"When girls' breasts start growing does that mean they can get pregnant?"

"If they don't have breasts do they not get pregnant?"

"Why do guys have breasts, too?"

"Guys don't have breasts, we have chests!" shouted Carlotti.

"Carlotti! Ten laps. Now everybody calm down and one at a time." Two beads of sweat raced down the coach's forehead and crashed into his bushy eyebrows. "First of all, women have breasts so that they can suckle their babies, and before anybody asks suckle means feed their babies. Their breasts produce milk for the child."

"It's the father's child, too. How come men don't produce milk?"

"We just don't," Coach Harris answered.

"Then why do men have nipples?"

"I—I don't know. God just planned it that way, I guess." The coach mopped his brow with a handkerchief pulled from his back pocket. "Now girls can get pregnant before their breasts start to develop. But most don't because of their age."

Matt raised his hand again.

"Matt?"

"What I don't understand is, if man and woman are both created in the image of God, why can't we look at them?"

"Look at them?" Coach Harris looked confused.

"Why can't . . ." Matt searched for the words. "Why do they wear two-piece swimming suits? Why cover up their breasts?"

"Ah, well, breasts . . . tend . . . to excite men to want sex."

"Aren't we supposed to have sex? God said go forth and multiply and—" Donny began to ask.

"No. Well, yes. We are supposed to have sex. With our wives. Under the sanctity of marriage. Sex is a beautiful thing and it is supposed to be shared with someone you love in a sacramental fashion."

"Is that why they call it the missionary position?"

"Carlotti, twenty laps."

"Yes, Coach."

"There's positions?" A boy's voice squeaked. "Is that going to be on the test?"

"Yes, there are positions and no, they will not be on the test. Plumbing only," Coach replied.

"So why do we cover them up?" Matt repeated.

"Some men, at the sight of women's breasts get excited." He gazed out at a room of blank faces and a smirking Carlotti. "Excited means, you know, when you have an erection."

"Do you mean a hard on?" someone asked.

"Why?"

"That's something you should discuss with your dads, guys." Pools of sweat began to show under the coach's arms. "Just understand it is illegal for women to show their breasts in public."

Matt spoke. "I don't understand the paranoia. My mom takes my *National Geographics* and cuts all of the pictures of naked women out of it."

"How do you know they're pictures of naked women?" Carlotti asked.

"There's a place called a library, Carlotti." Matt turned back to the coach. "When Mom started cutting up my magazine, I went to the library to see what she was cutting out. And I don't get it. Those pictures didn't get me excited."

"What's the name of that magazine?"

"Carlotti!" the coach barked. He went to the chalkboard and picked up the chalk from the tray, pointing with it at the football player. "I have warned you."

"Yes, Coach, I know. Thirty laps."

"Breasts. When you are with a woman you love, and she takes off her clothes and you sleep together—that's when a woman can get pregnant."

A hand shot up.

"Yes, Andy?"

"When we travel, I always have to sleep with my sister. Is she going to get pregnant?"

"That's different."

Someone whistled in the back row. "How?" asked Andy.

"You love your sister with a noun. You don't love her with a verb."

"What?" came Andy's puzzled reply.

"Love. It's a noun and a verb."

"So where it is in a sentence makes a difference between if a woman gets pregnant or not? That doesn't make a bit of sense, Coach."

The coach unbuttoned the top button of his shirt. "When you go to bed with a woman, you are both naked, right?" Kids nodded. "You get real close and sort of start rubbing up against each other. The man gets an erection. The sperm come out and sort of go into the woman and she gets pregnant."

"Coach?"

"Yes, Carlotti?"

"In the drawings you show us of women and their parts? The vagina? Is that the right word?"

"Yes."

"The vagina is always shown as a little tiny line." Carlotti leaned forward in his chair. "How do they get in there?"

"The sperm?" the coach asked, glancing at the clock.

"Yeah, the sperm."

"Maybe they're tricky," someone offered.

"No, the vagina swells up and, ah, gets bigger, wider and the sperm get in."

"So, Coach," Carlotti went on, "You're in bed with a naked woman and how, exactly, does the sperm enter the vagina?"

"You're rubbing around with the woman—"

"Clinging?"

"Yes, Donny. Clinging." Coach Harris looked at the clock again. "And the woman's nipples and vagina start to swell. And the male penis starts to swell and then it kind of explodes and the sperm get out into the vagina and—bang—she gets pregnant."

"Our penises explode?" Donny cried out.

"Not really. Kind of like a volcano. Pressure builds up and you . . . sort . . . of explode."

"Is it painful?" Donny asked.

"Most people think it is wonderful," Coach offered lamely.

There was a tap at the door.

"One last question," Coach said with relief in his voice.

Matt raised his hand. "How do you know when you're done?"

✖ ✖ ✖

Sister Maria Tomas stood in front of the classroom holding the piece of chalk the coach had handed her. She waited a moment for the class to calm down. Serenely, she surveyed the room. Everyone was sitting up straight, eyes focused on her.

"I am delighted to see that Coach did not need to put any names on the board. The one thing I would like you to remember as you grow older is that sex is an awesome gift from God. With it comes wonderful and sometimes frightening responsibility. Also, with it come consequences, consequences that can last a lifetime." She turned and put the chalk in the tray.

"Remember, tomorrow we will announce the winners of the science project. First place winner goes to the National Science Day Dinner at Moffett Field. Also, report cards come out tomorrow. Your homework is on the board. Have a pleasant evening. You may go."

The students gathered their books and coats.

"Matthew? May I see you for a second?" She smiled and waited for the other students to leave. "Two weeks ago the coach talked to your class about personal hygiene and secondary sex characteristics, didn't he?"

"Yes, Sister Tomas, he did. And I've been bathing regularly."

She smiled. "Matthew, I asked him to suggest to you that you might want to try shaving."

"He did."

"And?" she asked.

"I told Mom, but she said he should mind his own business."

Sister took in a breath and let it out slowly.

"Mom said that what I have was peach fuzz and she thought it was cute."

"You are a little past peach fuzz, Matthew," Sister said in a kindly voice. "Parents sometimes have difficulty letting their children grow up." She looked Matt in the eyes. "Try again, tonight. If you are unshaven tomorrow, I will assume she has said no. Will you do that, Matthew?"

"Of course, Sister." He turned to leave, then stopped. "Thank you."

Outside Dave was waiting for him at the door.

"So are you in trouble?"

"No, Dave. Why?"

"They said Sister wanted to talk to you."

"Oh, that was nothing."

"Did she tell you you won the science project?"

"No. Why would she do that?"

"Everyone says yours is the best. The terrarium, the slides, the maps and display, plus your research redrew the lines of a state park in Palm Springs."

"The Coachella Valley."

"Yeah, that. I mean, it's kind of far out, you know."

"It was no big deal. I spent six weeks with my aunt in Rancho Mirage and visited the zoo there. They needed volunteers to study the kit fox. I volunteered. The guy in charge let us decide what we wanted to research. I decided to look at what they eat. After I learned that, I realized that the proposed area for the park wouldn't include some of the areas that held the best feeding grounds for kit foxes. So I told them."

"Cool. Maybe they'll name something after you."

"Like maybe the outhouse." Reaching the bike racks, Matt put his books in the rack and slammed the holder down. "Damn."

"Don't let Sister Tomas hear you say that, Matt."

"My bike tire is flat again."

"Again?"

"Yeah. Look." Matt pointed. The tire had three thorn heads embedded in the rubber. "I've got to stop taking that shortcut through the empty lot. I always pick up a thorn there." Matt looked up at Dave. "You wouldn't happen to have a tire patch kit with you, would you?"

Dave shook his head. "No. And we aren't allowed to have matches anyway."

"With all the candles they light around here, someone would have matches."

"Sorry."

"I don't really mind the walk. And I'm in no hurry to get home."

Both boys spun their combination locks and began walking, the flat tire scrunching as they walked. "So, what did you get out of Coach's talk?" Dave asked.

"I don't know." Matt frowned. "It all sounds kind of confusing and gross."

"You know it. And he really didn't tell us anything, did he?"

"I don't get what the big secret is. And he never answered my last question."

"What was it?"

"How do you know when you are done? Sister knocked on the door then and he stopped talking."

"You know," Dave said conspiratorially, looking around to make sure they were alone, "he didn't tell us the worst of it."

"Worst?"

"You bet. My cousin, Angelo, got married two months ago. We *were* kinda close. He's only three years older than me. Anyway, since he got married he's never around."

"So?"

"I saw him the other day at a family dinner. We shot some baskets for a bit. Anyway, he says that sex is terrific and, you won't believe this, but we actually put our cocks in the girl."

"Cocks. How is that word short for penis? And penis. That's just a terrible sounding word. Pee-nus."

"Did you hear me?"

"I heard you and I don't believe you."

"Why not? Angie is married. He should know."

"He's got to be lying."

"Why?"

"Or pulling your leg. Because I can't believe that something we need to wash our hands over every time we use it is anything an intelligent girl wants you to put into her. That just doesn't make sense."

"Angie says it's true. You put it into her and push it in and out. He says it's great. He says he has sex every day he wants it."

"I don't believe it. How does it get in?"

"He wouldn't say."

"Coach says that the girl's vagina swells to the size of a softball during childbirth. So I guess it's possible." Matt looked worried.

"What?"

"If they expand that big and if we put it in there—" Matt looked uncomfortable.

"Yes?"

"I don't know about you, but it doesn't seem like a very good fit." Matt held his hand in a circle, about softball distance apart. "I'm not that big."

"We're still young. Maybe we grow into it."

"I don't know. It seems unbelievable. Like I said, confusing and gross."

"Angie said he likes playing with his wife's tits."

"What does that even mean? Playing with. What would you do with them?"

"I don't know. He said I'll find out."

"I still think he's pulling your leg."

"Could be."

"Why do adults make such a big secret out of it? Why don't they just come out and tell us what it's all about. The truth can't be any worse than the stories and crap we hear."

Dave looked at Matt. "Did Coach seem nervous?"

"He was sweating buckets. Again, why? It's a basic bodily function. We will all find out about it except maybe Don, since he's going to be a priest. Why the secrets?"

"He was real nervous in our class, too."

"Even my dad won't answer direct questions. I asked him what an orgasm was and he spent the next two hours waxing the fenders of his 1939 Studebaker. The only one who seems to know what she was talking about was the nun."

They walked on a while in silence.

"You gonna watch *Batman* tonight?" Dave asked.

"Of course. I've got to figure out how he will escape from the trap the Riddler put him in yesterday."

"Oh, he'll pull out some Bat-thing and escape. He always does"

"Sure, Dave, but it's still fun to watch."

"That lady who plays Catwoman is a fox."

Matt laughed. "That's a mixed metaphor."

"Well, she is hot."

"Wrapped in that leather outfit anyone would be hot."

They stopped at the intersection of Willow Street and Lincoln

Avenue. "See you later, Matt." Dave crossed the street, mounted his bike and took off.

"Bye."

Matt stood at the corner with his crippled bike waiting for the light to change. The bus pulled up beside him. Hearing a knocking at the window he looked up to see Stacey Moore waving at him. Awkwardly, balancing his bike one handed, he waved back. The bus lurched off belching a plume of blue exhaust. He watched it accelerate away.

"Wow," he said, amid coughs.

Chapter Three

Matt pushed his bike with the flat tire up the driveway to the garage door. He tugged, gaining momentum and strained to lift the heavy door. Finally, the counterweights engaged, and the door nearly flew out of his hands as he backed out of the way.

Gazing across the workbench, Matt sought a tire repair kit. He spied the bright orange can and shook it. There was a dull thud in the can. He popped off the top and dumped out the contents. No glue. No matches. Nothing but a rectangle of rubber patch with a large circle already cut out of it. Matt sighed, shoving the useless patch material back into the can and posed, balancing on the balls of his feet, and shot. Swish! A perfect two point shot into the wastebasket.

He looked at his dad's old Studebaker. It had been Matt's grandfather's car, a man Matt never knew. His dad's dad. And his dad was determined to restore it. Other than needing a new paint job and new lining in the trunk, the car was in pretty good condition. A note was sitting on the driver's seat. "Your father called and asked that you have the battery charged before he comes home tomorrow."

"Tomorrow. Well, thanks Dad."

Grabbing the battery charger, he plugged it in, being sure to keep the cables and their alligator jaws wide apart. Then he lifted up a side panel of the hood. Bluish white corrosion encrusted the battery terminals. Taking a 7-Up bottle from the dented little refrigerator on the work bench, Matt popped the lid with a can opener magneted to the side. A plume of white fog escaped the bottle, hissing as it went. Matt took a swallow, then walked back to the car. Carefully he poured a little soda on each battery terminal, watching the hungry bubbles eat up all the corrosion. When they were clean, he took a rag and wiped both posts off. After affixing the correct cables to the proper posts, he turned on the battery charger. The light in the garage dimmed briefly as the charger began to hum. With a satisfied smile Matt backed away, pausing only to shut the garage door.

He entered by the side door of the house, stepped into the service porch, peeling off his school shirt and throwing it onto the pile of dirty clothes. One step brought him to a sliding door and into his small room. Kicking off his leather school shoes, he dropped his pants and stepped out of them. The breeze from the window cooled his body and Matt stood a moment, a smile on his face. Fishing in a dresser drawer, he found a pair of cutoffs made from last year's corduroy uniform pants. As he pulled them on, he stepped into a worn pair of Keds. Once bright red, the shoes were now a kind of muddy pink. He pulled on a white t-shirt over his tanned chest, as he stepped back into the service porch and out into the back yard.

"You're late."

"Hi, Mom. Hey, Letty!" He bent down to tussle with the apricot-colored French poodle that was trying to climb up his leg. The pompom on her tail wiggling frantically, the dog squirmed and licked at his fingers, eager for attention.

Mom was lying on a chaise lounge wearing a zebra striped two piece bathing suit that contrasted sharply with her deep mahogany tanned skin. She glistened with lotion beneath the hot California sun. A pair of dark glasses covered her eyes.

"Her name is Aletta and you are late."

"My bike had a flat again. And," he paused, "the patch kit in the garage is empty."

"Buy another."

"Any chance you want to give me the thirty five cents?" Matt asked, still playing with the dog.

"You get an allowance."

"Occasionally."

The sunglasses were snatched away from her eyes in one violent motion. She sat up abruptly. "What is that supposed to mean?" she asked sharply.

"You 'forgot' to pay me last week. And twice in December."

"You got money for Christmas, didn't you?"

"Was that supposed to be my allowance? It would be nice if—"

"Don't start on this, Matty. You get plenty of money."

"My name is Matthew, or Matt. You know I hate being called Matty."

"I am your mother. I will call you whatever I want" she steamed. "How dare you suggest that I didn't pay your allowance?"

"But you didn't. You said the milkman raised his rates on a gallon of milk and since I drank all of the milk anyway, you were taking my allowance to make up for the difference."

"You do drink all of the milk."

"That's not the point—"

"That is the point!"

"Matteo!"

Matt spun around to see his grandmother tottering out of the back door. Her wrinkles accordioned into a wide smile.

"Come here, *vita mia.*" She beckoned with outspread arms. Coming up only to his chest, she embraced him.

"Grandma, what are you doing here?"

"I came to vacuum the house for your mother."

Matt's glance went from his frail white haired grandmother to his mother, now reclining again on the chaise, the glasses back over her eyes.

"You lugged that old Kirby around. That thing is heavy."

"Itsa not so bad. I took down the living room drapes. They need a wash."

"I told you not to do that," snapped Matt's mother.

"Yolanda. They needed a wash. When were you going to do it?" The sunglasses turned toward her mother and peered at her.

"You shouldn't be doing our housework, Grandma," Matt objected.

"There was dog hair everywhere. The house needed to be vacuumed."

"Poodles don't shed, Momma," Yolanda said.

"Something does. And I cleaned all the cupboards in the kitchen."

"Mother! Last time you did that I couldn't find anything for a week."

"You had mustard in there that was turning brown."

"What did you do with it, Momma?"

"I threw it away."

"It was brown mustard, Momma. Very expensive. It is supposed to be brown." His mother's voice was rising. "Matty, go dig it out of the garbage."

"But—"

"Don't argue. Go!"

He left.

"Momma, I've told you a thousand times when you come over to clean the house only do the things I have asked you to do. Last time I couldn't find any pillow cases for days."

"That's because they smelled. I put them all in the washing machine. They were folded on the dryer."

"That's not the point."

"All you had to do was look in the laundry room."

Matt stepped back out of the house.

"Did you find it Matty?"

"Yes, in the refrigerator where it belonged. The mustard Grandma threw out was old yellow mustard that turned some brownish sludgy color."

"Whatever, the point is you —"

"The point is you should be grateful," Matt interjected.

"Matty."

"Isn't that what you were just telling me?"

"How dare you!"

"Matteo! You have a hole in your shirt," Grandma said.

"What?" He craned around until he spied a rip in the left side of his shirt. "That's okay, Grandma. I only wear this when I'm doing yard work or going down in the creek." He glanced at the fence separating him from his goal.

"That doesn't matter. Yola, I give you enough money to buy him decent clothes."

"It's a work shirt, Momma."

"And those shoes. You should buy the boy new shoes."

"But—"

"It's all right, Grandma. I have better shoes in the house. These are only work shoes. I don't want to ruin my good ones when I play around in the creek. I can wade in these without worrying about broken glass."

Grandma sniffed. Mom simmered.

"Matteo, you shouldn't be down in that creek anyway. Why do you let him go into that place, Yola?"

"I—"

"Grandma, how are you getting those curtains home?'

"Rose and I will carry them."

"Aunt Rose is here?"

"She came to make you some spaghetti sauce. You need to eat more, Matteo. You're too skinny."

"Grandma—"

"I don't want you taking the curtains, Mother. Anyone will be able to see in the living room window."

"Unless you're running around the house naked what difference does it make?" Grandma asked.

"Momma! I never—"

"Maybe if you did, I'd have more grandchildren like Matteo."

"Momma!"

"And Matteo. You got a girlfriend?"

"Ah, no, Grandma."

"No? Yola, what is the problem here? Matteo should have girlfriends. At his age his grandfather had many girlfriends."

"He's too young."

"No. He is Italian. Italians are never too young." Grandma paused. "Matteo, you are not thinking of becoming a priest, are you?" she ventured hopefully.

"No, Grandma."

"Why not?" she asked. "It is the only reason not to have girlfriends."

"Dad said if I decided to become a priest, he would kill me."

"You should have married a good Italiano," Grandma said to Yolanda. "Not that—man. So Matteo, why don't you have any girlfriends?"

"I don't —"

"You said it yourself, Momma. He's too skinny. And with that oily complexion." Yolanda ran her hand along his shoulder, found a bump and squeezed it. Matt winced and watched a small bloody spot begin to form on the shirt. "His acne is awful. The dandruff is worse."

"Stop it!" Matt pushed aside his mother's hand reaching for his head. "Just stop it."

"Don't tell me—"

"There is no reason for a boy not to have a girlfriend. Unless," Grandma's brow wrinkled even further. "He's not *finocchio*, is he?" she whispered.

"Momma! Of course not."

"How would you know?" Grandma asked.

"I," Yolanda stammered, confused. "I . . . would know."

"I'm pretty sure I am not," Matt ventured. "What is a—?"

"It's a man who—" Yolanda stopped and whirled toward him. "You don't need to know. Why are you even asking?"

"I'm being accused of something and I'm not even allowed to know what it is? Incredible! How fair is that?"

"Fair! You talk about fair. Me running this house and a son to raise without a husband here to help me—that's unfair. That is grossly unfair."

Matt glanced again toward the creek.

"So, Matteo, are you going to help me bring the curtains to my house to wash?" Grandma asked.

Matt glanced at his mother who shrugged. "Now, Grandma? I was hoping to go into the creek."

"No, your aunt just started the sauce. It will take some time to cook and simmer."

"So, I can go to the creek?"

His mother lay back in the chaise, the sunglasses snapped down like the visor of a knight's helmet.

"Be back in about an hour, Matteo."

"Thanks, Grandma."

Matt escaped down the canyon walls into the creek. At the bottom, he paused, pulled off his shirt, took a deep breath and let it out slowly. He examined the pimple on this shoulder his mother had popped. It was already beginning to scab over.

"Hard day?"

"Mr. Giannini, you startled me."

"Sorry."

"You are the only adult I ever see down here. Except for that time my dad came down to clear out all of the poison oak and caught it so bad his arms swelled up like balloons."

"Just working on the retaining wall. Don't want the canyon walls to collapse. That would bring all of that," he said and nodded toward the rim of the canyon, "down here."

"Wouldn't want that to happen." Matt hesitated. "Mr. Giannini, what is a *finocchio*?"

Giannini looked up. "Why do you ask?"

"My grandmother just accused me of being one since I don't have a girlfriend and I don't know what it is. The only thing I do know is that it's worse than being a priest."

Giannini snorted back a laugh.

"So, what is it?"

Giannini glanced at the shirtless boy. "It's something that you probably need to ask your father about."

"Oh. Then it's something dirty."

"Why would you say that?"

"The only time adults say 'you should ask your father,' it's something dirty."

"I'd say personal, not dirty. It's just something very personal." He looked at Matt. "So why *doesn't* a strapping lad like you have any girlfriends?"

"Why would I bring any girl into that?" Matt gestured with his head toward his house. "Even the guys I know don't like to come over. She always does something that either embarrasses me or my friends. Once for a 'treat' she gave us vanilla ice cream with maple sugar, canned peach juice and raisins on it. It was gross. And she stood there watching, with that smile of hers as we choked it down. Duane has never come back."

"Ugh."

"Believe me. It was awful in more ways than one. And where would I find a girl who would be interested in me? My complexion.

I'm too fat or too thin depending on the day and the relative. Dandruff. Bad breath. Crooked teeth. Acne. The list goes on and on."

"Listen." Giannini stood and looked Matt in the eye. "You are a perfectly normal young man. You are neither too fat or skinny. In fact, you're in pretty good shape. There is nothing wrong with you, nothing that every other young man hasn't faced at some point in his life." Giannini appraised him. "I see a handsome young man, who looks a bit like Sal Mineo. You will find a girl when the time is ripe for you. Not your mom, your grandmother or anyone else. Do you understand?"

"I guess so. I mean I know Mom is—whatever. But it goes it's hard to ignore."

"What happened to your shoulder?"

Matt shrugged. "Nothing. It will heal."

"Those kinds of wounds heal quickly."

"Thanks, Mr. G."

"Matt. In a couple of weekends, I'm going on a little trip. Robert might be in or out but could you keep an eye on the fish tanks?"

"Sure." Matt hesitated. "You have some exotic fish. Are there any special feeding instructions or anything?"

"Only for the piranhas."

"You got piranhas?"

Giannini nodded. "Every household has to have a man-eating fish in it somewhere."

"Far out!"

"Take care, Matt."

Matt took off down the creek. Balancing carefully, he step-stoned across the shallow flowing water.

He came to the broken concrete piles and began to climb. From a recessed space, he dug out *The Lost World* wrapped in aluminum foil. He bunched his t-shirt into a pillow, put it behind his head and opened the dog-eared novel to the third chapter, immersing himself into the adventures of Professor Challenger. Like a lizard, he soaked up the sun's rays. A slight breeze brought the pungent tang of eucalyptus. Bamboo shivered below him. In silence Matt read, the second hands on him Timex erasing the minutes.

"Matt!" His mother's voice intruded on his solitude. "Your grandmother is almost ready to go."

"Coming."

He wrapped the book carefully, using a eucalyptus leaf as a bookmark, and returned it to its hiding place. Not bothering with step stones, he waded the shallow water and emerged at Giannini's steps, his white socks bagging around his Keds. Giannini was gone. Scrambling quickly he climbed the canyon wall, entered his fort and emerged in the back yard.

"She's inside," his mother said from her chaise lounge.

Matt pulled off his wet shoes, grabbed a pair of sandals and stepped into the cool of the house while pulling on his t-shirt. "Smells good, Aunt Rose, as always."

Rose acknowledges the remark with a thin smile. "Thank you, Matty. Nice to be appreciated."

"Where's Grandma?"

"In the living room."

Matt found her in the living room bundling up the drapes in a king-sized sheet. She tied it at the top. "Gee, Grandma, if you had a stick, you'd look like a hobo."

"Ay?"

"Never mind. Let me lift that for you." He threw the bundle over his shoulder like Santa and headed toward the door. "Ready, Aunt Rose?"

"Yes. Let's get out of here. I have a lasagna baking at home." They walked out in silence through the courtyard, down the driveway and onto the cracked sidewalk shaded by overarching elm trees.

"Aunt Rose, why does Grandma come and do Mom's housework? It's not like we're that messy."

"If I had it my way she wouldn't."

"Why *does* she?"

"My mother spoiled your mother rotten. She is the *bambino*—the baby of the family. She got everything she wanted—including your father."

"How'd she meet Dad?"

"They were very young, about your age. You father's family moved in across the street from the apartment on Willow Street. They started seeing each other. Your grandfather got very sick. He went into the hospital and never came out. He died of complications to an operation."

"For what?"

"It was so long ago. Something to do with the arteries. Anyway when Papa died, Mom decided she couldn't handle a young girl with raging hormones, so she had them get married."

"Were they in love?"

"I don't know. It just seemed a good idea at the time."

"So why is Mom so much younger that her other sisters?"

"You're full of questions."

"Aunt Rose, who else would tell me? I may not like the fact that I have to put my dog out every time you come over, but I always know where I stand with you."

"You're right," said Rose. "Nobody in this family will tell you anything. Family secrets you know." She paused. "There are four of us sisters, with Leo between us. There was a sixth, a boy. You have to understand, an Italian woman loves her daughters. But a boy, he is king. His name was—it doesn't matter. He died two days after he was born. Your grandmother's grief was . . .she was . . ."

"I understand."

"No, you don't. A son keeps the bloodline going. A son takes care of his mother when the father dies. The son is the breadwinner, the hope of the future. To not have a son is a dishonor. To lose a son is—"

"Bad."

"Bad," confirmed Rose. "So your grandmother, in her grief, vowed to have no more children."

"Then Mom came along."

Rose stopped walking. Matt matched her. Rose watched as Grandma tottered on ahead, unheeding. "No. Your mother was the third to come along after that. Then Papa died and there were no more."

"Third?"

"She aborted them. With the corner of the dresser in her bedroom. As soon as she learned she was pregnant."

"Grandma?" Matt asked incredulously.

"Yes." Rose started walking again.

"And Mom?"

"Papa knew what she had done. He begged her to let your mother be born. He even brought a priest to talk to her. And so, your mother was born. And whether it was guilt or something else, your grandmother lavished her with everything. And she's trying to do the same to you. Don't let her."

"Spoil me? I don't think I'm spoiled."

Rose humphed.

"Am I?"

"No. Somehow you have avoided that. Your father may be a louse in a lot of ways, but he has given you an even keel. And the nuns. Never forget the influence of the nuns."

"Matty, how are you?" came a sultry voice from across the street.

"Hi, Mrs. Morgan. How are you?"

"Hello, Rose."

"Helene."

"How are the dogs, Mrs. Morgan?" Matt called.

Rose starred pointedly at the dogs, daring Mrs. Morgan to come any closer. She didn't.

"Matteo, come up here with me," his grandmother said.

"See you, Mrs. Morgan." He hurried to catch up with his grandmother.

"Why do you talk to that woman?" asked Grandma.

"I've taken care of her dogs whenever she is out of town."

"She is no good. Stay away from that *puttana*."

"What's a *puttana*?"

"Ask you father."

"That's twice in one day."

"What?"

"Nothing, Grandma."

They walked on in silence. Half a block later they were in front of Grandma's house. Rose opened the door and stepped inside, holding it for Matt and her mother. Matt carried the load of drapes into the service porch and dropped it on the washing machine. He untied the knot holding the bundle together, then stepped into the living room to leave.

"Matt. It goes without saying—"

"Don't worry, Aunt Rose, I never heard a thing you said."

Rose smiled and handed him a bag. "Biscotti. Fresh. Just baked them this morning."

"Gee, thanks." He clutched the bag in his hand. From down the hall, a toilet flushed, then moments later his grandmother walked into the living room.

"Matteo, here. This is for you." She pressed something into his hand. "For carrying the drapes for me."

"Thanks, Grandma. You didn't have to give me anything."

"I know, I know. You're a good boy, Matteo. Put it in your college fund."

"I will, Grandma."

"Your Aunt Victoria gave you fifteen thousand dollars in that fund. How much have you been able to add to it, Matteo?"

"Almost six hundred dollars. Mostly money I make taking care of the neighbors' yards and pets and stuff."

"You should get a job. Your grandfather, may he rest in peace, work from the day he was born."

Matt smiled. "I've heard this story before, Grandma." In a mock Italian accent, he continued. "He wassa saint. A saint, who worked his fingers to the bone so that his family coulda be successful in America."

"And as a result of working so hard, he died at an early age. Your grandmother seems to always forget that," Rose chimed in.

"I don't forget. I never stop praying for that man. But you must work hard to get ahead and college is the way to do that in America. My father wove fishing nets. You wanna weave fishing nets, Matteo?"

"No, Grandma."

"Then," she said triumphantly, "you have to go to school. Be glad your Aunt Vicki can help you. God knows your father won't be able to."

"Grandma! He owns six hotels," said Matt.

"Six hotels. Six hotels! That's why he isn't home to take care of you and your momma! That's why there is never any money to pay all the bills. That's why I had to buy your mother a new stove and dishwasher and refrigerator in the color she wanted."

"Grandma, I don't want to argue with you. Dad is trying to provide for the family."

"Your father should be home every night. He belongs here, in San Jose. Not in Idaho running a bunch of hotels."

"They're not all in Idaho," Matt said. "Two are in southern California."

"But not in San Jose."

"All right, Grandma. I gotta go. I'm sure Mom is cooking—something. Thanks for the biscotti, Aunt Rose." Matt headed toward the door.

"Your grandmother also brought in the mail." Rose said. "There were some magazines for you. She tossed them on your bed."

"Cool. The *National Geographic* came. They're featuring an article on humpback whales in this issue."

"You and animals."

"See ya, Aunt Rose. Thanks again. And thanks, Grandma."

He stepped out the door and ran down the steps. Pausing at the sidewalk, he looked to see what his grandmother had given him. Two crumpled dollar bills slowly unfolded. He shoved them into his cutoffs pocket and smiled.

"Matt," Rose called from the door.

"Yes?"

"Tell your mother that your Aunt Vicki is coming into town tomorrow. She just called."

"I will. Bye." Matt began his walk home whistling. Pausing to kick a dandelion ball, he watched the seeds float away in the gentle breeze. His grandmother's house was only six blocks from home and without the bundle of drapes, he made the trip quickly.

Opening the garage door, he checked the battery charger he'd left on his dad's car. The needle was well into the charged zone. After turning off the charger, he carefully removed the cables and put them away. He closed and latched down the hood, then crawled into the driver's seat of the Studebaker. Matt found the key under the floor mat on the passenger side of the car. Inserting the key, he settled back, reached for the primer and pushed the button, squirting gas into the carburetor. Three pushes, his dad had taught him. Too many flooded the old engine. With one foot on the clutch and the other on the gas, he shifted the gears to neutral and turned the key.

The ignition engaged and the engine roared to life then backfired, blowing a gout of black exhaust into the garage. Matt adjusted the mix and the engine smoothed out to a loud purr. He revved the engine a couple of times and, hearing nothing to worry about, switched off the car. The engine chugged to a halt. He pulled the key out of the ignition and started to slide it back under the floor mat, then paused and hopped out of the driver's seat. Opening the hood, he found a small niche near the rear of the engine and slipped the key in that spot instead. After re-latching the hood, he left the garage.

The smell of his aunt's sauce greeted him along with his dog, Letty. His mother stood over the stove with a wooden spoon stirring a boiling pot of water. Steam fogged the kitchen window. She stopped to pick up a bunch of spaghetti, deftly snapped the uncooked pasta in two and dropped it into the cauldron of bubbling water. The bubbles immediately ceased.

"Hey, Mom, Aunt Rose said that Aunt Vicki called and she's coming into town tomorrow for a couple of days."

"Oh, good. Matty, bring me the olive oil."

"Okay." Matt opened the counter near the refrigerator and pulled out the metal gallon tin of olive oil. He turned—not fast enough.

"You will never—" The wooden spoon she had grabbed arched through the air smacking him hard on the left shoulder. "Ever—" The spoon struck again, his elbow. "Embarrass me in front of my mother like that—" She swung again. This time Matt blocked the spoon with the can of olive oil. It thunked loudly. "Again." She swung the spoon wildly, hitting him as often as she missed. Trapped in the angle between refrigerator and counter there was no escape.

"Stop it. That hurts." Matt dodged and ducked, unable to avoid his mother's paroxysm of anger. He tried to shield himself with the can. She swung savagely, connecting with the can and with a pop the wooden spoon snapped, the larger half flying across the kitchen.

Mom stood there panting, strands of hair falling across her face. In a low voice she growled, "You broke my spoon."

"Me? You were the one—"

"You broke my good wooden spoon." She straightened up. With a flick, she tossed hair back where it belonged. "Bring it to me."

Matt put down the oil. Without turning his back to her, he retrieved the broken spoon.

"Give it."

She snatched the spoon fragment out of his hand. Examining both pieces, she turned with a scream of rage and hurled them against the counter. They slammed into a salt and pepper shaker set, shattering them. Several cans of opened tomato sauce flew like bowling pins. What sauce that was left in them splattered everywhere, blood from a shotgun blast. Yolanda visibly got herself under control. "Clean up the mess," she snarled. "Then go to your room."

Mom stalked out of the room.

Silently Matt went to the sink and got the washrag, then turned to the debris. He picked up the cans and dropped them into the garbage. Gingerly, he picked up the larger pieces of glass from the broken salt shaker and they joined the cans in the garbage. He wiped the counter.

"Ouch!" A shard of glass embedded into the pad of his palm. He pulled it out, swearing softly to himself. A ruby of blood welled up.

He washed down the wall behind the counter. Stepping back, he searched for tomato blobs he might have missed, then he hook shot the balled washcloth into the sink.

Angry oval red welts blossomed on both arms. He picked up the olive oil and the bag his aunt had given him. He carefully measured out a teaspoon of olive oil and added it to the spaghetti.

"I put in the oil," he yelled. There was no reply.

He stared into the chaos of boiling pasta for a moment, then turned and went to his room. He slid the pocket door shut and shoved a pencil from his desk between the door and the track, ensuring no surprise visits. He threw himself on the bed, scooping up the dog. Letty licked his face tentatively.

"Good old Letty. She really laid into me." The dog whimpered sympathetically as Matt examined his welts. "She did a number on the tin can, too." His grip on the dog tightened. "No matter what, I never want to be like her. Never." He choked back tears.

Turning over, he kicked off his sandals. Lying back on the bed, he felt something under his back. He rolled over to find two magazines. He peeled off the brown paper wrapper that held his *National Geographic* and glanced at it quickly. With a puzzled frown, he looked at the other brown wrapped package. Addressed to his father, it had no return address. Shrugging, he ripped the cover off. *Playboy.*

"Hey, dog. Dad subscribes to *Playboy.*" He began thumbing through the magazine, stopping at the fold-out.

"Wow, Letty. Even at the Elks swimming pool I've never seen anyone who looks like that." Faintly he heard the dinner bell ring. After a pause it rang again, a sweet fairy sound. "Come on, Dog. It's dinner time."

He took the *Playboy* and tossed it on the top shelf of his closet with its wrapper. Grabbing the *National Geographic,* he pulled the pencil from the slider and headed for the kitchen.

Mom was already seated, shaking freshly ground Parmesan cheese onto her pile of spaghetti. She didn't look up as he approached. "Grandma said this had come. She threw it on my bed."

Mom glanced at the magazine and paused, fork midway to her mouth. "Is this the only magazine that came?"

"It's the only magazine we subscribe to, isn't it?" Matt looked at his mom. She looked away.

Matt scooped a mound of spaghetti and slapped it into his plate. Then he ladled the thick aromatic sauce onto it. A blizzard of cheese followed.

"Do you want wine?"

"No, Mom." He wound a bunch of noodles around his fork. "Thank you," he added.

"Your father called. He will be in Saturday instead of Friday."

"Oh, rats."

"The car is ready?"

"Yes, it runs like a charm."

Forks scraped against plates.

"You have homework?"

"Just math. I'll do it while I'm watching TV."

"I don't understand how you can do that."

"What?"

"Watch television and study."

"I don't know. I just can."

Mom spooned up seconds. "Did you ask anybody to your cousin's birthday party?"

"No." Matt took a deep breath. "I really don't want to go. Joe is a freshman in college. He doesn't need a high school kid like me hanging around. And everybody's bringing a date. I don't have anyone to bring. And Joe and I never got along. He just brags about all the expensive gifts he gets. And it's a dance. I don't dance."

"I could teach you."

"You dance?"

"Your father and I used to dance a lot when we were younger."

"The Twist? The Frug? The Watusi?"

"No," she sighed. "Ballroom dancing. Real dancing."

"I don't want to go."

"You were invited. The family expects it."

"Aunt Paula invited me. Not Joe."

"You don't know that."

Matt used a piece of garlic bread to sop up sauce on his plate. "I really don't want to go."

"You're going."

Matt stood to leave. "I haven't excused you."

He sat back down. "Can I be excused?'

"Ask nice."

"Can I please be excused?"

Silence.

Matt gritted his teeth. "May I please be excused, oh beautiful mother? Pretty please, with sugar on top?"

Mom turned and smiled coldly. "Yes. Don't forget your plate."

"Come on, Letty."

"Her name is Aletta."

Matt took his plate and left, dog trailing. He scraped the plate leftovers into the sink and placed it in the dishwasher. Then he went to his room. The pencil back in place blocking the sliding door from opening, he took down the *Playboy* and thumbed through it again. From his desk drawer he pulled a letter opener and a rubber band.

Hunching down under his window, he located the small section of paneling the carpenter hadn't nailed into position. He carefully pulled back the vinyl floorboard and inserted the blade of the letter opener between the pieces of paneling. One panel pulled forward, revealing a hiding place already containing two silver dollars. He rolled up the *Playboy* and slid it in the space, carefully replacing everything. He checked to make sure there were no telltale signs, then went back to his desk and began his homework.

Chapter Four

Matt's arm swung down and hit the snooze button on his clock radio, silencing Peter, Paul and Mary for at least another five minutes. He flipped his pillow and buried his head in it, snuggling in the blankets for warmth.

"Matty."

"Ohhh—"

"Get up Matt, it's late."

Matt stretched his long legs, dislodging the sleeping dog between them. Letty jumped down with an indignant yip. When Matt's legs hit the linoleum floor he levered himself up to a standing position, yawning widely. He stumbled to his dresser and removed a card——a queen of spades—wedged in the crack between the drawer and dresser. He fished for a pair of matching black socks. Replacing the card carefully, he closed the drawer and then repeated the routine with his t-shirt drawer. Shrugging on a shirt, he shuffled sleepily through the kitchen to the bathroom. Mom was at the kitchen table sipping coffee. The morning gauntlet had begun.

"Really brush your teeth this time. Do you have Mass today?"

"Yeah."

"Then don't forget your tongue. I don't want any priest telling me you opened your mouth for Communion and your tongue was white. Scrub your face with that pumice soap I bought for you. It is supposed to be wonderful for skin like yours."

"Yes, Mom."

"Are you showering?"

"No, Mom."

"You should."

"I showered last night and yes, I used soap and the acne cream."

"The new dandruff shampoo?"

"Yes."

"Good, maybe we can save that face of yours."

Matt walked down the hall into the bathroom. After relieving himself, he turned to the sink. Through blurry eyes he examined his face. Finding a lone blackhead he squeezed it hard, leaving a bright red mark. He quickly brushed his teeth, taking time to brush his tongue. Then he peered in the mirror again. The red from the squeeze mark was fading. He pinched himself again. Not enough. Reaching into the drawer, he pulled out a needle. His eyes fixed on his thick eyebrows. Holding the needle in one hand, he tensed and stabbed. Dropping the needle into the drawer, he squeezed around his wound. A small bead of blood appeared. Matt appraised the results, then he headed back to his room.

Mom exacted her toll. "Let me look at you."

Matt stepped over to her as she stood up.

"Move into the sunlight. And stoop down, I'm not that tall." Mom glanced at the squeeze marks on Matt's face. Her eyes passed without comment. "Stick out your tongue."

Matt did.

"Good." She glanced at his eyebrows. "Oh, Matty, how could you leave the bathroom like that?" She picked up a napkin and wet it with her lips. "Lean down here and let me get that."

Matt leaned forward and his mother cleaned the drop of blood off with the tip of the napkin. Hands on his chest she pushed him erect. "There. I took care of that." She smiled. "What would you do without me?"

Matt shrugged, a crooked grin on his face.

"Hurry up. You'll be late."

"I don't have to leave so early today. Remember? My bike got a flat. I'm taking the bus."

"Did it? Well, then. There's oatmeal on the stove and raisins. Have some of that."

"Good idea."

He helped himself to the oatmeal, drowned the concoction in

cold milk and began spooning it into his mouth. "We get our grades today."

"Oh." Mom turned the page of the daily paper. "Matty, would you like me to read you Ann Landers?"

"Sorry, Mom." He dropped the spoon into the empty bowl. "I got to get dressed."

He headed into the bedroom, pausing to feed the dog and to grab his books and the sack lunch his mother had made for him. He pulled out two of his aunt's biscotti for his lunch bag and shoved the bag of remaining cookies under his bed. Petting the dog goodbye, Matt headed for the door.

"Did you forget something?"

"No, I—" He froze when he saw his mother puckering her heavily lipsticked lips.

"Oh, yeah."

He stepped over to his mother and gave her a quick kiss on the lips. Out the door, he hastily wiped the waxy lipstick feel off his mouth and headed to the bus stop at the entrance of Willow Street Park, a block from his house. Thick juniper bushes and ornamental bamboos flanked both sides of the sidewalk going into the park. Three grammar school kids in maroon uniform sweaters and corduroy pants clustered, gathering snails. The boys put them on the white stripes of the crosswalk, whooping it up when cars drove by crushing them.

Matt looked on, frowning. "You guys shouldn't be doing that," he said.

"Why not?" The tallest of the three boys responded. "They're just snails."

"Just snails? Surely you don't think that." Matt stood tall. "Snails are remarkable little beasts."

The boys stopped tossing the snails and looked at Matt.

"In fact, those very snails that you are throwing out in the street were imported all the way from France, in Europe."

"Really? Why would anybody want to bring snails here?"

"It happened back in the days of the California Gold Rush. A businessman—I can't remember his name—imported these snails from France. He figured, with all the money the gold miners had, they might be interested in some good food."

"Food! Ugh."

"You see, in France, they eat those very snails. They scoop them out of their shells and cook them up in garlic and charge people a lot of money to eat them. Those snails are called escargot."

"You had to pay to eat 'em?" one of the boys asked.

"Yes, in fine restaurants you could order them. Well, this businessman made a mistake. Snail might be considered food in France, but nobody in California wanted to eat them. They wanted steak or chicken or burgers."

"That's right. I don't eat bugs."

"They're mollusks, actually. So these snails escaped."

"Escaped? Who couldn't catch a runaway snail?"

"Who would want to?" Matt answered.

"True."

"And snails are hermaphrodites. Both male and female. Any two snails can make a baby. It doesn't matter what they are."

One of the boys looked at the snail he was holding quizzically. Then he bent to put it down carefully.

"That's weird," the boy said.

"You wouldn't know to call them John or Marsha," another piped in.

"Sonny or Cher," the tallest giggled.

"Besides, even though they are slimy, they got a right to live."

"There's the bus," the tallest boy called out.

The boys bustled about gathering up their lunches and books. Matt picked up a snail and placed it carefully in the bushes, snatched up his lunch bag and books and stepped up to the curb as the city bus roared up. The folding doors swooshed open and the three little boys jammed themselves on, dropping coins in the meter as they went. Matt followed, putting in his dime.

"Matt!"

Matt froze. It was Stacey Moore patting the seat next to her. Nonplussed, Matt walked back and slid in beside her.

"I don't see you on the bus very often." She said smiling.

"Ah . . . well . . . you see . . ." He took a deep breath. "My bike got a flat tire yesterday so I had to take the bus until I get to Sears and buy myself a tire repair kit. My mom wouldn't take me yesterday so I'll go sometime this weekend."

Stacey laughed. "Slow down, sport."

Matt smiled. "Anyway, I either have to take the bus or walk until I fix it."

"Today's the big day."

"Big day?"

"They're going to announce the winners of the science project competition. It's kinda exciting. I mean we are up against the all the schools in the diocese and some of the public schools, too."

"I guess."

"Aren't you excited?"

He shrugged. "Not really."

"Why not? Everyone says yours is the best of the bunch."

"It was just something I did over the summer. I didn't do it to win a prize. I did it to help the kit foxes."

"Maybe that's why it's good."

"Why?" he asked, puzzled.

"It's authentic. Everyone else was doing another old school project. You worked on something you love."

"Maybe."

"Why are you so interested in animals anyway?"

"I don't know. Maybe—maybe because they're honest."

"Honest?"

"Yeah," he said, warming to his topic. "With a dog you can always see the signs. If it wags its tail, things will be okay. If it lays its ears back, you know you're in trouble. Animals always give you signs."

"Did you watch *Star Trek* last night? I mean I just assume you're the kind of person who would watch *Star Trek*. Aren't you?"

"I watched it. I watch it every Thursday night like clockwork. You watch it too?"

"Isn't Spock the coolest? Those ears and those eyebrows." She gushed a little. "Spock's my favorite character and Bones."

"Mine, too." He thought a minute. "And I like Sulu and Scotty."

"Why do you like Spock?" She asked.

"He's logical. My dad and mom were fighting and when it was all over, Dad turned to me and said, 'You just can't argue logically with a non-logical person.'"

"Spock's not like animals. He doesn't give you signs."

"But he doesn't have emotions. He won't explode on you."

"Oh, he has emotions. They just simmer there, inside."

"I know." Matt reflected for a moment. "But he isn't controlled by them."

"What do you think of Cathy Donatelli?'

"Huh?"

"You know, the freshman who lives a block over from you. What do you think of her?"

"I—I guess she's okay." He paused. "I really don't think about her too much."

"Good."

Matt looked confused.

"You should come over after school today. My dad wants to meet you."

"Me? Why?"

"I told him about you." She glanced away. "I told him that you liked to read and what you were reading." Swiveling back she said, "He's got a great library. I bet he'd loan you some books."

"They're also announcing the winner of the writing contest today. You'll win. Since I won last year I got to judge. I read your poem. It was cool," Matt said.

"You think so?" She dislodged the books balanced on her lap and they fell to the floor.

Matt bent to pick them up and found himself staring at her uncovered knees. Grabbing the books, he straightened, "Yep. It was seriously very cool."

"Thanks!" She blushed. "I really want to win."

"You will."

"I write every day."

They talked until the bus arrived at the school. Matt stepped back into the aisle, letting Stacey out first. He followed. When Matt jumped down from the bus stair he was greeted by Dave.

"Matt, I figured you'd be on the bus today. Was that Stacey Moore?"

"Yeah."

"Did you talk to her?"

"Yeah." Matt turned and looked at Dave, face glowing.

"How was it?"

"It was freaking fantastic."

"What did you talk about?"

"I don't even know. *Star Trek* . . . some other girl . . . her dad's library. I don't know."

"Some other girl? Who?

"Cathy, Cathy Donatelli. Stacey wanted to know what I thought about her."

"Man, this is awesome! She was fishing."

"Fishing?" Matt asked quizzically. The bell rang. Everyone on the school grounds froze, then began walking to their classes. "What do you mean, fishing?"

"Got to go, Matt. Mr. Ryan marks us down if we aren't in our seats before the bell stops ringing."

"But—"

Dave ran off.

Matt ran into Sister Maria Tomas during breaks between his science and math classes. She stopped him in the hall near his locker.

"Matt." She eyed him closely. "I take it your mother still won't allow you to shave."

"Sister, honestly, I forgot to ask her."

"You promised."

"I know, but yesterday just wouldn't have been a good day to bring it up. I promise, really promise I will talk about it with her this weekend. Maybe with Dad coming home, she'll be in a better mood."

"You have bruises on your arms."

"Yes." Matt made ineffectual attempts to cover his arms with his books.

"Would you like to tell me how those happened?" she asked kindly.

"No, Sister. I really—I'd rather not talk about it."

"I might be able to help."

"I appreciate that, Sister. I know you mean it. But it's no big deal." Matt shrugged. "It's just the way things are."

"Matt—"

"Sister, I've got to go. You know how Mr. Ryan is." He looked at her pleadingly.

She smiled. "See you last period then, Matt." He bolted down the hall and into the math room, shutting the door behind him.

At lunch, Matt sat alone on the school bench looking with dismay at another avocado sandwich. This one had cold bacon on it. The bacon grease had congealed into blobs like frozen sweat. Matt chucked it into the garbage then dug into his lunch sack and pulled out the biscotti his aunt had given him the night before.

"More avocado sandwiches?" Dave asked, sitting next to him.

"Threw it away. This one had bacon."

"Bacon's good."

"Not cold, greasy, green bacon. It looked like great green gobs of green greasy gopher guts."

"What's that from?" Dave asked while chewing peanut butter and jelly.

"I think it's from a kid's song. That's all I remember from it,"

"You're in trouble, you know, Matt?"

"Why."

"You know Peter Delvechio?"

"Is he the guy in my language class with the big ears?"

"Yeah, that's him. Could be Icabod Crane in a play or something."

"Yeah, all arms and legs and ears."

"That's the guy." Dave finished his sandwich and fished out some chocolate chip cookies. "Want one? My mom makes them and she puts walnuts in them."

Matt took one and bit into it. He grunted thanks to Dave.

"Anyway, I heard Pete saying to some of the guys in my Spanish class that he liked Stacey Moore."

"So?"

"Somebody told him that they had seen her talking to you yesterday. And that you two were together on the bus."

"So what?"

"So Pete said that he would have to look into that." Dave punctuated that pronouncement by biting into another cookie. "He thinks he likes Stacey, too. He said he thought he might ask her to the Spring Fling. You going to ask her?"

"I don't know. I hadn't thought about it."

"Man, you got bruises up and down your arms. What happened?"

"My mother really tied into me."

"Your mother did this? What did you do—rob a bank or something?"

"Nope. You know my mother. She just goes off"

"Those must have hurt."

"Sister Tomas asked about them. I didn't tell her what happened."

"You didn't lie to a nun did you? They know! They have nun-senses."

"Is that like spider sense?" Matt asked.

"Kind of. They always seem to know if someone lies to them."

"I didn't lie. But what good would telling her do?"

"She's a nun!"

"Sure she's a nun. But she's only king here," Matt said. "Here she has control and authority. Once we step off the school grounds, where's her authority?"

"She could talk to your mom."

"And as soon as she leaves, Mom would go off on me again. I can't hide every wire hanger or shoe my mother has. No. It's better just to live with it." He paused and thought for a moment. "And she is my mom. I wouldn't rat her out over this."

"I still think Sister could do something."

"What? It will take more than a black dress and rosary beads to change my mother."

Matt watched a cloud of pigeons circle the steeple of the church.

"Want to shoot some baskets?"

"Sure."

Student anxiety rose as the day dragged on. Report cards and announcements about the winners of the two contests were coming out. As the hands of the clock crawled toward three, the fidgeting, whispering and number of passed around notes rose, defying the best efforts of the teachers to control it. At 2:30 the intercom squawked, a roar of scratchy static. The principal's tinny voice announced, "Teachers, pardon the interruption. Pardon the interruption. I am pleased to say that there are a couple of winners that need to be announced."

The classroom door opened and Monsignor Cochetti entered, resplendent in his black robes with red linings, a portly man with a round smiling face. He walked up to the desk and whispered to Sister Tomas as the class stood to greet him. He turned to the standing class.

"Please be seated," the monsignor said, indicating the intercom.

"As you know, we are in competition with several of the schools in the diocese as well as some of the public schools including Willow Glen High School. I am proud to say that St. John Bosco High has acquitted itself very well."

Students squirmed, looking from the monsignor to various people in the classroom. The principal's disembodied voice continued, "In the writing contest we did very well. Third place went to Andrew Miller in Mrs. Baldwin's sophomore writing class. Second place went to Amy Cravats at St. John Vianney Prep. And first place went to our own Stacey Moore."

The classroom erupted in chaos as students congratulated Stacey, who managed to look surprised, humble and very self-satisfied, all at the same time.

"Quiet," the monsignor said.

The class quieted.

"—place goes to Anthony Girabaldi at Willow Glen. And first place goes to our very own—where is a drum roll when you need it—Matt Connors."

The intercom was drowned out by the tidal wave of noise that swept the room. The monsignor beamed, looking over the cheering students, letting the noise crest and recede.

"—will be a dinner for the winners of the writing contest and they will get their material published in local newspapers. Matt will be attending a banquet at Moffett Field where he will be presented a first place check of five hundred dollars by none other than Mercury astronaut Wally Schirra. Congratulations to all of the winners."

"Five hundred dollars? That's pizza for everybody," someone shouted.

"Ahem." The monsignor cleared his throat gently. "I came to congratulate the winners. I understand there are two in this classroom?" He turned and looked at Sister Tomas.

"Yes, Monsignor. Stacey Moore and Matt Connor. Would the two of you please stand?"

Stacey bounced out of her chair beaming. Matt got up reluctantly with a silly grin on his face.

"I have here the official letters announcing the winners. They also have information about the dinner or banquet you are going to be attending." He pulled two white envelopes from beneath his robe. He handed one to Stacey, who took it and shook hands with the monsignor. The class broke into enthusiastic applause. She turned smiling, her joy washing across the room. Matt stepped up, taking the proffered envelope awkwardly. He shook hands almost as an afterthought with the monsignor and mumbled a thank you. The lopsided grin never wavered as he looked at the class.

Sister silenced the students with a glance then turned to Matt and smiled. "The dinner is next Friday. Monsignor and I will be joining you and your parents. It should be a wonderful evening. You worked hard. You deserve it." She turned to the rest of the class. "Now, it's time to hand out the report cards. Stacey, Matt, will you help me?"

Matt nodded and stuffed the prize envelope into his pants pocket. Taking the envelopes Sister handed him, he began passing them out and acknowledged the thank you's and congratulations with a bob of his head.

Matt held out the last report card as the bell rang. Peter Delvechio snatched it out of his hand. "Suck-up," Peter snarled as he grabbed his books and left.

Matt watched him go.

"Ignore him. He thinks IQ is a flavor at Baskins and Robbins," Stacey said. He turned.

"Matt. Congratulations on winning the science competition," the monsignor said, walking over to shake hands again. "I had an opportunity to see all of the projects in the competition. Yours was well written and well researched, though the fish in the terrarium needed a bit of water. Hope you don't mind, but I put some in the little pond."

"Not at all. Thank you, Monsignor."

"How much time did you put into that?"

"About five weeks of field work. Observations and notes, things like that. Then about another three weeks to analyze my facts and fit them in with the proposed boundaries of the preserve. A couple of speeches before a bunch of park people. And then a week to make the backdrop and write up the report."

"Have you heard anything about the parks plans? Did you influence it much?"

"Yeah, he heard," Dave answered, coming in the classroom door and sidling up to Matt.

"And you are—?" The Monsignor asked.

"David Arreugo. One of my most colorful students," Sister Maria Tomas answered dryly.

Monsignor Cochetti turned back to Matt.

"So what did you hear?"

"Well, the planning board decided to accept some of my recommendations. They shifted the boundaries around a little bit, including some prime feeding territory for the foxes. Funny thing is—" He paused. "It ticked off my Uncle Silvio."

"Oh? How so?"

"Uncle Silvio builds golf courses. The new boundaries meant he had to move the golf course he was building. I don't think he was expecting that from me, since I was staying with him and my Aunt Vicki that summer."

"Probably not." Monsignor Cochetti chuckled. "Well, good job. You did St. John Bosco proud."

Cochetti turned and began talking to Sister Tomas.

"I told you that you'd win," Dave said.

"It's no big deal."

"It's five hundred dollars," Dave continued. "And since you ticked off your moneybags uncle, you may need it."

"I told him we'd both win today, too," Stacey added.

"You two better be careful. You're sounding serious."

"Come on," Matt protested.

"Matt," Stacey put in. "We better hurry if we want to catch the bus."

"You're right." Matt said, "Sorry, Dave. We got to go."

Dave leered at Matt mouthing the word "we." Then he turned and sprinted to the bike rack.

Matt and Stacey trotted to the bus stop. Looking down the street they could see it a mere block away.

"We made it," Stacey said, breathing hard.

"Not by much," Matt added.

"Are you happy?"

"I guess so." He paused and thought a second. "Yeah, I guess I am. Happy."

"I'm delighted. I'll be published. Sometimes after the paper publishes it, a magazine like *The New Yorker* or something will pick it up. I could even get paid."

"It was a wonderful poem."

"You really did read it?"

"Of course. I love ballads."

"Like *The Highwayman*?"

"Yes." The bus rumbled to a stop and they got on, sitting together. "Look for me at moonlight. Watch for me by moonlight. I'll come to thee by moonlight though Hell shall bar the way."

"Sad. And very romantic." Stacey sighed. "Come to my house."

"Okay."

"Dad's home and it's just a few blocks past your stop."

"Sure." Matt did some calculations in his head. "As long as I'm home by five there shouldn't be any problems."

"What's at five?"

"My Aunt Vicki is coming over. We eat promptly at five o'clock whenever we have company."

"I'll get you home on time."

"I'm the one who is supposed to say that."

Stacey laughed and Matt watched his stop slide by, a shiver of freedom coursing through him.

They got off the bus talking and laughing as they walked to Stacey's house. Several times their shoulders bumped together. Matt shifted his books from his right arm to his left, leaving the one nearer Stacey free. Moments later Stacey changed her books to her right hand. After a few bumps, fingers awkwardly intertwined. Matt stopped walking and looked down, a slight blush spreading across his face.

"Is there a problem, Matt?"

"What? A problem?" He looked at her and smiled. "No. I don't think there is any problem at all."

They walked on, pausing before a Victorian mansion, the weathered paint cracked and peeling.

"Dad says once all the paint has peeled off, then he will paint it. Until then it'll just have to look like this."

"It has an Addams Family kind of charm," Matt said gallantly. "If he needs any help, I'm pretty close."

Stacey skipped up the stairs, opening a massive wooden door with a stained glass window in it. A rainbow of color arced across the hall as the door closed behind them. "Dad doesn't skimp on the inside at all."

Burnished hardwood floors lay before them. Stacey pointed to the right. "That's the living room. Color TV and a stereo hi-fi."

"Wow. You can watch *Star Trek* in color."

"And *Bonanza*. It's great." She led him deeper into the house toward the sound of typing. She paused before a set of paneled sliding doors. "This is the inner sanctorum-my father's combo study and library." She pushed apart the doors. "Hi, Dad." The typing stopped as a blond, athletically built man with deep blue eyes looked up.

"Stacey." He glanced at the clock then at Matt. "This must be Matt." He got up extending an arm. Matt stepped closer and shook his hand. The grip was firm. Mr. Moore's eyes appraised Matt quickly. "Stacey has told me a great deal about you, Matt."

"She has?"

"And most of it was good," Stacey said, seating herself on her father's desk.

"Actually, all of it was good." He smiled at Matt.

Matt nodded. He eyes wandered to Stacey and then to the shelves of books that covered every inch of wall in the room. Sunlight flooded the room and Matt turned in a short circle, taking it all in. The walls were eighteen feet high, oak shelves heavily laden with hundreds of books everywhere. Two ladders attached to a track graced either side of the room. Between the two picture windows a set of animal horns were hung.

"Like it?" Stacey asked.

Mr. Moore regarded the boy with a smile. "Those mountain goat horns were given to me many years ago by Ernest Hemingway. He enjoyed hunting now and again."

"Begging your pardon, sir, but those are ibex horns, not mountain goat."

"He's right, Daddy. You've always told me they were ibex."

"Most people don't know a mountain goat from an ibex, so I go with mountain goat. It's an easy out." He regarded Matt again. "Would you like a tour?"

"Sure."

Mr. Moore walked to the right side of the room. "These are the first editions. Authors whose books I review send them to me. A lot of them are signed." His arms swept over a half dozen shelves. "are the books I have reviewed. Those," he turned and pointed across the room, "These are my personal books. The stuff I like to read."

"Wow."

"What do you like to read?"

"A little of everything. I like science fiction and mysteries a lot. But I read biographies and history. A lot of adventure stuff—"

"Like *The Executioner*?" Mr. Moore asked.

"No, true adventure. Martin and Osa Johnson, Bernard Grzimek, Jean-Pierre Hallet, Dr. Leakey—that sort of thing."

"Well rounded."

"I try to be." Matt glanced at Stacey. "My grandmother says you need a good education to make it in this country." He grinned. "I learn more from books than I have from most of the teachers I've had."

"Stacey's right. You are a rather remarkable young man."

"How do you review nature writing?" Matt asked

"I look at it critically. I reflect on what I believe an author can do and should do, and I try to be honest." He paused, "That's all any of us can do when we review an author, isn't it? Trust in what we believe?"

"Enough of my father," Stacey chimed in. "My bedroom is upstairs. Do you want to see it?"

Matt found his throat tightening

"It's okay, Matt," Mr. Moore said.

"Oh. Okay."

Stacey hopped off the desk and grabbed his arm. She led him out the sliding doors and up an oak circular staircase. Turning to Matt she said, "My bedroom is in the turret."

"Of course." He smiled up at her. "Isn't that where all princesses live?"

"And what room would the prince live in?"

"I'd be in the dungeon."

Stacey laughed and opened the door to her bedroom. Painted a pale yellow, with sunlight flooding through the wrap-around windows, the room was warm and bright. Book shelves lined the walls. Matt walked over to the windows.

"Great view. You can see almost the whole neighborhood from here." Stacey stepped up to his side. He turned. "Nancy Drew. I wouldn't have pegged you for a Nancy Drew reader." His eyes wandered over the worn brown books. "And they're the old ones, too."

"Too?"

"I have all the Hardy Boy books. The old ones. And a few of the very old Tom Swifts. The old ones had more—" He paused, searching for the right word.

"Charm?"

"Maybe. And originality. The new ones are too much the same formula."

Stacey shut her bedroom door and sat on the bed.

"Should you shut the door?"

"Why not? My dad trusts me."

"But does he trust me?" Matt asked.

"I trust you." She pointed across the room to a chair in front of her desk. Matt sat. She plumped up some pillows and leaned across the bed beneath a framed painting of a unicorn. "So, who's your favorite Hardy Boy character?"

"Fenton Hardy."

"The dad?"

"He isn't around much, but he always manages to give his sons the vital clue they need to solve the case." They talked for a long time.

Both of them were on the floor together, leaning against the bed, laughing. A book slipped off of Stacey's lap and thumped lightly on the floor between them. Matt looked at the clock and then did a double take. It was twenty minutes to five. Then another thought struck him.

"You know what we forgot to do?"

"What?" Stacey picked up the book and tossed it behind her onto the bed.

"We forgot to tell your dad about our winnings."

"You're right!" Stacey bounded up. "I'll be right back."

"I've got to go, too." He pointed at the clock. "It's almost five."

"Cinderella at least got until midnight." Together they trouped down the stairs. "Dad."

Mr. Moore opened the study doors and looked up at this daughter.

"What is it, Stacey?"

"We forgot to tell you."

"What?"

"I won the writing competition—"

"That's wonderful." He swept his daughter up in his arms and gave her a big hug. "Wonderful. You'll get published."

"Maybe you can review my poem."

"I'd have to be honest."

"It's real good, Mr. Moore," Matt said.

"You read it?"

"He won last year," Stacey explained. "Third place, but enough to be one of the judges, Dad."

"And I'm not just saying that," Matt said. "It is good."

"Stacey, that's great. You know the banquet will have several authors present. One of them is Ray Bradbury."

Stacey showed her father the letter announcing her win. "And," she added, "Matt won first place in the science competition. Show Dad your letter."

Matt pulled the crumpled letter out of his back pocket and handed it to Mr. Moore.

"Five hundred dollars, very impressive." He scanned the letter. "Uh oh."

"What is it, Dad?"

"Both of these dinners are the same night. You won't be able to cheer each other on."

"I didn't know I was invited—"

"Of course you were invited." Stacey said. "But if we can't—"

"Next time, Stacey," her father said.

"Nice to meet you, Mr. Moore. But I got to go. If I'm not home at five—"

"He turns into a pumpkin."

They walked him to the door, and Stacey brought Matt his books. The two men shook hands and Matt said a goodbye to Stacey. "I'm glad I came."

Chapter Five

After he turned the corner from Stacey's house, Matt began to run. He relaxed as he came within sight of his house. A new Lincoln Continental, white with gold trim, eased up to the house as he arrived and parked alongside the other car in the driveway. Matt waited politely as his Aunt Vicki and Uncle Silvio got out of the Continental.

"Matt. It's good to see you." Vicki engulfed him in a hug. The fur of her mink tickled his nose.

"I'm good, Aunt Victoria. How are you, Uncle Silvio?"

Silvio examined the crease of his pale yellow golf slacks and the shine of his white leather shoes before answering. "I'm good, Matthew. How are you?" Not waiting for an answer he went on, "Is your dad here?"

"Nope. Something tied him up. He's supposed to be here tomorrow."

"That's disappointing."

"How long are you staying this time?"

"Oh, not long, not long." He brushed lint from his cashmere sweater. "Your aunt and I are going to Morocco. Possibility of building a golf course there in the desert."

"Hey, if you see an Arabian oryx or an impala take a picture for me, will you?"

"Yeah, sure thing. I'll do that. Your Uncle Leo here?"

"Don't know, Uncle Silvio. But I think that's his Cadillac."

Silvio looked at the Cadillac: last year's model. "That's what he's driving." Silvio pumped himself up, looking from his Continental to the Caddy. "Well, this could be interesting."

"Silvio, don't," warned Aunt Victoria.

"Oh, Mommy. Let me have some bragging rights." Victoria relented. Silvio walked away toward the house.

"Matthew, I want to give you this while nobody is around." She reached into her purse and pulled out an envelope. "That's a hundred dollars to go into your college account."

"Thanks Aunt Victoria." He took the envelope and stuffed it in his pocket. Then he bent to kiss her.

"And here." She thrust three silver dollars into his hand. "Your uncle will never notice."

"Wow. This one is from 1888. Cool."

"Put them in your pocket. Your uncle is coming."

Silvio stepped out of the house into the courtyard. They could hear his voice bragging. Uncle Leo trailed behind him. "Nah, didn't pay a thing for it. The dealership gave it to me for a year. They like to have their cars driven around the country club by people like me." With an expansive wave of his hand, Silvio introduced the Continental. "Heck, Larry Welk bought one because he saw mine. Of course with all that champagne music he sells, he can afford a dozen of them."

Uncle Leo walked around the new car. "Nice car," he said.

"Nice!" Silvio countered. "Look, it's got air conditioning, AM/FM radio, an internal antenna control, a tape deck. It's a beautiful car."

"Yes, it's a very nice car. Hi, Matty. I didn't know you were here."

"I just got here, Uncle Leo."

"You mother has been wondering where you were."

"A *very* nice car?" Silvio exclaimed.

Matt turned and thanked his aunt again, then ran into the house. "Hey, Mom, I won—"

"Where have you been? Take the tongs and get the artichokes out of the pot and then I need you to get the table set. And get that dog out of here. Your Aunt Rose just called and they are on their way. You know she hates dogs."

"She used to own a dog."

"Don't argue with me. The artichokes are done."

Matt scooped up the dog and carried her into his bedroom. He pulled the three silver dollars out and looked at them. Two he tossed into a jar on his desk. The third he slid into the secret panel with the *Playboy* and his other treasures. Quickly he changed shirts and stepped back into the kitchen.

"The artichokes," his mother insisted.

Grabbing tongs and a platter Matt pulled the lid off of the stock pot, ducking out of the angry wash of steam. One by one he plucked the bloated artichokes out of the boiling water and placed them in a pyramid on the platter. "Hey Mom, I—"

"Done?"

"Yes."

"Dump the water into the sink. Then fill the pot with water and put it back on to boil." She waved hair out of her face. "My momma won't eat anything but pasta, pasta, pasta."

"At school today—," he started as he did what he was told.

"Yes?"

"I was going to tell you—"

The front door opened.

"Yola. Where are you?"

"In the kitchen, Momma. Damn it, Matty, if you had been here on time the table would be set."

"Can I help?" Matt's grandmother asked, at his elbow.

"I think I have it handled, Grandma," Matt replied, putting salt and oil in with the cold water on the pot.

"Don't forget a bay leaf," his grandmother added, watching him intently.

"Momma, I know what I'm doing," Mom said.

"The table isn't set," came a brusque voice.

"Hello, Rose. Yes, I know. Matt was late. He'll get it done."

"I hear barking. Is that dog penned up, Matty?"

"Yes, Aunt Rose. It's in the bedroom and as long as—"

The door opened again. Silvio and Leo entered, arguing about the respective merits of their cars. Victoria entered the kitchen, hugging her sister Rose and kissing her mother. "Smells good in here," she said.

"I'm broiling some T-bones. Rose, what are you doing?"

"Getting the dishes down, Yolanda. What does it look like I'm doing?"

"I have things handled."

"Matteo, that's not enough bay leaf."

Matt pulled out two more and checked with his grandmother. She nodded and he dropped the two leaves into the pot. "It'll be a couple of minutes before it boils Grandma. Want to help me set the table?" She nodded again.

Matt got down glasses and handed a few to his grandmother, who put one besides each dish. Matt pulled open the silverware drawer and counted the forks.

"How many are we, Mom?"

"Let's see. There's Victoria and Silvio. Leo's wife couldn't make it. That's—"

"Seven," Rose stated.

Matt looked at his mom. She nodded.

"Is Paula coming?" Victoria asked, entering the room.

"No, the boys had a baseball game and she couldn't get them out of it."

"Not even for a family get-together?"

"Aunt Victoria, Joe and Jimmy are the pitcher and catcher. Without them you don't have a game," Matt said.

"Oh," Victoria said vaguely. "Do you have anything to drink, Yolanda?"

Yolanda was trying to put together a salad. At Victoria's question her knife blade slipped and a tomato rolled off the cutting board and onto the floor. "Hell!"

"Mom, I'll take care of the salad," Matt said. "Why don't you take the wine into the living room and get everybody a drink?"

"Very well. Come on everybody, my son has just ordered everyone out of the kitchen." She gathered herself together and pulled a bottle of white wine out of the cupboard. Matt pulled down wine glasses and put them on a tray.

"I'll take those."

"Thanks, Aunt Victoria."

"Your water's boiling, Matteo."

"Okay, Grandma." He opened a drawer and took out a bag of spaghetti, measured it with his thumb and forefinger and snapped it in two, dropping it into the pot.

"Is your mother using my sauce or her own sauce?" Rose asked.

Matt looked into the cluttered sink and pulled out a piece of aluminum foil with a name written on it.

"Yours I think, Aunt Rose."

"Good." Rose turned on her heel and started to exit the kitchen. She paused before leaving. "You better check the steaks. Your mother has a tendency to burn them."

Popping open the oven door, Matt tested the steaks with a fork. Red blood oozed up from the wound he made. He sprinkled garlic, salt and pepper on them, then shut the door and turned off the heat.

"Almost perfect," he said.

"Where is the garlic bread, Matteo?"

Matt looked around. "By the refrigerator, Grandma."

"Get me a knife like a good boy."

Matt found a knife and handed it to his grandmother. Then he picked up the tomato, rinsed and sliced it, and tossed it into the bowlful of lettuce. He found a can of olives and a jar of artichoke hearts, which joined the growing salad. A white onion, celery and carrots were tossed in with the rest. Matt saw his grandmother laboring to cut the garlic bread.

"Here, Grandma. Let me finish that." Gingerly he removed her thin fingers from the knife handle and smiled.

His grandmother squeezed his cheek. "You are my favorite grandchild, Matteo."

"Thanks, Grandma." He sliced up the bread and put it on another platter, then opened the stove and removed the steaks. In the refrigerator he found a tray of salami, beef tongue, cheese and pepperoncini covered with wax paper. Matt put them on the table.

"Napkins, Matteo?"

"Here, Grandma."

He handed her a stack of napkins and she set to work. With one last trip to the refrigerator Matt brought forth cruets of vinegar and olive oil. "I think we're done, Grandma. Why don't you go tell everybody and I will get a couple more bottles of wine."

Matt found two bottles of wine and put them on the counter. From the refrigerator he snagged the gallon of burgundy his grandmother always drank and the carton of milk. After pouring a glass of wine for his grandmother and milk for himself, he stood behind his chair at the table as the family milled in.

"John Brodie is by far the best quarterback the 49er's ever had," Uncle Silvio declared.

"I don't know. I think that quarterback for Pittsburg—"

"Uncle Silvio, take the head of the table please. Grandma, your glass of wine is right there." Matt pulled the chair out for his grandmother. "Everyone, please be seated."

"Well, aren't you the perfect little host?" his mother breathed as she sat down, precariously balancing her glass of wine.

"Mom, would you like to say the prayers?"

"Do I have to get up again?"

"*Nel nome del Padre, e del Figlio, e dello Spirito Santo, Amen.*" Grandma settled the prayer issue with a hasty sign of the cross and kissing her thumb. She picked up her glass of burgandy. "*Salute.*"

She hefted the glass and clinked it with the others. Matt picked up his glass of milk.

"You can't make an Italian toast with milk," Silvio said, grabbing an empty glass. He poured a generous dash of white wine into it. "Here, drink this."

"But, I—"

"Do what your uncle says, Matty," Mom interjected.

Matt took the glass and lifted it. "*Salute.*"

The family toasted in response. Everyone except Matt drained his glass.

"That's an Italian toast," Silvio approved, smiling at Matt. "So Matt, what do you think of the 49er's chances?"

"Matteo, where is the pasta?"

"It should be just about done, Grandma. I'll get it. Excuse me, Uncle Silvio."

"When is Douglas returning?" Victoria asked.

"Ha! Last I heard tomorrow. If something else doesn't hang him up."

Matt poured the spaghetti into a colander. Steam erupted, fogging the windows. He slowly poured the bubbling sauce into a serving dish and brought them both to the table.

"Is your dad in Idaho?" Leo asked.

"Yes, he's at the North Shore, the hotel he bought last year."

"Beautiful spot," Leo replied. "I enjoyed our visit there last year."

"It certainly has a lot of developmental potential," Silvio agreed.

"Have you considered moving there like Douglas would like?" Victoria asked her sister.

"To Idaho?" Yolanda gasped.

"It's not the end of the world. God knows I thought the desert was the end of the world when we moved down there but now—"

"With the golf courses I've built and the country club, it's booming," Silvio said. "Hell, we had Dean Martin at the club playing a round of golf. Bob Hope has moved into the area."

"Really? Bob Hope?" Leo asked

"I played golf with him a week ago. The desert is close enough to Hollywood that we are attracting a lot of big names, and it's far enough away they can relax."

"Idaho is close to nothing," Yolanda said.

"Yolanda, Douglas has the ability to make it succeed."

"Yola is not moving to Idaho," Grandma decreed. "Neither is my Matteo."

"*Your* Matteo?" Yolanda asked.

"I raised him like my own son."

"Mother, I raised him. He is my son.'"

"Who nursed him when he got sick and you had to go play golf?"

"Momma—"

"Matt. Got a bunch of girlfriends calling?"

"No, not really, Uncle Leo."

"Why not?"

"I just—"

"Matteo." Grandma pushed her glass toward him.

Matt opened the burgundy and refilled the glass for her.

"*Gracia tante*," she said raising her glass.

"So why no girlfriends?"

"Uncle Leo, there just hasn't been—"

"All he does is read books and hide in the creek." His mother drained the glass of wine and refilled it just as quickly.

"I do have some news," Matt offered.

"What is that, Matt?" Rose inquired.

"I—"

"I have news too. I signed up for a mosaic tile class," his mother said.

"Mosaic tile? What's that?"

"It's an art class, Rose. You make a design and you cut tile and —"

"Yolanda, didn't you just finish a copper engraving class?"

"Yes, Rose, I—"

"And flower arranging? And watercoloring?"

"Yes, Rose, I—"

"I have yet to see any results from any of these classes."

"I—Rose, sister dear, I just have so much free time, I have to find something to do with myself."

Rose opened her mouth to respond.

"If you took good care of Matteo—" Grandma said.

"Momma, I take the best—"

"I have some news," Matt exclaimed. Silence descended. All eyes turned to him. His mother finished her glass of wine. "Well, two things actually. I got my report card today and Aunt Rose, you'll need to grease up those cookie sheets."

"You got those straight A's."

"Absolutely."

"Congratulations," Silvio raised his glass. "To Matthew."

Glasses clinked.

"What are you going to do with all that education?" Leo asked.

"Have you been looking at colleges yet? I know it's early but it never hurts," Victoria started.

"He's going to be a doctor," his mother said.

"Wonderful," Silvio said.

"Actually, a doctor is what *you* want me to be. I want to go into wildlife preservation."

"Wildlife preservation? What is that?" Rose asked.

"I want to be a zoologist."

"What's that?" Victoria asked.

"I would like to travel the world and help save those animals that are facing extinction. Like the Phoenix Zoo is doing with the Arabian oryx or even what I did with the kit fox."

"That cost me a pretty penny Matt," Silvio said.

"Silvio. You know you made a profit on both the sale of the land to the county for the reserve and on the new land you bought. If anything you should give Matt a cut," Victoria said.

"Can you make any money as a zoologist?" Leo asked.

"That's why he spends all his time in the creek. He catches lizards and frogs and crawdads and all sort of stuff and sneaks it into his zoo out there." Mom gestured with her wine glass, spilling some on the tablecloth.

"I don't know about money," Matt replied to his uncle. "Marlin Perkins seems to be doing okay."

"What college are you planning to attend?" Leo asked.

"Stanford," mother and grandmother announced simultaneously.

"What's the tuition at Stanford?" Leo asked.

"Last I looked, it was fifteen hundred a year. Not including room and board," Matt said.

"You wouldn't need that, Matty. You'd live at home," Yolanda said.

"Maybe. But some of the best zoology programs in America are in Arizona. Florida has a great program and so does a school in Grays Harbor, Washington. The best schools are in London and Germany."

"What makes you think I'd let you go to Germany?"

Matt just looked at his mother. "And, I just won the district science project. The banquet is in four weeks on a Friday."

"My mosaic class is on Friday."

"It's a great honor—" Matt said.

"Honor doesn't pay any bills," Rose added.

"First place receives a five hundred dollar check, which I will put into my college fund."

"Five hundred dollars? That is great Matty," Aunt Victoria said, raising her glass.

Yolanda turned to Matt. She grabbed his cheek, squeezing it. "My little sugarplum won a five hundred dollar prize," she giggled. "Isn't that wonderful? Five hundred dollars!"

"Matteo, how much did I promise to pay you for your A's, you know, on your report card?"

"It was a dollar an A, Mother," Rose answered. She slyly winked at Matt.

"And here." Silvio dug into his back pocket and pulled out his wallet. "Here's twenty more. So you can become a zoologist or whatever."

"Wow, thanks," Matt said as his grandmother pulled crumpled one dollar bills out of her black leather purse.

"How many do I owe you, Matteo?"

"I got eight A's, Grandma."

She counted out the eight and slapped them on the table.

"There. A toast. To Matteo—the doctor. *Salute!*"

Chapter Six

Aletta whimpered and looked up at the bed where Matt was sleeping. Jumping onto the bed, she walked on Matt's back and began digging at the covers. She looked intently at Matt. No response. Aletta barked and jumped off the bed, heading toward the door. Matt rolled over and moved no more. The dog trotted back to the bed and jumped onto it. She stood on Matt's chest and barked. Nothing. Barked again. Nothing. Aletta leaned forward and barked directly in Matt's face.

Matt's eyes fluttered open and he winced.

"What do you need, you silly ole dog?" he asked rubbing her head. She barked again. "Ugh. Dog breath." Aletta jumped off the bed and ran to the door once again, pausing to look back. Matt hadn't moved. She barked again.

"All right. All right! Geez, everybody wants a piece of me." He got up and stumbled to the door, down the hall to the back door. He opened it, squinting at the bright sunlight. "What time is it?"

He padded barefoot into the kitchen past the pile of dinner plates in the sink. Opening the refrigerator, he pulled out the milk and took a big gulp, then closed the carton and returned it. "Mom?" he called.

A glance out the kitchen window ascertained that the morning paper was still there. He turned and read the clock through blurry eyes. "Nine o'clock. Nine o'clock. Damn!" He ran down the hall to his mother's room and pounded on the door. "Mom. It's nine. You have a tee time today, don't you?"

The bedroom door flew open. "Why the hell didn't you wake me sooner?" she snarled as she ran past, buttoning her blouse.

"Letty just woke me up. She had to go outside."

"I'll never make it."

"You could call."

"Sure, smart ass, but that won't save my tee time. And on a Saturday—"

Matt wandered about the kitchen, found an untouched piece of
garlic bread and tore off a hunk.

"You're in your underwear," his mother said.

"Yeah, Mom. I just got up."

"These dishes will need to go into the dishwasher."

"I'll do that when I get back," Matt said.

"Where do you think you're going?"

"I have to walk to Sears to buy a tire patch kit. And some rope. If
you want those rocks, I'll need to buy some rope."

"I want the dishes done before your father gets home."

"I'll try. But if I'm walking, I'm walking while it's still cool."

"Don't ask for any money. I don't have time to look for any money
for you."

"But, it's your rock project."

She stopped and glared at him. "You live here too."

"Fine."

"I've got to put some makeup on. See if you can find my keys."

She hurried out of the kitchen. Matt heard the bedroom door
slam. Wandering over to the kitchen table, he spied a slice of salami,
wrapped it around a piece of cheddar cheese and stuffed it into his
mouth.

"Are you looking for my keys?" his mother yelled from the other
end of the house.

"Yes, Mom," he yelled back through a mouthful of food. "They're
not on the table," he muttered to himself. He spotted a bowl with olives
in it, tossed an olive into the air, then caught it in his mouth. Several
more followed. Several steaks, cold and pebbled with coagulated
grease, sat on a platter. Matt pulled out a knife and hacked off a bite.
Skewering it with the knife, he salted the meat then ate.

"My purse. I think the keys are with my purse."

Matt cut off another chunk of steak.

"Did you hear me?"

"Yes, Mother." He cut off several hunks of meat and forked them into his mouth. Chewing, he glanced around the kitchen. On the corner table near the green wall phone sat his mother's purse, next to it the keys. He picked up another piece of garlic bread, pulled out the soft center, ate it, and tossed away the crust.

"Find them?"

"Still looking."

"Damn it. Where did I leave them?"

"Did you look on the dresser?"

"Of course I did. What do you think I am? Stupid?"

Matt smiled, pulling the center out of the last piece of garlic bread.

"Well?" Yolanda yelled.

"Well what?"

"My keys!"

"Still looking." He walked over to the phone table, picked up the keys and purse and walked back to the door. Mom hurried down the hall.

"Did you find them?"

"Yep." He offered them to her.

Grabbing them she said, "You're still in your underwear."

"I was looking for your keys, Mom. So you wouldn't be late."

"Yeah, well, thanks. Get dressed and get yourself something to eat."

"Have a great game," he called, watching her race to the garage. He laughed as he turned back to the kitchen. On the middle of the table was half a chocolate cake. "Ah, cake. The perfect breakfast food." He helped himself to a huge slice.

Letty was barking at the back door and Matt let her in. "Smart dog, waiting till she left. It's safe to come in now. Here." Matt offered the poodle a piece of his cake. The dog swallowed it in one bite. "Good girl." He dropped another big crumb down to the dog.

In his room, he slipped on a pair of Bermuda shorts and a t-shirt, white sport socks and his favorite red tennis shoes. Taking a moment, he sat at his desk. The money from his aunts and uncles for his grades he placed in the secret panel under his window with the *Playboy*. The half-naked woman on the cover stood guard over his silver dollars, cash, and his other treasures including a Meerschaum pipe. The other silver dollars he tossed into a Mason jar on his desk, making a total of eight. The official notice of his science project win he propped against a dictionary. Checking his pockets, he counted five dollars in bills and change. More than enough for a tire patch kit and a hundred feet of rope. He could even stop at the Race Street Market and buy a fish sandwich. Letty looked up at him expectantly as he stood and grabbed the house key.

"Sorry girl, I can't take you with me." With a last glance around, he headed for the door.

✂ ✂ ✂

The return trip from Sears was hot. Sweat beaded on his forehead and hung there. He slurped up the last of his Coke and dumped the cup in the trash can outside of Lincoln Lane Market. Rounding the corner onto Glen Eyrie, he stepped into the cool mottled shade of the tall elms that lined the street. Even though it was only March, the trees were already leafing out. Matt shifted the scratchy hemp rope on his shoulder. The tire repair kit didn't weigh much but the two pounds of bird seed he purchased for the zebra finch that lived in his museum was getting heavy.

"Matt!"

Matt whirled and saw his friend, Fred. Fred waved and pumped his leg, stood on his skateboard and coasted up to Matt. "Hey, Matt. How are you?"

"Hey. Fred."

"Look what I got." Fred picked up his skateboard. "My dad bought it for me at Sprouse-Reitz yesterday."

"He *bought* a skateboard?" Matt exclaimed looking at the toy.

"Yeah, why not?"

"I always made my own skateboards. You know, a scrap of two by four and an old pair of skates. You break the skates apart and nail the wheels to the board."

"I've made them too."

"Why do you need to buy something you can make?"

"Well, it's got better balance. And the wheels are aligned better so you're not fighting it all the time. And the guy at the store said that the bearings are better so the wheels don't wear out like an old pair of skates wheels do."

"Cool."

"And it's quieter. The wheels aren't just metal. I don't know what they are but they don't make half the noise of my handmade boards. And look!" Fred stepped down on the back of the board, flipping it up and catching it.

"Far out!"

"Yeah, I could never do that with an old two by four skateboard. And look at the flames. That's painted on, not a cheap decal."

"Enjoy it while you can, Fred."

"What do you mean?"

"It'll never catch on. I mean most of us are outgrowing skateboards and looking at cars. Skateboards are like hula hoops and pogo sticks. Fun for a while then people move onto the next toy. It'll never catch on."

"The guy at the store says he's selling a lot of them."

"How much are they?"

"Twelve dollars."

"Twelve *dollars*? I can build one for about twenty-five cents. Believe me, they'll never catch on."

"Hey, you want to come over for a bit? I got my train set up in my room."

"Sure, for a little bit. And I need to use the bathroom."

"Okay, see you in a few minutes. Nobody's home but me so come on in."

Matt opened the front door to Fred's house. The interior was cool and dark and solemn. A large Chinese vase graced the tiled entry. Stepping inside, Matt called, "Fred?"

"Back here."

Matt followed the voice to Fred's bedroom. A piece of plywood was set on the extra bed, covered by painted streets and grasslands. HO railroad track made a huge oval circuit past miniature trees and a brick depot. Fred knelt near the train, carefully aligning the locomotive's wheels on the track.

"Matt. Hook up the transformer, will you?"

"Sure." Matt sat on the floor and picked up the two leads that dangled from the transformer. "You got a screwdriver?"

"Nah. I always use a dime."

Matt fished in his pocket and found a dime, and tightened the screws down. Then he plugged in the transformer and turned the dial. The transformer began to hum. Wheels on the locomotive turned and the engine chugged around the track.

"Okay. Turn it off," Fred said and began attaching cars to the locomotive. "In the box under my bed there's a bunch of buildings and towers and stuff. Can you pull that out?"

Matt reached and found the dusty box, grabbed a water tower and placed it on the board with a farmhouse and a bag of tiny cows. "This is really cool, Fred," he said. "But I really need the bathroom."

"It's down the hall. Second door on the left. The first is a closet. Don't pee in there."

Matt headed down the hall. The second door was open so he stepped on in ignoring the slightly steamy atmosphere of the room. Standing in front of the toilet, he lifted the seat and unzipped. He sighed with relief as his bladder began to empty itself.

"Can you hand me the towel?"

Startled, Matt turned to see Emily, Fred's older sister, standing naked in the bathtub. Wet ebony hair coiled around her head and shoulders. Water ran in rivulets down her torso, molding to the contours of her flesh, flaring at the bell of her hips, rushing through the v of her thighs, slowing at the forest of dark hair, cascading down her long, long legs to pool at her feet. A breeze from the window goose bumped her arms and hardened her nipples. Her nipples. Matt stared at her nipples. The size of quarters, they topped her pale round breasts like a cherry on a vanilla sundae.

"The towel?" Emily pointed to the towel rack beside the toilet. Matt stared. "Today."

Trying to cover himself and check the flow with one hand, he reached behind him and groped for the towel.

"Up a little," Emily said.

Matt tore his eyes away from her breasts long enough to grab the towel and handed it to Emily. "Thanks." She said.

She stepped out of the tub, all grace and sinuous muscle, her breasts bobbing slightly. Posing, she took the towel, gathered up her hair and wrapped it in a turban. Matt's head bobbed with her breasts. Smiling, she turned and walked out of the bathroom, her hips undulating with the sure knowledge that she was being looked at and appreciated. Matt watched ignoring the pain in his groin. Opening her bedroom door she turned and looked at Matt.

"You might want to put that away." Her eyes fell to his crotch. She smiled at him again and shut the door. Matt stared at the door until the click of the lock broke his trance. Turning, he finished peeing. Hastily zipping up he flushed and ran from the bathroom. Faint female laughter accompanied him back to Fred's room. Matt stood there, lost.

"Here." Fred tossed him a bag of little people. "Put them on the board."

"I—I got to—um—go."

"What? You just got here."

"I know, but my mom will be home soon and I got to go." Matt dropped the bag of people on the bed. "Sorry, man. But I really need to go" He headed to the front door with Fred trailing.

"Maybe I can come over to your house?"

"Later. Maybe. I got chores to do and my dad's coming home today."

"See you later, I guess." Fred watched him leave. "Feel free to come over to pee anytime."

Matt hefted the rope back on his shoulder and began to run home. It was only two blocks but the running calmed him down. Breathing hard, he found the key and went inside. Ignoring the bouncing dog, he threw himself on the bed.

"Matt!"

"What, Mom?"

"The dishes haven't been done."

"I know, Mom. I just got home."

"What took you so long?"

"Sears is a longer walk than I thought it would be. And I stopped to eat."

"Get them in the dishwasher."

"In a minute, Mom. Geez. Give a guy a minute to get his breath."

"What?"

"In a minute!" Matt leaned down and picked up his dog. "You know what, Letty? The coach said in class that all those pictures in *Playboy* are fake. Nobody looks that good. It's all makeup and lighting." He scuffed the dog's head. "But you know what? He lied. There are girls out there that look that good. There really are."

Letty didn't answer.

Matt stood up and headed for the kitchen.

✂ ✂ ✂

He washed off the table top, poured soap crystals into the dishwasher and popped it closed with his foot. He hit the start button and waited for the machine to engage. Only two pots remained unwashed on the stove.

His mom popped into the kitchen. "The steaks?"

"I wrapped them in aluminum foil and put them in the refrigerator."

"How many were left? I'm going to the store. What do we need?" she asked.

"There's enough artichokes for dinner, but I think we are out of mayonnaise."

"How are we on salad?"

"I don't know. You'd have to look in the fridge."

"How are we on salad?" Mom repeated in a harder voice.

Matt walked over to the refrigerator, opening it. Leaning in he pulled open the vegetable drawer. "Looks like half an onion. No lettuce. No celery. Some leftover olives. One . . ." Matt pulled out a furry blob and carried it over to the trash. "No tomatoes."

"Any potatoes?"

"No, I don't see any potatoes, Mom."

"I'll need to get something for dessert."

"There's still some chocolate cake. Enough for three of us for tonight."

"*If* your father comes home."

"You haven't heard?"

"Not a damn word." Matt's mom was scribbling a list of things on a piece of paper. "Maybe some nice Swiss chard." Matt winced as his mother wrote things down.

"How about some lunch meat for my school lunches?" Matt ventured.

"That's right. I'm out of avocados."

Matt slammed the refrigerator door shut.

"You seemed full of good news last night."

"Oh, yeah. Got my report card. And—"

"I found your report card."

"You went through my drawers again."

"Didn't you see the little cards on the floor?"

"That's not fair. You shouldn't be going through my things! I have a right to privacy like anyone."

"I am your mother. I decide what rights you have."

"I don't go through your things!"

"You damn well better not! I am the adult. That's the way it is. You don't like it, you can lump it."

Matt glared.

"About your report card. You had an A minus. In spelling I think."

"An A minus is still an A."

"Minus."

"Are you going to pay me?"

"You got paid yesterday."

"You didn't give me any money."

"Your Aunt Victoria gave you twenty dollars at the dinner table. So did your Uncle Silvio. My mother gave you eight. That's forty eight dollars. That's enough."

"But—your word isn't worth—"

Her hand whipped out and slapped him across the face, hard. "How dare you!"

"Slapping me doesn't change anything. Your *word*. That should mean something."

"I'm your mother."

"So it should mean even more, shouldn't it? Go ahead. Hit me again. It doesn't change a thing."

"Wait until your father gets home."

"Trust me. I can't wait." He turned to leave.

"Oh, I forgot to tell you. I have some news too. I got a date for you."

"What?" He turned toward her. "For what? With who?"

"For tomorrow night. Your cousin's birthday party."

"I didn't want to go to that."

"Well, you are going." She enunciated each word. "I even bought a present for you to give him."

"You got me a date. With who?"

"One of my golf partners has a daughter named Margaret. So, I told her about how you couldn't get a date—"

"I couldn't get one because I didn't want to go!"

"And she and I talked about it and Margaret will be your date."

"I don't even know this girl."

"That's what dates are for, to get to know someone."

"I don't *want* to know this girl. I don't want to go. Joe is four years older than me. What will we do?"

"Whatever young people do on dates. That hasn't changed that much since I dated your father. I'm only in my thirties."

"I am not going." He enunciated each word. It didn't work.

"Yes, you are. Mrs. Paris said Margaret bought a new dress for this date."

"So? Wait a minute—Margaret Paris? Margaret Paris! Really? She's in junior high school. What grade is she in? Eighth? You're sending me to a college age party with an eighth grader? No way, Jose. There is no way that is going to happen."

"You're going and I don't want to hear another word about it."

Matt ground his teeth and shook his head, then stalked out the front door.

"Don't slam that—"

He slammed the door.

"—door."

Matt took refuge in the garage. He upended his bicycle and examined the flat front tire. With a screwdriver he carefully began prying the tire from the rim, reached in with his fingers and grabbed the inner tube. He pulled the air valve through the hole in the rim and pulled the whole inner tube out. Then he felt under the tire, all the way around the rim until he found the three thorns. Using the blade of the screwdriver, he pushed the thorns out of the tire and tossed them into a coffee can. He unscrewed the lid of the tire repair kit and used the rough top to scratch up the inner tube surface, and cut a patch that would cover all three holes. After squeezing out the glue onto the inner tube, he lit the glue on fire with a wooden match. The fire burned briefly before he blew it out. Testing the glue for tackiness, he grinned, pleased. He pressed the patch onto the glue, flattened out the edges and picked up a five pound weight from a broken scale. With it he began pressing the patch into the glue. After several minutes, he inspected his work. It looked good. He threaded the valve back through the hole in the rim and stuffed the inner tube back inside the tire. Using the screwdriver, he reattached the tire to the rim, then put away the kit. He pulled the air pump off of a hook on the wall and pumped up the tire. After checking for leaks he opened the garage and rolled his bike down the driveway.

"Matty, I need you—"

Ignoring his mother Matt jumped on his bike and took off.

"Matty, I know you can hear—"

Matt was around the corner and gone. He pumped the pedals of his bike as hard as he could until his mother's voice faded away. Then he sat back on the seat and relaxed. He coasted, enjoying the warm air and the wind in his face.

"Matty!"

Directly in front of him were Mrs. Morgan and her dogs. He stomped on the brake, sliding to a stop inches from them.

"You laid rubber," she observed.

Matt looked back, seeing an eight foot black skid mark. He smiled. "Cool."

"You need to watch it, Matty."

"I'm sorry, Mrs.—"

"No harm done." She smiled.

Matt looked at her, smiling back. Her white v-neck blouse was exposing more of his neighbor than he had seen before. He fidgeted, balancing his bike between his legs.

"Excited about your dad coming home?" she asked.

"If he comes home today. Mom hasn't heard."

"Oh, he'll be here. He called me from the Nut Tree."

"He called you?"

"He needed to set up an appointment with me. He's doing my accounts, you know, for taxes."

"Oh."

"And since he isn't going to be in town too long, he called to set up an appointment." Mrs. Morgan tugged on the leash of her dogs. "Heel," she commanded.

"How long ago did he call?"

"About an hour ago."

"So he should be here in about a half hour," Matt mused. "I hope he's wearing armor."

Mrs. Morgan looked up and smiled. "Mom in a bad mood?"

"You know, the usual 'wait until your FATHER gets home' stuff." He looked down perplexed. "I just wish that just once when he came home there wasn't a—"

"A what?"

"A fight."

She looked at Matt kindly. "I don't know what to tell you, Matty."

"I know. Thanks. See you later." Matt rode off.

Chapter Seven

Matt coasted a long curving arc into his driveway. Slapping the kickstand with his foot, he hopped off his bike and walked into the courtyard shadows. His mother was there in the one spot of sunlight, tanning.

"The dishes."

"I know, Mom. I'm doing them now."

Matt walked into the house, through the kitchen and to the back door. He let the dog into the house. Letty beelined to her water dish where she sloppily began lapping up water. "You poor thing." Matt patted the dog. "You were thirsty weren't you?"

The dog wagged her tail and kept drinking. Matt stepped into his room, peeled off his t-shirt and saw the Mason jar on his desk. Empty. He knelt down under his window, removing the piece of paneling that hid his treasures. Intact. Everything was there.

He picked up the jar and went to confront his mother. "Mom."

No answer. She lay in the sun like a Komodo dragon soaking up the life-giving rays.

"Mom!"

Slowly her head turned and she peered at him through green lenses.

"My silver dollars. What happened to them?"

The head rotated back. "The paperboy came today."

"So?"

Languidly, she reached down and picked up a glass of water beside her and took a sip.

"So, Mom?"

"So?" She replaced the water on the concrete. "I paid him."

"With my silver dollars? Why?"

"I couldn't find my purse."

"You," he sputtered. "Those were silver dollars!"

Mom licked her lips.

"Those were *mine*. This is such a rip off, Mom. You had no right using my silver dollars to pay . . . to pay a paperboy!"

"I owed him for several months."

"And the paper cost what, a dollar twenty-five a month? You paid him eight silver dollars for a four dollar bill?"

"It was five dollars and seventy-five cents."

"So? Eight silver dollars?"

"It was his fifth trip to collect the bill." She paused and swiveled toward him, the sun glinting on the lenses of the dark glasses. "I thought he deserved a tip."

"A tip. You thought he deserved a tip? Do you have any idea what a silver dollar is worth? Any? Just for the silver alone they are worth twice face value! They haven't made any for what? Fifty years?"

"Matt, do the dishes."

"The *dishes*! You had no right to take—to steal my stuff to pay the damn paperboy."

She tensed. "Watch your mouth with me, little man. I am you mother. You will not swear at me."

"You stole my money. Aunt Vicki gave me those. They can't be replaced."

"I'll pay you back someday."

"In silver dollars?"

She reached again for her glass. "From what I understand, they're not made anymore." She sipped and returned the glass to the ground.

"Mom."

"We are done with this conversation, Matty." His mother rolled over on the chaise. "Unhook my top."

"What?"

"Unhook the top of my swim suit. I don't want any tan lines."

Fuming, Matt grabbed the fabric and struggled with the hooks on her bikini top. Unclasping them, he stepped away and headed for the front door.

"Don't forget the dishes, Matty."

It only took about ten minutes for Matt to put the dishes in the dishwasher. He headed outside.

"Where are you going?"

"Putting my bike away." He walked down the sidewalk to the driveway as a big Jaguar sedan rolled in.

"Dad!"

Mr. Connors stepped out of the Jag. Running up to him, Matt embraced his warmly. "How ya' doing, Sport?"

"Great to see you, Dad. Where did you get that?"

"It's a Jag sedan. Wood grain dash, leather interior. Look, it has fold-down rests for your drinks and the last owner installed a new eight-track cartridge player. Though to tell the truth, I only have one tape and four hours through the Palouse with no radio reception and only the Loving Spoonful was driving me crazy."

Matt replied, "Well, glad you survived. So is this the new car? For keeps, I mean?"

"No." Dad lit a cigarette. "I traded my old Beechcraft for this and I'm trading this for the last of the restoration work on the Studebaker."

"You should see it, Dad. I've got the battery charged and turned it on. It purrs like a kitten."

"All right. But I guess I better see your mother first. She wouldn't like playing second fiddle to car."

"You got armor on?"

"That bad?"

"The last three days have been nothing but 'Wait until you father gets home.'"

"Do you deserve them?"

"Some of them, maybe. But she fixed me up with a date with a thirteen year old and gave my silver dollars to the paperboy!"

"Wait. Wait, wait." He waved his son to silence. "I guess I better hear it from your mother first."

"Sure."

"Oh, I got you something." He reached into the interior of the car and pulled out brown bag and thrust it toward Matt, who took the bag with a quiet thank you and opened the bag.

"*Two in a Bush* by Gerald Durrell. Thanks, Dad!" Matt said, "I've read a lot of books of his. He's funny. A real great writer. And he built his own zoo in England—"

"Did you bring *me* anything?"

Father and son looked up to see Yolanda, standing rigid, hands on hips at the gate to the courtyard, sunglasses reflecting the sun. Douglas smiled.

"Just my undying love, dear."

He walked up and kissed her on the lips. She didn't unbend at all. As the kiss broke, she said, "A fat lot of good that will do."

"Honey—" he said.

"Don't honey me, Doug. You left me with no money for how many weeks? If my mother hadn't given me some cash last week there wouldn't be any heat on in this house."

"Yolanda, its 78 degrees out right now."

"It gets frigid in that bedroom at night, Douglas."

"Don't I know it."

"And I gave a party you were supposed to be at. Everyone wondered where you were. Silvio and Leo were asking about you. What was I supposed to tell them?"

"That I was out trying to make a living to support you in the fashion they have made you accustomed to?"

"Are you blaming my family for the fact that you weren't here?" She shook her head, the light reflecting from the glasses flashing into Doug's eyes.

"No. I'm not blaming them. I am simply explaining what I was doing, dear."

"Buying hotels in Idaho!"

"Yes, buying hotels in Idaho. That's how I am supporting you. You think we could afford this house on the pay I got as a milkman?"

"At least the checks were regular."

"And the dairy industry is dying, dear. Over half of my route canceled service. Everyone buys milk at the store now. It's cheaper. Even with selling Kirby door to door, it wasn't enough."

"So, how much did you bring home this time?"

"The car—"

"I can't buy milk with a car."

"And—" He reached into his coat pocket and pulled out a wad of bills. Peeling off a five, he tossed it to Matt. "Seven hundred and—" he counted, "thirty-eight dollars."

Mom relaxed a little. He waved the bills at her.

"So, how about a real kiss?" They kissed, Yolanda a bit more warmly than before. "Maybe," he whispered, "we won't need the heat on in the bedroom tonight."

She stepped back. His smile lingered. Matt coughed.

"And your son," she began.

"Our son."

"Your ungrateful son has been mouthing off at me. He accused me of stealing his silver dollars."

"Matt mentioned that."

"Well, if you had left me with anything in the checking account—"

"There was over a hundred and fifty dollars in the checking account. What happened to that?"

"There were groceries for the party and everyday. The electric bill—"

"The electric bill is, what, about three dollars a month?"

"That shows what you know. It was four eighty-seven last month."

"That still doesn't explain—" Douglas said.

"The paperboy—" Mom interrupted.

"You used my money for that, Mom," Matt said.

"Matt," Dad warned.

"You see what I have to put up with?" Yolanda said.

"She signed up for mosaic tile lessons and has a carload of tile in the trunk."

"Matty!" she shrieked.

"Sorry, but it's true."

"You're not helping, Matt," Dad said.

"Sorry."

"He fights me about everything. He refuses to do his chores when I ask him to."

Dad looked around. "Looks like all of the chores are done. No brown spots on the lawn. It's been cut."

"You *would* take his side."

"I'm not taking anyone's side. I'm just commenting things look pretty good." He stepped back and let his gaze wander over his wife's bikini. "Including you." His arms went around her.

"You need to do something."

"I'm hoping to."

She squirmed out of his grasp. "About your son."

Douglas sighed and stepped away from his wife. "All right. Let's go inside and talk about it."

She turned around and stomped across the courtyard and into the house. Pausing at the door, she yelled over her shoulder, "Matt, clean up the courtyard."

"But—"

"Just do it, son." Doug followed his wife into the house. "Damn it, Yolanda. Just once couldn't you meet me at the door with a smile instead of all—"

The door slammed, cutting off his father's voice.

Matt stared at the mess. A towel, a glass and a tube of suntan lotion. He walked to the chaise and picked up the towel, damp with sweat and lotion, and hung it on the clothes line. He could hear his mother yelling and the placating tones of his father. The din grew louder as he brought the glass and lotion inside, so he simply kept going, out the back door, across the yard, over the fence and down the creek.

Silence. Quail skittered by. Breezes stirred the leaves. Matt leaned against Mr. Giannini's retaining wall and sighed. A mockingbird sprang out of an elderberry tree and winged out of sight. Matt wandered down to the stream and pulled off his sneakers and socks. Plunging his feet into the cool water scattered a school of minnows. Hopping from bleached rock to rock, he crossed the stream. His toes dug into the warm earth on the opposite bank, then he climbed the giant shards of concrete that littered the creek wall. Balancing carefully, he found his cave and reached in. Next to a battered statue of the Virgin Mary given to all sixth graders many years ago were his slingshot and a roll of BB's. Fitting a BB into the sling's pocket, he looked for something to shoot at. A blackbird glided by, landing by the creek for a drink. Matt aimed. He didn't fire. "Shoo, bird. Bring me a can or something."

"I would have shot it."

Matt jumped and turned.

"Careful, bwana. Don't fall on my account."

"Robert. You startled me."

Robert laughed. Clad only in cutoffs and sneakers, he seemed perfectly at home in the creek bed. Fine blond hair covered his muscular arms and legs and his blue eyes regarded Matt. "Your dad got home?"

"Yes."

"And the fight goes on."

"Yes. How do you know?"

"Come on. You mom could put a banshee to shame. When she gets up to full volume half of the neighborhood knows."

Matt chuckled. "She is loud."

"How do you put up with her? Some of the things she says to you—and your dad—I just don't understand how you guys put up with her."

"I don't know. It just is."

"My mother was like that."

"A screamer?"

"Yeah. Nothing was ever good enough for her. Nothing. I mean, look at me. I was quarterback on my high school football team and she never came to a game."

"Mine, either."

"You play football?"

"I played a couple of games. She never came. Not even to pick me up afterward. I had to catch a ride with friends."

"What position?"

"Coach alternated me between running back and tight end." Matt smiled. "Coach couldn't figure out what to do with me."

"Story of my life."

"Just didn't seem to fit."

Robert smiled. "I know what you mean."

"Is that why you are here?"

"Here?"

"Here. With your uncle, Mr. Giannini."

"Oh yeah. My uncle lets me come down on weekends. Home cooked meals. Away from the dorms. You know."

"Do you miss your mom?" Matt asked.

"Miss her? No. Maybe. I miss what we could have had, sometimes. But what we had—"

"I know what you mean. Sometimes when I watch tv and see, oh, I don't know, *Donna Reed* or *Leave it to Beaver*. It would be great to have a mother like that. Someone who supports you instead of—"

"Instead of cutting you off at the balls." Matt and Robert shared a moment.

"Matty!" Mom's voice broke it.

"The banshee wails, Matt."

"I better go." Matt began climbing down and waded across the creek. He paused to pick up his shoes and socks. "Bye." He waved at Robert. "Nice talking to you."

"Good luck, kid." Robert called from the opposite bank.

His mother waited for at the top. "Who were you talking to?"

"Robert."

"Who?"

"Mr. Giannini's nephew."

"Right, his nephew." Mom headed for the house. Over her shoulder she called, "Your father will deal with you."

Mom pushed past Dad who was standing in the doorway. He stepped out. "Let's go to the garage, Matt."

"Is it that bad?"

"Nah. Show me the Studebaker."

Matt led the way, turning on the light as they entered the garage. He leaned against the Dodge Pioneer as his father inspected the other car. "Looks good, Matt. For a non-mechanic, you've done a good job."

"I wish I knew more. Are you going to be around enough to teach me more?"

His father stiffened. "What do you mean?"

"How long are you in town this time?"

"Oh." Dad relaxed. "A couple of weeks. I've got to go to Mexico to look at a hotel, and one in Guam."

"Guam? Why Guam?'

"I bought a chain of fourteen hotels and one of them is in Guam, another in Acapulco."

"Does Guam even *need* a hotel? I mean, who takes vacations in Guam?"

"Doesn't matter. I've got to go look the place over."

"Can you teach me more about the car while you're here?" Matt asked.

"We'll see." Dad said. "Look, your mother is pretty upset."

"I could tell."

"Tell me about the silver dollars."

"Aunt Vicki gives me money now and then and some of it was in silver dollars from casinos in Tahoe. I kept them in a jar on my desk. I didn't want to take them to the bank because I'd never get the silver dollars back. They are worth more than a paper dollar."

"Okay." His father ran his hand across the curved hood of the car.

"I get back from being out and the silver dollars are gone. She used them to pay the paperboy and tipped him the extra ones for, I don't know, coming back a bunch of times."

"She said she had no money."

"That doesn't matter. She shouldn't have taken mine," Matt insisted.

"You're right. She shouldn't. I can pay you back."

"Dad, it's not the money. It's the principle of the thing."

"Okay, that's done. Nothing I can do about that." Dad turned. "The date?"

"I told her I didn't want to go to Joe's party. He's in college. All his friends are in college. I'm a junior in high school."

"You two used to be pretty tight."

"Because we were the only boy cousins. But he's, what, four years older than me? The invitation said BYOB. It means bring your own bottle. What am I supposed to do? Bring a bottle of Coke?"

Dad chuckled. "Look, this is the nitty gritty. You have to go. Your mother lined you up with a date."

"She's thirteen. I've never even met her."

"Your date's all excited. She and her mom went out and bought a new outfit for this. This is her first date."

"So I have to go because it would disappoint this girl, whatever her name is?"

"That's about it."

"Because it's the right thing to do."

"You got it."

"Okay. But it will cost you."

"How do you mean?"

"I've got to get Joe a present."

"Your mother bought something for him."

"I know. I've seen it. Now I've got to go get something he might really like."

Chapter Eight

The bells in the church steeple rang, scattering pigeons, as Douglas unlocked the family car. Waving goodbye to some of the other church goers, the family slid into the 1960 Dodge Pioneer.

"I don't understand why we couldn't drive the Jag," Matt's mom complained.

"You know my theory," Dad answered. "Never let the church know you have any money."

"But we don't *have* any money. All we have is that damn car," Mom pointed out.

"It's the idea, honey. It's not like they don't already nickel and dime everyone to death. If it's not the first collection, then it's a second collection to put a roof on the convent or—"

"The Pope's Poor Children fund or the St. Mary's Blessing for Orphans," Matt said.

"But I don't see why it would have harmed anything to show off nice things when we have them," Mom said.

"If the church thought we had money, they would be after us all the time for donations for one thing or another. Like your sister Victoria and that altar."

"What about Aunt Vicki and the altar?" Matt asked.

Doug glanced at his wife. "Matt, I wasn't Catholic when I married your mother. I wasn't really much of anything. But to get married the church insisted that I convert to Catholicism. Now, I didn't agree with a lot of what they taught."

"Your father was very anti-church."

"Yeah, I guess I was, and still am somewhat."

"I didn't know that, Dad." Matt said.

"He's never around enough to know what he's thinking," Mom added. "About anything."

"Anyway, shortly before you started grammar school, Father Leopaldi and I got into a major fight."

"You punched a priest?" Matt asked, shocked.

"No. I hit him where it hurt, his pride. He was preaching the usually peace and good will stuff at a Fathers of the School meetings and I brought up the Aztecs."

"The Aztecs?" Matt asked.

"In the days of the conquistadors, the Church forbid killing people unless they were Christians."

"That doesn't make sense." Matt said.

"They didn't want to have the sin on their soul of killing anyone unless that person had the opportunity to know Jesus and go to heaven. So the Spanish brought padres with them into war. They would ride up on a tribe or village and send in the priests. The priests blessed and baptized the entire tribe and then got out of the way so the soldiers could come in and slaughter them all."

"Is that true? That doesn't make any sense. Those Indians didn't even know they were being baptized. That's phony," Matt said.

"It's phony as hell. And the church did this time after time, tribe after tribe."

"Were did you learn this?"

"Not in a Catholic school. Matt, there is another reality out there."

"Douglas!"

"It's true. History is written by the winners. That doesn't always mean it is absolutely true." Doug rolled down the car window. "Father Leopaldi and I had a very public debate about the church and he swore that he would never let me in a church again, me or my family.

"When he refused to let me register you for first grade, I went and talked to my sister," Mom chimed in.

"Your mother was in tears. After all, everyone in the family went to Bosco's from first grade until they graduated high school. And Vicki told your mother not to worry about it. She would take care of it."

"Are you saying Aunt Vicki bribed Father Leopaldi with an altar just to get me into school?"

"Yes, Matt. That's what happened. If you walk up to the altar there is a little plaque on it saying it is a donation from Victoria and Silvio Lambretta. Quite a nice bribe."

"A twenty-thousand-dollar bribe imported from Italy. Solid marble," Yolanda said.

"And now it's not even the main altar anymore," Matt said.

"Nope, Matt. Vatican Two did it in."

"It's a crying shame. That beautiful altar sitting in a side hall of the church. The new altar looks like a damn card table," Yolanda said

"It's not very majestic," her husband admitted.

"I kind of like the new Mass," Matt said. "At least now you know what the priest is saying."

"Somehow," Yolanda said wistfully, "it just sounded grander in Latin."

"But you couldn't understand it," Matt said.

"Sometimes the image is greater than the reality. In Latin it had mystery and awe. Don't you think it's a little—I don't know—common now?" Doug asked.

"No. I like it. I like to know what's going on."

"I felt odd about being handed the host. Didn't you, Douglas?" Yolanda asked.

"I didn't think about it much." The car came to a halt.

"Are we having lunch at Grandma's?" Matt asked.

"No. Your mother and I are going to the store to pick up a few things."

"Your grandmother called and wanted you to pick up the drapes. We figured you could carry them home," Yolanda said.

"When you get them there, if you'd rig the ropes like we talked about so that we can haul rocks out of the creek for your mother's project, we'll get right on it when I get home." Doug said.

"Sure." Matt hopped out of the car and dashed up the walk. As usual, his aunt was at the door waiting.

"They're not coming in?" Rose asked in a dry whisper.

"No, they have to shop."

"Your mother lives to shop." Rose stepped into the house, allowing Matt to enter.

"Matteo, you come for the curtains?"

"Yes, Grandma." He bent and kissed her. His aunt came from the back room with the carefully pressed pile of drapes.

"Now, Matteo. You carry them very careful. They are cleaned and pressed and ready to hang up, *capisce*?"

"I *capisce*, Grandma."

She held the door open for him.

The house was empty when he got home. Like most of the other houses on the street, the front door was unlocked. Matt entered and carefully placed the folded drapes on the couch. Then he headed to his room to change. His dog bounded about in greeting.

"Hiya, mutt. Come on now Letty, get out of the way girl. I gotta change." She trotted happily after him into his room. Tie, dress shirt, sport coat all hit the bed and he changed into t-shirt, cutoffs and sneakers. He headed to the garage and grabbed the rope. Over the edge of the creek grew an old, gnarled elderberry tree. One strong limb with bark like elephant skin hung over the edge. Matt climbed up the tree with the rope over his shoulder. The branch sagged, but held under his weight. He hung the rope over the branch then dropped it on either side. Catlike, he walked back down the limb and jumped the six feet to the dirt below. Grabbing a large metal bucket out from under some bushes, he tied one end of the rope to the handle, then he pulled on the other end of the rope. It would work.

Matt turned and began collecting basketball sized rocks. He grunted and heaved them into a pile near the bucket. Thirty or forty stones later, he paused. Sitting on the pile Matt whipped off his shirt. The quiet and peace of the creek enveloped him and he soaked in the sunlight like a flower ready to bloom. Overhead a towhee hoped from twig to twig and cocked his head to peer at him. Matt glanced back.

"Making you nervous, bird?" he asked.

The pudgy brown bird flitted to another slim branch, clutching tightly with both feet as the limb bobbed. It looked down at Matt sideways.

"Matt? You ready?"

"Yeah, Dad. I got a couple dozen down here waiting."

"Good. I'll go get the wheelbarrow. Why don't you start hoisting up a load while I go get it?"

"All right."

Matt hefted a chunk of granite and dropped it into the bucket with a metallic thud. He fisted the ropes and pulled, muscles bulging. Slowly, testing the rig, the bucket rose. He pulled it until it was level with the cliff edge, then wrapped his end of the rope around an exposed root of a pine tree. The bucket swayed gently. His father stopped the wheelbarrow at the edge of the cliff and a riffle of loose dirt filtered down in a silent cascade. Douglas clenched the trunk of the elderberry tree with one hand and reached out, snagging the rope and bucket. He dumped the rock into the wheel barrow.

"That's heavy."

"Yeah, Dad. I guess they're about thirty, forty pounds each."

"If we do this one at a time this could take all day."

"I can fit two, maybe three in the bucket but I was worried about the handle."

Dad examined the bucket and its handle. "Let's do two at a time. And both of us watch the handle. I think it will be okay." He let the bucket go and it swung in a wide arc. Matt lowered it, chunked two more large stones into the bucket, grabbed the rope and began pulling. The branch creaked but held.

Dad grabbed and emptied the bucket. "Two more."

"That old wheel barrow going to be able to take it?"

"Probably better than I will."

Matt and his father repeated the process, then Douglas trundled off with the ungainly burden. Matt dropped the bucket and threw in two more stones and waited.

"Your mom came out to supervise," Douglas said over the edge. "She thinks she'll need about a hundred rocks this size and at least that many smaller ones. Then she's going to want six or eight really big ones, four to five times the size of what you got so far."

"Did you tell her those won't fit in the bucket?"

"That's when she blew up. We're going to take the half of the fifty gallon drum and rig it for the bigger ones."

"I don't know if I can pull up that much more weight."

"We'll deal with that when we come to it."

"I'll need a ramp."

"What?"

"A ramp. To push the bigger ones into the barrel. I can't lift them over the edge. We're talking one to two hundred pounds."

"Can you make a ramp out of littler rocks?"

Matt looked around. The creek floor was covered with an inexhaustible wealth of river rock. The excavation they were planning wouldn't even be noticed.

"Yeah. There's tons of rocks down here. I'll be okay."

"Good. Well, let's haul away."

Matt loaded rocks as his father unbuttoned his shirt and threw it on a branch where it hung like a flag. They toiled on.

About an hour later, Matt's father yelled down. "You thirsty?"

"Yes. And hungry."

"I'm sending down a Thermos in this bucket. It's just water, but it's cold." He dropped the thermos into the bucket and Matt began to lower it. "Last load. I told your mother to make some sandwiches."

"Please tell her no avocado and fried egg or peanut butter or sliced bananas." Matt stopped the bucket and pulled the thermos out. Unscrewing the lid, he upended it. The cool water poured down his dry throat and chin, creating muddy rivulets. Matt turned and pulled his shirt off of the rock pile, mopping his face.

"Keep the Thermos until its empty. I got the garden hose."

"Mom doesn't let me drink out of the garden hose. She's afraid there's a mouse in it."

"Well, don't tell her then. That's what I filled your Thermos with."

"Let's get another load up. Have you been keeping count, Dad?"

"I think we're about done with the medium sized rocks. So, during lunch I'll switch out the bucket with the barrel. You can still load the smaller stuff in that."

They were able to get up three more loads before Mom appeared with sandwiches, diagonally cut on paper plates and adorned with quartered sections of oranges and peeled carrots cut in fours lengthwise. Matt bit hungrily into his sandwich.

"Avocado!"

"And roast beef. She's nothing if not creative."

"In an evil sort of way."

"Here." Dad pried the green slice of bread from the roast beef and used it to wipe the avocado off of the meat, then tossed the offending piece of bread into the creek. Matt followed suit. Folding over the remaining piece of bread and meat, he ate hungrily. Lunch vanished quickly. Matt sent the empty plate and a rock up in the bucket.

Dad said, "I'll tie the barrel on this and lower it down. You scoop up some dirt and rocks and build yourself a ramp. Will you be able to roll some bigger rocks to where you need to load them?"

"Yeah, I already tried. They roll, but they don't lift worth beans."

"Then start building your ramp."

Pushing and piling the loose river rock, Matt was quickly able to make a usable ramp, then headed about thirty feet away toward a much larger chunk of granite. He could see the individual sparkling particles on the rough surface of the mottled stone. Matt pushed upward. It budged. Resetting himself, Matt heaved again. This time the rock tilted out of the small depression it was sitting in, toppling itself. Once over, the stone rolled a bit easier. Struggling on hands and knees, putting every ounce of strength into it that he could, Matt inched it over to the ramp. Above him, the black circle of the barrel hung suspended.

"Ready?"

Matt nodded, watching the barrel float down. The sides of the metal barrel had been cut about eighteen inches from the bottom. Matt pushed the barrel with his feet and grinned with satisfaction as the edge and the ramp lined up.

"Is it going to work?"

"If the ramp holds, it should. The ramp's a bit taller than the barrel."

Putting his shoulder into it, Matt began pushing the stone up the ramp. The rocks shifted and the base of the ramp widened. Slowly, reluctantly, the granite rose until it was teetering on the edge of the barrel. He pushed. The stone fell into the barrel with a deep clang.

"That's one," he said.

"Are you going to be able to hoist that?"

"I don't know," Matt answered.

"Try wrapping the extra rope around that tree trunk. That'll take most of the weight. Then use your legs against the tree."

Matt followed his father's directions, then yelled, "Here goes nothing."

Matt pulled. The rope tightened. The barrel stirred. It rose a couple of inches. The stone shifted. The barrel slammed to the ground.

"Well, that didn't work."

"You okay?" his father yelled.

"Yeah. Let me try again."

The second attempt mirrored the first.

"One more time with feeling." Matt strained. The load lifted. One foot. Two.

"Hey, Matt."

Matt wrapped the rope around the root. It held. Hands on knees and panting, Matt looked up to see Mr. Giannini and Robert. "Yes?" he huffed.

"Look, I talked with you a week ago about taking care of my fish."

"Yeah, in the garage, right?"

"It's this coming weekend. I'm leaving on Thursday and will be back—," he looked at Robert in silent consultation. "Sunday night."

"No problem," he said. "Any new fish? Or instructions?"

"I've got some discus. They eat brine shrimp. I'll write out all the instructions and leave them on the desk by the door."

"Glad to do it."

"Hey, Matt." Fred appeared.

"Hi, Fred. Want to come down to help?"

"No, that looks too much like work. And besides, Mom is taking me shopping. I got to go."

"So, you just come by to see me sweat?"

"No, my mom said I could ask you if you wanted to come to the cabin with us on the weekend."

"Cool? Could I, Dad?"

"I don't see why not."

"Great. Thanks, Fred. Oh, wait a minute, this weekend?"

Fred nodded.

"Mr. Giannini, if I fed the fish early Saturday and later on Sunday, will that work?" he asked.

Giannini smiled. "Sure, they aren't on a time clock. As long as you don't forget, they'll be fine."

"I won't forget."

"Gotta go, Matt." Fred said.

"See you. Thanks."

"Looks like you and Matt could use a little help," Mr. Giannini said. "How many of those big rocks you planning to haul up out of there?"

"About five. Yolanda said it had to be an odd number, for aesthetic balance."

"Six," Yolanda's voice piped in. "Helene wanted you to haul her up a rock, too."

"So, six?" Giannini broke the silence. "Robert and I could help."

"That would be great, Tony. I'm not sure Matt and I could manhandle this by ourselves."

"What are neighbors for?" Giannini asked. He motioned to Robert. "You're the strongest. Go give Matt a hand."

Shinnying down the rope, Robert hopped down next to Matt. "So," he said with an easy smile, "we meet again. Show me how this thing works."

Bracing himself, Matt unhooked the rope from the root and accepted the weight of the load. "You just pull."

Robert seized a portion of the rope and the two heaved. The barrel rose higher.

"One, two, three," they said in unison and heaved again. The barrel continued its rise. Doug and Tony grasped the lip of the barrel and pulled it into the yard. Together they dumped the rock into the protesting wheelbarrow.

"We're clear," Dad yelled. Manning the handles, he and Mr. Giannini headed to the front yard.

Matt turned to Robert. "Let's find another one." They both looked around.

"That one," Robert pointed to an obese bluish stone setting on the edge of the creek.

"It's a pretty one. But we'll have to get into the water to move it."

"We'll dry, Matt."

They waded into the shallow water and pushed. The stone pulled free with a great sucking sound. The bottom was wet and muddy. Translucent patches of snail eggs dotted the underside like boils. This stone was rounder than the first and rolled a little easier. Still, by the time they reached the ramp, both were panting.

"I got to reinforce the ramp sides with flatter stones," Matt said, catching his breath.

Together they clawed the blue stone up the incline and into the container. Then to the ropes, dragging the rock skyward. "Two!" Matt yelled.

Robert shook his head. "Man, that's a job"

"Only four more."

"Clear!" his father yelled.

✂ ✂ ✂

The final rock went up far more slowly than its brothers. Matt was soaking in sweat and grime covered his arms and chest. He yelled to his father, "Is that it?"

"Yes, thank God. That is it."

"Mom hasn't changed her mind again?"

"Nope, we are done." Doug turned to Tony and they shook hands. "Thanks. We never could have managed that without help."

"Hey, Dad? You mind if I wash up down here?"

"Sure. Go for it."

"You know a good spot?" Robert asked.

"Follow me."

A half mile down the creek was the eucalyptus grove. Towering silver-green trees rose, arcing together in cathedral-like symmetry. The temperature dropped a good five degrees as they stepped into the cool shadows. The smell of eucalyptus scented the air. Across the creek the body of one of the huge trees had fallen. Scrambling over the carcass, Matt found his pool. "Come on."

There in a puddle of sunlight was the pool. The fallen tree made a curtain of brown leaves making them invisible to anyone else. Matt sat on a branch waiting for Robert. Robert climbed the massive trunk. Leprous scabs of pale bark peeled off as he climbed.

The pool was mirror calm and about the size of a card table. A skiff of fallen leaves littered its surface and water gliders skimmed about peacefully.

"Here, help me." Matt stepped in sinking up to his shoulders and began splashing the leaves out of the pool. "It's about five feet deep and there are a couple of rocks Fred and I rolled in here to sit on." He searched with his feet.

He boosted himself onto a rock and sat, leaning back to soak in the sunlight, arms spread on either side.

"Is it cold?" Robert asked.

"Not after you've been in it awhile."

Robert stuck in a tentative toe. "You're crazy. It's cold."

"You got to get in all at once or else when it creeps up to your balls, you'll chicken out completely."

Robert looked at him a second. "What the hell." He slid into the pool submerging then shot up spraying water everywhere."

"Here's the rock." Matt nodded to his side. Robert climbed up. Captured in the thick blond hair on his chest, dewdrops of water broke the light into miniature rainbows.

"It's cold," Robert groused.

"But it feels good, right?"

Robert relaxed and allowed himself a smile. "Yeah, it is nice. Cold and nice."

Both closed their eyes enjoying the sunlight. A sky blue dragonfly hummed by, regarded them both and then decided to light elsewhere.

"The creek has lots of secrets like this. Most of them are good. There's a five-foot waterfall that way beyond the Lincoln Street Bridge. Most of the year the water there is warm. A bit further there are the slide rocks where the water narrows going over granite. If you sit in it right, the water pushes you downhill for about forty feet."

"And—?" prompted Robert

"Well, of course, there are secrets that aren't so nice."

"Oh?"

"I know where most of the poison oak is. There's a family of skunks that live over at that pile of rocks," Matt pointed. "Under the Locust Street Bridge is a bunch of really foul graffiti. There's a guy on up about a mile that slaughters his own sheep and throws the bones and heads down in the creek. I can also tell you who drinks in the neighborhood and how much."

"Those are the bad secrets?"

"Pretty much," Matt nodded, turning to Robert. "Where you expecting more?"

"You're crawling around people's backyards a lot. Yeah, maybe I expected more."

"Fred and his brother told me once that they were climbing around where the bamboo grove is and watched a lady and her gardener making out." Matt paused. "I haven't gone to look. Tell you the truth I come down here to get away from it all. I don't want to climb out of here with more secrets than I came in with. I already have enough."

Robert spread his arms out, interlocking them with Matt's and leaned back, his head against Matt's arm. The breeze stirred the curtain of dry fragrant eucalyptus leaves sheltering them from view. A water strider rowed across the calm surface of the pool.

"Matty," his mother yelled.

Matt flinched. "My God, her voice has power." He pulled his arm gently out from under Robert's head.

"This is a great spot. It's like nothing can touch us here," Robert said.

"Matty!"

"Except that. Sometimes I think no matter where I go that voice will find me."

Matt climbed out of the pool, reaching back to help Robert out.

The two stood there, dripping wet, smiling.

Robert smacked Matt on the shoulder. "Thanks, Matt. Mind if I come back?"

"The creek belongs to everybody."

Robert nodded.

"So you heard your mother call?" said Matt's father as he scrambled up the last part of the creek bed.

"Yes, Dad."

"She's wants you to take a proper shower for your date tonight."

"You have a date?" Robert asked.

"I was hoping they would forget. My mother picked the girl. How much fun can that be? See you, Robert. Thanks for the help. You know, hauling rocks."

"Don't forget Mr. Giannini's fish."

"I'll be by on Wednesday for instructions."

✖ ✖ ✖

Matt fiddled with his tie as he rode in the Jag with his father.

"Great car isn't it, Matt?" He looked at his son.

"Uh-huh." Matt shifted a small white box from hand to hand.

"Quiet ride, comfortable interior, hugs the road, kinda makes you wonder what the rich folks are doing tonight, doesn't it?"

"Uh-huh." Matt unbuttoned his coat. He stared blankly out the window.

"Cat got your tongue?" Douglas turned toward his son and only got a blank stare. "Earth to Matt? Beam me up, Scotty? Come on Matt, talk to me."

"I really don't want to do this."

"It's done. Get over it."

"It's baloney."

"I know. Is it the girl or the event or the fact your mom set this up that upsets you?"

"Yes."

"Okay, Son. You can be mad at your mother, that's fair. She shouldn't have done this. But it's not fair to be mad at the girl. It isn't her fault. If I get wind that you have done anything to embarrass her or do anything other than ensure she has a good time I will be greatly disappointed in you. Do you understand?"

"Yes."

"It's also not your cousin's fault. You are not to be the dark cloud in the corner grousing through this whole evening. It is his party. Help him celebrate it his way. Again, I don't want any reports about you ruining anything because you're ticked off at your mother. Do you understand?"

"Yes."

"Believe it or not, your mom's doing this for your own good."

"My own good?"

"She wants you to get out of the house more and meet more people. She wants you out of the creek. She thinks you're a hermit. And she wants you to see your cousin. He's successful. He's in college. This will give you an idea of what's ahead of you."

Matt said, "Dad, I understand what you said. I'm just having trouble relating to it. Mom wants me to interact, be more social. So she sends me to a party with an eighth grader, overdressed in a double breasted suit, with a corsage. I don't even know what to do with this thing."

"You pin it on the girl."

"Pin it? Where?"

"On her strap. You know." Dad pointed to his chest. "About here."

"Who wears a corsage to a birthday party?"

"Matt," Douglas warned, "Remember what I said. We're here." Dad nodded toward the front door. "There is some good news"

"What?" asked Matt, opening the door.

"I talked to her mother and she has to be home by eight. She has a nine o'clock bedtime."

"So, if the party starts at six," Matt said, glancing his watch, "we will only be at the party for two hours."

"Two hours. You can handle that can't you?"

"Guess so." Matt got out of the car, paused, then began walking toward the door.

"Matt," his father cried, getting out of the car. Matt turned. "Don't forget this." Doug lobbed the corsage box to him. Matt caught it with both hands.

"Thanks, Dad."

Margaret was wearing a knee-length bright yellow dress with polka dots and a deep rounded collar. Leather sandals that tied half way up her pencil-thin calves covered her feet. A simple string of pearls graced her throat. Her light brown hair was cut short and held in place with a yellow head band. In the middle of a growth spurt, she was a puppy—her feet and hands were too big for her, she was all angles with knobby knees and elbows. A bright floral ring adorned her right hand.

Matt fumbled with her collar trying to pin on the corsage. The point of the needle disappeared into the yellow fabric and embedded itself firmly into Matt's finger. Jerking his finger from behind her collar he watched a bubble of blood grow. He sucked off the blood.

"Hope blood doesn't stain your dress. You look very nice."

Margaret giggled.

The second try was more successful. The yellow rose hung lopsidedly on her collar. "There," Matt declared triumphantly.

"Let me just fix that," Margaret's mom said, stepping between them and attaching the flower more firmly. "Now you know this is her first date." Margaret giggled shyly. "And she has to be back between 8 and 8:30. Any later and her father will be on the porch waiting."

"Yes, ma'am."

"You're mother said you're a good boy, so I'm trusting you to take care of my daughter." Mrs. Paris turned and kissed Margaret. "Have a good time, baby."

They walked to the car in silence. Matt opened the back door for her then walked behind the car and opened the front door for himself. Through the smoke of his father's cigarette, his father glared at him.

Matt mouthed "What?" as his father indicated with the jerk of his head the backseat.

"Oh." Matt shut the door and opened the back door, sliding across the cool leather.

"Nice car."

"It's my dad's."

"I figured that."

Douglas started the car, exhaling smoke out the driver's side window. He flipped his cigarette out the window and glanced in the rear view mirror.

"So, ah, Margaret. How are you?" Matt asked.

"Fine."

"Your first date?"

"Yes. And now that Mom has let me go out with you, she'll have to let me go out with Andrew Culligan."

"Andrew?"

"Yeah, he's my boyfriend. We've been going steady for the last three weeks after he broke up with Andrea King. You know the big tease in seventh grade. Well we've been going together ever since then and last week he asked me to a movie and my mother, you know how she is. She said no, she didn't know his family or anything about him. So she asked if I wanted to go to this thing. What is it?"

"My cousin's birthday party."

"Yeah. So when she asked if I wanted to go to this I jumped at it. I got a brand new dress."

"It looks nice on you," Matt said.

"Yeah it does. And I got these awesome sandals and she let me shave my legs and she said if I go I can get my ears pierced this week. Isn't that just peachy?"

"Peachy."

"So how old is your cousin?"

"Twenty."

"Awesome. My girlfriends are going to be so jealous when they hear that I'm going to a college party with a high school boy, even if it's just you. I mean, you're cool and all, but if you were on the football team that would be just awesome."

"I'm on debate."

"What's that?"

"Never mind."

Margaret leaned over and whispered to Matt. "Do you think they will have beer?"

"I don't know."

"I hope so. The girls would be so jealous if they had beer."

Matt rolled his eyes.

He opened the car door for his date once they arrived.

"Cool car. What kind is it?"

"It's a Jaguar sedan."

"Rich people drive these, don't they?"

"Yeah, I guess so."

"Too cool. They're going to be—"

"—so jealous." Matt finished for her. Margaret giggled. Matt slammed the door shut as his Uncle Leo and Aunt Paula came out of the house.

"Douglas, missed you the other day," Leo said.

"Hello, Leo. Got caught up in something. You know how it is when you're trying to make a living. What's up?" Douglas asked.

"The little lady and I thought we'd give the kids some private time. You know, for the party. So we're going to the country club. You and Yolanda want to join us?"

"Sorry, Leo, but thanks. Margaret there needs to be home at eightish."

"Eight o'clock sharp, her mother said," Matt corrected. "And I promised her mother."

"Matt, go on in," Leo suggested.

Matt hesitated. Margaret grabbed his arm and tugged. "Come on."

As his father stepped out of the car, he called to his son. "Matt, just a minute." Matt paused. "Excuse us, Margaret." Dad separated the two.

"This is going to be a disaster," Matt said.

"Here, I got something for you. No young man should go out on a date without some money in his pocket."

"This is Joe's house. What do you expect me to spend it on?"

"And here." Doug handed his son a blue foil packet.

"What's this?'

"You never know when you might need it."

"Trojan," Matt read. "It's a prophylactic? What's that?"

"You'll figure it out."

"You sound just like Coach. Let's see, lactic means milk in Latin?"

"Matt, come on," Margaret called. "I hear music."

"Good God," Matt groaned.

"Have a good time," Dad said.

"Thanks." Matt stuffed the money and the foil packet in his pocket. Margaret grabbed his arm and in they went.

"Is that a color television?" Margaret asked.

"Actually, there's four of them." Joe stepped into the entry. Dressed in jeans, a white t-shirt and moccasins he leaned casually against the entry door.

"Hi, Joe."

"Matt, how are you? Long time no see, little Cuz. Two presents? For me?"

"One's from Mom."

"Let me guess—a sweater?"

"Yes."

"Ugly?"

"Green and yellow argyle with matching socks," Matt said.

"God. How did you know? Did you peek?" Joe asked.

"She bought me one, too."

Looking at each other they both said, "I'm sorry" in unison and laughed.

"Hey, where's the bathroom?"

"Down the hall, little lady, second door on the left."

Margaret left.

"Robbing the cradle there aren't you, Matt?"

"Mom set up the date."

"That's too bad, Matt. There's some really hot—and easy—chicks here tonight. I bet a stud like you could have scored before the night was done. If you didn't have, you know."

"Man, oh man. A groovy marble bathroom. Green." Margaret giggled from down the hall.

"You need to get out of that establishment suit you're wearing, Cuz. You got a t-shirt on under all of that?" Matt nodded. "Well, peel that shirt and tie off and join us."

"That is an unbelievable bathroom!" Margaret said returning.

"Joe, this is Margaret Paris."

"A pleasure to meet you, little lady. Should we join the party?" Joe turned and headed toward the sound of music.

Matt sighed and slipped his hand behind Margaret, guiding her down the hallway after his cousin.

Chapter Nine

As the mismatched couple followed Joe through the large house, pausing in the kitchen, where Joe picked up a six packs of beer.

"Hamm's, the beer refreshing," Joe sang. "Want a beer, Matt? Margaret?"

"No, thanks," Matt replied.

"Sure," Margaret said.

"Joe. She can't have a beer. She's only thirteen."

"Oh. Here. I have something you might like. Try this." Joe grabbed a tall bottle and poured something red into a tumbler. "Here." He offered it to Margaret.

"What is it, Joe?" Matt asked.

"Boone's Farm Strawberry Hill." He watched as Margaret sipped her glass.

She smiled. "It tastes like strawberries and something fizzy."

"Don't worry Matt. It's pretty harmless."

"It tickles my nose," Margaret giggled. "It's groovy." She downed the glass and motioned for Joe to refill it. He did.

"Matt, there are a couple of bags of potato chips and pretzels and junk on the counter. If you get that, I'll bring the beer." He hefted three six packs. "Oh, Matt, grab the brownies off of the oven." He nodded toward the stove. "One of the guys made them."

"Guys made them," Margaret giggled. "I want to try one."

"Matt's hands are full with the munchies. You get them, Margaret, and have a couple."

Margaret swallowed her drink and headed to the stove. Pulling the wax paper off of the brownies, she picked one up and took a tentative bite. She smiled.

"They're good. Just like my mom makes."

"Trust me, girl, they are not just like you mom makes unless your mom is way cool."

"She's not."

"Have another. Want one Matt?"

"Sure."

Matt polished one off in two bites.

"Okay troupe, onward to the party." Joe indicated a hall leading off the kitchen and ending in a closed door. With hands full the trio took off. The driving strains of Sam and Dave's "Soul Man" pounded to a halt as they opened the door, to be replaced with the Rolling Stones "Satisfaction."

"This is the place," Joe yelled over the music.

Drawn curtains cut off the sunlight, making the room dark. Bluish smoke hung in the air. Glowing black light posters covered every inch of the walls and most of the ceiling. A strobe light pulsed at the far end of the cavernous room. Matt's eyes were drawn to an orange black-light poster of Jesus smoking a cigarette. Quiet clusters of people shared bean bags and a love seat. Three were on Joe's bed, oblivious to the others in the room as they made out.

"The birthday boy is here," Joe shouted over the nose. Someone shuffled to the hi-fi and turned down Mick Jagger's repetitious refrain. "Let's get to the most important part. Presents and cake!"

Joe sat on the love seat near a pile of presents. Matt put down the bags of chips and pulled his two presents out from under his arms. Munching another brownie, Margaret put down the platter.

"Gather around, children, while I examine my booty."

Matt looked around and sat on the floor, Margaret beside him sipping noisily. Nobody moved off the bed. Though fully clothed their hands were very busy.

"Thanks, Mario," Joe cried, pulling the wrapping off of a box. He pulled out a long tall bottle with a lot of tubes running out of it.

"What is it?" Margaret asked, burping softly.

Joe held it up. "It's a hookah." Joe winked at Mario. "We'll break this in royally a little later."

Joe picked up another present. Slipping the bow off of the tube he unrolled it, read it a minute and broke out laughing. He held it up so that everyone could see it. Simple orange silhouettes of an overly endowed man and a buxom woman in various sexual positions under the caption of "Fly United."

"I love it," Joe declared over the laughter of his friends.

"I don't get it," Margaret whispered.

"I'll explain it later, maybe," Matt replied.

"Pour me some more strawberry juice." She lifted her empty glass.

"How many have you had?"

"Only three. They're just juice." As Matt got up she called, "And another brownie."

One after another Joe opened presents until at last there were only a few left. He held up the box Matt's mom had wrapped. "Sweater," he said with his hand to his forehead and eyes closed. "The Great Karnack sees a sweater. No, make that an ugly sweater—with equally hideous matching socks."

Joe tore off the paper and opened the white box. With two fingers he pulled out the sweater while holding his nose with his other hand. Holding the offending item as far away as possible, he looked at it with exaggerated horror. Then he laughed and turned to Matt.

"She got you one of these, too?"

Chagrined, Matt just nodded.

"Wow. You mother has the most abysmal taste in clothing," Joe said. "I'm not even sure what shade of yellow that is."

"Urine!" somebody yelled. People laughed

"You can throw it away," Matt ventured.

"No, you know the rules, Matt. She has to see me wear it at least once. Then, I can do whatever I want with it." Joe picked up the other box, more crudely wrapped than the first. "Your mother again?"

"Nope, that one's from me."

"Cool!" Joe ripped through the paper and opened the box. Opening it, his eyes went wide.

"Matt, is this—? Matt, this is great!" Joe held up a right-handed baseball glove. "How did you—?"

"Uncle Leo was talking the other day that since you are a left-handed pitcher, you were having trouble finding a right-handed glove."

"They are *way* hard to find." Joe fitted the glove on his hand and slapped his fist into it. "Way hard. Where did you get it?"

"A sports store in Town and Country Village. It's the Jim Bunning kind." Matt beamed, pointing at the signature.

"This is great, Matt." Joe looked at his cousin. "Thank you."

Matt smiled.

Joe banged his fist into the mitt again, then reluctantly pulled it off and set it aside. "It fits perfect, thanks a lot."

"Open mine!" The voice from the bed sounded familiar, and Matt turned. Pushing her way out from under two young men was Matt's cousin, Agnese.

"Aggie? Is that you?"

"Me in the flesh, Cuz." Aggie adjusted her tie dyed t-shirt and leather fringe vest. She smoothed out the long brown peasant skirt she was wearing. "How have you been, cousin?"

"Me? I'm fine, I guess." Matt indicated the two guys getting up off of the bed, "You looked—busy."

"I am, cousin, I am." She hugged the first guy. "This is Bug."

"My name is really Bugliosi, but everybody calls me Bug." He reached over and shook hands with Matt. Aggie pulled his other arm around her and placed it on her stomach, where it immediately began moving. "I don't know the other guy's name."

"That's Angelo. He plays outfield for my team," Joe said. "Bug here is first baseman."

"Joe said he has great hands," Aggie murmured, "and he was right."

"What are you doing with these guys?" Matt asked.

"I'm a liberated woman now, Cuz."

"How liberated is it to be laying under two guys?"

"Still going to Catholic school? Life is more real than that, cousin. I was exploring my sexuality."

"So were they," Matt pointed out.

"Have you opened my present, Joe?" Aggie asked.

"I got it right here." He held a small box in his hand. He tore off the paper: a small white jewelry box.

"It's not jewelry," Aggie said, snuggling against Bug, whose hands were roaming freely across her torso.

Joe pulled off the box top. A small chalky yellowish cube lay there. "Awesome!" Joe leaned over and kissed his cousin full on the lips. "This is awesome. Is it what I think it is?"

"Of course, Joe. It's a block of hash. Perfect for that hookah you got."

Bug's hand were exploring under the hem of the t-shirt. Aggie turned around and leaned up to kiss him. They both fell into a bean bag chair.

"I'm hungry," Margaret said.

"Have some chips," Matt replied, unable to turn away from Aggie. "I don't understand what happened to Aggie."

"She is a fully liberated woman doing what comes naturally," Joe explained.

"She was going to become a nun!"

"Well, if virginity is a requirement, she doesn't meet the qualifications anymore," Joe said. "Don't be too upset with her, Matt. Sex is natural. It's fun. Hell, I even have had a shot at her."

"You made love to my—our cousin?" Matt exclaimed.

"Oh, I wouldn't call it making love. It was pure, horny, out of control, drug induced slam, bam, thank you ma'am passionate, animalistic sex. Yes."

"With Aggie?"

"Of course with Aggie. Hell, half of the baseball team has had a go at her." Joe said. "You're the animal guy. Animals were created by God and they just do what they were put on earth to do. Eat, fornicate and die."

"It's wrong. She's your cousin."

"In bed it doesn't make any difference. The parts all work the same."

"But Sister says—"

"Here's a bit of advice Matt. Don't go to professional virgins for advice about sex. What do they know? Have they ever had sex? If they did, I guarantee that they wouldn't take that vow of celibacy." Joe smirked. "No matter what, sex is too damn much fun."

Matt just stared.

"Loosen up, Matt. Let's get some cake."

"Cake!" Aggie pried herself out from under Bug.

Bug said, "I brought brownies. Marijuana brownies made with the finest stuff I could find. All flowers, buds and new leaves, no stems."

"I'm hungry," Margaret wailed.

"Matt, how many of those brownies did your girlfriend eat?" Aggie asked.

"She's not my girlfriend," Matt said. He peered down at Margaret sitting on the floor. A tumbler rolled away from her hand trailing wine. "I don't know, maybe three."

Margaret dropped the bag of Fritos. "Six," she slurred. "I had six and three glasses of this groovy juice." She fumbled for the glass, found it and held it up. "Can I have more?"

"Wow, Matt, she's stoned."

"This is wrong, wrong, wrong, so wrong. I am in so much trouble," said Matt.

"Matt, calm down," Joe said.

"Calm down? Calm *down*? How can I calm down?" He pointed. "Look at her. She's bombed. I've got to take her home in an hour, and what am I going to tell her mother?"

"Don't panic, man. All you got to do is get her to puke," Joe said.

"Great first date. Drugs and puking. How am I supposed to get her to puke?"

"Well, Matt, looking at how green she's getting I don't think puking is going to be a problem," Joe said, smiling.

Matt looked at Margaret, who was licking Cheeto dust off her finger. A long orange stripe marred her left cheek. She stopped licking and turned to Matt.

"You don't look too good, Margaret," Joe observed.

"I don't feel too well, either."

"Matt, get her to the restroom," Aggie said.

"Down the hall, Joe?"

"No!" Joe pointed in the other direction. "Take her to the one off of the service porch. There's no carpet that way."

Matt steadied Margaret and began walking her down to the bathroom.

Bug walked up to Joe with the hookah. "Hey, man. Where do I get some water for this thing?"

"Follow Matt."

Bug walked off, following Matt.

Matt stood behind Margaret, one arm around her middle. Cradling her against his chest, he supported her with his hips. The other arm held her head over the open toilet bowl. Margaret was panting and groaning.

"Hey, man. Don't mean to intrude." Bug pointed to the sink. "Just need some water."

Margaret wailed, "Matt, I think I'm going to die."

Aggie pointed. Margaret had both hands on the toilet bowl and was bucking against Matt's hips. "She's a little young, Cuz."

"Aggie! You have a dirty mind. She's just heaving. Help me out here, Bug."

"Man, I'm just here for the water." He unscrewed the bowl of the hookah and put it aside. The neck and the vase of the hookah were larger than the little sink. Bug picked up a Dixie cup and began filling it. "Do your own thing, man."

"I'm not doing my own thing. I'm doing hers."

"That's what it looks like, Matt," Joe said from the doorway.

"Come on! Who has sex with someone who's throwing up?" At that point Margaret noisily threw up, proving Matt's point. "See?" Matt declared triumphantly. "Puke."

Margaret redoubled her efforts, bucking against Matt. Joe looked at Aggie. "I think he's right. Looks like puke to me." He turned to Matt. "Good job, Matt. Try to keep it in the bowl."

"Joe, we just rolled some joints. You got any matches?" came a voice from the other room.

"On the table by the cake. Don't eat it until I get there. It's my birthday." Joe looked at Matt. "Some party, eh Matt?"

Matt was leaning against the bathroom wall, still holding Margaret.

"I think I'm feeling better now," Margaret said.

Matt let her go and she stood on her own power.

"Groovy party." She burped softly. "Got anything to eat?"

"No brownies!" Matt, Joe and Aggie all said together.

❈ ❈ ❈

"Your dad's here," Joe said to Matt.

Matt sipped a Coke quietly in an armchair. He looked at the clock. "Only forty-five minutes late. Great."

"Uncle Doug is here?" Aggie sprang up as a sliding door opened and Douglas entered. "Uncle Doug!" she exclaimed, jumping up and hugging her surprised uncle.

"Aggie. This is a pleasant surprise." Matt's father sniffed the air. "What's that smell?"

"Incense, Dad. It's just incense," Matt said.

"You must be burning a lot of it," said Douglas.

"It's groovy, isn't it?" Margaret looked at Matt. "Come on, Matt, we got to go. My mother is going to be livid that I am late."

"Don't worry," Matt's father said. "My wife called and said we would be a little late."

"Forty-five minutes?" Matt said.

"Your mother and I were having a discussion."

"Peachy."

"Hey, Unc!" Joe and Douglas shook hands.

"Happy birthday, Joe. You're what, 21 now?"

"Yep, I am a legal adult now."

"Me, too," chimed in Aggie, leaning toward her uncle.

"Dad, we need to go."

"You're right, Son." Douglas unwrapped himself from his niece. Goodbyes were said and the three walked to the car. Joe followed.

Joe hooked Matt's arm and waited as Margaret and his uncle continued down the path.

"All that about—you know—Aggie and me, the drugs—"

"Don't worry, Joe. I won't say anything. I'm good at keeping secrets."

"Here." Joe handed Matt a small paper bag.

"What is it?"

"Acapulco Gold. Good stuff!"

"I can't." Matt handed the bag back.

Joe tucked the bag into the inner pocket of Matt's coat. "Who knows? Someday you might want it."

"What did Joe have to say?" Douglas asked as Matt opened the car door.

"Nothing, Dad." Matt climbed into the backseat with Margaret. "He just wanted to thank me for the mitt again."

Dad started the car. Margaret leaned against the other door and fell asleep.

"So how was your first date?"

Margaret snored softly. "I may never date again," Matt said.

Chapter Ten

"You recovered from your date yet?" Dad walked into the kitchen and glanced at the clock.

"I don't *even* want to talk about it," Matt replied, screwing the top back on the jar of mayonnaise.

"Didn't your mother make you lunch?"

"Sure did." Matt nodded toward the brown paper bag on the kitchen table. "You're welcome to it. Avocado and sliced tomato."

"What's with her? I bought lunch meat."

"Yeah, I found it. Also found the salami. So, I'm making the best sandwich in the world. White bread, salami sliced thick and gobs of mayo."

"No cheese?"

"I'm a purist."

"Aren't you late?"

"No. There is a teacher meeting this morning. Don't need to be there until nine." Matt stuffed the sandwich in a bag, then threw in an apple and a couple of cookies.

"So you're taking the eight thirty bus? Its eight twenty now."

"I know. I gotta boogey. Fortunately Mr. Costella drives slowly. I should make it."

"You shouldn't count on other people's mistakes. What if he's on time?"

"Then I'll come home and ride my bike." Grabbing books and lunch, Matt rushed out the door and down the street just as the bus huffed to a smoggy stop. Matt stepped aboard.

"Hi, Matty."

Matt stared stupidly at Margaret and two of her friends crammed into the first bench seat of the bus.

"Margaret—what are you doing here?"

"Teacher meeting. So, I don't got to take the regular bus." Margaret purred, "I can see you again."

"Good. Yeah. Great."

"That's him?" one of Margaret's friends asked.

"Move along, Matt," the bus driver said.

"Yeah, sorry. See you, Margaret." Hastily, Matt slid into the empty seat next to Stacey. "Hi, Stacey."

"Looks like you got a fan club." Stacey indicated the three giggling girls who were turned around and watching Matt.

"I'm doomed."

Margaret waved. Matt weakly waved back. The threesome giggled.

"So, how was your date last night?"

"How did you—?"

"See the girl by the window, the one with the freckles?" Numbly Matt nodded. "Well, Margaret there is one of her best friends and her sister is a good friend of mine."

Matt looked at her blankly. "So?"

"So, I got the call about nine thirty last night."

"Why did she call you?"

"Margaret has a phone in her room. She was up half the night calling all of her friends telling them about the groovy party she went to last night. Half of her friends have brothers and sisters in high school."

"Oh, God!"

"By nine fifteen the whole school will know."

"I am so doomed!"

Another wave of giggling erupted from the front of the bus.

"Just shoot me now." Matt slumped in his seat.

"We can fix it, you know."

"How?"

"Why didn't you ask me?"

"I would have. But my mom, even though I told her I did *not* want to go to the party, decided that I was going. She set the whole thing up." He glanced toward the front of the bus, "Including Margaret."

"He said your name!" Freckles declared, causing more giggling.

"Oh, please!"

"So you didn't pick Margaret over me?"

Matt turned and looked at Stacey, stunned. "Of course not! I didn't pick anything. I didn't know that I was even going until Saturday. And when I told my mom I know somebody I could ask she said it is too late. Everything is set."

"Then I know how to fix this."

"How?"

"Keep your eyes on the girls." Matt turned forward, meeting the stares of the three. "Are they looking, Matt?"

"Yeah, it's not helping."

"All three are looking at you?"

"Yes. No, wait. One of them is looking out the window."

"Wave or something. We need all three looking. Tell me when they are."

Matt waved. The middle girl nudged the one looking out the window. She turned around. "Okay. They're all—"

Stacey leaned over and kissed him on the cheek.

Three mouths dropped open. Two heads whipped around, but Margaret lingered, a triumphant smile on her face. "No kissing on the bus," Mr. Costella's voice boomed.

Silence reigned in the bus. "Who was kissing?" someone whispered.

"You kissed me!" Matt said.

"Yep," Stacey said proudly.

"Why?" Matt asked. "Half the school is on this bus. So is my mother's butcher."

"Your mom has her own butcher?"

"And Mr. Rizzo works at the gas station my dad goes to. Everyone is going to know you kissed me."

"Yep. And you'll never have problems with Margaret again." Stacey looked at Matt. "Look, Margaret is a manipulator. Trust me. You gave her exactly what she was hoping for. Matt, she's not interested in you."

"Oh, she made that pretty clear. Then why this show?" He indicated the girls. One of them had her arm around Margaret. The other was staring daggers at Matt.

Stacey laughed. "The little drama queen got what she wanted. And she got it in front of an audience. Believe me, she is very happy."

The bus rolled to a stop in front of the high school. Matt followed Stacey out. At the steps of the bus he glanced at Margaret. Margaret looked up, sharing a secret smile, then buried her head in her arms and began sobbing.

"Way to go, Killer," Mr. Costella said.

"Hey, Matt."

"Hi, Dave."

"Hey, Stacey. How are you?"

"Fine, Dave. Look, Matt, I got to go. See you at lunch?"

"Sure."

Both boys watcher her go. "Fixed your bike, didn't you?"

"Yeah. Why?"

Dave just smiled.

"She kissed me."

"Really? She kissed you?"

"Yeah."

"Where?"

"Right on the bus."

"No, you idiot! On the bus: why?"

"Well, she was doing it to save me from Margaret."

"Margaret? You got two girlfriends now? That's not even fair."

"Margaret is *not* my girlfriend."

"So tell me."

Matt did as they walked into the school and meandered to their lockers.

"Ah, I understand," Dave said.

"You do?" Matt opened his locker and threw in his books.

"Sure. She was just marking her territory." Dave slammed his locker shut and ran off as the bell rang.

"Marking her territory? She thinks I'm her territory?" Matt smiled, then his smile faded. "Wait, isn't that what dogs do to fire hydrants?"

At lunch Matt looked for Dave in the milk line, got a milk and went out into the yard, settling on the same bench he sat on every day. Moments later Dave joined him. "Got a weird sandwich again?"

"Nope, made my own." Matt pulled out the sandwich and unwrapped it.

"Salami. The king of meats. Good job, Matt."

Matt bit into the sandwich and smiled, chewing. Hungrily, he took another bite. "Yep, best sandwich on the face of the earth."

"Uh, oh. Trouble headed this way," Dave said.

"What?"

"Carlotti. He's been telling everyone that he's going to be taking Stacey to the Fling. Have you asked her yet?"

"No."

"She's already turned down two guys, Al Camadora and some guy in her Geometry class. She's waiting."

"For what?"

"The right guy to ask her, you idiot!"

"So what's Carlotti's problem?"

"He thinks he's the right guy."

"Hey, Connors." Carlotti sauntered up and stared down at Matt. "I heard about you and your date with Mary Poppins. How old is she, ten?"

"She's twelve or thirteen or something."

"Twelve or thirteen. A little young isn't she, Connors?"

Carlotti straddled the bench and sat down.

"I wouldn't sit there if I were you," Matt warned.

"Is that a threat, Connors?"

"No, it is not a threat, Carlotti. I'm just telling you I wouldn't sit there, if I were you."

"Well, you're not me, Connors. You are nowhere near me. And that's why we're gonna talk." Carlotti leaned forward. "See, a chick like Stacey deserves a guy like me. Not a pansy like you."

"What the hell do you want, Carlotti?"

"I want you to know that I'll be taking Stacey to the Fling."

"And what about Stacey?"

"What about her?" Carlotti sneered.

"Does she get a choice?"

"No way. She's going with me."

Matt got up. Dave followed.

"We'll see."

"Oh, you want to let the best man win, Connors? Well, I am the best man here. I always win."

Matt turned to walk away. "Hey! I'm not done with you." Carlotti stood up quickly, his pants snagging on a nail head. They ripped.

"I warned you not to sit there."

"You did this!" Carlotti pushed and Matt fell backward onto a trashcan, stumbled and fell across the bench.

"Freeze, Carlotti!" Brother Amaldi yelled from across the yard.

"He started this," Carlotti shouted, pointing to his torn pants.

"Tell it to the office, Carlotti," Brother Amaldi said firmly. "You, too, Connors."

Two uncomfortable wooden chairs held the boys as they waited for the vice principal. Hostility crackled between them as they sat in silence before the polished mahogany desk belonging to Sister Maria Tomas. She stepped in quietly. Both boys rapidly stood.

"Sister, Connors started this whole thing."

"Silence!" She raised her hand. "I am a nun, Mr. Carlotti, not a fool. I have investigated this incident."

She turned toward them.

"You, Carlotti, are not unexpected. But you, Matthew Connors. You're a bit of a surprise."

"Sorry, Sister Tomas."

"So tell me what happened and remember that I have done my research, Mr. Carlotti."

"Connors here, he threatened me and he got up to get me—"

"Enough. Mr. Connors, can you explain how Mr. Carlotti tore his pants?"

"He came over to Dave and me—"

"David Arreugo?"

"Yes, Sister. Anyway, he came over to talk and I warned him not to sit on the end of the bench. Dave and I sit on that bench all of the time and, we knew that the bench had nail heads poking through it."

"Did you tell this to Mr. Carlotti?"

"I tried."

"Is this true, Mr. Carlotti? And keep in mind that I have spoken with Mr. Arreugo."

"Yes, Sister."

"So, can I assume you got up and tore your pants on the bench?"

"Yes, Sister."

"Then what happened, Mr. Carlotti?"

"I got up and sorta fell against Connors."

"Fell? Brother Amaldi says you shoved Mr. Connors against a garbage can."

"We were just messing around, Sister," Matt said.

"Oh?" She whirled on Matt. "Messing around?"

"Yes, Sister. You know, guy stuff. I wasn't hurt. I fell against the can and stumbled over the bench."

"You're bleeding." She indicated Matt's elbow.

"It's okay. I used to get worse than this playing kickball on the blacktop in sixth grade."

"So this is all a big misunderstanding?"

"More or less, Sister Tomas."

"So, Mr. Connors, Mr. Carlotti, as there is no real problem, there won't be any real punishment."

"So we can go, Sister?" Carlotti asked.

"Not so fast. This incident did bring one thing to my attention." She reached into her habit and pulled out a hammer and a paintbrush, handing one to each. "We have some very unsafe benches that need to be fixed. Consider it community service. You, Mr. Carlotti, will pound in the nails and do a bit of sanding. You, Mr. Connors, will repaint the benches. Do you both understand?"

"Yes, Sister," they said in unison.

"You'll work one hour after school each day until all the bad benches are fixed, starting today."

"I have football practice," Carlotti objected.

"Mr. Carlotti, I have already talked to your coach. And both of your parents have been called. They will pick you up at four, sharp."

"You may go." The boys stood in silence. They turned and left the office, closing the door behind them.

"I am going to kill you, Connors," Carlotti growled and stalked off.

"I am doomed."

Sister Tomas blew the whistle at exactly four o'clock. Tapping the lid back on the taupe paint can, Matt carried it over to Sister. With a movement of her head, she indicated where he was to put it. "I'll see you boys again tomorrow."

"Yes, Sister."

"You, Mr. Carlotti, may leave."

"Yes, Sister." He turned and ran off.

"You, Matt, need to stay. Your mother just pulled up."

Mom stepped out of the car and stalked over to them, her high heels clicking on the asphalt. "What did he do?" she demanded.

"Pardon me, Mrs. Connors?" Sister Tomas arched one eyebrow.

Mom hesitated. Then she did an awkward little curtsey. "Sorry, Sister Tomas. How are you?"

"Fine, Yolanda. Let's step into my office."

For the second time, Matt found himself on one of the uncomfortable hardwood chairs. Nervously he rubbed his hands together.

"Matt is not in trouble. He volunteered to do some community service. A project he helped to bring to my attention," Sister Tomas began.

"So why am I here? He could have taken the bus home."

"I wanted to talk to you about Matt's shaving."

"What?"

"Matt needs to shave. I've asked him to talk to you about it and haven't seen any results."

Yolanda bristled. "Sister Tomas, with all due respect, I am his mother and I will decide when Matty will be old enough to shave."

"Matt," Sister said, eyes locked on his mother, "would you mind stepping outside? And close the door please."

Matt got up, looking from woman to woman. He backed out of the room and closed the door behind him, then opened it a crack.

"All the way, Matthew."

Matt shut the door. He could still hear them talking.

"Sister, this really isn't any of your business. You don't have children and . . . and I won't have you telling me how to raise my son."

"Funny." Sister Tomas leaned back in her ancient leather chair. "That's exactly what your mother said when? About twenty years ago?"

"What are you talking about?"

"Yolanda, surely you haven't forgotten the eleven year old girl who came to me in tears because she was getting teased."

"That was different."

"Different? That little girl was being teased by the other girls because her mother wouldn't allow her to wear a brassiere. Day after day she came into my classroom avoiding the other girls—and boys, who were giving her a bad time. The Lacurto girls were particularly catty, as I recall."

"They were awful."

Again, the eyebrow rose.

"Are they teasing Matty?"

Sister Tomas merely nodded. Yolanda dropped her head, then looked up. "Is it bad?"

"How bad does it have to be?"

"Those girls were awful. Non-stop."

Sister Tomas nodded sagely.

"Maybe it is time he shaved, now and then."

"I agree."

"Is there anything else?"

"No." Sister Tomas got up and shook hands with Matt's mom. "Please send Matthew in for a minute. And shut the door."

Looking confused, Matt stepped into the room.

"All the way," said Sister Tomas.

The door clicked behind him.

"Is the nonsense with Mr. Carlotti over with, Matt?"

"I think so, Sister."

"Very well." Sister Tomas started to turn from him. "She loves you, Matt. Sometimes it's hard for mothers to deal with change. Some want their children to stay children forever. Her mother did."

"May I go?"

"Yes, Matthew."

"Thank you, Sister." Matt took a step to the door, opening it. "Do you want it shut?" he asked. Sister Tomas nodded. He shut it, all the way.

Chapter Eleven

"Matt, I haven't seen you much lately," Stacey said. "You weren't on the bus the last couple days."

"Sister Tomas has me doing some community service. I painted all the benches in the school yard."

"I heard there was a fight." She looked at Matt. "Over me."

"Yeah, kinda. It was a guy thing."

"Who won?"

"Nobody, I guess," Matt replied. "Carlotti ended up pounding nails for the last three days and I painted. I've seen enough taupe for a lifetime."

"Carlotti's a jerk."

"He thinks he's the best thing since white bread. He thinks every girl in school lives for the day he asks them out."

"Not every girl."

"I haven't seen you at lunch either, Stacey."

"Softball practice and team meetings. They have me playing shortstop."

"That's pretty good."

"It's great! You don't know much about softball, do you?"

"Not really. I've not been much for team sports. I prefer single sports, you know, where you compete against yourself. Like bike racing and swimming."

"But you're not on the swim team."

"Yeah, well, there are other reasons."

"Your mother?"

"How—?

"Dave. He and I talked a little the last couple of lunches." Stacey paused, "He's scared of her, I think."

"She's scary sometimes."

"I'm not afraid of her."

"You haven't met her," Matt said.

"I'd like to."

Matt looked at her with surprise. "You're the only person I ever heard say that."

"Your stop is up ahead," Stacey said. "Since you've seen my inner sanctum . . ."

"Inner sanctum?" Matt asked.

"You've seen my bedroom."

"Oh, yeah. The turret."

"Maybe I should see yours?"

"My bedroom?" Rising, Matt grabbed his stuff. Stacey got up, too. "You're serious?"

"Of course, I'm serious." Both of them got off the bus. "Come on, Matt. Show me where you live."

"I got a better idea. Come with me."

Hand in hand they walked down the block. "That's my house." Matt nodded at the blue rancher across the street. "This way." Turning right, they walked about half a block. "This is the empty lot." Matt paused. "It belongs to the crabby old lady who lives next to the store. She hates us going in it."

"But we're going in it, right?" Stacey said with a smile. They waded through thigh high weeds. The back of the lot sloped into the creek. "Down there?"

"Yes," Matt urged. "Come on."

Slinging his book bag down the incline, Matt hollered and ran after it. Balancing precariously, he glissaded down the steep slope, coming to an abrupt and breathless stop on the sandy bottom.

"Come on!" he shouted up at Stacey.

"I'll fall."

"No you won't. Lean back as much as possible. Besides, I'll catch you. Toss down your books."

The book bag arched in the air and landed about halfway down the hill. It slid the rest of the way. Matt picked the bag up and tossed it aside.

"You ready?" Stacey asked.

"Ready."

"You better catch me."

"I will."

Wide eyed, arms pinwheeling, she careened down the hill. "This is steeper than it looks," she screamed.

They collided together in an untidy heap. They hugged each other, as Matt stopped and steadied her. They laughed, hearts pounding.

Stacey looked around, brushing hair out of her eyes. "What is this?"

"This is the creek. It's my world." Matt let go of Stacey and stepped back.

A wide ribbon of silver water split around a large boulder. Eucalyptus swayed, creaking, casting dappled green-silver light across the water. Twittering birds darted in and out of branches overhead. Bamboo undulated to its own song, dry leaves rasping. Emerging cattails spread out along the creek bank.

"What is this?" Stacey asked again.

"This is where I live. You wanted to see it, right?"

"It's like a fairy tale. And in most fairy tales I've read, the princess kisses the frog and he becomes a prince."

Matt looked around at the water. "Sometimes a frog is just a frog. Come on, I want to show you something."

Matt picked up the book bags, handing one to Stacey. He helped her cross the stream, and picked up a flat stone. Sidearm he flung it.

"One, two, three—not bad," Matt said. "Want to try?"

"Sure."

Matt handed her a flat stone. "Try to throw it level with the surface."

She did. The rock hit the water perfectly, skimming across the water in six bounces.

"You've practiced."

"Dad and I vacation in Tahoe a lot. He showed me how. Is this why you come here, Matt?"

Matt thought a moment. "No. I come here to get away from it all. The creek gives me everything I need. There's food. See that?" He indicated a lacey leafed plant. "That's anise. Here, smell." He broke off a small piece. She looked at it and sniffed.

"It smells like licorice."

"It tastes like it, too. There's black walnuts and prickly pears and all sorts of things. There's shelter, too." He grasped her arm. "This way." They hiked to the cliff of broken concrete. "Up there." They climbed, Matt leading. Brushing aside some shrubs, Matt uncovered an opening. "In here."

Matt scrambled in. Stacey followed. Indicating a rock, Matt invited her to sit down. "This is my place."

Stacey looked around, eyes pausing on the plastic Mary sitting on a rock shelf.

"I won that in grade school. One of the hinges is broken, but I keep her here."

"This isn't what I expected."

"I can light a candle."

"No, what I mean is, most guys wouldn't have a Mary statue. They'd have beer or something."

"I'm not—"

"What's this?" She pulled at a small package wrapped in aluminum foil.

"That's my favorite book."

She handed the package to Matt and he carefully unwrapped it.

"What is it?" she asked.

"*The Lost World* by Doyle."

"The Sherlock Holmes guy?"

"That's him," Matt said. "There's somewhere I want to take you. It's one of my favorite places."

"Let's go."

"We can't. It's not ready yet." Matt looked at Stacey. "Give me a week or two. It's a beautiful, peaceful spot. You'll love it."

"Okay. Whenever you're ready, Matt." She scooted closer to him as he rewrapped the book and placed it back on the shelf. He turned and found her very close.

"Matty!" The call echoed down the canyon of the creek.

"Damn."

"Your mother?"

"My mother."

"Ignore her?" Stacey asked.

"I wish."

"Matty!"

"Matty?" Stacey asked.

"Yeah. I hate being called that. Come on. We need to go."

They scrambled out and Matt replaced the brush covering the door, then he helped her climb down. Together they waded the shallow stream. A few steps brought them to the base of Matt's yard.

"This is my place." Matt pointed up.

"Matty!"

"Yes, Mom," he called back. "Come on up. We've got to go."

Matt's mom walked to the cliff edge and looked down. "Oh."

"We're coming up, Mom." He turned to Stacey. "You first. I'll help you. Grab the rope and climb. Use the holes in the wall as steps until you get to the roots. Then climb up." Matt grabbed the rope and handed it to her. "I'll carry the backpacks."

"You sure?"

"I've done it a million times."

Stacey took the rope and looked at the cliff. "The first step is pretty high."

"Here, I'll boost you." Hands on her rear, he pushed. She stepped into the hole with one foot and began climbing. Up she climbed, under the watchful eyes of Matt's mother. Matt clambered up behind her. Stacey reached out, offering her hand. Matt took it and stepped up into his yard.

"Who is this?" came the clipped tones.

"Hi, Mom, this is Stacey."

"And do you find many girls in the creek?"

"No, Mom. Stacey goes to my school. We ride home together on the bus." He turned to Stacey. "This is my mother, Mrs. Connors."

"How do you do, Mrs. Connors?"

"I'm fine." Mom turned away from Matt and Stacey. "Come along, Matty. We have dinner with your aunts. Say goodbye to your little friend."

"I was planning to walk her home."

Matt's three aunts came out of the house.

"Hi, Aunt Vicki, Aunt Rose, Aunt Rita." Matt turned to Stacey. "These are my aunts. This is Stacey."

"Pleased to meet you all," Stacey said.

"There's no time to walk your friend home, Matty," his mother said. "You know we always eat at five, and its four forty now."

"But, Mom, you and Dad always taught me that if you are out with someone, you make sure they get home safely. Right?"

"Right, but—"

"So, I am walking her home. It isn't far. Won't take twenty minutes."

"I promise I won't bite him, Mrs. Connors."

Mom didn't smile. "Your Aunt Rose eats at five, Matty. You know that."

"I couldn't go without changing anyway, Mom. These clothes have poison oak on them."

Yolanda stepped back. "Stacey, is it? We eat at five and—"

"Hi, Aunt Yo," a chipper voice chimed in.

"Aggie!" Matt greeted his cousin.

"The front door was unlocked."

"Agnese. I was just telling Stacey—"

"Yolanda." Aunt Rose's voice was firm. "Since Aggie is here, she can take Matt and the girl home and meet us at the restaurant."

"Yeah, Mom. That would work. I could change in a minute and Aggie can drive us."

"I don't want to be a bother," Stacey said.

"You're not a bother," Aunt Rita said. "Any friend of Matty's could never be a bother. And since Aggie is here, everything is solved. Right?" Rita looked at Yolanda.

"Right," Yolanda clipped.

"Elmer's Restaurant? I mean, it's always Elmer's, isn't it?" Matt asked.

"I don't want any damn poison oak. Be there in fifteen minutes, Matty."

❊ ❊ ❊

Matt ran around the car and opened the door for Stacey. He ignored his cousin's facetious grin, and walked with Stacey to her door. "I am really, really sorry, Stacey. Nobody should have to face my mother without a mirror, shield and sword. Not to mention the aunts."

"Really, it wasn't that bad." Stacey held out her hands and flexed her fingers. "And I don't seem to have turned to stone yet. I'll live."

"Still, my mother—"

"Your aunts seemed nice."

"They're okay. Aunt Rita is an airhead. Vicki is the moneybags of the family. Rose can be intimidating, if you're not ready for it."

"It wasn't that bad."

"My mother—"

"Was being 'The Mother.' Trust me, I've seen worse."

"Really?"

Stacey thought for a moment. "No," she admitted. "But I've read about worse. Mostly in Grimm's Fairy Tales."

"Most of those mothers are described as 'wicked step.' They have an excuse."

"Is there a test tomorrow, in English?" Stacey asked.

"Yes. First five chapters of Homer."

Stacey nodded. Spinning around, she gave him a peck on the cheek, and ran up the porch. "See ya tomorrow, Matt." She waved and disappeared within. Matt, bemused, stood staring at the door.

Chapter Twelve

Aggie leaned on the car horn. "Come on, Cuz. We don't want to be late. The coven has convened."

Matt hurried back to the car and slid in beside his cousin. Aggie backed out of the driveway, then fixed her cousin with an appraising grin.

"What?" Matt asked, uncomfortable.

"She's a step up, Cuz," Aggie remarked. "I'm impressed."

"Impressed?"

"She's a real step up from the jailbait you brought to Joe's party."

"Margaret." Matt sighed.

"Just so you know this new one is real fine. Pretty and smart and—"

"Not scared of my mom."

"Aunt Yo? She's a real peach. Why would anybody be afraid of her?"

"You're kidding, right?"

"No. She's always been good to me."

Matt stared at her. "She's on my case constantly. She's *always* telling *everyone* about my zits or whatever. She searches my room daily."

"What's she looking for?"

"I don't know, but I hope she never finds it."

"You riding that filly yet?"

"What?"

"You banging Stacey yet?"

"Aggie!"

"It's just a question. Though if you're not, you're a fool."

"I don't even think of her in that way!"

"Nonsense. You're male. That's all that males think about."

"The guys you know."

"All men."

They rode on in silence for a minute. "So, Aggie, given up on that whole nun thing?"

"God, yes! I couldn't be trapped in a male dominated world like that. Can you imagine me with a vow of silence?"

"No."

"I've decided to free myself from the artificial bonds imposed on women. I plan to experience everything the world has to offer. And to screw as many beautiful men as I can."

"But why? What do you gain by screwing as many men as possible?"

"Look, Cuz, sex is fun. I enjoy it. I have sex for the pure unadulterated pleasure of it. It's my body. I can do whatever I want with it. And guys tell me I'm a great piece of ass."

"I always thought you wanted to be more than a piece of ass."

"Like what? One of those television mothers like June Cleaver?"

"No, but a piece of ass. Just look at the words, Aggie. Each time you have sex with a guy, you become a piece. Each time you are giving the guy a piece of yourself, your time, your dignity, your body, maybe even your soul. What happens when you wake up one day and you've got nothing left? If you give it all away, you become, what? Empty?"

"It's not like that, Cuz."

"And what have you got to give your husband? What is there left to give to him and just him? And after your marry, he has to measure up to all those others you gave a piece of yourself to? And if he doesn't, what's to keep you from going out and getting some more? I mean, if marriage is—"

"Marriage is a farce. It was developed by men to control women. Besides, real women don't need men for anything. I am never going to marry. No piece of paper would ever legitimize my love for a man."

"Maybe that's not how it works."

"Meaning?"

"Maybe a piece of paper can't legitimize a man's and a woman's love. Maybe their love legitimizes the piece of paper."

Aggie stared out the window. "God, Cuz, you are depressing. We better go. Aunt Rose will have a fit."

They walked to the restaurant. The four sisters could be seen sitting at one half of a round table. The cousins paused. "Look at them, Cuz," Aggie said.

"It's like looking at four snappers on ice in the butcher shop," Matt said.

"All they need is someone to put a sign in front of them saying a dollar nineteen a pound." Laughing they entered the restaurant.

"There they are!" Waving a napkin, Aunt Rita shouted, "Agnese, we're over here."

"They can see us, Rita. We're the only people in the restaurant," Rose pointed out dryly.

"Oh, well. I just wanted to make them feel welcome."

"You're finally done with your little friend?" Mom asked.

"Mom, you always said a gentleman walks his lady to the door."

"And you'd be proud of him, Aunt Yo. He walked her to the door and very chastely said goodbye."

"You're late."

Matt glanced at the clock on the wall. "Aunt Rose, we are only three minutes late and since the menus are still on the table—"

"And my mom hasn't made up her mind yet," Aggie said.

"There are so many choices, Agnese," said Rita.

"The waitress hasn't come to take orders yet. So everything is right with the world."

"Matthew, you know I eat precisely at five o'clock. If Aggie didn't have to take you and your friend home, we would be eating by now," Rose fumed.

"Can I take your order?" asked the bemused waitress who had come up behind Matt and Aggie.

"There are so many choices." Rita peered at the menu uncertainly. "What are you having, Aggie?"

"I'll have . . ." She glanced at her aunts staring at her raptly, mouths slightly agape. "Maybe not the fish. Lamb chops. That, baked potato, Thousand Island dressing and a roll."

"I'll have that, too," Rita said, closing her menu.

"Yolanda, tell the waitress what you want," Aunt Vicki said.

"I was thinking of the rack of lamb, but—"

"I'm paying," Vicki added.

"The lamb."

"Rose?"

"I can pay for my own, Vicki."

"Next time."

"You said that last time." Rose looked at the waitress, "I want the filet of sole. No spices. Poached with no butter. No roll. Do you have corn bread? Okay, I want that, no butter, but I do want honey. Baked potato."

Vicki looked at Matt. "You ready?"

"Liver and onions. Baked. Blue cheese dressing."

The waitress looked at Vicki.

"Lobster. No potato. Extra vegetables."

After getting the drinks order, the waitress left.

"Who is that girl you dredged up out of the creek?" Yolanda asked.

"That's not a very nice way—"

"Quiet, Rita," snapped Yolanda. "Who was she, Matty?"

"She *is* a girl from my school."

"Who just happened to be down in the creek?"

"No, we walked home together and she wanted to see the creek."

"Because?"

"Because what? We rode the bus home together and she got off at my stop and we walked home. She wanted to see the creek and I took her down there. What's the big deal?"

"Is she Italian?" Vicki asked quietly.

"I don't know. Her last name is Morgan. That doesn't sound Italian. But I'm half and my last name is Connors."

"How long were the two of you in the creek together?" Matt's mom asked.

"Not long. I didn't time it."

"Time enough to have your hands all over her."

"That's not true," Matt said.

"I saw your hands on her rear end as she was climbing the rope."

"A boost. I gave her a boost so she wouldn't fall. That's all."

"I know what I saw. What were you two doing in the creek?"

"You're right, Mom. We were up to no good. Sinful me. We waded in the water, we skipped stones and—I am sorry to say—I showed her how to avoid poison oak. I gave her a boost. That's all." The waitress came with a tray of salads and passed them around. "I didn't do anything wrong," Matt said after the waitress left.

"She's not good enough for you," Yolanda said.

They sat in silence eating.

"How can you say she's not—"

Aggie squeezed Matt's leg as the waitress approached. "Now, who had the lobster?"

Vicki raised a finger. "Let's see, you had the plain sole, and you two had the chops." She placed steaming plates in front of each person. "And you had the liver and onions."

"How can you eat that?" Aggie exclaimed.

"I got a tough stomach. Besides, I love it."

"Did you hear me, Matty? I said she wasn't good enough for you."

"I heard you and I don't understand how you can say that. You've only talked to her for what, three minutes?"

"First of all, she isn't Italian."

"So? Dad isn't Italian. Did people tell you he wasn't good enough for you?"

"I did," Aunt Rose said.

"Me, too. Sorry, Matty," Aunt Rita added.

"We all did, Matt," Aunt Vicki confirmed.

"Because he isn't Italian?" Matt demanded.

"That was not the only reason," Rita said.

"Secondly," Mom went on, "any girl you find in a creek—"

"I didn't find her in the creek like a discarded bottle or a bull frog. She asked to see the creek and I brought her into my creek. It's not like I found her in the dump or a bar or something."

"Thirdly, I didn't care for her attitude."

Matt furiously swallowed a mouthful of meat. "Her *attitude*? All she said was hello," Matt continued, "You were the one staring at her like an owl at a mouse."

"I did no such thing."

"This sole could be warmer," Rose said.

"Rose, really!" Rita exclaimed.

Rose stabbed a piece of fish with her fork, brought it to her nose and sniffed, then ate it. "It could be warmer. But, Yolanda, you were rather cold and Matt wasn't pawing her. If he hadn't boosted her, she would have fallen."

"I saw what I saw," Matt's mom declared.

"I don't think it had anything to do with being Italian, or the creek. I think it's very simple." Matt looked his mother in the eye. "She . . . wasn't . . . afraid of you. You did your best, I don't know, cold fish imitation, and it didn't work. She smiled and talked pleasantly and didn't run for the hills. That's what you didn't like."

"Matty, this is not the time and the place."

"Then why did you start it, Mom?"

"When your father—"

"How's your meal, Matt?" Aunt Vicki asked. She pulled up her purse and began rummaging for her wallet.

"Great, Aunt Vicki. Really good, thank you."

"And yours, Yolanda?"

"It's all right." Mom signaled for the waitress. "Can I have a doggie bag?"

"Absolutely. Anyone else?"

"I'll take one, if it's all right," Rita said.

"Is everyone finished?" Vicki asked.

Everyone nodded.

Vicki dug into her purse and pulled out two fifty dollar bills and handed them to Yolanda. "Here. Go pay the bill and keep the change."

"What about a tip?" Rita asked.

"I'll take care of the waitress," Vicki said.

Sticking one of the fifties into her pocket, Yolanda got up and headed to the register.

"Agnese, dear, I'm heading to the little girl's room."

"I'll come with you, Mom." Aggie looked at Matt, rolling her eyes.

When they were gone, Vicki pulled a twenty out of her purse and slid it over to Matt.

"What's this for?"

"Your mother said some cruel things, Matt. I thought this might help."

Matt stared at the twenty and then looked up at his aunt. "Aunt Vicki, you have always been one of my favorite aunts and not just because you are so generous in handing out money. I like the money, but I really like you. You're fun and you let me do pretty much what I want when I come down to visit you. And the horses are cool, too. So, please, don't feel offended, but this time money isn't going to help. I can't take this."

"Are you sure? You could go buy a—"

"I'm sure. I appreciate the offer, but it won't help and I wouldn't feel right taking it."

Vicky reached out and traded the twenty for three fives.

"That enough for a tip?" she asked as she got up. She leaned over to Matt, whispering, "I liked your girlfriend." Straightening up, she walked off.

"I've never seen anybody refuse money from your Aunt Vicki." Rose looked at Matt with a thin smile. "There might be hope for you yet."

Chapter Thirteen

"Aggie said she would take me home, Mom."

"Get in the car."

"But –"

Yolanda whirled, facing her son. "After that display in the restaurant, do not argue with me!"

Head slumped, Matt followed his mother to their car. She slammed the door and stabbed the key into the ignition. Matt crawled in beside her. Throwing the car into reverse, she backed out of the parking spot and slammed on the brakes. Rita scurried out from behind the car.

"Yolanda," she shouted, waving wildly.

Matt's mom rolled down the window. "What, Rita?"

Rita held up the doggie bag and handed it to her baby sister. "You forgot this."

Without saying a word, Yolanda snatched the bag out of Rita's hand and rolled up the window. She peeled out of the parking lot as Rita waved a vague goodbye.

"Mom, I—"

"Don't. Say. A. Word."

Matt stared through the reflection of his face forlornly out the window. His mother swerved wildly through traffic. Finally, she pulled into the parking lot of Lincoln Lane, the local grocery store.

"Sister Tomas thinks you ought to shave."

"I know."

"Did your Aunt Vicki give you any money?"

"She offered me twenty dollars. I refused it."

"You refused?"

"I hadn't done anything to earn it."

Yolanda looked at her boy appraisingly. "You're telling the truth."

"Yes."

"She gave me some."

"I know."

Yolanda reached into her purse and pulled out some bills. She carefully counted out six ones. Handing them to Matt she leaned toward him. "Buy a razor and a can of shaving cream. Your father likes Gillette razors and Burma Shave, but the Gillette shaving cream is cheaper. I also need some toilet paper." She turned away from her son. "And pick up a quart of milk. We might be out of hamburger. Ask Max for a pound of hamburger. I'm sure I am forgetting something." She turned back toward Matt. "And I want my change."

"Yes, ma'am."

He headed for the store, grabbed a cart and found the nonperishables. He flipped the toilet paper into the cart after making sure it was two-ply. The choice of razor was easy: the store only carried the one brand. Shaving cream was more difficult. Ten choices in a rainbow of colors and sizes all promising the smoothest possible shave. Matt picked the cheapest.

"You buying that for yourself or for your father?"

Matt looked up and saw Mr. Acevedo, the manager of the store walking down the aisle toward him with a large box of napkins. Acevedo stopped and began unloading the packages of napkins onto a shelf.

"Sorry?"

"It matters, you know, if you're buying if for yourself or for your dad." Acevedo looked at Matt. "I'm guessing you have what they call a light beard. First shave?"

Matt nodded.

"Try this." Acevedo picked up a red striped can and handed it to Matt. "It's for sensitive skin. Your first time, your skin is likely to be sensitive."

"Thanks, Mr. Acevedo."

"Welcome to the club, kid."

Matt hurried by the butcher and grabbed a pound of hamburger, then to the dairy for milk. Passing the freezer compartment he glanced at the ice cream. Reaching in, he pulled out a half gallon of ice cream, then headed for the checkout.

"My change," Matt's mom said as he opened the car door.

Matt handed it over as he settled in the front seat.

"There should be more."

"Toilet paper wasn't on sale. It was a dollar twenty-nine for the four rolls."

"Everything is getting so expensive."

He reached into the shopping bag and pulled out the ice cream. "It's your favorite."

"Maple nut?"

"Yep."

She started the car and headed home.

Standing in front of the mirror with the can of shaving cream in his hand, Matt examined his face and neck. He glanced down at his dog who was watching him. "Well, Letty, this is it. I wish Dad was home, but he's coming in late, so . . ."

Matt held the can in one hand, pointing it at his face, and depressed the nozzle. Shaving cream flew over his shoulder, splattering on the floor. His dog leaned over and sniffed it.

"That didn't work."

Matt held out the palm of his hand and leaned the can toward it. Awkwardly, he thumbed the nozzle. An apple-sized pile of shaving cream exploded onto his hand.

"That came out faster than I expected."

He put down the can and turned on the hot water. Splashing hot water on his face, he applied the cream in thick blobs. "Great, dog. I look like the Joker." Using both hands he spread the cream around, covering his entire face. Looking into the mirror, he nodded with approval.

"It's the end for you, Dynamic Duo," Matt said in his best Joker impression.

Looking closely in the mirror, Matt was puzzled. "How are you supposed to see what you have to shave?" His dog provided no answer.

He twisted the bottom of the handle, opened the razor head, injected a blade into the razor and twisted the opened ends shut. He looked from his face to the razor and back. Turning his arm, he ran hot water over it. Carefully, he shaved an inch and a half swatch of hair off of his wrist. He shrugged. "Looks easy enough."

Gingerly he scraped an inch of foam away from his cheek. Then, he placed the razor near his ear. "Here goes nothing." He swiped downward two inches. Pulling the razor back, he examined the two inch area he had cleared. "No damage done, dog." Letty wagged her short tail, encouragingly.

Matt made another pass at the smooth plain of his cheek. He paused to look at it and grinned. "This isn't too hard."

Tilting his head, he swung the blade along his jaw line.

"Ouch. Geez, dog, I cut the head off a pimple. Damn. That hurts!" He stared at the growing circle of pink foam.

He tried again, without drawing blood. "There's no point in slicing open my neck. I don't have any hair there." Letty, bored, sighed and lay down.

❊ ❊ ❊

"Mom!" Matt cried.

"What?"

"Come here."

"What is it? Cronkite's on."

Matt waited until he heard her footsteps outside the bathroom door. She opened the door and looked at her son.

"You did a number on yourself there, Matty."

His face was bleeding from a half dozen self-inflicted wounds. Matt cried, "How do I stop the bleeding?"

Matt's mom chuckled, smiling despite herself. "Your father uses toilet paper."

Matt reached around and pulled off about three feet of paper.

"No. No. No. Just little pieces, Matty. Thumbnail size." She watched as he dabbed at his face. "Just put them on the bloody spots and let them soak it up."

"How can I go to school like this tomorrow?" he wailed, staring at his reflection. "I look like a reject from some mummy movie."

"Your father heals very quickly. You probably will, too. You favor him in that way. If they are real bad, I have some base makeup."

"Makeup?"

"Your dad uses it sometimes."

"I look awful."

"It'll heal. Wait here." Mom turned and left, coming back a few moments later with a bottle a quarter full of green liquid. "Your father splashes this on after he shaves. He says it's soothing." She turned and left.

Matt pulled the bloody paper wads off of his wounds. The bleeding hadn't stopped. He poured some of the green liquid into a cupped hand, then splashed his face. His scream sent the dog running out of the bathroom.

❆ ❆ ❆

"Why didn't you wait until I got home?" Douglas asked.

"Mom said you would be late."

"Seven isn't late."

"She just said late and sometimes for you, late is late."

Douglas took his son's face in his hand and turned it right and left. "You didn't do too badly."

"Did you cut yourself the first time?" Matt asked.

"And the second and many, many more times."

"Why do they call them safety razors? There's nothing safe about them at all."

"Just a name, son. Really, you didn't do badly. I cut the hell out of my face and I'd practiced on a peach for two weeks."

"A peach?"

"Why do you think they call it peach fuzz, son? My dad gave me a peach, a razor and some shaving cream and said that when I could shave a peach without cutting the skin, I would be ready."

"Were you?"

"No. I could shave a peach clean as a whistle, but your face isn't a peach. You shave your face in a reflected surface and it has peaks and valleys. No, I sliced myself up pretty darn good, especially on the lip under the nose."

"I look awful."

"Not really. Most of the cuts are on the jawline. Nobody will notice. And, they're pretty small. Just nicks."

"What about . . . makeup?"

"You know the acne cream she bought? That stuff is skin colored. A bit of that rubbed in really good should do the trick."

"Thanks."

"Now, tell me what happened at the restaurant. Your mother jumped me with it the minute I walked in the door."

"There's this girl, Stacey."

"Cute?"

"I guess so," Matt paused. "I walked her home the other day, so today she decided to walk me home. She lives on Cherry Street. She wanted to see the creek. So I took her down there. We talked and stuff for a while–"

"Any fooling around?"

"Dad!"

"Okay."

"Mom yelled and we came up through the backyard. Stacey had never climbed up the creek bank before and I—I boosted her."

"Your mother said your hands were all over her."

"No way. She was above me and slipped a bit. I put one hand on her butt and pushed. That's all. You can ask my aunts. They were all there."

Douglas smiled. "I believe you. But your mother didn't see it that way."

"I know. And she was rude and said Stacey wasn't good enough for me."

"Look, your mom is pretty pissed off about the whole thing. Especially this argument and then something that happened with Sister Tomas."

"Yeah."

"Care to explain that one?"

"No. But it wasn't my fault."

"Tell you what. I have to walk over to Mrs. Morgan's house. She needs help with her taxes and some business stuff. Why don't you come with me? It would get you away from your mother while she cools off. You can bring your homework and work on it there." Douglas paused, "And today's Thursday, isn't it?"

"Yeah."

"She's got a color television. Tonight's *Star Trek*, isn't it? You could watch it in color."

"Wow! That would be cool."

"Get your books."

"I don't have any homework, but I gotta go next door and feed Mr. Giannini's fish."

"How long will that take?"

"About twenty minutes. He has a lot of fish."

"I'll meet you in the front yard in twenty minutes. I have to go tell your mother."

The darkness in Mr. Giannini's garage was partially dispelled by the light from twenty-three fish tanks that bubbled gently on sturdy wooden shelves lining two walls. Matt walked to the one unlit tank and switched on the light. A blizzard of brine shrimp exploded mindlessly in all directions. Finding a net, Matt scooped out two netfuls of the struggling crustaceans. Pouring them into a Dixie cup, he began feeding those fish that needed live food. Discus and angel fish flashed through the water, snapping the shrimp in two and gobbling up the bits. From another tank he took three gold fish and plopped them into the arowana's tank. The long sluggish silvery predator turned and regarded them with baleful eyes as the goldfish tried to retreat to the farthest corner. He began dropping fish food into the tank of neon tetras.

Matt put away the fish food and headed for the door. He paused, glancing back to make sure everything was all right. In the biggest tank, the arowana had a struggling goldfish by in its mouth. Matt watched as the larger fish gulped and the tail of the goldfish disappeared.

Chapter Fourteen

Matt stopped at the sidewalk, watching his parents.

"I don't want you to go."

"Damn it, Yolanda, I have to go."

"Why tonight?"

"Does it matter?" Douglas stepped forward, searching his wife's face. "Will tonight be any different than any other night?"

She backed away from him. Douglas turned, seeing Matt. "You done?"

"Yes."

"Have Matt home on time. It's a school night." She slammed the metal courtyard gate and seconds later the front door.

"Let's go, Son," Douglas said.

They walked half a block in awkward silence.

"You and Mom fight a lot. Why do you fight so much?"

"I don't know. It's a combination of things."

"Like what?"

"Oh, money is a big issue. What are you studying in school right now?"

"In religion we are reading about the Virgin Warrior, Joan of Arc."

"Virgin warrior, huh? Led the French army to victory."

"Yeah. No experience. No education. She ran on faith alone. Why is money an issue? We seem to be doing fine. Are we broke?"

"No."

"I mean Mom got all those new green appliances."

"That was your aunt."

"What was?"

"The appliances. She decided that we needed new ones like the ones she got. So, she went to Sears and ordered us new ones. She made the down payment and the delivery fee."

"So? A free stove and refrigerator. It's a nice gift."

"Wasn't a gift. I have to make the payments and I wasn't consulted." Douglas kicked a rock and it skittered down the sidewalk. "Burned her at the stake, right?"

"In Rouen. Then they dumped her ashes in the river. I'm sure she was only trying to help."

"Of course. But the prince was vain and insecure. A real man would have accepted her help and rewarded her for it. Instead, he threw her to the wolves."

"I was talking about Aunt Vicki," Matt said. "She doesn't mean any harm,"

"I know. In a lot of ways your mother should have married your Uncle Silvio and Vicki should have married me."

"You're kidding, right?"

"Your mother wants to be rich without the burden of having to work for it or manage it. Vicki wanted nothing more than to be married and have children."

"Why don't they?"

"Have kids? I really don't know. Something medical. The church turned on her, too."

"Vicki?"

"No, Joan of Arc. They were jealous of her influence and her ability to lead. They called her a witch and railroaded her. Forced a phony confession from her, which she recanted, but they executed her anyway."

"Is that why Aunt Vicki is so generous to the cousins and me?"

"Maybe. Your mom is the baby of the family. And you're the baby's baby. So everyone doted on you."

"I didn't ask for it."

"Didn't matter." Douglas sighed. "And I was the awful father, right from the first."

"No, you weren't."

"You weren't there. Well, yes, you were. Your mother labored for twenty-six hours to bring you into the world. And there was her mother and your aunts and their cousins all crowded in the hospital room saying rosaries in Italian. Your grandmother was clutching her scapular and swaying back and forth calling on God to bring you safely into the world. Your mother was screaming. My God, you would have thought someone died."

"You were there when I was born?"

"No."

"Why not?"

"Believe me, I was there for twenty-four hours of it. I was with her the whole time. Holding her, encouraging her. Finally, I fell asleep. Silvio woke me up and convinced me to go into the next room and get a couple hours sleep. He assured me that they'd come and get me when the time came. Your mother seemed calm and I agreed. Just next door. One room away."

"They didn't get you?"

"Contractions began again. The female mafia ordered the men out of the room and bingo, there you were."

"Her heart didn't burn."

"Who?"

"Joan of Arc. They say she never screamed or cried out as they kept throwing oil on the fire. Her entire body burned to ash except her heart."

"I'm sure that gives Joan a great deal of comfort."

"They made her a saint."

"First they burn you, then they laud the hell out of you. Make a fortune on the souvenirs."

"Most saints die terrible deaths."

"I think it's a requirement. And it allows the Church to enthrone the virtue of suffering. And guilt. Catholics are big on guilt. You want to know my theory on how to make a bundle of money?" Douglas asked.

"What?"

"You buy a worthless piece of land, preferably one with a grotto, or a cave. Maybe a spring. Then you hire a group of folks to claim they saw the Virgin Mary there and were healed."

"Then you build a hotel and rent the rooms to pilgrims?"

"No. You deny it. Tell everyone who will listen they are liars and fakes. You build a huge fence around the place and hire guards to keep people out."

"How will that make money?"

"They'll figure you wouldn't build a fence unless you were protecting something valuable. Someone will pay you millions for the property and probably donate it to the Church."

"You make millions—"

"—and the Church won't want to admit its stupidity so they'll build a shrine and sell souvenirs to the pilgrims."

"Might work," Matt admitted.

"Has worked," Douglas affirmed. "We're here."

"So the prince was a weakling and a coward."

"Absolutely."

"And an innocent woman paid the price."

"Leaving nothing but her heart." Lighting a cigarette, Douglas rang the doorbell.

Helene Morgan swung open the door. "I wasn't expecting the two of you," she said with a smile. "I might have some milk and cookies, Matty. Do you like Oreos?" She ushered them into the house.

"They're my favorite."

"Good. I'll be right back," she said, heading for the kitchen.

"So, what shows are you going to watch?"

Matt glanced at the grandfather clock. "*Batman* comes on in seven minutes. Followed by *F Troop*, which is in color now, too, and then *Star Trek*."

"When is that over?"

"Nine thirty."

"*Batman*?"

"It's the second part. They end with a cliff hanger and then solve it in some cheesy way."

Helene turned on the television and changed the channel. "If it's cheesy, why watch it?" Doug asked.

"Cheesy's fun."

"Here you go, Matty." Mrs. Morgan placed a plate of cookies and a glass of milk on the coffee table as the theme of *Batman* began to play. "Can I get you anything, Douglas, before we begin?"

There was an explosion from the television set and all three looked up to see Batman and Robin escape from another diabolical device.

"How'd he get out?" Douglas asked Matt.

"He's always got the exact Bat-something he needs to escape."

"We better get started, Helene." Douglas ground out his cigarette in a teepee shaped ashtray. "Her office is that way, Matt. That's where we'll be."

"Okay." Matt turned back to the screen. "Hey." Both turned back to him. "Where's the bathroom?"

Helene pointed down the other hallway.

"Okay, thanks." Matt turned back to his show as the theme song ended and relaxed against the sofa cushions.

A half hour later, Matt stuffed the last Oreo into his mouth and washed it down with the final warm dregs of milk as the announcer said, "Next week. Same Bat-time. Same Bat-channel." He picked the glass up and headed for the kitchen. On the counter sat the box of Oreos. The glass went into the sink. He reached for the Oreos, his hand pausing halfway there. Frowning, he looked around. There had been a sound – a low urgent groaning sound. He shrugged, seeing nothing. There is was again. The same low groan followed by a sibilant *yes*. Matt glanced out the kitchen window, then around the living room. Nothing. No sound emerged from the halls leading to the bedrooms. The groan repeated, coming from the office. Matt followed the sound to a door left open a fraction of an inch. Light spilled from the door. Light and another deep groan.

The room contained a desk, now empty with a lamp on it. Across the room was a small leather couch. Mrs. Morgan lay on the couch naked, one leg raised over the back, the other dangling to the floor, her full round breasts lolling back and forth, nipples taut and expectant. Matt gasped. Mrs. Morgan's head rolled to the side, beaded with sweat. Her eyes were glazed over momentarily before focusing on Matt. Eyes alight, she licked her full red lips. She smiled, winking. Matt's eyes were riveted to the motion of her heaving breasts. He watched as she lifted her leg from the floor. Matt's eyes flowed from her dainty painted toenails, past her delicate ankle, along her smooth muscular calf, her dimpled knee, up her well-formed thighs to . . . his dad!

Gasping again, he shut the door and leaned against it. He walked away, down the hall, past the cookies in the kitchen and settled on the sofa. He arrived to the raucous trumpet theme of *F Troop* just as the big cannon went off and the ball slammed into the guard tower, sending it crashing to the ground.

Douglas joined his son in the living room about an hour later. He eased himself onto the sofa and lit a cigarette. Inhaling deeply, he turned to Matt. "Good show?" he exhaled, blowing smoke between Matt and *Star Trek*.

"Yeah, I guess."

"You guess?"

"Not as good as last week's."

Mrs. Morgan joined them, sitting on the arm of the sofa near Matt's dad.

"Is this almost over?" Douglas asked.

Matt glanced at the clock. "About five minutes."

Douglas got up and stretched. "I've got to hit the can."

Helene watched him go, then turned to gaze at Matt. "Matt—"

"Don't."

"I just wanted to—"

"Is there anything you can say that will fix it?"

"No," she said hesitantly.

"Then don't."

"I told your father you saw. I thought he deserved to know."

Matt turned and looked at her. "I get cookies and he deserves to know." Matt got up as his father entered the room. "Let's go."

"*Trek*'s not over."

"So?" Matt opened the door.

"Will you be back tomorrow so we can finish our paperwork, Doug?"

Matt shook his head and muttered to himself, "Mosaic class."

"Maybe."

"He'll be here," Matt said. The adults both looked at Matt. "Mom has mosaic class until, what, ten? What is there to stop you?"

Douglas looked from Matt to Helene and sighed.

"Goodbye, Helene. I guess we better go."

Matt started down the sidewalk, several steps ahead of his father.

"Matt, wait up."

"You used me as camouflage to hide this whole thing."

"Matt, I—"

"'Nothing will happen,' you said. 'I'm taking Matt.' Thanks a lot, Dad."

"What are you—"

Matt whirled on his father. "Don't lie to me, Dad. I saw you fucking Morgan."

Matt didn't even see his father's hand whip out and slap him across the face. "Don't you talk about her like that, Matt."

"Did you hit me because of the word, or because it's true?" Matt asked softly.

Douglas sighed.

"And it wasn't the first time, was it, Dad?"

Douglas tensed, looking at his son. He took a hit off of his cigarette, holding a moment and exhaling slowly. "No. How did you know?"

"There were four Marlboros out in the ashtray on the coffee table."

"A lot of people smoke Marlboros."

"What's the name of our hotel chain?"

"The Indian Inns. What the hell does that have to do with anything?"

"You shouldn't leave teepee ashtrays in your mistress's house."

Doug chuckled. "You're right, Sherlock."

"You taught me to be observant and to question." Matt paused. "You also taught me to obey vows and be loyal."

"I don't know what to say, Matt. You weren't supposed to see that."

"*That* wasn't supposed to happen." Matt turned away from his father and continued walking home.

"Matt. Stop."

Matt stopped, facing away from his father.

"Where do we go from here?"

"I'm going home."

"You know what I mean."

"Yeah, I know." Matt turned toward his father. "Do you? You've put me in a no win situation. You know Mom will be at the door asking what happened. So I have been given a choice. I can tell her what I saw which will probably result in a divorce, right?"

"Your mother is proud. Yeah, a divorce is a possibility."

"Is it what you want?"

Doug looked into his son's eyes. "I don't know."

"Would you marry Mrs. Morgan?"

"Helene is a friend. A good friend who takes care of my needs. Needs your mother should take care of and doesn't."

"That's more information than I need."

"Your mother is beautiful. Always has been. One the outside anyway. She was so beautiful. I was a farm boy fresh from Kansas and she had this exotic beauty. Brown eyes that flashed when she laughed. Ebony hair. A smile that wouldn't quit. Beautiful olive skin. My family moved across the street from hers. For me, it was lust at first sight."

"Lust?"

"Yes, lust. I wanted her from the moment I saw her. We dated for about six months and your mother was as pure as snow. She never let me touch her." Doug paused. "I took her to Santa Cruz one day. We strolled the surf and found ourselves under the pier. We made love that day, to the sounds of the crashing waves and boardwalk music. I don't think anyone had told your mother anything about sex. She had no idea what was going on. Schools didn't have sex education back then. We were just swept away by the moment and our hormones."

"Again, do I need to know this?"

"I drove her home at sunset. The house was empty. We sat on the couch and began making out. Your mother may have been inexperienced, but she was willing to learn more. Rose came home and found us. Not as far into it as what you saw, but enough. Rose began screaming that their father had had a massive heart attack and here we were screwing on the couch in her father's living room. We weren't, but sometimes people see what they want to see."

"I know."

"Her father died before I could get her to the hospital." Douglas sighed. "It devastated her. She adored her father and he doted on her." He pulled out a cigarette, lit it and inhaled deeply. "She cried for weeks and refused to see me. I think she blamed me for his death, as if she had been here should have done something. Anyway, Rose told her mother her version of what she had seen and your grandmother decreed that we had to get married. She didn't ask. She didn't discuss. She ruled."

"But you said it wasn't . . . you weren't screwing her."

"Nope. But who are you going to believe – a hormonal teenager or a respected adult like Rose?"

"Rose said she was against you marrying Mom."

"Maybe it was because I had a reputation as a lady's man. Your mother was not my first."

"Or your last."

"No."

"Have there been others?"

"No."

"If I answered a question like that, that fast, would you believe me?"

"No, Son, probably not."

"So there have been, are, others?"

"Yes." Douglas dropped his head. "I am not proud of it."

"It won't stop, will it?"

"Probably not." Douglas looked at Matt. "A man has needs, Matt. You know that. You're old enough you should be feeling those needs."

Matt just looked at him.

"When I turned fifteen, my dad brought me into town and to the local whorehouse. He selected a woman for me. A girl, really. She looked to be very young. He paid her three dollars to teach me to be a man. Then he went off with the madam. I hear she was five dollars."

"What was it like?" Matt asked, in spite of himself.

"Scary as hell. Embarrassing and wonderful. It was a lot of things. But it was just sex, not love."

"So, the very same moral grandfather who forced you to marry Mom took you to a whorehouse when you were fifteen?"

"It was my birthday present. He'd done the same with all my other brothers. There's seven of us. Sometimes I think he kept fathering boys just so he could go to that whorehouse."

"Do you think he went other times?"

Douglas looked sideways at his son. "Your grandmother did."

"And she didn't mind?"

"After carrying seven boys, I think she was relieved he was cultivating someone else's crop."

"Wow. For my fifteenth birthday I got a bb gun."

"It's what you wanted."

"Yes."

"But maybe not what you needed."

"That still doesn't explain—why?"

"Your mother is what is called frigid. Sex just doesn't happen with her."

"It did once," Matt said.

"And that led to one lengthy and extremely painful pregnancy. Look, she relates sex to her father's death and twenty-five hours of delivery pain."

"So, I'm to blame for you and Mom not having sex and you fulfilling your 'needs' with Mrs. Morgan?"

"No, Matt. This has nothing to do with you."

"It does now. Either I tell Mom what I saw and divorce follows or I lie and hide what you did. Thanks, Dad."

"I didn't mean—"

"You were the one who taught me to take responsibility for my actions. Are *you* going to tell Mom?"

"No."

"Why not?"

"In a divorce, you would be stuck with your mother. No, we will stay together until you leave the house."

"So again it becomes about me. You stay with a woman you don't love. You don't really love her, do you?"

"I did once," Douglas said.

"You stay in a phony marriage because of me. Mom doesn't have sex in part because of me. You're screwing her friend because of me. I get to choose liar and hypocrite or cause of divorce. Just peachy. And you get off scot free."

"If you'd had sex, you might understand."

"I don't need to kill someone to know murder is wrong," Matt said.

"What about this girl, Stacey? Any possibilities?"

"I've just met her."

"You interested?" his dad asked.

"Yeah, kinda. Wait. Shouldn't someone be giving someone a speech of responsibility here? And shouldn't it be you? Shouldn't you be more concerned about your affair instead of encouraging me to have sex with everyone in sight?"

"I'm not encouraging you to have sex with everyone in sight. You should have sex responsibly."

"And who should my example of that be? Another 'do as I say, not as I do' moment? Like smoking? 'Don't smoke, Matt, it's not good for you.'"

"Not having sex isn't healthy, either."

"You had a vow. You made it before God and witnesses. I'm part of that vow." Matt looked Douglas in the eyes. "You weren't here for my fifteenth birthday. Or my fourteenth. Giving me advice about sex—I think that boat has sailed."

"We're almost home. What are you going to do?"

"Lie."

"Good. I'm proud of—"

"I'm not proud of me and you shouldn't be either. This is survival, that's all."

They walked up the path to the cast iron gate of the courtyard. Matt opened it and they both stepped through. Letting it go the gate slowly swung shut.

"What took you so long?" Yolanda sat on a porch bench in the dark.

"Hello, dear." Douglas leaned down to peck her on the cheek. She endured it stoically.

"Well?"

"There were good shows on, Mom. You couldn't expect me to leave before *Star Trek* was over, could you?"

"You watched TV, too, Douglas?"

"For a bit. Then we went into the room off her kitchen. She converted it into a neat little office and we worked on her taxes there."

"The whole time?"

"Of course, dear. Her husband left her with substantial investments and it takes a lot of time to go through all of it. Her taxes are quite a headache."

"She has a great color TV. The Riddler's costume is the same green as the sweater you bought Joe."

"So you watched TV the whole night?"

"That and ate cookies."

"Cookies?"

"Oreos and milk."

"Oh, Matty. You know that those are not good for your complexion."

"I know."

"And?" she prompted.

"After Batman I ran out of cookies. I went into the kitchen to ask Mrs. Morgan for more. The door to the office was open—"

"They left the door open?"

"Yes. I stepped into the room and found them hard at it. In fact, Dad was so deeply into what he was doing, I don't think he even knew I was there."

Douglas made a strangled sound.

"Mrs. Morgan gave me permission for more cookies and when I left they were banging away at it."

"Banging away?"

"The nine-key adding machine, dear," Douglas added hastily, shooting a look at Matt.

Matt's mom studied her son's face intently. "Well, then, best we get inside. Tomorrow is a school day, remember?"

Chapter Fifteen

Coach Harris looked up at the clock and continued. "No more questions on sex ed? What about you, Mr. Connors? You always seem to have a lot of questions." Coach looked at Matt. Matt apparently hadn't heard. "Matt? No questions?"

Matt looked up dumbly. "Ah, no, Coach. Sorry."

"Well, we are almost out of time and there is one thing that I have to say. This is only sort of related to the sex ed class. Some of you young men will soon be turning eighteen. If there is one thing that the recent offenses of the northern Commies in Vietnam has taught us, it is that they are not ready to give up yet. This terrible war may go on for many more years. So remember, on your eighteenth birthday, you become eligible for the draft. You have to register for the draft at your post office."

"What about the lottery?"

"Lottery or not, registration is required. It's the law."

Weasel-faced Leo Pinetta shouted from the corner of the room, "What about a deferment? I'm Catholic. Thou shalt not kill. Doesn't that qualify us for a deferment?"

The coach just looked at him. "Ever hear of the Crusades? The War of the Roses? Catholics have waged war for centuries. I doubt that being Catholic will get you much of anything. But you are welcome to try."

"Shouldn't it though, Coach?" Matt asked. "If we really believe what we've been taught, shouldn't it count?"

"The world doesn't work that way, Matt." He paused. "I have never heard of anyone getting a deferment for being Catholic."

"You could volunteer to be a medic, can't you, if you don't think you could kill someone?" someone yelled from the back of the class.

"Yes," Coach answered slowly. "But let me say this—a medic is out on the battlefield in the heat of the battle. He's dodging bullets and trying not to get killed just like every other poor guy out there. The difference is that the medic usually only carries a pistol. And he wears a big white helmet with a red cross on it. He's wearing a target on his head. The life span for most medics is very short."

"But they're not supposed to shoot at the red crosses," Matt protested. The bell rang and everyone started to leave.

"A lot of things aren't supposed to happen, Matt. But they do."

Matt gathered his books slowly. Last to leave the classroom, he shut the door behind him and slipped into the coolness of the hallway. He walked to his locker and dialed his combination. He whipped the locker open, ignoring a note that fell out onto the floor. After stuffing his things into it, he slammed it shut, twirled the dial on his lock and leaned his head against the cool smooth surface of the locker. He closed his eyes tightly.

"Hey, Matt," Dave softly said behind him.

"Dave," Matt acknowledged, not moving.

"You all right, man?" Concern showed in Dave's voice. "You been like a zombie all day."

"I'm all right."

"You got one of those righteous migraines you've told me about?"

"No."

"Talk to me, man. What's up?"

"Nothing, Dave. Thanks, but it's nothing you can help me with. I just got a lot on my mind and it all caught up with me today."

"Where were you at lunch today? Stacey was looking for you."

"Oh." Matt rolled his head on the locker door to look at Dave.

"Yeah. She seemed worried when she couldn't find you."

"I went to Confession." He rolled his head back.

"What the hell did you do? Kill the Pope?"

"I actually didn't do anything."

"So why are you so bummed out?"

Matt straightened up. "If you knew that someone was doing something really bad, would you rat them out?"

"Depends on what you call really bad. Smoking a little pot, probably not. Getting drunk every evening and driving around, maybe."

"What if telling would cause a bigger crapload of problems for a lot of people? What if those people are actually better off not knowing?"

"This is serious, isn't it?"

"Very."

"I don't know, Matt. It depends on the situation."

"What if telling the truth would cause more problems for you, personally?"

"Jesus, Matt. What did you do? Witness a murder?"

Matt laughed dryly. "No. Nothing like that."

"You're not in any trouble, are you?"

"No. I guess not. Want to come over? Maybe we could go to a movie or something?"

"I got to go to see Ada."

"Ada?"

"Annonciado Pelligrenno. Sister Tomas talked her parents into hiring me as a tutor for her in math."

"Annonciado Pelligrenno. There's someone I haven't thought about in a while."

"You know her?"

"Sure. She and I went to grade school together. Sacred Heart. She left in the seventh grade. She wasn't very happy there. She was always chubby and shortly after transferring in she came down with head lice—you know—cooties. It went downhill from there."

"You should see her now. She's not the girl with the pear-shaped bod anymore. She got into track, lost a bunch of weight. She's a fox, if you know what I mean."

"I'd like to see her again. I'd want to, even if she still was pear-shaped. She was a decent person." Matt paused. "Sure you don't want to come over? I need something to keep my mind off of everything."

"Nope, my friend. Ada awaits."

"See ya Monday, I guess."

"You better hurry. You're going to miss the bus, again."

"I think I'll walk home. The walk will help me get my head together."

"Good luck with that, whatever it is." Dave turned and left.

Matt leaned back against his locker. After a moment or two, he headed out. Ignoring everyone, he crossed the blacktop of the school grounds and walked past the bus stop. He glanced back down the street. No bus was coming. Quickly the sounds of the traffic were drowned out by his own thoughts. Out of the shade of the over-arching olive trees he began to feel the force of the sun. Off came the maroon uniform sweater. He tied it by the sleeves around his waist. A half block later, he opened the top couple of buttons on his white collared shirt. He looked up. Two blocks ahead he saw the sign for Baskin-Robbins. Matt didn't look up as the bus swept by.

"Matt."

Surprised, Matt looked up and saw Stacey. "How—?"

"I was on the bus. When we passed you, I pulled the cord."

"Why weren't you on the early bus?"

"The softball coach called all the players in to tell us we are having a practice at the college. He's got the college girl's coach willing to work with us for one day. It ought to be cool."

"I . . . I'm trying to think of something clever to say."

"How about good to see you?"

"It is good to see you. I've been bummed out all day. It's *really* good to see you." He smiled and walked up to her. "Want an ice cream?"

"You buying?"

"Absolutely."

"One scoop or two?"

"Come on."

They walked the block to the store hand in hand. Matt opened the door for Stacey and waved her in. They stepped into the cool interior and looked at the various flavors.

"Have you ever counted to see if they really have thirty-one flavors?" Stacey asked.

"I have," Matt admitted, with a smile.

"Can I help you?" a bald man in a pink and white shirt inquired.

"You ready?" Matt asked.

"I'll have one scoop of Pralines 'n Cream, please." The counterman picked up a scoop and carved out a baseball-sized scoop and patted it into a cone.

"A woman who knows her mind. I like that," Matt said.

"That'll be thirty-five cents."

"I'm paying."

"Okay, sir. What can I get you?"

"Rocky Road. One scoop, please."

The counterman handed the cone to Matt, who licked it and pushed it down with his tongue. "Seventy-three cents, with tax."

Matt paid for the ice cream and grabbed a handful of napkins. "Thanks." Turning to Stacey he continued, "So, you got off the bus to see me?"

"Duh. Why were you such a hermit today?"

"Bad stuff at home."

"Oh." Holding up her cone, she licked around the top, catching any melting ice cream attempting an escape.

"You want to walk down Lincoln Lane with me? Maybe catch a movie or something?"

"Won't your mom scream?"

"Nah. As late as it is she's getting ready for her mosaic class. In an hour she'll be gone. And who knows when my dad will come home. If he comes home."

"What's playing at the Garden?"

Matt bit into the ice cream, slowly chewing marshmallow and nut. "I think it's an Elvis movie, *Easy Come, Easy Go*. Or maybe it's the other way around."

"I'm not a big Elvis fan."

"I thought all girls liked Elvis."

"I'm not like all girls."

"I noticed."

They stopped at the light, then turned down Lincoln Lane. Stacey crunched into her cone, "What do you want to talk about?"

Matt watched her tongue dart out and lick the ice cream off of her upper lip. "What?"

"Talk about, Matt. Don't you think we should get to know each other a little better? Heck, I don't even your favorite color."

"Blue. And I really like black."

"I don't think black is a color."

"Isn't it all colors?"

"I think so."

"It's my favorite."

"Why?"

"I don't know. Shiny black just looks cool. Fury—you know, the horse —was black. And Black Beauty was black. The Batmobile is black. I have a black turtleneck my aunt gave me and I like it, a lot."

"Blue," Stacey said, and crunched another bite of cone. "Sky blue, powder blue, navy blue. Doesn't matter, I just like blue."

"Cool." Matt took three quick bites of his cone and chewed, cheeks bulging. They walked a few more paces. "Got a favorite song?"

"No. I like everything from musicals to opera to rock," Stacey said.

"I can live without opera, though I like some of it. My mom forced me to go see *Madam Butterfly* when I wanted to stay home and watch the second part of something on TV. And I actually liked it. But only in small doses."

"What's your favorite song?" Stacey asked.

"I like 'Secret Asian Man.'"

Stacey looked at him, puzzled.

"You know, by Johnny Rivers?"

She laughed.

"What?" he asked.

Stacey popped the last of the cone into her mouth and chewed rapidly. "You mean 'Secret Agent Man.'"

"Agent? Are you sure?"

"Yes. 'They've given you a number and taken away your name.'" She smiled. "It's 'Secret Agent Man.'"

"That makes more sense."

They paused by the entrance to the Garden Theater. "You were right, Matt. Elvis Presley."

"Next week is *Casino Royale*."

"I've heard that's good."

"Maybe next week we should go," Matt said.

Stacey turned and looked at him. "You mean, like on a date?"

"Well, yeah. Like on a date. Maybe we could ask Dave and somebody—"

"No, you don't. Don't you *dare* weasel out on this," Stacey said.

"Okay, a date."

"Just the two of us?"

"Just the two of us."

"That would be cool."

Both stared at the posters of Elvis. Matt turned to Stacey. "Want to go to the park?"

She nodded. They walked. "So was Margaret really your first date?"

"She wasn't a date."

"I know."

"I almost had another date," Matt volunteered.

"Almost?"

"Her name was Letticia. She's the colored girl on the basketball team."

"I know her."

"I've known her since about seventh grade. We graduated from Sacred Heart together. We'd been in a lot of classes together and sort of hung together at lunch. So one day, back in October, I asked her if she'd like to go to a football game together."

"What happened?"

"She said I'd have to talk to her father. So I went to her house and sat on the porch for a half hour waiting for him to come home. He was a huge black man and he wanted to know why I wanted to date his daughter. I told him just because we were friends. He looked at me long and hard. Finally he said no."

"Why?"

"He didn't want his daughter dating a white boy. He said that I may not have a prejudiced bone in my body, but the rest of the school wasn't that way. That dating me would cause his daughter and me pain and that he didn't want his daughter to have to face that." Matt took a couple steps in silence. "She never talked to me again. She was beautiful."

"And stacked."

Shocked, Matt stopped and looked at her.

"Well, that's what you guys say about girls with big—," she traced an hour glass figure with her hands.

"Yeah, but I didn't expect to hear it from you. You're not one of us guys."

"I'm glad you noticed."

"I noticed."

She smiled at Matt sweetly as they crossed into Willow Street Park. Four older men were playing bocce. They watched as one man rolled a ball toward the others and the balls clunked together with a wooden kiss.

"You ever play, Matt?"

"My Uncle Silvio showed me how," he replied. "I never got too worked up over it."

"What do you like to play?"

"Ping pong."

"I play ping pong a bit," Stacey said.

"My family is really into tennis. Silvio's made a fortune opening swim and racket clubs all across the state."

"So you found a game you wouldn't have to play with your family?"

"Yeah, how did you—"

"I don't like to say duh too often in one conversation, you know."

"Kind of obvious, I guess."

They both laughed. They walked past the playground full of screaming children.

"I used to love climbing on that metal elephant," Matt said.

"My favorite was the giraffe slide."

"Let's cut across the tennis courts," Stacey suggested.

Matt pushed open the gate into the tennis court. They crossed the smooth surface quietly. In the far corner, six nets away, a lone woman served balls into a cement wall.

"That's Mrs. Morgan," said Stacey. "She has great form."

"I guess," Matt said, stopping. "You want to go back?"

"Heck, no." Stacey waved. "Hey, Mrs. Morgan, how are you?"

Mrs. Morgan stopped, mopping her brow with her arm. Seeing Matt and Stacey, she smiled.

"Stacey . . . and Matt? Nice to see the two of you."

"Your serves are getting faster and more aggressive. You're getting a lot better," Stacey said.

"Thanks. Now if I can just control my aim. Against the wall I'm awesome. Against an opponent I have a tough time maintaining control." Helene glanced at Matt. "Glad to bump into you, Matt. That rock you dug out of the creek for me—I'd like two more. Is that possible?"

"I guess."

"I'll pay you. I decided I need three rocks of various sizes to create the effect I want. And I don't need them for a couple of weeks yet. Unless?"

"Unless what?" Matt asked.

"I had to fire my gardener. He just wasn't doing the job I wanted. He hasn't cleared out the corner I want to put the rocks in and it's been a couple of weeks. Plus he was getting expensive. If you'd like a job, I'm in the market. You'd just be mowing lawns, weeding, trimming bushes, that sort of thing. And clear the corner for my rock garden. Interested?" She tilted her head expectantly. "I'll pay."

"Sure, I guess so. Thank you."

"Can you start tomorrow?"

"Actually, no. I'm going to Santa Cruz with my friend, Fred. But if you just need the lawn done this weekend, I can do it on Monday after school."

"Great. See you then."

Helene picked up a tennis ball and slammed a wicked serve into the wall. Matt and Stacey watched for a minute.

"She's got great form," Stacey observed.

"She sure does," Matt agreed, "and her backhand isn't bad either."

"Matt!"

"Well, it's true." Matt smiled. "Come on." They waved goodbye and exited the tennis courts. "Let's go to the hill," Matt urged.

The hill was a gentle grassed slope dotted with dandelion puffballs and yellow flowers. Stacey picked a seed ball gently and held it before her lips.

"My father calls these wishing flowers." She blew. Seed heads separated and drifted away. "There go all my wishes," Stacey murmured.

"Any about me?"

"You can never tell your wishes aloud. That ruins them." She smiled slyly.

"Want to roll?"

"Head to head?"

"Absolutely, holding hands for as long as we can."

They lay on the grass, head to head, hands stretched over their heads. Matt grasped Stacey's hands, fingers intertwined. Matt rolled his eyes back until he could see the top of her head.

"Ready?"

"Let's go."

They turned downhill and the hand of gravity grabbed them. Rolling. Turning. Tumbling down the long hill. Flashes of blue and green flickered by. Laughing. Screaming, they gained speed. Fingers tightened, holding the bond together. Accelerating joyously they bumped and bounced down the hill, exploding wish seeds into the air, coming to a gentle stop on the grass, gasping for breath. Both stood up swaying dizzily. They stumbled toward the rock wall of the stage. Matt boosted Stacey up, then jumped up beside her. She bumped his shoulder and he bumped her back.

"You caught some wish seeds in your hair." He reached up and brushed dandelion fluff from her hair. He looked into her incredibly blue eyes. He turned away, wiping leaves from his pant legs. "Does this mean we're like girlfriend and boyfriend?"

Stacey smiled. "Duh. It kinda looks that way, Matt."

Matt gave her a smile. "I think I'd like that."

"I'm glad."

Matt busied himself with grass fragments on his shirt and looked away.

"What? Cold feet already?" Stacey asked.

"No. Absolutely not. I just—I just wondered, of all the guys in that school, why you picked me." He turned to her.

She studied his face for a moment. "Because of all the guys in school, you're the only one who would ask me that, Matt."

He smiled. "Wow."

Perched together on the edge of the rock stage they leaned together. Stacey's head rested on Matt's shoulder. Matt's arm snaked behind her and rested on her hip. Stacey giggled.

"Double wow."

Chapter Sixteen

Matt slowly swung out of his bed in response to Letty's whining. Padding to the back door, he let the dog outside. She shot out, barking boisterously at every bird in the back yard. Matt smiled sleepily. From the living room came the voice of Eddie Fisher singing "Oh! My Papa." Matt shook his head and headed back to his room and slipped on a pair of shorts, then headed for the kitchen. His mother sat at the table staring into a cup of coffee.

"Hi, Mom," he said. His mother didn't look up. Matt opened the refrigerator, pulling out the milk, then walked to the cupboard and grabbed a glass. He sat across the table from his mother.

"Mom, hi." Again she didn't respond. "Mom!"

Slowly she looked up. Her eyes glistened. "What?" She focused on Matt.

"Why do you do this to yourself? Play that song? Every time you put on that song, it makes you cry. Why do you keep doing it?"

"I'm not crying," she said, wiping her eyes and turning away.

"Right. Every Saturday it's the same thing. You wake up early, put on Eddie Fisher, pour yourself a cup of coffee and sit there crying."

"I said I'm not crying."

"How many years ago did Grandpa die?" Matt asked.

"Twenty-two. Twenty-two years ago this month."

"That's a long time, Mom," Matt said gently.

She looked at him. "It's an eternity. He was a . . ." Her voice choked a bit. "It was a long time ago, and I still can't get over it."

"It's hard to let things go. But sometimes you have to."

Mom took a sip of her coffee and sat up straighter. "Thank you, Ann Landers."

Matt took a gulp of his milk. "You're welcome, Yolanda from San Jose." He smiled.

She glanced at him and turned away. "Want some toast?"

"Sourdough?"

"Of course."

"Sure, I'd like a couple of pieces."

"Get the butter and garlic salt, if you want it. I'll start the toast."

Matt leapt up and got the butter and garlic. He also grabbed some napkins and returned to the table.

"Get the paper," his mom said.

Matt headed out, passing through the courtyard and found the newspaper in the center of the driveway. Mrs. Morgan was walking by with her two dogs.

"Hi, Matt. I thought you were headed to Santa Cruz."

"I am. Heck, it's only, what, seven?"

"About that."

"I've got a few chores to do, feed Mr. Giannini's fish and get packed. I'm heading to Fred's about ten."

"Have a good time."

"You, too."

She looked at him quizzically.

"I mean tonight. I mean, you know, have a nice day," he ended lamely.

He fled back into the house, tossing the paper on the table. A plate of steaming toast was waiting. He grabbed a knife and slathered the warm bread with butter and then sprinkled garlic salt on it. Crunching into it, he savored the sour tang, smiling. His mother sat down and began to butter her bread.

"So, Matty, what are your plans for the day?"

"I'm going to pick up the dog doos, mow the lawn. Then I got to take care of the fish next door. Then throw a few things together. Do we have a small suitcase?"

"Why do you need a suitcase?"

"I'm heading to Fred's about ten. He invited me to Santa Cruz this weekend."

"What!"

Matt looked at his mom and swallowed the last of his toast. "Yeah, Fred asked me last week, when I was digging the rocks out of the creek for you and Mrs. Morgan."

Mom got up and headed to the sink with her empty plate. She slammed it on the counter. Matt got up with his plate and glass. "And you didn't think to ask me?"

"No, I—"

"I have things I need you to do."

"What? I already told Fred I'm coming."

"There are eight boxes of mosaic tile in my car." She turned from the sink, facing Matt. "They're heavy and I can't get them out. I want you to get them out and start cutting them into diagonals."

"Diagonals?"

"I need triangles. I am making an orange sunburst and need triangles."

"Can't I do it Monday?"

"No."

"But—"

"I said no!"

"That's not right. I told them I was coming and they are expecting me."

"Are you arguing with me? I said no."

"Mom, look I could—"

Her hand whipped out and grabbed a spatula, swung and connected.

"Ouch! Stop that!"

Her hair flying, she swung again and again. The metal edge of the spatula slashed his arms and side, stitching livid red welts as he yelled in protest.

"When." Swing. "I." Swing "Say something." Swing, swing. "I expect." Swing. "You to." Swing. "Do it."

"Stop it!" Matt cried. "Stop hitting me."

"What the hell is going on?" Douglas thundered.

Yolanda stopped swinging, panting. Matt nursed his battered arm and side.

"What is going on?"

"Mom is beating me because I told her I was going to Santa Cruz."

Douglas turned to his wife. "I have plans for him," she yelled. "I have tiles that need cutting."

"Damn, that spatula really hurt," Matt said, rubbing his arm.

The spatula slashed out, slamming into his shoulder.

Douglas grabbed her arm. "Stop, now." He paused, "I told him he could go." He stared hard at his wife. "Put it down, dear."

Reluctantly, she put the spatula on the counter. "You should have told me."

"You're right, dear. I should have told you. But he is going to Santa Cruz with his buddy."

Mom turned and stomped out of the room.

Douglas turned to his son. "You all right?"

"That stinking thing really hurt."

"She nailed you good." Douglas examined Matt's arm and side.

The doorbell rang. Douglas answered it.

"Hi, Uncle Doug. How are you?"

"Joe, fine. And you?"

"Great, Unc. I was passing by and thought I'd see how Matt was."

"He's fine. Matt!"

"Hey, Joe." Matt walked to the door.

"You got a minute?" Joe asked.

"I guess so." Matt looked to his dad, who nodded.

"Come on outside."

"Dad, I'll go over and do Mr. Giannini's fish now, okay?"

"Go ahead. I'll go calm down your mom."

"Good luck with that." Matt closed the door behind him. "Come on, Joe." They walked next door in silence. Matt opened the side door of the garage and they both stepped in. Matt turned on the lights.

"Wow! This guy's got a hell of a lot of fish," Joe said.

"He's got a bunch."

"What are these?" Joe asked, peering in a tank. "Piranhas?"

"No," Matt laughed. "Those are discus. The piranhas are in there." He pointed at a large tank on the next shelf.

"No shit? Real piranhas?" Joe asked. "They don't look so bad."

"Want to put your finger in?" Matt asked, spooning brine shrimp into a tank.

"Ah . . . no."

"So, what's up, Joe?"

Joe turned away from the fish and faced Matt. "I wanted to—What the hell happened to you?"

"Mom flipped out and did a number on me."

"She sprout claws?"

"Metal spatula."

"She must have whaled on you."

"She gets that way sometimes."

"What did you do to deserve this?"

"I'm going to Santa Cruz."

"Wow, heinous."

"So, why are you here?"

"Ah, yeah." Joe looked uncomfortable. "I was with Aggie last night and . . . nothing happened."

"So?"

"Nothing happened, man. I was expecting to score again, you know, and . . . nothing. Apparently you talked to Aggie."

"Yeah, we talked about my girlfriend and stuff."

"Not the skinny—"

"No. I got a real girlfriend."

"Cool, Matt. You—ah?"

"No!"

"So what did you say to Aggie? She was talking about a bunch of junk I didn't get."

"I don't know. I had a lot of questions about sex and stuff."

"Why didn't you ask me?"

"You weren't there."

"Point."

"She met Stacey and we just talked."

"Well, I don't know what you said to her, but she gave me a bunch of bullshit about it's her body and she didn't want to give it to me."

"It *is* her body."

"And?"

"And I told her if she gave a piece of herself to everyone, what's left for her?"

"Whatever you said, she's not—look, I need you to talk to her."

"Why? Aren't you the guy with a chick on both arms?"

"She's hot." Joe stared into a tank of fish for a moment. "Look, Matt, I—" He paused and hung his head. "I'm not the stud everyone thinks I am. In fact, most girls don't like me for very long."

"Just long enough to—"

"Usually, just long enough to try to bed them. Usually they leave after I try. And, truth to be told, I don't score that often."

"Maybe you're trying too hard. Maybe girls want something more. You know . . ."

"Whatever, I need you to talk to her again, man. Soon."

"Okay, I'll talk to her, but I don't promise anything."

"Thanks, man." Joe glanced at his watch. "Look, I gotta go." Joe started out the door, then glanced back. "Hey, Matt, with all of those cuts you might want to avoid the ocean."

Puzzled, Matt looked at him.

"You know, the salt water. You're going to burn, man."

"Probably. See you, Joe." Matt dropped some goldfish into the piranha tank. The fish swarmed their meal, leaving only a small cloud of blood.

Chapter Seventeen

Matt took a deep breath and dove to the bottom of the swimming pool. Scouting along the tile floor of the pool he scooped up one of the pennies he had thrown in earlier. Kicking upwards, he raced bubbles to the surface and breached like a whale, blowing a plume of spray from his snorkel. He adjusted his snorkel and spit into his face mask; dipping the mask into the water, he washed off the condensation and pulled it back over his head. He tossed the pennies again and dove. He dolphined through the clear water, scooped up the coins, and blew to the surface again.

"Nice snorkel you have there."

He turned in the water, responding to Emily's voice. She stood on the side of the pool, tanned and lovely in a yellow bikini. Beside her stood Margo, her best friend. Margo was as tall and as attractive as Emily. Chestnut hair flowed down to her shoulders. Her pink polka dot bikini strained to keep her covered. Both girls looked at Matt appraisingly.

"Thanks, it's new."

"What's that thing on the top?" Emily asked.

"It's a cage for a ping pong ball. The ball floats on top of the snorkel tube. Underwater it seals the tube. On the surface, you blow it aside and can breathe."

"There's nothing more that I like than a half-naked man holding a big, red snorkel in his hand," Margo said. Both girls laughed.

Matt snorted, stuck his snorkel in his mouth and dove underwater. Surfacing again, he saw the two girls lying on their stomachs on matching chaise lounges. His eyes followed the line of their tanned legs, stopping a moment at the bright fabric wedged in where their thighs met and lingered even longer over their rounded butt cheeks. He tore his gaze away and tossed his pennies back into the pool. Launching from the side, he glided through the silent water, hovering a moment nearly weightless, then shot down, snatching up the copper coins. Surfacing, he blew great gouts of water from the snorkel.

"Matty." He ignored the singsong cadence of Emily's voice, intent on tightening the strap on his facemask. "Oh, Mat . . . ty. Come hither, Little One."

"Kipling. What do you want?"

"Do you know what it's from?" Margo's husky voice asked.

"Sure. 'The Elephant's Child.' It's what the crocodile says to lure the elephant child down to the river before he grabs the elephant by the trunk."

"I thought it was an alligator," Margo said.

"No way. Alligators only live in America. 'The Elephant's Child' took place in India."

"I told you he was smart," Emily said, turning toward her friend.

"And sorta cute, too," Margo said, squinting into the sun and appraising him. "All wet and dripping."

Emily's hand searched the concrete beside her chaise. Finding a tube of Coppertone, she lifted it up. "Here. I want you to put suntan lotion on my back."

"Ah." Matt stared at the tube of lotion. His eyes shifted from the little girl whose dog was playfully tugging down her bathing suit to the young woman stretched out on the chaise beside him. He emerged from the water and took the tube of sun cream from her.

"I told you he was smart," Emily said, silkily.

Margo watched as he squirted a dab of the white cream onto the palm of his hand. Starting at Emily's shoulders he began to work the cream into her soft flesh. He applied more to her neck and began massaging her shoulders. "That feels good. You have strong hands," Emily purred.

Matt worked his way down the flat of her shoulder blades and encountered her swim suit strap. "Unhook it," Emily said softly.

"But—"

"Unhook it. Surely you've unhooked a girl's bra before."

Matt grasped the thin fabric and pushed the two ends together, twisting. Exposing the underside, he could see where the metal tongue slipped into the groove. The unsnapped strap snapped apart, revealing a narrow inch of pale skin. Matt stared. His eyes followed the untanned path of skin, dwelling on the pale bulging of her breasts against the chaise.

"Hurry up and finish her. I need my back done, too," Margo said.

Matt squirted more lotion onto his palm and returned to Emily's silky smooth back. He rubbed lotion onto her body, palms and fingers working their way down the bumps of her spine. Reaching the swell of her buttocks, he rubbed the remainder of the lotion onto the soft curve of her cheeks.

"How about . . . ah . . . lower?" he asked.

"My legs? No, that's okay. I can get them myself."

"My turn," Margo declared. She sat up, cupping her bikini top to her bosom and reaching behind her, unsnapped the bikini clasp. Then she lay back down, pancaking her breasts beneath her alluringly. "Same routine, snorkel man."

Matt slathered more lotion on her back and began working up her spine and down her ribcage, each pass getting closer and closer to the sides of her tits. Reluctantly, he pulled his hands away and kneaded his way down her spine, approaching the hem of her swim suit bottom. Margo shifted a bit, her legs spreading.

"You can do my legs, Matt." Matt's hand trembled as he reached for the Coppertone.

"Hey, Matt!" Matt jumped. "Mom's back from the store. How about helping unload the car?"

"Sure, Fred." Matt slowly drew away from Margo. He screwed the lid back onto the suntan lotion and dropped it between the two girls, adjusted his cutoffs and headed over to Fred.

"Matt."

He stopped at the sound of Margo's voice. "Thanks, snorkel man. Maybe we'll have a chance for you to finish the job later."

Matt smiled crookedly and joined Fred. "She's stacked, isn't she?" Fred said.

"Who?"

"Margo, of course," Fred said. "My brother had a real thing for her. Said she was built like a brick outhouse. I'm not sure what that means, but I think it means he liked her. Maybe when he gets back they can get together."

"Maybe," Matt agreed. "Your sister's built pretty good, too."

"I know. She's always walking around the house half naked. Drives my mother crazy."

"I can see that," Matt said, still staring at the two girls.

"Fred? A little help." Fred's mother's voice drifted from the garage.

"Good thing Dad didn't see you rubbing up his favorite daughter."

"I thought he went shopping with your mom."

"Nah. He always takes a little nap after he gets here."

"My God. I thought he was gone."

"Fred?"

"Coming, Mom," Together the two boys walked out to the driveway. Fred's mom was holding a box full of canned goods. "Here. One of you boys take this."

Matt stepped up and took the heavy box from her. She straightened up and let out a sigh. "That was heavier than I thought."

"You got a lot of food for one weekend," Matt said.

"That's not all for this weekend. We're only here for one night." She brushed a strand of hair out of her eyes. "We're coming back in two weeks for spring break. I wanted to get my shopping done before all the tourists descend on town."

Fred grabbed a bag of groceries and headed for the door. Matt shifted the box up onto his shoulder, stepped into the cool kitchen and placed the box on the counter. He pulled out a can and examined it.

"Garbanzo beans? I thought only Italians ate garbanzo beans."

Fred looked up, grimacing. "Mom likes to put them in salads. I hate them."

"I only eat them when I'm at my grandmother's. She puts them in salad, too. She says I should eat them because they put hair on your chest. I've never understood why grandmothers are so interested in having hair on their grandson's chests."

"My sister eats them."

"There's certainly no hair on her chest."

"Fred!" his mom called from outside. "A couple more bags."

Both boys trouped out. Fred's mom handed him another sack and lifted a small one for herself. Fred headed for the kitchen. "Let me get that." Matt reached out, taking the small bag and shutting the car door.

"Thanks, Matt." She smiled at him.

"Mrs. Tipton, I have a question. Fred is always talking about his brother. Always saying when his brother gets back they're going to do this thing or that. I was wondering – when is his brother coming back?"

Fred's mom didn't answer. Her eyes fixed on the crack in the driveway at her feet.

"I mean, he's been in the Army for a—"

"He's not. He's not coming back."

"Did he reenlist?"

"No." She looked at Matt intently. "You remind me of him: young, smart, intense. You truly don't know, do you?"

"Know what?"

"He died in action over a year ago. He flew helicopter rescue. He'd picked up a few wounded from some godforsaken hill in that damn country and was evacuating them to a hospital when his helicopter was hit." She paused for a second. "No one survived."

"I'm—"

"Sorry?" She looked at Matt and forced a smile. "I know you are. I just heard it all a long time ago."

"I didn't mean to bring it up, to hurt you."

"I know. You're kind, Matt. A lot like he was."

"Doesn't Fred know?"

"Of course he knows. He was with us at San Francisco Military Cemetery when they buried Dean with full military honors." She paused and looked to the tree tops. "It is such a beautiful spot. You can see the Golden Gate Bridge from his grave. Beautiful . . . until you look around and see row after row, mile after mile, of identical white markers in every direction, each one of them with a name and a grieving family and each one representing such promise, such hope.

They're like marble exclamation points ending too short a life." She sighed deeply.

"So why—?"

"So why does my son think his brother is coming back?" She straightened and looked at Matt. "We all cope in different ways. His dad hasn't said a word about it. I cried myself dry for weeks. Emily discovered boys and had slipped from one to another looking for . . . something. Fred knows. It's just easier for him to pretend that his brother is coming back. You've been a big help to him, Matt."

"How?"

"Just being a friend. He doesn't talk about Dean as much when he's with you." She composed herself quickly. "He's coming."

"Matt, want to head down to the beach?" Fred asked.

"You are not going to the beach barefoot, young man," his mother said firmly

"Oh, Mom."

"No arguing. It's over a mile to the beach and there is broken glass everywhere. Besides, you haven't gone barefoot since last summer. Your feet haven't toughened up."

"Mom!"

"Get your thongs." She turned to Matt, "You, too, Matthew."

"Are they in the bedroom?" Fred asked.

"Yeah. They're in the bag of stuff I brought."

"I'll get them for you," Fred said as he dashed off.

"Matt, if you could just continue to be a good friend to him. That's what he needs more than anything else. Just be his friend."

"I can do that."

"Thank you, Matt." She headed for the kitchen door. "And Matt." She turned, eyes shining. "Try to stay out of this damn war."

Chapter Eighteen

The boys skipped down the concrete steps and jumped into the warm sand of the Santa Cruz beach. Matt took off his thongs and slipped one sandal in each of the back pockets of his cut offs.

"Why don't you just wear them?" Fred asked.

"I can't stand the gritty feel of the sand against the rubber. On sand, I'd rather be barefoot." They walked toward the shoreline. Wave after wave roared in, flung itself on the unyielding sand and hissed away. The cold water licked at their feet and ankles while depositing an ever-changing treasure trove of broken shells and rounded rocks about them. Gulls screamed overhead and sails danced on the horizon.

Fred bent over, picking up half of a sand dollar. "My mom loves these. Hope I can find her a whole one."

"I found one that still had the spines on it. It was cool."

"Mom makes them into things."

"Your mom is awesome. My mom—"

"I know. Your mother has fits at the drop of a hat."

"Fits?" Matt mused. "That's a nice word for it. My dad calls them conniption fits. The sisters just try to ignore them."

"Want to head up to the wharf?"

Matt nodded. The boys walked in silence, watching the water foam in and out, stopping occasionally to pick up a shell or piece of polished glass. "Ever hunt for sand dabs, Fred?"

"Never even heard of them. They're not like snipes, are they?"

"No," Matt laughed. "They are real. They're kind of a little crabby thing that rolls itself up in a ball like a sow bug."

"You sure they're not related to snipes?"

"Positive. Look." Matt pointed to the receding surf. "See those bubbles? Next time a wave starts to wash out, spot a bubble and dig. Dig real fast." They waited as another wave crashed ashore, surged landward, lost energy and was sucked oceanward again. Bubbles popped up under the retreating water. They fell to their knees and began scooping out wet gouts of sand.

"There," Matt yelled. His hand shot down into the water-filled hole and pulled out a sand dab. About two inches long, it began to curl on Matt's palm. Matt nudged it over onto its back. Multiple sets of legs and pincers waved futilely.

"What do you do with them?"

"I've heard some people eat them."

"Ugh. That's just gross."

"Once, my dad took me to Point Reyes to explore tide pools. A bunch of Mexicans were pulling sea urchins off of rocks, cracking them open and sucking them down."

"People will eat anything, I guess." Fred peered closely at the sand dab. "Is it a beetle?"

"No," Matt answered. "It's a crustacean – like a crab or lobster."

"Well, you may be into that stuff, but I'm into mammals. Like those mammals there."

Matt looked up and immediately dropped the sand dab onto the wet sand where its jointed legs flashed quickly and it burrowed out of sight. Matt stared in the direction Fred was looking. Three girls in bikinis were jogging toward them. Slim and trim, their breasts danced invitingly, threatening to escape the confines of their tops.

"I love the beach," moaned Fred.

The girls ran toward them, laughing and talking. Matt and Fred stared as they pounded by. One of the girls glanced at the boys and smiled, then turned back and laughed. They flashed past and headed down the beach. The two boys stared, as intrigued with the girls' goings as with their comings.

Fred sighed heavily. "Come on, Matt, let's head to the wharf."

The Santa Cruz wharf stretched nearly a half mile from the beach into the ocean. Matt slipped his thongs on when he reached the top and looked questioningly at Fred.

"This way," Fred responded.

They headed toward the ocean. Exhausted mothers with baby buggies and tired old men with fishing poles competed with sea gulls and the occasional pelican at the rails. The gulls screamed at each other.

"My family and I used to come down here all the time," Fred said. "Dad would try fishing and sometimes Mom would take us to look at the Cement Boat in Aptos. The boat used to be bigger. I think a piece broke off last year during a big storm." The ocean breeze brought them the scent of sea salt and dark deep places.

They reached the end of the pier where a rusted chain link fence festooned with dried kelp labored to support a cracked and peeling No Trespassing sign.

Matt watched as two gleaming black sea lions flung themselves from the surf onto the stained gray deck of the wharf. Others sprawled across the crossbeams of the wharf, barking at each other or waving a fin like overheated mandarins. "The seals seem to like it here," Matt observed. One scarred old bull reared himself up and surveyed the deck solemnly, his long mustached drooping.

"Let's go," Fred said, turning from the abandoned pier toward the sounds of laughter and screams from the roller coaster riders. The sound of the waves pounding against the wharf surrendered to the lilting melodies of the Looff Carousel. A bevy of bathing beauties walked by giggling and children shouted and laughed everywhere.

"I love the Boardwalk," Fred said with a big smile as he watched the laughing girls. "I love the girls, the swim suits, the cotton candy, the girls, the hot dogs and, oh, did I mention the girls?" A juggler rode by on a unicycle, pausing and balancing, tossing and grabbing bowling pins. Catching them all, he doffed his hat and rode off.

"Boycott grapes! Don't eat grapes or drink wine," a group of voices chanted.

"What's that?" Matt asked.

"Oh, it's spring break at the colleges and all of the causes show up on the boardwalk to recruit members or whatever. It's a bummer because it makes the boardwalk real crowded."

Matt walked over to the La Causa booth and picked up a brochure. He asked, "Why shouldn't we buy grapes?"

A burly man wearing a bandana turned to him. "The wine barons like Earnest and Julio Gallo are exploiting the migrant farm workers. The Mexicans provide the sweat and labor and the wine makers and stores like Giants and Safeway make all the profits. It is unfair and we want people to stop buying grapes and wine until we bring those capitalist pigs to their knees. Viva Cesar Chavez!" the man shouted. Matt backed off. "Are you with us, brother? Because if you aren't with us, you are against us!"

"Yeah, I guess so. I don't like grapes anyway."

"Right on. Here," he handed Matt a button with a purple "boycott grapes" symbol against a yellow background. "Wear this, man. Show your solidarity with the workers."

The boys wandered on. "Gee, Matt," Fred said, "your grandmother would disown you if she knew you were boycotting grapes and wine."

"I'm not going to boycott anything. I'm Italian. I can't boycott wine," Matt said as they walked away from the La Causa booth. "It's a cool button though." He pinned it on his t-shirt.

Chants of "Hell, No, We Won't Go" and "Bring Our Boys Home" competed with one another outside the entrance of the Big Dipper.

"Want to ride it?" Fred asked.

"Sure, but let me get a button." Matt dashed away for a few minutes and came back with two more buttons.

"You sure you want to ride the roller coaster?" Fred asked nervously, after the roar of the cars and the screams of the passengers crashed down upon them. "There is a ride here I like much better than the roller coaster. The Wild Mouse. Have you ever been on it?"

"I love the Wild Mouse!"

"Let's go."

They pelted down the boardwalk past booths for other causes. Matt collected buttons from each and shoved them into his pockets.

"You're not going to vote for some of that stuff, are you?"

"I'm not old enough to vote, Fred. Neither are you." Matt skirted the Woman's Rights group, snagging their button and headed to the Legalize Marijuana booth, grabbing another. "How far is the Wild Mouse?"

"It's down past the Tilt-a-Whirl," Fred replied. As Matt put the new buttons on this t-shirt, Fred darted away. "I'll be right back."

Matt wandered over to a booth proclaiming that we should ban pesticides. He glanced at grainy pictures of dead pelicans and walked away after discovering no buttons.

"Do you know Jesus?" a pretty girl with light brown hair asked him.

"I'm Catholic."

"But do you know Jesus?" She hooked her arm in his and began walking. Matt stared. The girl's low-cut linen blouse was very thin, failing to hide her braless breasts.

"I've read the Bible."

"So you know He ordered us to love our fellow man?"

"Yes."

"Want to be my fellow man?"

"Okay," Matt said, mystified. "Why?"

"I have a friend named David and he said we should believe that sex is the best way to know Jesus and to love our fellow man." Matt's eyes widened as she continued. "We just got to California and are camping a mile or two from here. If you'd like to visit us, we could be together. Or, if you like, we have men, too." She smiled.

"Men, too?"

"Yeah, that is, if you like guys." She looked at him and smiled. "I hope you don't like guys." She rubbed her torso against his arm.

"I'm a Catholic."

"We've established that. But the Catholic Church has lied to you. They know that sex is the truest way to show God's love and they have spent centuries controlling sex. Beating down the natural urges between people to enjoy their bodies and to fully embrace the love God has in mind for us." She let go of his arm and stretched, straining the buttons of her linen shirt. "You're afraid. I understand that, I was afraid, too. But once I woke up to the beautiful love Moses David offers his children—"

"Your religion lets you have sex?"

"Let's us?" Her laugh peeled. "It *encourages* us to have sex. All the time. With anyone that Moses David tells us to have sex with. It's all in the name of Jesus and is his way of bringing people into the family of Christ."

"So if I go with you, we could have sex? Now? Today?"

"Yes!" She grabbed his arm and pulled. "Come on, the van is waiting."

Fred returned with a pink cloud of cotton candy. "Come on, Matt, the Wild Mouse is this way."

"She wants to have sex with me. Now."

"It's a bunch of kooks, Matt," Fred reasoned. "They lure people in with the promise of sex and then they make them into sex slaves to lure in others."

"We are not sex slaves! We share the love of Jesus," the girl said.

"She's just fishing. I've seen her here a lot. She takes on anybody. You're just a number in a quota for her."

"You are obviously not ready for the enlightenment of Moses David and our theology," she sniffed.

"I want to be enlightened. I really do."

"Matt! Really?"

The girl whirled away from Matt and stepped up to an elderly man. "Do you know Jesus?"

Matt and Fred watched her hook her arm through his as the couple walked away.

Matt sighed.

"Come on, Matt. The Wild Mouse is this way." Fred began walking and Matt followed after a last glance at the girl, who now had her arms around yet another man.

"Want some cotton candy?"

"Sure." Matt ripped off a hank of the pink fluff and stuffed it into his mouth.

They wandered past more booths as they got closer to the Wild Mouse. Fred picked up a couple more buttons and gave them to Matt. Matt stopped at the Save the Whales display and talked with a bearded man there. That group's button was added to his t-shirt's collection.

"There it is," Fred said reverently. Both boys stood before the ride and looked up at it in awe.

"Best ride on the boardwalk," Matt said.

"The most awesome ride in the world," Fred replied.

"I love the way it feels like it is ready to leap off the tracks before it jerks you back and shoots you down a drop."

"Yeah," Fred said in a hushed tone. "This is my brother's favorite ride. We would go on it over and over again until we were so sick we puked. Maybe when he gets back, we'll ride it again."

Matt looked at his friend's profile as Fred gazed at the ride, lost in memory. "Fred, why don't you ride it with him now?"

Fred turned to Matt with a puzzled look on his face. "I can't, Matt. He's not here."

"If you remember him, he's with you here. You know he's not coming back, don't you?"

Fred hesitated, eyes on the ride. "Yes, I know," he answered quietly.

"Then why—"

"Why pretend he's coming back? Why pretend? Fear. I've been afraid for a long, long time. Afraid when he enlisted. Afraid when he left. Afraid the whole two years he was in 'Nam."

A car of the Wild Mouse clattered to an end. The operator lifted the safety bar and two smiling kids ran off. Two other kids, one carrying a red balloon, replaced them.

Fred looked away. "Afraid at the funeral. And, I guess, most of all, afraid he'd never come back."

Fred watched the car clatter up the first rise, the red balloon trailing jauntily. At the top the Wild Mouse's front end lurched over the edge and the riders screamed as the car jerked them sideways, then plunged down the first fall. The balloon drifted skyward.

"And now he is never coming back, is he?" Fred asked.

"No, Fred. He's not," Matt said. Fred's eyes glazed. Another ride car rattled to a stop and laughing kids jumped off and swirled by. The empty car stood there. No one was in line.

"We'll never ride this together again."

"Ride it now, Fred. You and your brother. See him in your mind and ride with him now. Enjoy it with him now."

"Will you come with me?"

"The car only holds two. The ride is for the two of you. Once you've made this ride, we'll ride it over and over until we both puke."

Fred hesitated. "I guess I can ride it alone. Can't I?"

"You won't be alone."

Fred ran up the ramp to the empty car, hesitated, then slid across the leather seat leaving room for a second rider. The ride operator looked at Matt, who just shrugged. Slapping down the safety bar, he pressed a button and the car began chugging its way up the first rise. Fred turned to Matt and waved. Matt waved back, then turned away and headed for the nearest booth. The Save Capitola's Estuary League had no buttons. Disappointed, Matt turned, spotting someone he knew.

"Robert!"

Robert stood, shirtless, behind a table laden with brochures and papers. He was talking to the young man standing next to him.

"Robert," Matt yelled again, waving. Deep in conversation, Robert didn't hear Matt's call. Matt headed over. "Hey, Robert."

As Robert began to turn, a tall, thin young man stepped up behind Robert, put his hands around Robert and pulled him close. The young man's hands traveled up Robert's chest, ruffling through the blonde hair covering his sternum. Surprised, Robert laughed and turned as the thin man leaned over and kissed him – a long open-mouth kiss.

Matt skidded to a stop, wide-eyed.

Robert stepped away from the arms holding him. Turning to the young man, they embraced. Robert pulled him closer, chest to chest, and kissed him back. Breaking away from the kiss, Robert turned, seeing Matt.

"Hi, Robert," Matt blurted out.

"Matt," Robert said, shrugging off the thin man's attempt for another embrace. His paramour looked at Matt, huffed and walked off. Robert regarded Matt. "What are you doing here?"

"Me? I'm … ah … the Wild Mouse." Matt jerked his head toward the ride.

"No. I mean here." Robert indicated the booth.

"I saw you and came over for buttons." He indicated his shirt.

"I don't think you're going to want one of these, Matt," Robert said, holding up a white button with two pink male symbols interlocking side by side.

"Why not? I—"

"Hey, faggot!" a passerby yelled, "get off the beach!"

"Faggot?"

"Matt, this is a homosexual booth. We're distributing information on gay gatherings coming up in San Francisco."

"Dear Robert." A bearded older man in a too-tight Hawaiian shirt sidled up, putting his arm around Robert's shoulder. Gazing at Matt he purred, "Who's the chicken, Robert?"

"Nobody you'd be interested in, Vince."

"Oh, I think I'd be *very* interested, Robert."

"So, you're a homosexual?" Matt asked Robert, ignoring Vince.

"Yes, Matt."

"Oh, he's cherry," the bearded man said, circling around Matt. "A fresh chicken, and cute, too. I think I could be very interested."

"Back off, Vince. He's not available."

"Keeping him for yourself, Robert? Really? That's not fair, not fair at all." Vince put both hands on his hips. "Besides, Robert, I thought you were more interested in older queens."

"I don't get it," Matt said.

"Me, I like them young." Vince's hand trailed lightly across Matt's shoulders. Matt froze as Robert stepped out from behind the table. Vince leaned in close to Matt and whispered, "Would you like to come with me? I'll be gentle."

"I said back off. He's not on the market," Robert said.

"Very well, Robert. No need to act like a brute." Vince sniffed. "Keep him for yourself. There are other pretty boys on this beach."

"Just leave, Vince."

"Oh, I will." Vince turned and took a step. Stopping, he turned half back. "Just wondering, Robert, are you grooming him to be a top, or a bottom? He looks like a delicious bottom to me."

Robert stepped forward, fist clenched. "All right. All right. Be gentle with him, Robert." Vince sashayed away.

"I'm sorry about that, Matt."

"Who is he?" Matt asked, looking at Robert. "You were going to hit him."

"He's a chicken hawk. You're a chicken. He likes young boys— chickens. He cruises the boardwalk, to take them home for— Well, you don't want to know."

"Robert?"

"You shouldn't be here, Matt. It could make some people think that you're something you're not." Robert smiled at him. "Are you?"

"The ride is over. I need to find Fred."

"Matt, I'm sorry."

"Gotta go." Matt hurried off, and Robert watched him go. He shook his head and returned to the booth.

Matt raced to the exit of the Wild Mouse. Fred formed an island of silence about which noisy kids bumped and ran. "You have a good ride?" Matt asked.

Fred looked up at Matt. "I did. I really did."

"Want to ride again? Ride until we puke?"

"No. If you don't mind, I'd like to go somewhere else." Fred thought for a moment, "You up for the Fun House?"

"Cool."

"They got this big rotating barrel like twelve feet wide and you get a prize if you can run through it without falling."

"I know it. Let's go!"

They backtracked toward the other end of the boardwalk, passing Robert's table. Matt looked straight ahead.

"Matt, this table has some buttons." Fred pointed to a paper banner declaring Bobby Kennedy for President.

"I didn't think he was running."

A girl at the table looked up at Matt, her sunburned face radiating an earnest smile. "He hasn't declared yet, but he has been in California meeting with Cesar Chavez. Chavez thinks he's going to run."

"Maybe if he declares." Matt turned to walk off.

"Matt, want a button?" Fred called.

"No." Matt walked up to a litter barrel and began stripping off the buttons he had collected. "I don't think I want any of these things anymore."

He headed to the Fun House, leaving a confused Fred in his wake.

Chapter Nineteen

Matt jumped out of the station wagon. Grabbing his bag, he thanked Fred's parents and said his goodbyes. Emily threw him a kiss, and laughed as the car backed out of the driveway and took off in a cloud of blue-gray exhaust. He tossed the bag over the gate to the courtyard, trotted over to Mr. Giannini's house, pushed through the gate and entered the garage through the side door. He flicked on the lights and surveyed the fish tanks. Everything seemed in order.

Grabbing the can of fish food he dropped a pinch of flakes into an aquarium full of neon tetras. Rainbow-colored streaks of silver slapped against the surface as the fish fed.

"Hi, guys," Matt said to the side of the tank. The fish ignored him in their frenzy. "Hope you didn't get too hungry."

He moved to a tank where silver dollars swam lazily through forests of kelly-green milfoil. "Miss me?" Matt dropped in a little fish food and watched the somber fish slowly rise to the surface.

"I missed you."

Startled, Matt turned to the doorway. "Robert. I didn't know you were home."

"Just got here. Mr. G. was going to stay another night, but I have classes tomorrow."

Turning away from Robert, Matt tossed in a dab more food.

"You walked off without much of a goodbye, Matt."

"I . . . ah . . . I had to go find Fred." He tossed in a little more food. The fish retreated to their aquatic forest, waiting for the manna to end.

"Really?"

"Yeah. Look, I guess I should thank you."

"Thank me?"

"Yes." Automatically, Matt shoveled in more food. "You saved me, or would have, from that Vince guy."

"Vincent."

"The chicken man."

"Hawk." Robert smiled. "Vincent gives all of us a bad name."

"All of you—homosexuals?"

"All us queers," Robert agreed, stepping forward.

"I guess I don't understand, Robert." Matt took a step back.

"And there's something I don't understand, Matt."

"What?" Matt asked uncertainly.

"How much food are you going to give those fish?" The top of the tank was covered with fish food.

"Oh, crap." He slammed down the can and screwed the lid on. "Hand me that net. There by the angel fish."

"Which ones?"

Matt pointed. "The black and white striped ones over there. Thanks. There's another net by the goldfish. The ones that—"

"I know what goldfish are, Matt."

Matt scooped a net full of soggy confetti-like fish food. He handed the dripping net to Robert and grabbed the empty net Robert extended toward him. "Drop about a third of that in with the blind cave fish. No, the pink ones with no eyes."

"That figures."

"And another third in the tank above them and the rest in the swordtail tank. Here, switch." They traded nets and Matt scooped more flakes out of the tank. "That goes in with the, ah, see-through fish."

"See-through? Oh, I see them."

Matt stood looking at the silver dollar tank. Cautiously, the fish peeked out, and began to rise. They paused. Fins spinning, they turned slowly, continuing to rise.

"Your net's dripping."

"This I'll just have to throw away." Matt dumped the soggy mass into an open garbage can. "Thanks, again."

He walked over to Robert and took the net, putting both of them away. "Does Mr. Giannini know you are . . . you're—"

"Matt." Robert smirked, hands on hips.

Matt paused and looked at Robert. "Your uncle knows?" Matt closed his eyes and shook his head. "Let me guess, your uncle isn't your uncle, he's your—"

"Yes."

"Was he like Vince?"

"No."

"Why—I mean, how—"

"Honestly, Matt, that's none of your business. And I mean that in the best way possible. I don't pry into your sex life."

"I don't *have* a sex life. I barely have any life at all."

"That's why Vince zeroed in on you. He has a knack for knowing guys with no self-esteem, and virgins."

"Great, now complete strangers can tell I'm a virgin," Matt exclaimed. "Do I wear a scarlet letter on my forehead? Here goes a virgin, everybody! Look, the last virgin in the entire state of California!"

Robert laughed. "Matt, you walk around with your head down, never looking anyone in the eye. You're shy, smart and never take credit for anything you do. Really. You telegraph that you're insecure for miles and men like Vincent pick up on it. Hell, he thrives on it."

"Wow." Matt tapped the side of the tank with the piranhas. "Does Giannini know that I saw you?"

"I told him. And he's worried. He's concerned that things will change and that if you tell anyone, it could make things very uncomfortable."

"Who would I tell? My mother? No way."

Reaching into his pants pocket, Robert took out a pile of bills.

"We didn't talk about pay," Matt protested.

"Mr. G. insisted." Robert pulled out a five.

"That's too much. Look, this only takes about twenty minutes over four days."

"How much do you want?"

"I don't want anything. You don't charge friends. I mean, Mr. Giannini saved my science project when Mom threw it out. He's had me over to see the films he shot in Africa—the ones with the Kalahari bushmen hunting giraffes. Both of you helped me haul those damn rocks Mom thinks she needs for landscaping. You don't charge friends for something like this."

"Gay friends?"

"I—I guess so."

"Hug?"

"No," Matt replied quickly. "Nothing to do with you, but in my family, hugs are generally an omen of bad things to come. Like the kiss of death in those old Mafia movies."

"Matt! Where are you?" His mother's voice cut through the garage walls.

"Damn, that woman's voice carries."

"You better go."

"I was just about done anyway."

Running, he swept up the bag of clothes and burst into the house. His mother waited, arms crossed in the entrance hall, her one high heel tapping on the cold marble.

"Where have you been?"

"I told Mr. Giannini I'd feed his fish as soon as I got home."

"And I told you that your aunt is taking us out to dinner tonight. To Vahl's."

"What's the occasion? We never go to Vahl's unless it's something special."

The tapping stopped. "She'll be here in fifteen minutes and you know she is never late. Do you need a shower?" She stepped closer and sniffed. She pointed.

"There isn't time!"

"And use the dandruff shampoo."

❄ ❄ ❄

The shiny black Cadillac Brougham crunched silently to a stop in the gravel parking lot. Matt stepped out, holding the door for his Aunt Rose and grandmother. He slid his hand appreciatively along the long front fender of the car.

"Great car, Aunt Vicki. Change the front a little and it would look just like the Green Hornet's Black Beauty."

"Come on," Rose said. "I eat at five."

Vicki started to say something, clamped her mouth shut and marched to the restaurant's door. Everyone followed silently.

The hostess greeted them by name at the door and ushered them past the huge bar with its backdrop of dusty Jim Beam collector bottles into the main dining room, which was dimly lit by flickering candles. Sitting at a white-topped table was Aggie and her mother. "Matt!" Aggie jumped up and hugged her cousin, then Aunt Vicki.

"Hi, Aggie. What's up?"

"I don't know, but to tell you the truth, I don't feel good about this."

Waiting until his aunts and grandmother sat down, Matt took the remaining empty chair, on the end opposite Aunt Victoria. A waitress came with plates covered with thin slices of beef tongue marinated in sauces and shiny, plump green olives. Wine followed. Matt's grandmother raised her glass of port.

"*Salute!*" Crystal clinked musically all around the table. Matt sipped the dark red wine carefully, making a face.

"Matteo, drink up. It will put hair on your chest." Matt slugged down a large gulp, shuddering as he drank. His mother smiled.

"I'll order for everyone."

"But Victoria, you know I like the fillet of sole," Aggie's mother sputtered.

Vicki looked up at the waitress. "We'll have the lasagna, lamb chops with mint jelly and filet of sole." Vicki shot a glance at her sister. "Serve it family style. Baked potatoes and both the baked carrots and broccoli. Vin Rose with the dinner and we want spumoni for dessert."

"I hate spumoni," Aggie whispered, leaning over to Matt.

"I'll eat yours," he replied.

"Very well, then." Vicki shut the menu and handed it to the waitress.

"Can I have a glass of milk?" Matt asked.

"Matteo," his grandmother said, "Italian men don't drink milk. That is only for the bambinos."

Vicki shot the waitress a look. She nodded and left.

"Where's your husband, Yolanda?" Rose said. "I thought he was supposed to meet us here."

"God only knows, Rose. He went to Fresno last night to look after his hotel. He called this morning saying he was held over."

"He spends a lot of time away from home."

"I know, Rose. Let's not talk about it."

"You know, Yolanda, Ann Landers says if you just took the time to cook your husband a good meal and to meet him at the door and make him feel like a king, he'd come home every night," Aggie's mom said while popping an olive into her mouth. Oblivious to the stare she was getting, she gnawed the flesh off of the pit and pushed it out into a waiting napkin.

"So the divorcee and the old maid are giving me marital advice?"

"Hush up your mouth, Yolla."

"Momma, I—"

"Enough, Yolanda," interrupted Vicki. "Douglas isn't here and that's just fine. It will be just us girls and Matthew."

Dinner arrived. Steaming plates of pasta and meat, savory garlic bread and bowls of antipasto were heaped on the table. Victoria hoisted a tall glass of wine and proposed a toast. Everyone followed suit, clinking glasses, gulping down mouthfuls of wine. Matt toasted with his glass of milk, earning frowns from his grandmother and Aunt Victoria.

"Oh? Okay, Cuz—" Aggie reached for another bottle of burgundy and leaned toward Matt's empty wineglass, "Want me to refill that for you?"

"No thanks." Matt pulled his glass away. "One is enough."

"Not for an Italian man, Matteo," Grandma said. "But one is enough for now."

The meal was eaten in relative silence thereafter. As Matt pushed his plate away his mother exclaimed, "Matty, I can't eat all of this. Here, you finish it."

"Mom, I'm full."

"I can't let this food go to waste."

"Then get a doggie bag."

As the plate was passed to Matt, Rose added a piece of meat she couldn't finish onto it. "Mom, you're always telling me I am too fat. Why are you pushing food on me?"

"Just eat it, Matty."

"*Mangia,*" Grandma added.

"I'll tell the waitress to hold dessert until Matt is finished with his food," Victoria intoned.

"It's not my—" Matt looked up from the plate to see all eyes on him. Reluctantly, he picked up his knife and fork. "All right. I'll eat it. But no more fat comments."

No one said a word as he finished his mother's leftovers.

"Everyone got room for dessert?" Victoria asked, not waiting for answers. She nodded at the waitress, who scurried away to the kitchen. She returned, carrying a tray filled with iced metal dessert cups of spumoni. Victoria picked up her spoon, nodded, and everyone dug in. Matt's spoon scraped the sides of the metal dessert bowl, seeking every possible vestige of the green ice cream.

"Matt. Here, have mine. I really don't need anymore."

"No, Rose. He doesn't need more ice cream. He's heavy enough as it is. Did you see how much he ate?"

Rose looked from Matt to his mother, then scooted the bowl to Matt. "If he can eat your leftovers, he can eat mine."

"Thanks." Matt snatched the bowl from his aunt and plunged in.

"Now," Victoria said, "we should chat." Victoria focused her attention to Matt. "Matthew, Silvio and I were a little confused about what you want to do with your life."

"I want to travel the world and study endangered wildlife and find ways to protected species that will disappear if we don't do something. Did you know that the whooping crane is almost extinct? Experts believe that there are fewer than fifty in the world."

"Is there any money in saving whopping cranes?"

"Whooping cranes," Matt corrected.

"Whatever, Matthew. The point is, is there any money in this little adventure you are so enamored with?"

"I don't know. Dian Fossey's written a book or two. Merlin Perkins has a television show." He looked as his aunt, puzzled. "Does it have to be about money?"

"Silvio and I have given you some money for your schooling—"

"For which I am very grateful—"

"And we don't want to see it thrown away on some child's dream about saving the . . . whatever."

"Whatever? This isn't a child's dream. It's not like I'm saying I want to grow up and be a cowboy like the Lone Ranger."

"How is it different, Matthew?" Victoria asked. "You want to save condors and foxes and cranes in a job that offers no monetary support or security."

Wiping his mouth with a napkin, Matt balled it up and tossed it on the table, leaning back. "And what would you like me to grow up to be, Aunt Victoria?"

"Well, someone with grades like you could easily get into law school. Silvio and I would help. You could be a lawyer."

"A lawyer."

"Or a doctor. Doctors make very good money. One of my friends at the country club is a dentist and he is making a great deal of money fitting kids with braces—"

"A dentist."

"Or a businessman, like your Uncle Silvio. We want you to be happy, Matthew."

"And money makes you happy?"

"It makes life a lot easier. That's why we talked Agnese, here, into pursuing a teacher's certificate."

"Aggie?" Matt turned to her, "You want to be a teacher? I thought you wanted to be a journalist. That is, after you wanted to be a nun."

"Teacher's work very steadily and the pay isn't too bad," Agnese said.

Matt sat back in his chair. "You, Aggie? The bohemian who writes wonderful free spirited poetry and—"

"Poems sell for pennies a line, Matt," Aggie said. "I can be a teacher and write poetry on the side. Silvio says you have to have a vocation before you can afford an avocation."

"And teaching would make you happy?" He didn't wait for an answer, but turned back toward his aunt. "Money makes people happy. Tell me, Aunt Victoria, are you happy?"

"I belong to two great country clubs, have lots of tennis friends, eat well, drive a new car each year—"

"And this makes you happy?"

"I know that not having money makes me unhappy," Victoria said.

"Mom, what would make you happy?"

"A new car, golf clubs—"

"That's just stuff. I've watched you, Mom. It doesn't matter if it's mosaic, or macramé, or flower arranging, you seem happiest when you are creating something. You've made beautiful things, like your mom and her afghans. You've made things that people enjoy looking at. Isn't that when you're happiest?"

"Matty, don't argue with your aunt. You should be willing to listen to whatever she says."

"Yolanda." All heads snapped toward Rita. "Maybe you should just stop talking. I get so tired of hearing you talk." Rita tore off a fragment of bread and used it to sop up the sauce on her plate. She stuffed it in her mouth.

"Rita, how dare you?"

"I dare because I am your older sister. Not the rich one." She nodded toward Victoria. "Or the one who cooks." She looked at Rose. "But I am your older sister. And Matty, sorry, Matt is right. And this isn't just about your son; it is about my daughter's future, too."

"Way to go, Mom."

"Thank you, Aggie dear, but for now, hush. This is my moment." She regarded her sisters "Matthew is correct. Yolanda, the happiest I have ever seen you is when you are creating something. Like those flower arrangements you used to make. You were never happier. And the banks and dentist offices you made them for loved them." She pulled off another piece of bread and dabbed at left-over vinegar. "Rose, you are happiest in the kitchen, cooking up amazing food. And happier even more watching everyone eat the food you make.'

"We are talking about my son!"

"Oh, Yolanda, he's the son you use as a prop. She waved a hand dismissively. "Vicki. I've seen you at tennis tournaments with the royalty of tennis—Arthur Ashe, Rod Laver and hobnobbing with celebrities like that *Wild, Wild West* guy."

"You mean Robert Conrad, Aunt Rita. I love that guy."

"No, Matt, the other one. And it's still my moment." She wagged a finger at him and looked at Vicki. "You mix with the best of them, but the happiest I've seen you is curled up on your couch with a big bowl of sherbet watching your soaps and game shows. You should see her Matt. She's a whiz at Password."

"What's your point, Big Sister?" Yolanda asked.

"The point is that none of you are happy. Money hasn't bought you happiness. Marrying a rich man hasn't worked." She inspected her plate for any overlooked sauce. "You all embrace unhappiness like it was a lost lover. It hasn't worked. Why inflict the same thing on the kids? If Aggie wants to be a journalist—who are any of us to decide what will make her happy? Or Matt— if he wants to conserve kangaroos in Australia, let him. We've all had money. I'm all for giving the kids a chance at happiness." She tore the soft center out of a slice of French bread. "That's all." She smiled as she popped the bread into her mouth.

The waitress stepped up to the table.

"And who gets the bill?"

Chapter Twenty

Carefully, Matt twirled the lock, lining up the number on the dial to seven. He jerked. Nothing. Sighing, Matt worked through the combination again. Again nothing. "Come on."

The fourth time was the charm. The lock popped. Matt pulled the door open and tossed in his books. Pulling out a binder and several Pee-Chee folders, he slammed the locker closed.

"You taking the Spanish test today, Matt?"

"Hey, Dave. No, my class takes it tomorrow. But I got Ryan's math test sixth period today."

"Bummer. Study all weekend?"

"Nah, I went to Santa Cruz, remember? Besides, math is easy. I'll look over the chapter again at lunch."

"Sister Tomas says the test Wednesday will be over everything we covered since Christmas."

"I've got really good notes. I'm not too worried."

"Well, when you're a brainiac, it's easy not to worry."

"I'm not a brainiac, Dave."

Straight A's last report card, right?"

"Right." They began walking.

"Brainiac." Dave paused at a drinking fountain and slurped up a drink. Straightening up, Dave wiped his face with his arm. "Too bad about Stacey, huh?"

"Stacey? What—"

"That's right, you were in Santa Cruz. You probably don't know."

"Come on, Dave, spill it."

"There was an accident. She's in the hospital."

"What happened?"

"Her softball team went to the college to work out with their softball team."

"Yeah, she told me."

"Part of the workout was running the stairs at the stadium. She was running down the stairs and slipped. Crashed and burned head-first. Broke her arm, I think. She's at O'Connor Hospital."

Matt hurried back toward his locker.

"What are you doing, Matt?"

"Going to the hospital."

"You're cutting? You are going to be so busted."

"No, I'm not. They took roll in first period. They won't take it again until after lunch. If I'm lucky and get the transfers right, I'll be back by lunch."

Matt spun the dial of the lock and flung open the door. "Here, give this to Sister Rosalie. It's my homework."

"You got bus money?"

"Crap. Not enough." He looked at Dave. "You have hot lunch money?"

"Sure, Matt." Dave dug into his pocket, pulled out change and poured it into Matt's open hands. "Here."

"Thanks, Dave. I owe you." Matt started to close his locker.

"You got my lunch money. What am I supposed to eat?"

Matt reached in a grabbed his bag lunch. "Here." He thrust it at Dave.

Dave opened the bag, pulled out a sandwich, and pried apart the bread. "Avocado!"

"Sorry, Dave," Matt called, as he hurried off.

❁ ❁ ❁

Matt punched through the hospital doors, running to the admittance desk. After thanking the startled nurse, he began counting room numbers. The door to Stacey's room was shut. He took a deep breath and pushed in. He glanced quickly at Mr. Moore, slumped half asleep in the only chair, and turned to Stacey. She looked small. Great bruises racooned her eyes. A metal cage was taped with white tape over her battered nose. Her left arm was encased in plaster. Swollen lips parted in a pained smile as Matt entered the room. He stepped over to the bed.

"Hi."

"Hi, yourself."

"How are—. Sorry, that's a stupid question."

Stacey's smile widened, encompassing her eyes.

"She's doing fine," her dad said.

"Hello, Mr. Moore."

Stacey's father stepped over to his daughter. He and Matt shook hands. "I'm sorry I wasn't here sooner. I was out of town. I just found out half an hour ago."

"Santa Cruz," Stacey whispered, wetting her cracked lips with her tongue. Her father picked up a glass of water with a straw in it, and held it for his daughter. She sipped delicately, then lay back against the pillow.

"Have you eaten anything this morning, Dad?" she asked hoarsely. She coughed a little, clearing her throat.

"No. I haven't yet."

"Since Matt is here, maybe you should get a cup of coffee or something," she said.

Mr. Moore glanced at Matt and then at his daughter. "Sure. That would be a good idea. Take care of her, Matt." He headed for the door. "Do you want anything?"

"No, thank you."

"If the doctor comes, let me know. I'll be in the cafeteria for a bit."

"I'll be here until you come back."

The older man smiled, turned and left.

Stacey struggled to sit up a bit higher, folded her arms gingerly and smiled at Matt. "So, how was your weekend?"

"Less painful than yours. What happened?"

"We were running stairs. Great exercise they say. I slipped or something and wham, I'm tobogganing down the stairs on my face." Her good hand fluttered toward her nose. "I must look like hell."

"You look great to me."

"You'll have to confess that lie."

Matt laughed. "No. All the way here I kept picturing how you would look. Really, you look better than I thought you would."

"Thanks—I guess."

"And?"

"And I don't know. One of my friends said I caught my arm on the seats as I was falling. I guess that explains the broken arm. I've got a sprained ankle, cracked ribs and a broken nose."

"Cuts and bruises."

"Yeah, I split my lip and my face feels like tenderized meat."

"You're beautiful."

"Another lie."

"Okay, beautiful in a bride of Frankenstein sort of way."

"Oh, thanks." She laughed, which turned into coughing.

"Water?" Matt held out the cup to her and she sipped.

"Thanks, Matt."

Matt said, "You got a lot of flowers. I should have brought some."

"No, you shouldn't. They're pretty. But we're not bringing them home with us. Dad will have enough trouble getting me into the car."

"When are you going home?"

"Maybe today. Tomorrow at the latest. There was a lot of swelling. They want that to go down first. Carlotti sent flowers."

"He did?"

"Yeah. The daisies."

"Hmmm."

"He came yesterday. Dad wouldn't leave the entire time he was here."

"Good."

"Good?" Stacey cocked her head at Matt.

"Yeah, good. I don't trust Carlotti."

"Why not?"

"Because," Matt said, "because, he's *Carlotti*."

Stacey smiled. "Don't worry, Matt. I'm not a big fan of him either. He asked me to the Spring Fling."

"But you said no."

"I said no. Several times. He didn't seem to believe that I would refuse the opportunity of his exalted company."

Matt sat on the side of the bed and leaned down to her. "Would you consider going with me?" he asked, his eyes searching her face.

"You'd want to go to the Fling with the Bride of Frankenstein?"

"No, but I'd go with you, if you wanted to."

"Yes."

"I mean I don't dance very well. But I got an agricultural driver's license and I think that means—"

"Yes."

"Yes?"

"Yes. I've been waiting for you to ask."

"Really? Wow. Awesome. Cool." He leaned forward, searching for a place that wasn't bruised, and settled for kissing her on her forehead.

"I don't know if I'll have my cast off. It's only three weeks away."

"I don't care."

There was a gentle knock at the door. Matt straightened up as the door pushed open. Stacey's dad came in carrying a cup of coffee.

"The doctor hasn't been in?" he asked.

"No, haven't seen hide or hair of anyone," Matt said.

"Matt asked me to the dance."

"And you said?"

"Yes, of course."

"Of course." He smiled at his daughter. Turning to Matt, he said. "Shouldn't you be in school?"

"Yeah, I sort of cut classes when I found out about Stacey."

"Aren't you going to get into trouble?"

"Maybe, if I'm caught."

"How'd you get here, Matt?"

"The bus and a couple of transfers. I hope to get back by lunch."

Mr. Moore glanced at the clock. "That doesn't give you a lot of time."

"You're not trying to get rid of him are you, Daddy?"

"By no means. I just don't want him to get into trouble at school."

Matt squeezed Stacey's good hand as he got up. "Your dad's right. I should go."

"Matt," Stacey called as he headed for the door. "Can you get all my homework for me? You can bring it by the house once they let me out."

"Sure. I'll take care of it." He headed for the door. "Bye Mr. Moore. See you, Stacey."

The door clicked shut behind him.

Matt jumped off the bus a block from the school and ran up to the Foster's Freeze. With his extra nickel he couldn't afford a cheeseburger but he could get a small Foster's soft serve—chocolate dipped. He took the cone and a napkin and headed to school with twenty minutes to spare. He bit off the chocolate swirl at the top of the cone and sucked some of the creamy vanilla out.

"Connors!"

Matt looked out from behind his cone. "Crap," he muttered. Carlotti and a couple of his friends were loitering outside the gates surrounding the school's playground. "Carlotti," he responded warily, crunching through the chocolate in a big bite.

"Saw that chick, Stacey, the other day."

Matt responded by taking a second bite.

"Man, she was totally messed up."

Matt stopped chewing, and regarded Carlotti evenly.

"She did a face slide down the stairs at the stadium. Man, there was blood everywhere. It was so uncool. And to think, I was going to take that bitch to the Fling. I mean, she was so messed up."

"You weren't going to take Stacey anywhere," Matt said quietly.

"She used to be the best looking chick on campus. Of course, I'd take her. But I wouldn't go with that slut now, if she begged me."

"Cool it, Carlotti. There's Sister Tomas," Carlotti's friend warned.

"I'm not afraid of that withered old prune either. In fact, teacher's pet here's probably doing her. He's probably banging both the nun and the crip—"

Matt's ice cream cone hit the ground about the same time as his fist slammed into Carlotti's mouth, knocking the football player to the ground. "Don't get up, Carlotti," he said.

"Geez, Connors," Carlotti said, spitting blood. "What did you do that for?"

"Cheese it, Carlotti. The nun's coming." Carlotti's friends scattered.

"Mr. Connors, why did you hit Mr. Carlotti?" asked Sister Tomas.

"I'd rather not say, Sister."

"I didn't do anything, Sister!" Carlotti said.

"Mr. Carlotti, I will inform you when it is your turn to speak." Sister Tomas turned to Matt. "Did he hit you?"

"No, Sister."

Sister Tomas folded her hands in front of her. "We will not leave this spot until I know what happened."

"He insulted a friend of mine," Matt said.

"You hit him because of an insult?" she asked.

"Yeah, he hit me for no reason," said Carlotti.

"Matthew, that doesn't sound at all like you. Is it true?"

"I did hit him and he did insult a friend."

"What did he say?"

"He—he called Stacey a slut."

"The truth, Mr. Carlotti. Did you?"

"Yes, Sister."

"And he called her a bitch."

Sister shook her head and tsked. "There's more?"

"He suggested that you and I were—you know, having sex. That's why you rewarded me for the science fair. And he said that Stacey and I were—"

"That's enough, Mr. Connors. I get the picture. Mr. Carlotti, follow me."

"But what about him?" Carlotti protested.

"I will deal with Mr. Connors later."

"But he hit me."

"With good cause, apparently." She walked off without a backward glance. "Come along, Mr. Carlotti." Sister Tomas stalked off with the defeated football player trailing behind her.

Dave came up. "That was awesome. You nailed him with one punch."

"Dave, are they gone?"

"Yes."

"Good." Matt winced, hugging his fist. "That hurt like hell. Ow! Ow! Oh, ow that hurt." Matt tried to shake the pain out of his bloodied knuckles.

"Hey, Matt. You're right handed right?" Dave asked.

"Yes, ow. Why?"

"Father Donnetti's test."

"Yes."

"It's an essay test."

Chapter Twenty-One

There was no response to the doorbell at Stacey's door. Matt shifted his shoulders, readjusting the double load of books in his backpack. He retreated down the stairs and saw Mrs. Morgan across the street.

"Hi, Matt." She waved.

"Hello, Mrs. Morgan."

"She's not back yet. Her dad called and said she'll be released tomorrow, after the doctors see her one more time."

"I've got her homework."

"I have a key to their house. We watch each other's places whenever we go away. You could leave her stuff here, with me. And after I finish watering the yard, I'll take it over."

"That'll be great."

"Put the books on the porch." Mrs. Morgan pointed with her hose, then turned, put her finger across the mouth of the hose and began spraying her roses.

Matt dug out a piece of paper and wrote a note. "Mrs. Morgan?"

"Yes, Matt?"

"I'm leaving a note in her history book. It's got today's homework on it and what tests are coming up."

"Okay, I'll see she gets it. Oh, Matt?"

Matt looked up expectantly.

"You have my rocks?"

"Yeah, I found three about the color and size you wanted. I'll put them in the wheelbarrow and bring them over."

"Saturday would be fine."

"I'm mowing the lawn then anyway, so that will work." He paused. "I'll be over Wednesday after school and finish the weeding and rake that spot level. Have you bought the sand?"

"Yes. They'll deliver it tomorrow." As Matt piled the books on Mrs. Morgan's porch she bent over and tugged at a dandelion. The weed emerged, root and all. She straightened and said to Matt, "They come up easier when wet." She tossed the weed into a bucket. "Have you seen Stacey?" she asked.

"She's pretty banged up." Matt glanced at the books on the porch. "Her spirits are good. And she has her sense of humor."

"That's half the battle right there."

"I gotta go, Mrs. Morgan."

"See you Wednesday."

"I'll be here." He waved and headed home. Rounding a corner, he stepped into the shade of towering maples that canopied both sides of the street. Straight down the street, dead center in the T intersection was his house. The figure of his mother stood, hands on hips, at the gate to the courtyard staring up the road at him. He hurried down the street, crossed Glen Eyrie and hustled up the sidewalk.

"Hi, Mom."

"I got a call from Sister Tomas."

"Okay," Matt agreed warily.

His mom shifted her weight and the belt jiggled, the silver buckle flashing, "She said there was an altercation involving you and another boy." Her voice began to climb. "My son got in a fight and hit another person. What the hell were you thinking? You know I don't condone violence. Hell, I don't even let you watch the Three Stooges. I can't believe this."

His mother glared at him a moment. "It was that girl, wasn't it?"

"Yes."

"I told you I didn't want you to see her anymore. Look, she made you get into a fight. She's trouble."

"She's not trouble, Mom. Carlotti's trouble."

"So he insulted this little piece of fluff and you hit him?"

"He insulted Sister Tomas, too."

"Sister Tomas can take care of herself."

"You're right. Nobody messes with Sister. But that's just the point. You and Dad always taught me to stand up for yourself. He called Stacey a bitch and a slut and said that she and I were . . . screwing."

"Are you?"

"Mom! You can't ask me that. That's nobody's—"

The belt whipped out, catching him across the hip. Matt bit his lip, saying nothing.

"You need to stop seeing her. You are too young to have girlfriends."

"You were only a year older than me when you married Dad."

"Don't you dare throw *that* in my face."

A car pulled into the driveway and a mechanic climbed out. Mom calmed herself, with an effort. The Studebaker pulled into the driveway next to the first car. Dad jumped out.

"Hey, Matt, Yolan. Look. Isn't it a beauty?" He indicated the restored car.

"It's great, Dad."

His father walked over to the mechanic and shook hands. "I'll be back in a moment, Corky."

Douglas turned to his family, assessing the scene. "Something up?" he asked mildly.

"Your son got into a fight at school over a girl. Sister Tomas called me and told me about the altercation." She drew out each separate syllable.

"Really?" Dad said. "Who won?"

"I guess I did. I punched him and that was it."

"How's your hand?"

"Sore." Matt held up his right hand and his father examined his son's knuckles.

"Did you hold your hand like I taught you?"

"Yes. No fingers wrapped around the thumb."

"Good."

"Stop it! Just stop it!" The belt rippled in her hand. "He beat up some poor boy for insulting his—"

"He didn't hit you first, Matt?"

"No, sir."

"Matthew, you know I have taught you to never start a fight."

"You also taught me to never run away from a fight."

"Did the school suspend you or anything? I'd go in and talk to them if they did."

"No. Sister Tomas said that since the fight took place off the school grounds and Carlotti was being provocative, neither of us was suspended."

"I want him punished," Yolanda said.

"For defending his girlfriend? I can't punish him for that."

There was a simmering silence. Mom pivoted on her heels and stalked through the courtyard, slamming the gate behind her.

"I have a feeling I haven't heard the last of this," Matt's dad said.

"The car looks great though." The Studebaker's royal blue paint job gleamed in the sunlight, the black trim matching the polished black leather interior. "Did they fix the convertible top?"

"They had to replace the canvas. The old one was too far gone to patch."

"It's a thing of beauty. Really, it is, Dad."

"The shop did a wonderful job, Son. Is she worth it?" His dad smiled. "The girl, I mean."

"Yep."

"Okay, then. Corky here has to bring me back to the shop to pick up the other car. You might want to head down the creek for an hour before running into your mother again." Matt nodded. "Say, I almost forgot. You know about the hotel in Mexico, right?"

"Yeah."

"Want to go check it out with me?"

"Sure. That would be cool."

"Can you get out of school?"

"My grades are good. Most of the teachers would let me make up anything I missed. Where in Mexico is the hotel? Heck, I haven't even seen the one in Fresno yet."

He stepped away from Corky, pulling Matt along with him. "Look. You remember the story I told you about my father taking me to town to see the madam? Well, I've talked to the manager of the hotel. It's in Tijuana, just across the border, and he knows some people who have some girls about your age. Maybe we could, you know, visit them together and have a little fun."

"Sure. When do we go?"

"Thursday. I have a meeting scheduled Friday to look the place over and audit the books. The manager thinks he has a buyer for the place and everything has to be up to snuff." He looked at his son, "So Friday night we'll go out and meet a couple of senoritas. I'm surprised. I thought you'd be offended."

"Over a trip to Mexico?"

"Over me arranging a night at a madam's for you. Maybe you've grown up."

"I don't get you, Dad. One minute you're proud of me for defending a girl's honor and the next you're setting me up with Mexican prostitutes?"

"Not a prostitute. She's the manager's niece."

"I can't go. Friday I go to the banquet and pick up my check. Five hundred dollars, remember? And you said you were going to take me. You promised."

"I can't. There's a buyer. I can't miss the chance to sell one of these hotels. It'll turn everything around."

"You promised!"

"I'll talk to your mother. She'll take you."

"Right."

"She'll know how important this is for you. She won't refuse."

"How come *you* don't realize how important this is for me? And for you to be there?"

"I do. I just have to meet with the buyer Saturday. Won't they send you the check if you don't go to the banquet?"

"Maybe, but I want to go to the banquet."

"I thought your whole generation was the 'all you need is love' generation. You know—'if it feels good, do it.' Come on Matt, think about this. I'm told she's a lovely girl, brown hair, long legs and her mother is supposed to be a knockout."

"One for each of us?"

"Yes, just like my father and me."

"Sorry, Dad. This is a once in a lifetime thing for me." Matt paused. "I hope you make the sale in Mexico."

The mechanic opened the car door and slipped inside.

"I got to pick up the other car," his dad said. "Put the Studebaker away for me?"

"Sure."

His father tossed him the keys. "Be careful with it."

"I will." Matt smiled. Dad slammed the car door shut and the mechanic turned the key. It roared to life and backed down the driveway.

After parking the car and closing the garage, Matt walked into the house. A bucket of water sat beside a pile of rags on the table. His mother was pouring vinegar into the bucket. She screwed the lid back on the vinegar bottle and slammed it down on the table.

"Wash windows. Start in the living room. Inside and out, Matty, and no streaks or you'll do it all over again."

Matt knew better than to argue.

✄ ✄ ✄

The fight lasted for some time and was loud enough for Matt to follow most of the main points sitting on a bench in the courtyard. The front door opened and his father stepped out, pulling out a package of Marlboros and lighting up. He took a deep drag and let it out slowly.

"Mom didn't sound too happy about you going to Mexico."

Dad chuckled. "You could say she was less than ecstatic."

"You could have offered to take her with you."

Dad shot his son a look. "I took her to Mexico once. We ate, and danced, and had a wonderful time." The tip of his cigarette glowed red. "I thought she had a great time."

"What happened?"

"She said she never wanted to go back." His father exhaled quickly. "She said there were too many Mexicans there."

"Figures."

"So, I'm leaving Thursday for Mexico." Dad looked at Matt. Matt turned away. "Alone."

"I'm sure you will have a successful trip."

"I need to sell that hotel, Matt."

"I know. Is Mom taking me on Friday? To the banquet?"

"I'll talk to her about it." His father dropped the cigarette butt on the porch and crushed it.

Chapter Twenty-Two

Matt glanced at the classroom clock on the wall again. Beside him, Dave's fingers drummed on his desk top. Sister Tomas stood erect at the front of the class. She, too, glanced at the clock.

"Class, remember that next week will be midterms. Everything we have covered in the past five weeks will be on the test." The class groaned. "You need to organize your notes and reread the text and the other material handed out."

"Will we have time to review in class, Sister?" someone asked.

Sister Tomas stood quietly. A hand went up.

"Yes, Mr. Rossi?"

"Will we have time to review in class, Sister?"

"That is what homework is for, Mr. Rossi. We will take no classroom time to review."

"Thank you, Sister."

"The test will be Tuesday. And I will not give you any homework so that everyone has the weekend to review and prepare for this test."

Matt raised his hand.

"Mr. Connors."

"The test will cover the last three chapters and all the lectures on India. Will it include the Indian poetry that we read?"

"Good question. No, the test will not include the poetry I handed out."

"Thank you, Sister."

Dave leaned over to Matt. "It's almost ten, Matt."

"I know."

"Are we really going to do it? Walk out?"

"I wish it wasn't during Sister's class. But yes. We are going to walk out. At least I am. You coming with me?"

"Absolutely, man."

"Cool."

"Mr. Connors, is there something you want to share with the class?"

"No, Sister. Sorry, Sister."

A gong sounded over the speaker on the classroom wall.

"Your attention, please. Your attention, please." Static filled the room. "Please excuse the interruption." Again a cloud of static hissed. "This is Mr. Tucci. As you are all probably aware, there is a planned nationwide school walkout planned for today at ten o'clock. I am not here to comment on the merits of the war this walkout is protesting. I represent the diocesan administration in telling you that we cannot condone this walkout. As a school, we are responsible for the safety of all our students. Since this walkout is scheduled during school hours we cannot condone students leaving the school grounds to participate in what could be a dangerous protest. Your parents expect us to keep you safe. Consequently any student who attempts to leave the classroom and join the protest downtown today will face suspension and possible expulsion. There will be no exceptions. In order to keep you safe, we will use these extreme measures. Again, I know that many of you have strong feelings about the war. I appreciate that. But this is a school day. It is your job to be in the classroom and it is our job to teach you. I am sorry for the interruption. Good day."

Muttering erupted in the class. Sister Tomas clapped her hands sharply. "Class, we have another twenty minutes of class time left. Let's get back to work."

The muttering subsided. The minute hand of the clock skipped to twelve.

"Bummer," Dave whispered to Matt. Matt looked from Dave to Sister Tomas to the clock and raised his hand.

"Mr. Connors."

"Sister, we've spent the last week learning about Gandhi and passive resistance, correct?"

"Yes, that is correct."

"We learned that sometimes it is necessary to break rules in order to achieve a greater good. I mean, if Gandhi had marched across India gathering followers and stopped because the British police said this far and no farther, India could still be a colony, correct?"

"Yes. Your point, Matthew?"

"If we believe this is an unjust war and that America should leave Vietnam and if we let the possibility of being suspended stop us from expressing our belief, then we have learned nothing from Gandhi or Dr. Martin Luther King or Cesar Chavez or any of the others who stood up for what they believed in. Even the Bible states this. Jesus threw the men out of the temple, acting on what He believed in."

"Yes. But again, what is your point?"

"It is our right to peacefully assemble. It is our right to stand up and protest for what we believe in. Isn't that why we go to this school, to learn that we have these rights?" Matt stood, closing his book. "If there is one thing I have learned from Gandhi it is this." He took a deep breath and turned to the rest of the class. "Gandhi showed us that there is power in numbers. Principal Tucci said he would suspend us or maybe expel us all. I mean, if he expels all of us, they're out of jobs. They can't keep a school open without us. They need us." He turned back to Sister. "That's right, isn't it, Sister Tomas? You can't suspend all of us, can you?"

Sister met his eager eyes. "No, Matthew, I don't think the school administration would consider expelling everyone."

"Sister, I am sorry, but I am walking out now." Picking up his books, he looked at the class. Everyone's eyes were on him. "Is anyone coming with me?"

The class sat frozen. Then Dave jumped up. "I'm with you." Another stood. Then another and another. In moments the entire class stood up. Matt turned toward Sister Tomas.

Sister Tomas smiled. "Are you sure about this, Matthew?"

"Yes."

She stood silently, her hands folded before she tucked them into her sleeves. "Then I will not stand in your way."

Matt headed toward the door.

"Before you go, Matthew—"

"Yes, Sister?"

"I don't think you'll have any problem with the test."

"Thank you, Sister." Matt said and stepped out the door.

A trickle of students left the room silently. Other students in other classes saw the departure and the trickle turned into a stream, then a river, then a flood. Sister Tomas walked to the door and watched them go.

Chapter Twenty-Three

Matt struggled with the knot of his tie, finally giving up and let go a frustrated sigh. "Mom!" He tugged the tie, trying to adjust the knot but succeeding in making it larger. "That just shouldn't happen." He glared at the tie in the mirror. "Mom!"

"What's the problem?"

"This tie. I can't get the knot right."

"What do you want me to do about it?"

Matt turned and looked at his mother. "Help me fix it."

"I don't know how to tie a tie."

"You don't? Dad always wears ties to work. Don't you ever help him?"

"Your dad wears clip-on ties."

"Really?"

"He could never really tie a tie. So he bought clip-on ties. Fast and convenient. Totally phony." She stood with her hands on her hips. "Have you tried tugging the short end?"

"Yeah. It doesn't work."

"What are you all dressed up for?"

"Tonight's the banquet." He looked at his mother. Her blue capris matched her scoop-neck blue blouse. "Why aren't you dressed up?"

"For what?"

"The banquet. Tonight's the night that I go pick up my prize for the science project. At Moffett Field? Big dinner?"

"Oh, is that tonight?"

"You—you're driving me."

"I can't. I have my mosaic class. Tonight I give my presentation on my project for the class. As a matter of fact, I've got two boxes of purple mosaic tile and a round table top on the porch that I need you to put in the car."

"Can you at least drive me to Moffett Field? You can drop me off and I can probably get Sister Tomas to bring me home."

His mother tossed her head. "Moffett Field! That's twenty miles in the wrong direction. Can't you call Sister Tomas? Ask her for a ride."

"Mom!"

"I can't take you and that's that. Wasn't your father going to take you?"

"He said you'd take me."

"He did? This is the first time I've heard about it."

"I want to be there. I'm the guest of honor, Mom."

"Call Sister Tomas. She can pick up the check for you."

"Mom!"

"I'm not arguing with you, Matty. I have plans already made. You'll have to figure something out." She gestured toward the door. "The boxes are on the porch."

He stared into her unyielding eyes. "I have some calls to make."

Matt stormed to the wall phone. Pulling out the phone book he rifled through the pages and dialed. "Is Sister Maria Tomas there? This is Matt Connors. Yes. She has? No, nothing. Thanks." He slammed the phone down. He looked up at his mother. "She's already left."

"There is a bus that goes to Moffett Field. I can drop you there."

"No, thank you."

"How are you going to get there?"

"I'll ride my bike."

"It looks like it might rain."

"I'll chance it. What other choice do I have?"

After loading the tile Matt headed to the garage, folded the flared bell bottom on his right leg, then clipped the pants out of the way. Mounting his bike he sped off. Angry black clouds stacked up overhead. He stood on his bike pedals, pumping furiously, and sailed around a corner, coat flapping behind him like a cape.

"Where are you off to, Matt?"

"Mrs. Morgan." Matt skidded to a stop. "I need a really big favor.

I need to get to Moffett Field for the awards banquet. Mom was supposed to take me, but she had other plans. Can you take me to Moffett Field?"

"What time do you need to be there?"

"Six-thirty."

Mrs. Morgan glanced at her watch. "We don't have much time." She glanced at Matt. "Nice suit. Look, when we get to the house, you put the dogs away. I need to change into something more banquety. Wait for me in the living room. I won't be long."

Matt locked the two Dalmatians in their kennel, fed them and checked that they had water before heading into the house.

"Mrs. Morgan, do you mind if I turn on the news?"

"Go ahead."

Matt turned the television on, searching for news. A male reporter was covering war protests that had occurred downtown.

"Police estimate that more than thirty thousand students joined the boycott in the San Jose area alone. Every school we contacted reported a flood of students streaming out of buildings at the stroke of ten." The camera panned to show a large crowd of chanting people of all ages carrying protest signs. "Emotions were running very high. However, police have reported that there have been few arrests made and no injuries."

"Quite a commotion they're causing." Mrs. Morgan's voice caused Matt to jump.

"It was amazing."

"Did you join the boycott?"

"Yeah, I was there. I met those two runners who are going to the Mexico Olympics. And Godfrey Cambridge gave a speech and Joan Baez was—" He turned to Mrs. Morgan. "Wow."

She stood, fussing with the clasp of her necklace. A simple black evening gown clung to her body. Reaching behind her, she fastened the silver chain on which hung a single white pearl that fell into the valley created by the mounds of her breasts. She used both hands to smooth the gown along her hips, and looked up at Matt.

"You ready?" she asked, flashing him a smile.

"You look . . ."

"Yes?"

Matt swallowed. "We . . . ah . . . we should go, I guess."

"Just a moment, Matt." She stepped up to Matt and reached out her hand. "Let me fix that tie." She took the knot and tugged it, shaping it. She readjusted his collar and stepped back. "There. Much better."

Morgan turned, picking up a black leather purse that matched her high heels. "There's a white shawl in the hall closet. Grab that. I'll back the car out of the garage. Lock the door when you leave."

Matt grabbed the shawl and headed out, careful to lock the kitchen door. As he opened the car door, she swiveled to him. "Put your bike in the garage."

Matt did so, then jumped back into the car and put the shawl on the car seat between them. "Thank you, Mrs. Morgan."

As they pulled out onto the street, she looked at him. "That's what friends are for, Matt."

"I never thought of you as a friend, I guess. At least not *my* friend."

"Oh? What did you think of me as?"

"You're my mom's friend and my dad's . . . ."

"It's okay, Matt. We don't need to discuss what I am to your father. And as far as your mom goes, we've been friends for a long time. I still don't understand her."

"Me, either," Matt said.

"I assume your ticket to this thing is for two?"

"Yes."

"Good. I'd hate to get all dressed up for nothing."

"You look—very nice."

She glanced at Matt, smiling. "Thank you, Matt. That's the nicest thing anyone has said to me for a while."

Embarrassed, Matt turned and looked out the window. They rode on together in silence for several minutes. "Tell me what to expect tonight, Matt. It's a banquet. They are giving you an award."

"Me and a couple of others." Matt pulled the invitation out of his pocket. "Prime rib dinner. Baked Alaska for dessert. I've never had that before. What is it?"

"Ice cream with a sort of meringue coating. They light it on fire."

"Doesn't that melt the ice cream?"

"No. What else?"

"Dinner begins at six-thirty. Seven-thirty the presentations and speeches begin."

"Who's speaking?"

"It's not on the ticket, but Wally Schirra, the astronaut; Roman Vishniac, the photographer and Roman Gabriel, the quarterback for the Rams."

"That's an impressive lineup."

"It was a state-wide contest. Last year the dinner was in Sacramento."

"Anyone you know going to be there?"

"Sister Tomas will be there with someone from the diocese."

"How do you want to handle this?"

Matt looked at her, puzzled. "Handle what?"

"How do you explain me to Sister Tomas?"

"Oh."

"Yes. Oh."

"If I tell her who you are, she might mention it to my parents. That could get weird."

They slowed at the entrance to the air base. Matt handed his invitation to the guard, who looked at it and waved them through.

"It's invitation only. She'll wonder where my mom is."

"Tell her the truth."

"What about you? I can't explain you, looking like that. She's a nun."

Morgan smiled. "I'll leave you at the door, Matt. You go on in and find your seat. I have a plan." The car slowed to a stop before the lit-up dirigible hangar. Matt handed one of the tickets to Mrs. Morgan. Knots of people were smoking cigarettes and talking casually outside the hangar. "Good." Helene surveyed the scene. "Go on, Matt. I'll be there shortly."

He once again showed his invitation. The host called a waiter, who looked at the card and motioned Matt to follow. The hangar's massive interior swallowed the crowd of five hundred or more attendees. The waiter walked up to one of the front tables. Sister Maria Tomas looked up as Matt approached the table.

"Matthew. I was beginning to worry. The festivities are almost ready to begin."

"I had a little trouble getting here, Sister Tomas."

"Oh? Where's your father? Wasn't he coming?"

"Dad's in Mexico and Mom—she had other plans."

"How did you get here?"

"My bike."

"You rode your bike?" Sister looked incredulous. "That's at least eighteen miles. Monsignor." She turned to the priest sitting beside her, resplendent in black cassock and red sash. "Matt here rode from Willow Glen—on his bike."

"What did that take you, my son? An hour? An hour and a half?"

"Not quite that long." Matt looked at the sash. "Monsignor."

"I'm sorry, Matthew. Monsignor Cochetti, you remember Matthew Connors from my class? Matt, Monsignor Cochetti from the bishop's office."

A broad smile spread across the priest's patrician face. "So you're the young man we're all here to celebrate."

"Thank you, Fath—Monsignor."

The priest sat. Sister Tomas and Matt followed suit. Matt plucked at a napkin and dropped it on his lap. Cochetti grabbed a basket of bread and passed it to Matt.

"If you rode that far, you must be hungry."

Matt reached for a roll and a pat of butter. He pulled the roll apart and began buttering it.

"Is this seat taken?"

It was Mrs. Morgan. Matt and the others looked up at her. "I'm sorry to intrude, but they seem to have overbooked my table." She smiled at the young man standing next to her. "The waiter seemed to think there was an empty seat at this table."

"By all means." Cochetti stood, waving toward the empty chair. "Let me introduce you to everyone, Mrs.?"

"Randall. Helene Randall."

"Mrs. Randall." Monsignor sat and introduced her to the others at the table, saving Sister Tomas and Matt for the last. "And this is the man of the hour." Matt squirmed. "Matthew Connors."

Mrs. Morgan shrugged out of her shawl. The pearl caught for a moment on a wisp of yarn, then fell, gleaming gently. Every man's eye at the table followed the pearl.

"Mrs. Randall, is it?" Sister Tomas asked.

"Yes, Sister. I am sorry about the mix-up. I guess I'm just lucky someone didn't show up."

"Lucky," Sister echoed.

"Who's missing?"

"Matthew's mother couldn't make it."

"What a shame." She leaned back for a waiter and whispered something to him. He nodded and left. "Here it is—your big day—and nobody to share it with. That doesn't seem right."

The waiter returned with a tray holding flutes of champagne. Helene took one gently and turned to the others. "Anyone?" The priest and several others each took a glass. Sister Tomas shook her head. "How about you, Matthew?"

"Matthew's not old enough to drink, Mrs. Randall."

Helene's smile faded, a fact not lost on Monsignor Cochetti. "Now, now, Sister. I think that, given the circumstances, it is not out of order to toast Matthew. After all, he is our first representative from the diocesan schools to win this award in the last twelve years. I'm sure Matthew can handle a sip of champagne." The priest handed a glass to Matt. "To Matthew." He clinked glasses with the boy next to him.

"To our Lord," Sister Tomas said and sipped the champagne.

"To science," Matt said, lifting his glass and sipping.

"Well, Matthew, what do you think of the champagne?"

"It's better than port," he replied, taking another small sip. Helene laughed.

"Just a sip, Matthew," Sister Tomas warned.

"Ladies and Gentlemen, please take your seats. Please take your seats." A tuxedoed man stood on the dais of the stage. "In a few minutes we will begin serving a delicious dinner. But before then, there are some announcements I'd like to make. So, if you can take your seats we will be getting started."

Men began to mount the stage. Sister Tomas leaned over to Matt. "Isn't that Wally Schirra?"

Matt looked up at the man with the military haircut. "Wow. Wally Schirra."

❈ ❈ ❈

Matt stared at his check most of the way home. Mrs. Morgan glanced at him occasionally and smiled. Windshield wipers slapped at the pouring rain. "Almost home, Matt." Helene's smile faded. "What are you going to do with the money?"

"Put it in the bank. I'm saving it all for college." He turned to Mrs. Morgan.

"Did you have fun? I'm not sure Sister Tomas approved of me."

Matt glanced at her cleavage. "You're not exactly dressed for church, you know."

Helene glanced at Matt and then at the wiper sluicing water from the windshield. "Matt, we have a problem. Your bike ride would take you longer than the drive did. You shouldn't be getting home for another hour, at least." The car pulled into her driveway. She and Matt bolted for the house.

Matt stepped into the kitchen. Mrs. Morgan was nowhere to be seen. He heard a whisper of cloth against skin. Looking up, Mrs. Morgan stood before him, naked except for the pearl, the dress a dark puddle at her feet. She looked Matt in the eyes.

"Like what you see, Matt? But then it's not the first time you've seen me, is it?"

Matt swallowed. "Wow."

Chapter Twenty-Four

Bam! Bam! Bam! Matt was jolted awake by his mother banging on the door to his bedroom.

"Matty, open this door."

"What do you need, Mom?"

"I need this damn door opened, Matty. It's past ten thirty. You need to get out of bed and open this damn door."

Matt crawled out of bed and stepped over to the sliding door. Leaning over he grabbed a pencil jammed between the door and the wall.

"I think I see the problem, Mom." He pulled the pencil out. "Yeah, the wheels have skipped off the track again." He bumped against the door. "It should open now."

"Then open it."

"I'm still naked, Mom." He reached over and grabbed a pair of jockey shorts from an open drawer in the dresser.

The sliding door flew into the wall abruptly. Matt straightened up, zipping the Bermuda shorts he had just pulled up. Yolanda stood glaring at her son. "I don't understand why that door always gets stuck."

"It just slips off its track, Mom. What did you need?"

"First, it's late. Second, I've had two phone calls about you this morning."

"Oh?"

"Helene called."

"Mrs. Morgan? What did she want?"

"Matty, what am I going to do with you?"

"I—I'm sorry, Mom. I—"

"Matty." Her hands went to her hips. "I brought you up better than this."

"Mom, it wasn't my fault."

"Green shorts and a blue shirt?" She shook her head. "Blue and green simply don't go together. How many times have I got to tell you that?"

"What did she say?"

"Who?"

Matt pulled the blue shirt off and took a white t-shirt out of a drawer. "Mrs. Morgan?" He tugged the shirt over his head and down his chest.

"Helene wanted to know what time you'd be bringing the rocks over for her rock garden. That woman doesn't have an original thought in her head. I swear she copies everything I do."

"Not everything," Matt muttered.

"Then I got a call from the principal of your school. He wants me to bring you into school today."

"It's Saturday!"

"Mr. Tucci said it was urgent. I need to call your aunt."

❃ ❃ ❃

"Aunt Vicki's car is here," Matt said as they pulled up to the school.

"She always drives like a madman when she's angry."

"Why should she be angry? Why should she be involved in this at all?"

Yolanda stopped the car and turned it off. "We are family, Matty. Of course she is involved."

Victoria sat regally impatient on an oak wooden chair in the office waiting room. A secretary sat uncomfortably behind her desk, carefully avoiding everybody's eyes.

"How much longer do we have to wait?" Victoria barked.

"Hi, Aunt Victoria."

Victoria looked at him steadily for a moment.

"Mr. Tucci will see you now," the secretary said.

"It's about time." Vicki glanced at her sister. "Yolanda, are you joining us? He *is* your son."

Matt's mom put down the magazine she was leafing through.

Victoria burst through the door into Tucci's office like a battleship. Matt and his mother followed.

Victoria slammed her purse on the principal's desk. She scowled. "Are you going to just sit there or are you going to get up and get me a cup of coffee? Yolanda? Coffee?" Matt's mom shook her head. "One coffee, black."

She sat down abruptly. Matt sat beside her, awed as Mr. Tucci rushed out to get coffee. He hurried back moments later with the steaming liquid in a mug. He handed it to Victoria and smiled. "I'm sorry. I didn't expect you to come—"

"It's chipped."

"Beg pardon?"

"The coffee cup is chipped." She examined it minutely. "But it is clean. I suppose it will do."

Tucci composed himself and sat down behind his dark wooden desk. He fiddled with a few papers and looked uncomfortably at Matt. "I guess you all know why we are here."

"I want to hear why," Victoria stated, sipping the coffee and making a face. "Bitter."

"On Friday I made an announcement schoolwide."

"An announcement." She took another sip.

"I told the entire student body that because of safety concerns, the school could not allow any of our students to leave and take part in the protest."

"You took it upon yourself to abrogate the students' right of free speech?"

"It was a safety issue."

"And Matthew violated your decree?"

"Matthew and about five hundred more."

"Wow, five hundred," Matt said.

"Quiet, Matthew." Victoria turned back to Tucci. "Are they all being suspended?"

"No."

"Why not?"

Tucci swallowed and ran his hands through this thinning hair. "I made the decree on behalf of the administration. I am in charge of disciplinary matters. Decorum must be maintained so someone must be made an example."

"So this is a pissing contest."

"I am not used to being talked to in this manner."

"No, it has been a few years. Hasn't it?"

The door opened and Sister Tomas walked in. "Sounds like I arrived at just the right time."

"Sister Tomas! I didn't call you here."

"No, Mr. Tucci, you didn't. Victoria called me." Victoria just nodded. "We talked about air conditioning."

"Air conditioning?" Tucci asked.

"Yes, Victoria and her husband have been talking about purchasing air conditioning for the convent," Sister Tomas said. "Oh, and the rectory. Father is delighted. You know how hot the summers can get."

Tucci wiped his forehead and glanced at Victoria.

"I would have been here earlier," Sister Tomas said, "but I needed to talk to the reporter."

"Reporter? What reporter?" Tucci asked.

"Matt won an award yesterday, Mr. Tucci. He was the first student in years from the diocese to win. The diocesan newspaper wants to talk to him about his project. And I received a call from the Sierra Club. They were interested in talking to him. You're a celebrity, Matthew."

Tucci looked from the nun to Victoria.

Victoria spoke. "It wouldn't cost much more to air condition these offices."

Tucci face reddened. "This is blackmail."

"It isn't the first time," Yolanda said under her breath.

Victoria carefully crossed her legs. "Matty, haven't you ever read the inscription on the altar? What does it say?"

"Donated by Victoria and Silvio Lambretta." Matt turned to his aunt, who sat silently, her free leg moving slightly. "You donated an altar to get what you wanted."

Sister Tomas sighed. "You father and the former principal of the school didn't always see eye to eye. Your father questioned things that made a lot of people uncomfortable. When your mother tried to enroll you in school, the priest said no and the principal agreed."

"So you bought an altar and they let me in," Matt said.

"You are my most intelligent nephew."

"That's bribery."

"Excuse me," Tucci interrupted. "Am I to understand that you are willing to pay for air conditioning for the convent, the rectory and the offices—if Matt isn't expelled?"

Victoria turned to him and smiled. Tucci turned to Matt. "I will see you in school Monday, Matt."

Victoria stood. "Then our business here is done." She headed for the door.

"No, it isn't." Matt remained sitting, staring at Tucci.

"What do you want, Matthew?" Victoria asked.

"It stops." Matt turned to Tucci. "No scapegoat. Nobody gets expelled or suspended for anything."

"I can't do that," Tucci said.

Matt turned to Sister Tomas. "Where are the reporters?" he asked. "You think they would be interested in this entire story?"

Sister smiled. "It would create bad publicity for the school."

"Air conditioning the convent and rectory would be less expensive," Victoria said sweetly.

"Get out," Tucci growled.

"Do we have a deal?" Victoria asked.

"Yes."

"Very well, then." She turned to Sister Tomas. "Would you like to join us for lunch, Sister?"

"Yes, I think I would."

After lunch, Sister Tomas was dropped back at the convent. Matt and his mother drove home in silence after thanking Aunt Victoria. Once home, Yolanda ran into the house to change into her tennis togs and grab a racket. "I'll be back late this afternoon. Don't forget to haul the rocks over to Helene."

"I won't forget."

"Bye." She dashed off.

Matt changed into a pair of cutoffs and t-shirt. He folded an old blanket into the bed of his rusted Radio Flyer wagon, pulled it into the back yard and chocked the wheels with bricks. Then he took some two-by-fours and built a ramp. Shaking his head, he crouched behind the boulder and pushed with his arms and legs.

Planting his feet, he muscled the rock up the ramp. Grunting, he heaved and the rock tilted into the wagon, which creaked in protest.

Matt took a drink from the hose, and stepped back to the red wagon. He tugged. The wagon refused to move. Matt pulled the bricks away from the wheels, grabbed the handle with both hands and tugged. Slowly, the arthritic wheels screeching in protest, the wagon picked up a little speed. Matt headed out of the back yard and through the courtyard. He headed to Mrs. Morgan's house a block and a half away, and he paused at the gate.

"Hi, Matt."

"Oh, hi, Mrs. Morgan." Matt leaned against the rock, panting.

"How about if I get the gate? And maybe some ice water?"

"Ice water would be awesome, Mrs. Morgan." She trotted to the gate in a white crop top and matching pedal pushers separated by a thin red belt. "Could you move the hose, Mrs. Morgan?"

She leaned over, grasping the hose and coiling it on her arm. Mud left a dark smear on her top. Morgan looked down smiling and brushed at the dirt, smearing it even more.

Matt grabbed the handle and pulled the wagon to Mrs. Morgan's flower bed. The boulder rolled out and crashed to the ground with a thud.

"Before you touch that rock again, you will wear these." She pulled a pair of gardening gloves out of the back pocket of her pants.

"I'm not really good with gloves. I can't feel my fingers."

"Use them."

"Yes, ma'am."

"Do you need anything else?"

"No. I'm going to get the other two rocks."

She watched him walk toward the gate. "Have you eaten? I'll fix a sandwich or something after you get them all here."

Pulling the much lighter wagon he headed down the driveway. Stacey's dad was standing next to their car. "Stacey will be out in a minute. We're heading to the library," he said.

"You've got a whole houseful of books."

Mr. Moore laughed. "True. But I'm doing some research for a friend of mine and Stacey is looking for the next Ray Bradbury book. She met him at the award banquet last night. She'll have to tell you all about it."

"Matt!" Stacey bounced down the steps from her porch. "What are you doing?"

"Hauling rocks."

"We've got to go, Stace."

"In a minute, Dad."

"What are you doing tomorrow?" Matt asked.

"I've got a volleyball meeting."

"You're not playing, are you?" Matt glanced at the cast on her arm.

"No. Coach is making me the team's manager until I can play. In fact, that's the other thing I have to do Monday. They're taking this cast off and putting on a lighter one."

"Will it be off for the dance?"

"Probably not. You said you'd take me just the way I was."

"Just the way you are." His hand brushed her cast as they leaned closer together.

"We really have to go," Mr. Moore said.

"Coming." She backed away. "Enjoy hauling rocks." She headed toward the station wagon, ponytail swaying jauntily.

Matt turned, heading for home and the next rock.

Two rocks later, he wiped the sweat from his face on his t-shirt leaving a dirty smear across the front.

"Done?" Mrs. Morgan came out of the house.

"I thought I'd try to position them," Matt said, panting.

"No. Leave them. You can move them later. You've done enough. Come on in. Salami sandwiches with mayo on white bread."

"My favorite."

"Every Italian boy's favorite, I think. Do you want Coke or—," she hesitated, "a beer?"

"I'm not old enough for—"

"That's right. You're a stickler for rules."

"Not every rule." He paused.

"I find on a really hot day, like today, when you've been working hard there's nothing better than a cold beer." She held the door open. "But if you want a Coke—"

"No, I'll—I'll try a beer."

✂ ✂ ✂

Matt sat on the side of the bed, looking back at Mrs. Morgan. "You know, we can't keep doing this," he said, smiling at her.

"Why not?" she replied, raising up on one arm.

"Dad's coming back tomorrow."

"Monday. He called and he got delayed. He sold the hotel and needs to wait for Monday. Mexican banks aren't open on the weekends."

Matt got serious. "He's coming home and I don't know how I feel about sharing."

"Matt, I'm the other woman. One of the other women. Are you jealous?"

Matt thought for a moment. He stood and pulled up his shorts, zipping them. "No. You're only jealous over someone you love, aren't you? And you said we weren't in love. I just don't think that it will work as a father and son tag team."

"You could be right."

"I want you to know that I appreciate everything you have shown me."

"Matt, what we have had has been wonderful and precious. I will always remember it fondly. I want you to know, I will respect your choice. But also know I am here for you if you need me for anything. Your father may not want to share, but he doesn't own me. It is my life. I can share." She reached for his zipper. "But if this is going to be our last time," she said as she slowly inched his zipper down, "shouldn't we go out with a bang?"

Chapter Twenty-Five

Sister Maria Tomas stood by the double doors of the church, silently nodding to the goodbyes murmured at her from the students leaving morning Mass. "Quietly. Please leave quietly," she reminded them softly.

"Good morning. Don't forget to cross yourself." She indicated the Holy Water font and watched as a hand dipped in and made the Sign of the Cross. "Good. Hurry along. Class begins in a few moments. Hurry. Quietly."

She watched the last few stragglers, then looked toward the altar. A lone figure blew out one of the candles and paused. Sister Tomas began walking up the aisle toward the altar. "Hurry, Matthew. School waits for no man."

Matt slowly shuffled to another candle. Gazed at it. Blew it out.

Sister's heels echoed in the cavernous church as she walked us the aisle. "Matthew?"

He leaned over, staring at the flame on the end of the blackened wick, and blew. A question mark of gray smoke rose slowly upward.

"Matthew?"

"Sister?" He turned and offered a weak smile.

"School begins soon."

"School?"

"Yes, Matthew, school." She looked at Matt intently, head slightly tilted. "You seem a bit distracted, Matthew."

"Ah, yeah." He snuffed out the remaining candle and stepped down a step to meet Sister Tomas at the rail. "It was an interesting weekend."

"Still recovering from your big night?"

Matt looked up sharply.

"The banquet, Matthew. I imagine that could be rather heady."

"Heady." Matt barked out a bitter laugh. "Yeah, it was heady."

"Are you all right, Matthew?"

"Yeah, Sister, I guess so." He walked with her along the Communion rail, his hand caressing the polished wood. "They're going to tear it out, aren't they?" he said, eyes on the rail.

Sister Tomas glanced at the rail, "The Communion rail? Yes, the plan is to take out the rail. We will form a line and stand when we receive Communion once it has been removed. No more kneeling."

"Just like that."

"I suppose."

"Hundreds of years of tradition."

"Matthew?"

"Just like that." He looked up at Sister Tomas. "Just like that something happens in Rome and before you know it, bang, everything is turned upside down. Everything you know, tradition, out the stained glass window."

"Vatican Two was no whim, Matthew. The suggestions that have been put forth are to help modernize the church, bring it into the twentieth century."

"Maybe some things shouldn't change." Matt stepped over the rail and turned to the tabernacle and crossed himself. Making the Sign of the Cross, Sister Tomas turned off the lights. Sunlight poured through the windows, dappling the pews and tile with a wash of muted color. The red flame of the sanctuary lamp flickered patiently above the altar. Together, Matt and Sister Tomas walked out the side door of the church into a small garden.

"I've always loved this spot," Matt said.

Wedged between the outside walls of the church, rectory and garage was a small garden, shaded by two gnarled olive trees and a fig tree. Fountains of geranium and pansies, hibiscus and agapanthus bloomed.

"The priest's garden. The gardener has always done a fine job of maintaining it." Sister reached down, plucking a sprig of rosemary and rolled it between her fingers. She sniffed, rubbed her nose and smiled. "It is a place of peace, isn't it?"

Matt nodded. He stepped over to the back door of the rectory and picked up the topmost of two boxes of trash. "Father asked the altar boys to dump the trash after Mass," he explained. Two empty gallon bottles, formerly containing vin rose, shifted and clinked together cheerfully.

"Mass wine," Sister stated.

"Yes. Much better than burgundy." He glanced down at the second box of trash and froze. Then he looked at the nun.

Sister Tomas stared at two empty whisky bottles. She met Matt's eyes. "How imprudent." Matt picked up the second box and headed for the garage that made up the third wall of the garden. He stepped through the back door and dumped the contents of the two boxes into a trash can, returning to the rectory with the empty containers. He put them back at the rectory door.

"There's two empties every Monday, Sister. Sometimes three."

"And who have you told about this, Matthew?"

"No one, Sister."

She looked at Matt evenly. "Good. What people do in private isn't anybody's business."

"But he's a priest," Matt protested. "He tells us how what we do is right or wrong. He forgives our sins."

"God forgives sin." The wooden rosary beads at her side clicked gently as she turned. "Matthew, being a priest is very fulfilling. But it is also very stressful, and lonely."

"Isn't that true of being a nun?"

"Yes. But when the day is over I have a community, a family, to go home to. He has an empty rectory." They turned and started out of the garden.

"It's sin, though, right?"

"Venial sin," Sister said. "The Church teaches moderation and respect for our body and soul. So it could be considered a venial sin."

"Isn't it our duty to report sin?"

Sister Tomas stopped and looked at Matt for a long moment. "Father is a good man. That he drinks occasionally is unfortunate. But he is a good counselor, business manager, teacher and sacrosanct. The good that he does with the dying, giving advice, helping candidates for marriage or vocations far—"

"Outweigh the bad?" Matt finished.

"Yes." She regarded Matt carefully. "Talking could ruin a good priest's career. Matthew, I ask you to think about it."

"But what if a sin hurts others? What if the good doesn't outweigh the bad? What if there is no real good?"

"This isn't about those bottles is it? What is this about?"

A ruby throated hummingbird shot by and helicoptered to a feeder full of red liquid. It hovered a moment, tilting its head at Matt and the nun, then turned to feed. "The stuff Coach has been teaching us, I guess."

"Are we talking hygiene and human reproduction?"

"Human reproduction. It sounds so cold, so antiseptic. Insert tab A into slot B and, bingo, a baby is born. Sex education class, I guess. But we've been taught sex is sin."

"Sex isn't a sin. It is a gift from God when indulged in correctly."

"What if someone was sinning because of sex? And you know that telling anyone would cause more harm than good?'

"Are these questions about sex . . . because you and Stacey are—"

"What? No! Why would you think that?"

"She is an attractive young girl. You're male."

"And that automatically means we are having sex?"

"Often it does."

"Not this time. It doesn't mean that at all."

"I am relieved," Sister said.

"Hypothetically, if you knew someone was committing adultery, do you have an obligation to tell anyone even if you know that telling will cause major problems for everyone involved?"

"Hypothetically, I don't know."

"Come on, Sister Tomas, you know everything."

"Not true, but thank you anyway." She took a deep breath. "Objectively, yes you should tell. But there are many factors. Who would be hurt? How many innocents are involved? What is the cause of the sin in the first place?"

"Coach would say tell."

"He may be right. If he asked that on a test, tell is a good answer. But life is different from a test, Matthew. You know that."

"I know."

"Hypothetically, if the bad outweighs the good that telling would do, I'd say keep it quiet."

"I guess I just don't get it," Matt said. "We have all these rules and regulations. No meat on Friday. Women must cover their head in church. We enforce them to the letter and on big things—"

"I don't think anyone goes to Hell if they have a cheeseburger on Friday."

"But the big sins . . ."

"The big sins don't leave much wiggle room."

Matt turned to Sister Tomas. "Why is sex bad? I mean, God created the entire universe in His image. That includes all of the animals and plants and things. And I've studied nature. Animals do about everything that we do. God created animals to eat and drink and have sex. They don't get in trouble and they do it outside where everybody can see. Why are we prohibited from having sex?"

"It's a matter of free will. Animals don't have a choice about much. A zebra can't decide one day that today I am going to have a steak. Or today, I'm leaving the herd and taking polka lessons."

"Polka lessons?"

"Just as a zebra can't decide these sort of things, it can't decide on its partner or when or where to make love. In fact, they don't make love, they simply have sex. They breed, have babies and die. There are no real families, no caring parents. It's just part of the process."

"So because we can decide to have sex, we shouldn't?"

"Our civilization puts responsibility and sexual activity together. Children need parents to raise them. We have children and there needs to be a functioning family to care for them."

"I understand that. Family and children go together. But what about before marriage? Why is it dirty and bad and evil before it is blessed by a priest and good and fine once it is blessed by a priest? What has changed?"

Sister Tomas thought for a moment. "Do you have a car?"

"No, but I have a license."

"Think of sex as a car. If you go to the lot and see a car you want, wonderful. Pay the price and drive off as the owner of a brand new car. But if you come back at night and steal the car, well, it's the same thing. You still have gotten a brand new car."

"So a marriage license makes it legal?"

Sister nodded.

"There are lots of ways to get a car. And I can see your point about buying versus stealing a car. That's clear. But what if someone gives you the car? Or loans you a car? Or you just want to take it for a test drive to see how it works out? All of those are perfectly legal for cars, but if you apply it to sex it's a one way ticket to Hell."

"Matt are you sure you and Stacey aren't—"

"Yes, I'm sure."

"Then why all these questions?"

Matt sighed, "I'm just confused."

"Life is confusing, Matthew. And questions of morals are always confusing. Nothing is cut and dried."

"Religion class makes it sound easy. Do this. Don't do that." He nudged the empty boxes closer to the stucco rectory wall with his toe. "I mean, people never seem to know anything about other people. My mother always buys my dad powder blue shirts. Mom thinks that's Dad's favorite color. And she thinks it looks good with his salt and pepper hair. But, I asked Dad and he said his favorite color is maroon. So Mom is, with good intentions, forcing Dad to wear something he really doesn't want."

"A lot of people are like that."

"It's like living an illusion. People see in each other what they want to see. So all those happy couples we see at church each week can all be living an illusion, too?"

"That's why there is Confession, Matthew. Nobody is perfect, except God. We all do the best we can and try to live good lives that will be pleasing to God."

"But, how do we know? Hypothetically, if a man and a woman have sex, and they love each other, and nobody knows about it, and it doesn't hurt anyone, how is that wrong?"

"Maybe that's your answer."

"What?"

"It's hurting you just to know about it. If nothing else, it's making you late for first period. But more than that you feel guilt, you're conflicted, and you're questioning your faith. Somewhere along the line, it will impact decisions you make. Maybe not about telling, but somewhere. It is weakening your moral foundation. It may even cause you to question enough that one day you decide to leave the church. It is not a victimless sin, Matthew. Hypothetically, you are the victim. And so, too, are the people involved. There are probably others around them who may be affected."

"I would never leave the Church."

Sister smiled. "Maybe not. But maybe you will decide to say 'Well God, about those Ten Commandments? You know, those are pretty good but that one on adultery, so and so got away with it. I don't think that I'm going to follow that one and the one on stealing, well, it's not really stealing if it isn't noticed is it?'"

"So what do we do, Sister?"

"We do the best we can. Look to the saints. Each one of them was a real human being who overcame the very same problems we struggle with every day. Yet, overcome them they did. St. Augustine was mired in sins of the flesh and ego and overcame it all."

"Things were easier then, Sister. All you had to worry about was being fed to the lions."

"For as long as man has been on this earth he has been struggling with the same issues. Adultery, love, growing up: there is nothing new under the sun."

"It would be easier to have been born a zebra, Sister."

They stepped out of the garden. Sister Tomas shut the gate in the chain link fence separating the garden from the school yard. She turned to Matt and smiled.

"Then, at least, everything would be black and white."

Chapter Twenty-Six

Horns blared and brakes screeched as Matt cut across the lanes of traffic on Willow Street. He swerved up a driveway onto the sidewalk and peddled furiously, weaving around a startled mailman. He didn't slow as he approached the corner curb, but zipped across the street heedless of the cars waiting to turn. He took the next corner in a wide arc and sped down the last block straightaway to his house. Skidding to a stop at the garage door, he jumped off his bike and flung the garage door up. He walked his bike into the garage, kicking down the bike stand. It didn't catch. The bike tottered a moment and fell. Matt ignored it. He slammed the garage door down and headed to the back door, pulling the clip off his pant leg and flinging it across the room. It clattered noisily. Matt opened the door to the courtyard.

"Your bike fell."

"You. You're home," Matt said.

"I'm home. And your bike fell. You need to put it away." Matt's father sat on one of two wicker chairs in the courtyard. An ashtray with several cigarette butts in it was balanced precariously on the rim of a large vase holding an artificial palm. One of the butts had rolled out onto the tile. He exhaled a cloud of smoke and looked at Matt.

"Matt, when your mother gets home she could run right over it. Is that what you want?"

"What I want? When has that mattered?"

"Put the bike up, Son." His father took another deep drag from his cigarette and blew twin streams of smoke out his nostrils. "Now."

Without a word, Matt turned, walked into the garage and picked up his bike. He moved it further into the corner so his mother had plenty of space to park. Back in the courtyard his father sat amid a cloud of smoke.

"I've got big news, Matt."

"Great."

"I sold the hotel." Dad sat back proudly, blowing a series of smoke rings. Matt ignored them. "There was a time when you would have tried to catch those smoke rings on your fingers."

"I was a kid then, Dad."

"It wasn't that long ago."

"Times change."

"Bad day?"

"Very."

"Flunk a test?"

Matt stared at his father. His father continued blowing smoke rings, a smile on his face. "I went to the bank."

Abruptly, the smoke stopped. Douglas looked up at Matt. "Why did you go to the bank?"

"The awards banquet was Friday. They gave me a check."

"Sorry I missed that."

"But that's not the point, is it, Dad?"

"What is the point?"

"I went to the bank. The bank where I have an account. The account I had my college fund in. The college fund Aunt Victoria had put fifteen thousand dollars into. Fifteen thousand dollars for a college like Stanford or Notre Dame."

"I told you I would deposit your check for you when I got back, Son."

"Yeah, you did."

"Why didn't you wait?"

"I'm sorry, Dad. I was excited."

His father nodded, head down, tapping ash off his cigarette. It hit the tile, exploding silently. "And?"

"And the very polite bank teller told me my balance isn't fifteen thousand plus dollars. It's a little less. It's one thousand, two hundred nineteen dollars and fifty-six cents."

"Was she sure?"

"I had her check three times, Dad. Three times. And each time it came up a very polite one thousand, two hundred nineteen dollars and fifty-six cents. How did that happen, Dad? How did Aunt Victoria's fifteen thousand dollars and the money I earned baby sitting and mowing lawns turn into a measly one thousand, two hundred nineteen dollars and fifty-six cents?"

"Son, I—"

"The last withdrawal, Dad. The last withdrawal was two weeks ago, oddly enough the same day you brought money to Mom after you trip to Fresno. Coincidence, Dad?"

"I—"

"Interestingly enough, you are the only co-signer on that account, Dad. I trusted you, man, I trusted you. Why did you do that? Why did you steal money from me?"

"It wasn't stealing, it was . . . borrowing. I have every intention of paying you back."

"Right."

"Right, Matt. Look, you have every right to be upset. Every right. But look at it from my point of view. Your mother loves money." He mashed the cigarette into the ash tray, then pulled another from the pack. "She always wanted to be rich. I tried. I left a job I liked and bought hotels. I own fourteen hotels. None of them are making a dime. But your mother needs—she needed the money."

"And?"

"I needed these hotels to be successful and when they weren't, I needed to create the illusion that they were successful. So the membership at the Swim and Racket Club, the cabin at Elko, all of those things took money." He flicked this lighter. The tip of the cigarette glowed red.

"So, I began borrowing money. First to pay off debts, then to keep your mother happy. Money is the only thing that keeps your mother happy."

"So, you were going to pay me back. When?"

"Whenever I could."

"So you sold the motel in Mexico, right?"

"Yes."

"How much did you sell it for?"

"I made a thirty thousand dollar profit."

"Thirty thousand. Cool. Then you can pay me back."

"It's not that easy."

"Bummer," Matt's said. "Why not?"

"Well, some of it was in trade. I took in an airplane for six thousand of the thirty."

"That leaves twenty-four thousand."

"Part of the trade included a lot in San Diego worth about six thousand more."

"Eighteen thousand left. Plenty to pay me off."

"There are thirteen hotels, Matt. They have bills. Mortgages, utilities, payroll. It all adds up."

"How much?"

"Eleven thousand and change."

"And?"

"House payments. Swim and Racket. Tuition for you."

"How much did you give Mom?"

"Three hundred."

"Doesn't leave much for me, does it?"

"I will make it up to you."

"How?" Matt asked.

"I can make you an executive in my corporation."

"Thanks, but no thanks."

"I could sign over the airplane to you."

"You're the pilot. It's only worth six thousand, maybe. And I would have to sell it to make anything on it."

"I'm sorry, Son."

"You're sorry and my college fund is gone. I've gone from being able to attend Stanford or Berkeley or anywhere I want. Now, I am reduced to what? San Jose City College? Stinking City College?" The end of the cigarette glowed and Matt turned away. "You betrayed me, Dad."

"Look, I will pay you back."

"How?"

"I don't know."

They stared at each other in silence.

Matt glanced at the garage. "You only have one thing of value. One thing that I know really means something to you. The Studebaker."

His father took out another cigarette and paused in the midst of lighting it. "My father's car?"

"Yes. I want you to write two letters. One making me co-owner of the car and the other giving me permission to drive the car whenever I need to."

"You have a driver's license?"

"Shouldn't you know that?" Matt asked.

His father didn't answer.

"Learner's permit. And when I worked in the orchards last summer with Uncle Sal, he helped me get a farmer's driver license. It lets me drive farm vehicles—trucks, tractors, anything with a clutch and a PTO."

"The Studebaker doesn't have a PTO."

"But nobody knows that. It's old enough."

"It's not worth what I owe you."

A car drove up the driveway and honked. "Your mother is home."

The car door slammed shut. The click of high heels grew louder.

"Hey!" The courtyard gate squeaked open. "I've got bags in the car."

"We'll take care of it, dear."

Mom stalked across the courtyard and paused at the door. She fumbled in her purse. "Oh, Matty." She turned toward her son and pulled something out of her handbag. "I saw this in the cash register at Macy's." She handed Matt a coin. "It's not a silver dollar, but it is a silver half dollar."

"Uh, thanks."

She turned and headed into the house. Matt opened his hand and a Liberty silver half dollar lay on his palm.

"What is it?"

"A half dollar. A Liberty silver half dollar." Dad looked up at Matt in confusion. "She used my silver dollar collection to buy groceries and pay the paper boy. This must be payback. I guess." Matt stared at the coin a moment and began laughing.

"Why are you laughing?"

"I have no stinking idea. I don't understand anything anymore." He laughed even harder. "I don't understand a stinking thing."

Chapter Twenty-Seven

After clambering down the embankment, Matt sat against the rock retaining wall that protected Mr. Gianinni's property. An old pine stump encrusted with ancient sap would serve for a table. Matt settled down on the leafy floor and placed the bag his cousin Joe had given him next to the stump. Reaching into the crumpled bag, he pulled out the six hand rolled cigarettes, and a small box of wooden matches. The *Playboy* he propped against the stump.

Matt examined the six cigarettes. Five were plump and tightly rolled. The sixth had split a bit where the papers joined. Matt examined it. The interior looked like parsley. Matt sniffed it. His nose wrinkled.

He licked his finger and tried to moisten the paper and fix the split. The paper sealed. He struck a match on a rock, picked up the cigarette and tried to light it. Mimicking his father, he put the tip between his lips, leaned into the flame and inhaled. He coughed explosively, blowing out the match. He pulled the cigarette from his mouth and ground the match out carefully in the dirt. He watched the embers on the cigarette for a second then tried again. Taking a smaller breath, he was able to control his convulsing body and keep the smoke in. His throat burned. His nostrils quivered. A racking cough expelled the bluish smoke. Holding the smoldering cigarette between two fingers, he coughed and gagged repeatedly. Smoke trickled between his fingers.

"I recognize that smell." Robert walked toward Matt carrying a bundle of cattails.

"Robert, what are you doing down here?"

Robert nodded toward the cattails. "Mr. G. is doing a photo

shoot. He wanted some cattails."

"They're green," Matt responded.

"Ah, but with the magic of black and white photography they'll look perfect." He glanced at the burning butt in Matt's hand. "What the hell are you doing?"

Matt looked at the cigarette. "You mean this?"

"Yes, that. I didn't know you smoked marijuana. That doesn't seem like you, Matt."

"Maybe I don't want to seem like me?"

"But, weed?"

"My cousin, Joe, gave it to me."

"Have you ever smoked before?"

"I've watched my dad. It didn't look that hard."

Matt took another deep breath, drawing on the joint, and instantly coughed it out. "Maybe it's harder than it looks."

Robert dropped his bundle of cattails and sat next down to Matt. "You're doing it wrong."

"So what am I doing wrong?"

"Here, give it to me. I'll show you."

Matt handed the joint to Robert. Robert took it carefully in his fingertips. "First of all, when you inhale marijuana, you need to bring in a lot of air." Robert placed the tip of the joint between his lips and sucked in a long, tight breath. "Then," Robert whispered, holding his breath, "you hold in the smoke as long as you can possibly hold it." Robert held his breath a bit longer then blew it out slowly. "Cigarettes are more relaxed. Joints are raspier. You need the air so your lungs don't spasm and make you choke."

Matt nodded and took the joint.

"Hold it between your fingertips."

"Why?"

"With cigarettes you throw away the last inch or so. With pot, you smoke it down to the roach, the very end. And you don't want to burn your fingers."

Matt held the joint properly.

"Good. Now, put your lips together and hiss as you draw in air and smoke." Matt hissed in a focused stream of air and smoke. "Good, now hold it." Matt held it, and his eyes started to water. "Okay, let it out." Matt exhaled. "See, it worked. You didn't gag or cough."

"Cool."

Handing back the joint, Matt leaned back against the wall. "So when do I get stoned?"

Robert laughed and took another hit. He handed it back to Matt. "Go easy, Matt. Sometimes it takes more than one."

"What's being stoned like? I mean, am I going to see polka dot flamingos or glowing purple weasels or something?"

"Mostly, it'll just make you mellow."

"Mellow. I'd love to just be mellow."

"You haven't told me why you're doing this."

Matt turned to stub out the butt of the joint on the pine stump.

"You can put it out, but don't throw it away. What affects you in weed is THC. It collects in the roach." Robert reached over and took the smashed butt. "You eat it."

"Gross."

"It's what you do."

"Want another?"

"Well, I guess you need some adult supervision."

"Adult supervision? Don't make me laugh. I need less adult supervision, not more."

"Here, Matt. Let me." Robert took another joint and lit it, drawing in deeply. "This is good stuff."

Matt took a hit and held it.

Robert reached over and picked up the *Playboy*. He flipped through, finding the fold out and pulled it open. "Awesome."

Matt exhaled. "I didn't think you were into girls."

"Matt, I'm homosexual. That doesn't mean I can't appreciate a beautiful woman. I love to dance to rock and roll but that doesn't mean I can't enjoy classical. I'm a Beatles and Vivaldi man."

"I'm so confused," Matt said, inhaling and holding.

"So what's confusing you, Matt?"

"Oh, I don't know. My dad is having multiple affairs and expects me to keep it secret. My aunt had to buy an altar to get me into church. My mother is a bitch. My priest has a drinking problem. My cousins are having sex with each other. My father embezzled my college fund. My mother is a bitch. Sister Tomas helped my aunt set up my principal so I wouldn't get suspended. And me . . . I've changed. Oh, and the Mass I've been used to all my life is changing completely. Faith shouldn't change, should it? Something has to remain the same doesn't it?"

"You would think so."

"And me. I've changed."

"How have you changed?" Matt gave Robert a sideways look. "Oh, you got laid."

Matt nodded.

"Male or female?"

Matt winced.

"Just joking."

Matt took a long drag.

"So?" Robert asked.

"My father taught me not to kiss and tell." Matt laughed. "Kiss and tell. He kisses and I'm not supposed to tell."

"What's that supposed to mean?"

Matt turned to Robert and gave him a long look. Exhaling he said slowly and clearly, "I'm screwing my dad's mistress. How's that for the neighborhood nice kid?"

"It doesn't really fit the mold, Matt."

Matt laughed and handed the joint to Robert. "So, how was it?"

"Which time?"

"Which time? Matt, you stud." Robert took a drag and handed the joint back to Matt. "Your dad's mistress. That's a little complicated, man."

"Tell me about it."

Matt took a deep hit and leaned back against the rocks. He held his breath a moment then slowly let the smoke escape. Robert leaned closer to Matt, shoulders touching. "I broke it off. I told her I couldn't share. And before you ask, it isn't jealousy. I just can't be her fill-in for the nights my dad isn't around."

"I guess I can understand that. What did she say?"

"She's cool with it. She said she's always there if I need her."

"You going back?"

"Not today. Today I'm getting stoned. But tomorrow, I don't know. I hope my resolve holds."

Robert crushed out the roach between his fingers and offered it to Matt. Matt looked at it warily. "You eat it?"

"You got it."

Matt took the roach and placed it on his tongue. He chewed carefully. "It's like chewing autumn leaves." Matt reached for another joint and lit it.

"Wait a minute, did you . . . you know, screw your dad's mistress before or after he stole your college money?"

"Why does it matter?"

"I wondered if it was a revenge fuck."

"No. It was before. I only found out about the money today."

"Wow."

"I expected you to say something a little wiser than that."

"How about don't bogart that joint, my friend?"

Matt giggled and passed it over. "So everything is upside down. Like my mother, she replaced one of the silver dollars she took from my collection. Of course, she blew it. She can't tell a half dollar from a silver dollar, but she tried. And then she asked me what color my date was wearing to the dance."

"That cute blond I've seen you with?"

"Yeah, Stacey." Matt smiled. "When I asked her what difference it made she goes, Matty, Matty. You have to be color coordinated, otherwise nobody will know you're together. What if she's wearing a pink gown and you're wearing brown tux? It just wouldn't do, Matty. It just wouldn't do. It's like she's trying to help me. That's so weird."

"She's right."

"Really? See, it's weird. Then I said I wanted a tux with tails and she said no way. Tails are too much."

"She's right again."

"Hmm. Right twice in two nights. Too weird. You sound like you're talking from experience."

"I went to a ball or two in my day."

"Really? Boy or girl?"

"Girl."

"Girl? Why?"

"Truthfully, camouflage. I was a football player. We weren't allowed to deviate from the norm."

"That's hard, man." They passed the joint back and forth in silence. Robert ended with it.

"I don't know what to do," Matt said.

"Matt, you are the most intense kid I have ever known. You know right and wrong and have a better sense of who you are than many adults I know."

"So?"

"So—here, have another hit."

Matt took the joint and looked at it. "You know, they used to call cigarettes fags, and they call homosexuals fags." He held the joint away from him and compared it to Robert. "I don't see the resemblance." He broke out giggling.

"Gays."

"What?"

"We call ourselves gays."

"Why? What are you gay about?"

"It's just a word, Matt."

"Like pot used to be something you cooked in and now it's this." He held up the joint.

"Yeah, and dykes."

"What are dykes?"

"What are dykes? Aren't they what little Dutch boys stick their finger into?" Robert laughed. "Not any dykes I know. Dykes are homosexual women."

"There's homosexual women? Geez, the world is totally screwed up, isn't it?" Matt looked at the two unsmoked joints. "Should we smoke 'em all?"

"I think you've had enough, little man."

"You think so?"

"Yeah, I'm pretty sure."

"Cool." Matt climbed to his feet, using the rock wall as a crutch and swayed gently.

"You need to come with me, Matt."

"You don't think I can climb the rope, do ya?"

"Not really. Lean on me and go up the steps."

Matt leaned against Robert and giggled. "Don't forget your cattails."

"I'll come back down and take care of everything."

"You a good friend, Robert. A really super, duper friend."

"You're pretty stoned."

"I am?"

"Yes, you're really pretty stoned. You may want to stay away from your parents for a while. They might get suspicious."

"I spend half my life trying to avoid my parents."

"Then you ought to be good at it."

Matt laughed.

Chapter Twenty-Eight

Matt pedaled furiously. Head down and legs churning, he tried to catch up with the bus. "Stacey!"

A block away the bus slowed, letting off two students. Matt was gaining, just car lengths away, when, belching exhaust the bus roared away. Matt cursed softly and pedaled harder. Brake lights glared as a blue Impala pulled in front of it and Matt gained. Then the Impala turned and the bus pulled ahead, leaving Matt behind. Suddenly the bus stopped and the door shushed open. Stacey stepped out. Matt looked up in time and slammed on his brakes. Tires screaming, he laid down a smoking strip of rubber.

"St—Stacey!" he gasped out.

"One of the kids on the bus said you were following us."

"Yeah." He struggled to get his breath. "I've been chasing the bus since school got out."

"I didn't see you in class this morning or at lunch."

"I wasn't feeling good this morning. I woke up with my throat burning and a bad stomach. But I got better and came to school late."

"Flu?"

"No, I think it was something I ate. Last night I just was hungry. Didn't matter what I ate, I wanted more. It was weird. After dinner I ate a whole bag of Cheetos. Slept like a log though. Slept right through the alarm."

"You missed the test."

"No. I got to make up the test during lunch. So, that was kind of my day."

"And now you're chasing me?"

"Well, yes, I was."

"Well, you've caught me."

"Here, put your books in the basket," Matt said. She dropped the binder and books in. Together they began to walk.

"I brought you something, Matt." She reached into her handbag and pulled out a book.

"*S is for Space*. By Ray Bradbury! This is way cool!" Matt opened it and thumbed through a few pages. "He signed it! 'To Matt Connors, Dare to drink the Dandelion Wine,' signed by Ray Bradbury. Where did you get this?"

"My awards banquet. Bradbury was there and Dad knows him, so he asked him to bring a copy for you."

"This is awesome. Stacey, I can't—thank you." He closed the book and looked at her. "Wow. I haven't read this one yet."

They turned off the main road and started down a side street towards the empty lot. Arching sycamore trees shaded the quiet street, dropping the temperature several degrees. Manicured lawns spread wide in both directions.

"What did you think of Mr. Tucci's announcement?"

"What did he say?"

"Only that there wouldn't be anyone punished for leaving Friday. Odd, huh?"

"Maybe something happened over the weekend."

"Like what?"

"Oh, like my family." Matt related the story of his encounter with Mr. Tucci. Stacey laughed.

They came to a green space wedged between Fred's house and the Spano's house. "The Spanos own the lot. They have for years."

"You come here often?"

"When I was a kid, Fred and Peter and Tony and I played here all day long. It was the Wild West, Korea, alien worlds, a baseball diamond, a football field, anything we could imagine." He paused. "Now I just use it as a short cut into the creek."

He pushed the bike through the thigh high grass and weeds. At the back of the lot, near the corner of the fence, he laid down the bike. The weeds made it invisible. He extended his hand. She took it.

"Fred's dad dug some steps in. He wants to landscape his creek side, maybe put in a retaining wall, like Giananni did." He made a mock bow. "Follow me, my lady."

Hand and hand they navigated the crudely scooped out steps. Moments later they were on the creek bed. "See, not nearly so bad."

"No." She brushed golden hair out of her face.

He led her across the hard dirt creek bed cobblestoned with smooth river rocks until they came to the sluggish water. A swarm of iridescent dragonflies exploded past them as they pushed through a curtain of immature cattails. "We'll wade across here. It's shallow."

"What do you suggest?" she looked at Matt.

"I'm keeping the shoes on."

"Me too, then."

Matt waded into the water. After he took a step or two he reached back, offering Stacey his hand. Without any hesitation, she reached out and followed him.

They walked across in silence. Minnows darted, panicked, among the rocks and reeds. Clouds of silt rose with every step, engulfing the frightened fish, then flowed gently downstream. Matt dropped Stacey's hand and stepped up a foot onto a crumbling dirt slope. "Let me help you."

He grasped Stacey's arm and helped her up. They stood soaking in the warm sun. Matt wiggled his toes, forcing watery bubbles out of his sneakers. Stacey glanced down at her wet tennis shoes.

"The tops aren't even wet."

"I told you it was shallow." He turned toward a cliff wall of fractured concrete. "Now we climb."

Stacey said, "Where did all this broken cement come from? It looks like sidewalk."

"It is. On some of the slabs you can see an address inscribed onto them."

"So they just dumped this stuff here?"

"It doesn't seem to hurt anything and the animals love it."

A furry face exposed itself and flashed away in a blink of an eye. "What was that?"

"Ground squirrel. There are lots of them in here. Sometimes when I'm down here by myself, they'll come and collect acorns and stuff and let me watch them eat."

"Is there anything dangerous?"

"Not really. Black widows, but they're small. You can squish them. Maybe a rattlesnake, but I've never seen one," he added quickly. He started to climb, moving surely from jagged slab to jagged slab. "This way."

Nimbly they scaled the concrete rubble. At the top of the cliff, they paused, breathing heavily. Waist high grasses sighed as they passed through them. Matt stopped at a rough board fence.

"From this point on we crawl." He grasped two boards and pulled them apart like a curtain. He held them apart and nodded to Stacey. "Go in low and stay down."

"Where is this?" she asked.

"It's the orchard I work in during summer. It belongs to Mr. Romatta. He's got a thing about trespassers. I think he's worried about people breaking branches on his precious cherry and apricot trees."

On all fours, Matt and Stacey crawled through the weeds. He crawled on ahead of her parting the weeds as he went. "Almost there," he said.

The grass parted and they crawled out onto a little knoll. White and sky-blue butterflies flitted among the yellow mustard flowers. Streams of sunlight filtered through a canopy of pale pink flowers. Hummingbirds darted to and fro. The knoll was covered with fresh grasses and moss. A slow-motion rain of apricot blossoms fell gently on the knoll. Matt rolled onto his back, and Stacey lay beside him.

"It's beautiful," Stacey murmured. Quail scratched through the underbrush and doves cooed mournfully.

"I love it here, Stacey. It's like Eden on earth."

The wind rustled the mustard greens creating blizzards of yellow pollen. Apricot trees rocked slowly. "It's beautiful," she repeated, turning toward Matt.

"Yes, it is beautiful, isn't it?" Matt turned towards Stacey, their faces inches apart.

She smiled, blue eyes glowing. Matt smiled back, lost in her eyes, waiting for—

He leaned forward and kissed her, lips welcomed him. Matt's eyes widened as he pulled back, and rolled to kiss her again. Their lips met for several seconds, tongue tips dueling. They broke. "Where did you learn to kiss like that, Matt?"

"I . . . I read a lot of books."

She rolled onto him. Matt was submerged in a cascading waterfall of golden tresses. She straddled his torso and put both hand on either side of him. Her body stretched out, down his torso and legs. Her breasts mashed against his chest. She kissed him long and hard. They stopped, gasping for air.

"Wow. Where did *you* learn to kiss like that?" Matt asked.

"We must be reading the same books."

"Matty." His mother's voice pierced the silence. Matt sighed.

"We can ignore her, Matt."

He snaked a hand behind her head and pulled her down, kissing her hard and long.

"Matty!"

Matt rolled to his side, eyes never leaving Stacey's.

"We can ignore her, you know."

"I know we can ignore her, and God I want to, but we can't ignore them." He looked over Stacey's shoulder. Beyond her, the bushes rustled, footsteps came running toward them panting. Two Doberman pinchers burst into the clearing. Noses up and alert, their posture changed as they saw Matt. Immediately, their ears drooped and their bodies relaxed. Their stubby tails began wagging furiously and they squirmed with delight. "Stacey, meet Samson and Delilah." He reached out and ruffled their heads. "They belong to Mr. Romatta. And if they're out here, Romatta isn't very far behind."

"Show yourself!" a rough male voice yelled. The dogs whimpered, heads darting back between Matt and their master's voice.

"We gotta go. Romatta carries a shotgun. Tends to fire first and ask questions later. But don't worry. He only loads it with rock salt. But it still stings if he hits you." He got up on all fours. "This way. Stay low and don't make a sound. Samson. Delilah. Go home. Go home, guys!"

Matt and Stacey parted reluctantly and headed toward the fence.

"Show yourself. I know you're out there."

"Matty, are you in the creek?" his mother yelled.

"Come on," Matt whispered. They made it to the fence and Matt swung the boards apart. Stacey scurried through and Matt followed.

"I know you're out there!" Romatta fired. A thunderous explosion and a hail of rock salt exploded into the fence as Matt released the boards.

"Mr. Romatta. Is my Matty over there?"

"I don't know if it's Matthew or not. Somebody's in here, I think."

"Matty, is that you?"

"Don't answer her."

"Don't worry, I won't," Matt said.

Keeping low, they hugged the fence line. "We'll head through the bamboo," Matt said. "This path heads down to the creek bottom. Then we can walk to the Meridian Street bridge and climb out from there."

"Lead on, McDuff."

"I love an intelligent woman." He put his hands around her head and drew her close. Tenderly, he kissed her. "Come on." They turned and disappeared into the bamboo.

"Matty?"

"Can't she see us?"

"Nah. She never walks far enough out of the house to look over the fence. She just steps our and yells."

"What about—"

"Romatta? Nah, he's headed back to the house to reload."

They entered the hissing bamboo. The polished black stalks gleamed amid the soft green tissue-thin leaves. Fat green shoots had burst from the ground seeking sunlight. "It's another world," Stacey said wonderingly. "Where'd the bamboo come from?"

"People threw it down here. People throw all sorts of stuff down here hoping to never see it again. The problem is hiding it doesn't kill it. It just takes root and keeps growing." Something splashed before them. "Shhh," Matt hissed. Together they parted the bamboo and peered out.

"Who's that?" Stacey mouthed.

Matt stood and stepped through the bamboo. "That's my friend, Fred. Come on." Arm in arm they stepped out of the bamboo jungle. "Hey, Fred."

Fred looked up, startled.

"Hey, Matt." He picked up a can he had perched on a rock and walked toward Matt. "Who's this?"

"Fred. This is Stacey. She's my girlfriend." Stacey and Fred greeted each other.

"What are you doing down here, Fred?" Matt asked.

"Mr. G. wanted me to try to catch some crawdads for him."

"Why didn't he ask me?"

"He said he talked to your mom and you weren't in."

"Look, if you want crayfish you need to get into cooler water down by the eucalyptus trees. Find something like an old bird cage and put some meat in it. Pile a bunch of gravel up to the door as a ramp and wait a couple of days. You'll have a bunch of crawdads. Here all you will get is bluegills and sunfish."

"Cool. Thanks, Matt." Fred looked at Stacey. "When my brother comes home . . ."

"Fred," Matt warned gently.

"I'm sorry. My brother would have liked you. Not many girls have the guts to come down here." He glanced at Matt. "If Matt likes you, that's good enough for me."

"Did I miss something?" Stacey asked looking from Matt to Fred.

"Matt has been helping me. My brother died in Vietnam."

"I'm sorry."

"Me, too. Anyway, he's not coming back."

Matt looked at him fondly as Fred turned and started to wade away. "Fred?" Matt asked. Fred turned. "Do me a favor, man."

"Sure. What do you need?"

"I left my bike with our books in it in the empty lot in the grass. Can you walk it to my house? Park it by the gate where the garbage cans are."

"Sure."

"And Fred," Matt added, "make sure my mother doesn't see you."

"Absolutely." Carrying his can, Fred waded away.

Matt turned to Stacey. "Now we get to walk a bit." They wandered along the creekside, scrambling over beached rocks and drifted logs. The shadow of the bridge loomed above them. A truck rumbled overhead, startling a flock of pigeons and swallows. Obscene spray-painted graffiti covered the concrete bird-stained walls. Stacey eyed the anatomically enlarged nudes displayed there.

"Come here often, Matt?" she asked.

Matt blushed. "No. I hardly ever come this far down the creek. And I swear I never painted anything on the walls."

They climbed. Achieving street level they walked side by side.

Twenty minutes later they approached Matt's house, his mother appeared on the lawn. "Where have you been?"

"Walking."

"Where you in Mr. Romatta's orchard?"

"Not recently, why?"

His mother stared at Matt long and hard. Matt didn't flinch. "Dinner tonight at your grandmother's, Matt."

"What time is it?"

His mother glanced at her watch. "Four-thirty."

"Cool. I've got a half hour. I'll walk Stacey home."

"Hi, Mrs. Connors."

"And then I'll walk to Grandma's from there."

"You have lawns to mow."

"Come on, Mom. Our lawns are the size of card tables and I mowed them Sunday." His mother sputtered. "Look, I can mow them after dinner. But I am walking her home."

His mother wheeled around and stalked into the courtyard. Matt watched with amazement. "That never worked before."

"Maybe she's changing."

"Maybe," Matt said doubtfully.

Chapter Twenty-Nine

A week later, Matt was riding his bike home from the florist shop. A white orchard corsage rode in a white paper bag in his back bike basket. The yelling could be heard from several houses away. Matt parked his bike outside the courtyard and grabbed the bag.

"Again! You haven't even been home for what—two weeks?"

"I don't have a choice. I can sell the hotel—"

"I don't give a damn about your stinking hotels."

"You should, dear. I am doing this for you."

"All I know is that you are never home. Never. For all I know, you are screwing around every time you are out of town." She laughed harshly. "Hell, as far as I know, you have women everywhere in this town, too. You are a lousy, cheating, son of a bitch."

There was a slap and a thud. Matt was at the door and threw it open. His mother was crumpled against the wall, holding her cheek. His father loomed over her, staring down at his wife, panting hard.

"What the hell happened here?"

For a second nobody answered. His mother's head pivoted and she looked at Matt. "Your father hit me, Matty. Your hero hit me."

Matt looked at his father.

"It was only a slap, Matt," his father offered weakly. "She just wouldn't stop, Matt. She just wouldn't stop."

"So you hit her?"

"Just a slap. Honestly, I never meant to. It was just—a slap." His father offered his mother his hand. She ignored it and levered herself up.

"You told me that a man never hits a woman. No matter what."

"I know. I—"

"Maybe, you better step outside for a moment."

His father picked up his suitcase and stepped out of the house. Matt turned to his mother. "Are you all right?"

"Fine." She stalked off towards the bedroom, heels clicking on the tile.

"You're welcome, Mom."

Matt stepped outside. His father stood there head down, smoking. "Matt." He didn't look up. "I didn't mean to—"

"Don't apologize to me. I'm not the one you hit."

"I—"

"Look, I don't blame you. I mean, there are times I would love to clobber her. But you told me men don't hit women."

"You're right." Douglas blew out a stream of smoke.

"So, what is this all about?"

"I got a call today, from Guam. There have been two parties in a bidding war over the hotel there. I thought I'd be lucky if I could break even on a sale there. I mean, it's Guam."

Matt sat down next to his father. "The offer they are making is eleven thousand more than I thought I would get. But they need me there on Friday to seal the deal."

"That's tomorrow. Can you make it there by tomorrow?"

"I gain a day going over the international dateline."

"Oh, cool." Matt looked at the suitcase. "Leaving now?"

"Yes. Flight to Hawaii and then I've got connections onto Guam."

"But the dance is this weekend. You were my ride!"

"Look, here are the keys to the car. You're a good driver. At least that's what your Uncle Sal says. It's the best I can do, given the situation." Dad nodded toward the house. "I certainly can't go in there now and ask her to drive you. Take the key."

Matt took the key chain, unclipped the little chain and handed the other keys back to his father. "When do you get back?"

"Wednesday."

"Is that Tuesday in our time?"

"Yes."

"Don't you have to go?"

His father glanced at his watch. "Yes, the cab should be here soon. I've got to leave your mother a car."

"I guess."

A car horn beeped out on the street.

"I've got to go." Douglas threw down his cigarette and crushed it under his foot. He picked up the suitcase and headed down the walkway to the curb. Without a backward glance, he opened the cab door and got in. The cab drove off. Matt walked to the bike and pulled the white corsage out, then headed inside.

Chapter Thirty

Matt unbuttoned the tuxedo and looked himself over in the mirror. He frowned, adjusted his bowtie for the hundredth time and looked again. Fingering the cummerbund, he smoothed down his white shirt, rebuttoned the tux and examined the effect. He shook his head and sighed.

"Well, Letty, I can't tell which looks best. Any opinion?" His dog simply rolled over onto her side. "That's what I thought. I wonder what idiot invented the cummerbund. I just don't get it. What does a cummerbund *do*?" He examined his profile. "Maybe it you're overweight it'll hold you in a bit." The dog's ear twitched.

Matt looked at the clock on the wall and then at his wristwatch, walked into the kitchen and opened the refrigerator. The white box with the corsage in it sat undisturbed on the shelf, next to a quart of milk. He opened it and again checked that the corsage had a pin in it, placed it back carefully and glanced at the clock on the wall. From the living room, he heard the raucous brass of the theme song of *The Dating Game* blaring. He headed toward it. His mother sat on a recliner, feet tucked under her hips watching the TV.

"You sure you don't want to drive me?"

"I'm not your chauffeur, Matty."

"Dad was going to drive."

"Your father *said* he was going to drive, Matty. But he's not here, is he?"

"No." Matt walked back into the kitchen. Opening a cupboard, he fished around in a glass bowl, looking for the keys. He checked the clock again and opened the fridge, taking out the corsage. He headed into the living room again. "I'm going."

His mother didn't respond. "You hid the keys again, didn't you?"

Yolanda turned toward her son. "You don't have a valid driver's license, Matty. You know that. If there was an accident, our insurance wouldn't cover it."

"Dad said if I drove carefully—"

"I know what he told you. Maybe that's true, in Guam."

Matt pulled his father's key out of his pocket. "I'm not going to beg. This time I was prepared. Dad gave me his key."

Yolanda smiled. "I know."

Matt headed to the garage, the front door closing behind him. Inserting the key into the ignition he turned it. Nothing. Trying the ignition again resulted in the same result. Opening the hood of the Dodge he saw it—an empty hole where the battery should sit.

His mother stepped into the garage. "You think you won, Mom?" He turned the double latch on the left side of the Studebaker's hood and raised it. He pulled out a key that was attached by a magnet to the engine wall. Grabbing a rag off of the workbench he cleaned the key, then closed and latched the hood.

"You didn't win, Mom. There are things you can't stop. Things you shouldn't even try to stop." He picked up the white corsage box off the workbench and stepped into the vintage car. After pulling the choke, he primed the pump.

"That hunk of junk doesn't *work*, does it?"

"Watch." Matt turned the key. The engine grumbled. He pumped the hand pump again and pressed down on the clutch and feathered the gas. It grumbled again, then the engine sputtered and roared to life. Playing the choke and throttle he adjusted the feed and the roar mellowed to a purr. Matt said up and smiled.

"You lose, Mom." Switching gears, he eased off the clutch and released the hand break He backed down the driveway.

"You can't drive that, Matty!"

Matt reached forward and squeezed the bulb of the horn. The kettle drum headlights blazed to life, spotlighting his mother, now standing in the center of the garage.

"Come back, Matty."

"Bye. Mom." Matt waved jauntily, and headed off.

"This isn't over, Matty. It's not over."

Pulling up before the Moores' house, Matt came to a stop and pulled the handbrake. He jumped out of the car and got halfway up the walk before snapping his fingers and running back to the car. He grabbed the corsage box and ran up to the door. Hesitating, he glanced at his watch. The luminous dial said seven-fifteen.

"Perfect." Matt breathed and pressed the doorbell. Almost immediately, Mr. Moore opened the door.

"Matt, right on time. Fashionably early. She's upstairs pretending she's not quite ready yet." Mr. Moore leaned closer. "She's been ready for at least an hour. By the way, nice tux."

"Thank you, Mr. Moore."

"Come on in. I'm sure she knows you're here."

"Yes, Dad. I know he's here."

Stacey stood regally at the top of the stairs, one gloved hand resting on the banister, wearing a pastel blue prom gown with an empire waist band of dark blue. Her free hand held a matching dark blue clutch purse. Matching high heels completed the outfit.

"You look wonderful, Princess," her father said as she descended the stairs.

"Thank you, Daddy."

Matt just stared.

"Matt?"

Matt just stared.

"Do I . . . look all right?" she asked smoothing her dress down around her hips.

Mr. Moore elbowed Matt. "Say something kid. Don't blow it."

"You're—you're beautiful. I am totally blown away."

"Good job, Matt," Mr. Moore whispered.

"Thank you." Stacey blushed. "I wasn't sure."

"How could you not be sure? You're amazing."

Stacey stopped at the bottom of the stairs and the two drank each other in. Matt blinked first. "I got you something." He fumbled with the box and pulled out the orchard. "It's a corsage."

"Really?" Stacey teased.

"Yeah, I need to, to pin it on."

She stepped closer. Matt held up the corsage and paused.

"Need some help there, Matthew?"

"No, Mr. Moore, I've got this handled."

"Dad, could you get the boutonniere?"

"Sure, Stace."

Matt's fingers slipped under her dress's strap. He could feel her warmth, the velvet smoothness of her skin as he carefully attached the orchid and pinned it in place. Mr. Moore reappeared with a carnation wrapped in tissue paper. He handed it to his daughter. Stacey crept closer and fixed the flower to Matt's lapel. He watched. They raised their eyes simultaneously and flashed secret messages. They smiled.

"You should see the car he showed up in." Mr. Moore swept the door open.

"Wow!" Stacey exclaimed, stepping out on the porch.

Matt bounded down the porch steps and held a hand out to her. "Your carriage awaits, my lady"

"What is it?"

"It's a 1939 Studebaker. It was my grandfather's." Matt escorted her to the car and opened the door. Gracefully, she slid in. Matt closed the door and looked back up the porch where Mr. Moore stood silhouetted. He walked back up the porch.

"I have to be honest with you, Mr. Moore."

"Oh?"

"I don't have a regular driver's license. I have a farm equipment license. But I have driven a clutch like this for almost two years and I know the way to the country club by heart. My uncle's orchards are about three miles up the road from there. But if you want to drive us, I would totally understand." Matt looked up at him.

"Two years on a clutch?"

"And a learner's permit," Matt added. "But if you want to drive . . ."

Mr. Moore smiled. He looked at his daughter sitting in the car waiting. "You didn't have to tell me this, you know."

"I know. You need to know, I wouldn't drive her if I had any doubt at all that I can do it safely. Honest."

"I believe you."

"If you come to dinner with us though, you'll need to buy your own. I don't know if I have enough money for three of us."

Mr. Moore laughed, then grew serious. "You know if you do anything to hurt her, I will have to kill you."

"I know, sir. She means a lot to me, too."

The two men studied each other for a minute.

"Go."

"You're sure?"

"Go."

"Thank you, Mr. Moore."

"Thank you, young man."

Matt ran back to the car and hopped in.

"Matt, what do we do about my hair?"

"Oh crud, I forgot." He exited the car and unsnapped the tonneau cover, throwing it into the back seat. He grabbed the convertible top and pulled it forward. Sitting down next to Stacey, he pushed the top and windshield flush and latched it down. Reaching behind her he zipped up the two back windows.

"Ready." He flashed a big smile.

❈ ❈ ❈

Stacey and Matt broke from the dance, turning and clapping for the band. The lead singer stepped up to the microphone. "We're going to take a short break. There are some announcements to be made and prizes to be handed out. So cool it for about fifteen minutes and we'll be back to play the last three songs of the night."

A student emcee approached the microphone. Stacey had long since taken off her gloves and was now using them to wipe her damp forehead. "You want to step outside?" Matt asked, fanning himself with his tuxedo lapels.

"I'd love to cool off a moment."

"Come on. There's a bench on the first tee with a magnificent view."

They stepped out into the night. Floodlights splashed bright lights on the white stucco walls and red tile roof of the country club and palm trees swayed gently in the light breeze. They walked past a swimming pool where a couple sat on the diving board talking softly, then past a child's wading pool with a mosaic sunburst tiled into the bottom. Matt headed for a nearby stairway.

"Careful," Matt warned. "Looks like somebody broke a couple beer bottles." They headed down the step onto a concrete walkway. "This is the cart track. The first tee is this way."

A few steps later they found the empty bench, and sat to enjoy the view. The first fairway was a long black finger pointing ahead, bracketed by shadowy oaks. A swollen yellow moon glowed overhead in a star-studded sky. Sprinklers arched silver rainbows of water across the fairway, shimmering like diamonds. Beyond, the lights of downtown San Jose glowed like a distant tiara.

"I've never seen this before, Matt."

"I have. Sometimes if we eat dinner here, I come out here a look at the view."

"It's beautiful."

"Look." Matt pointed. "There's the green beacon on top of the Bank of America building."

"Cool."

"And that white glow over there? That's San Francisco."

She turned to Matt. "It's beautiful, simply beautiful."

"Yes, you are." Matt leaned forward and kissed her.

Back on the main stage the emcee asked, "Are you ready for the last three dances of the night?" The audience screamed its approval. "I can't hear you."

"Yes!" they roared back.

Matt and Stacey broke their kiss. "I bet that roar means that the band is coming back," she said.

"Yeah," Matt agreed reluctantly. Matt stood and helped Stacey up. "The last dance—we've got to be there."

Side by side with his hand around her hips, they ascended the steps. Two steps from the top, Stacey lurched, falling into Matt. He caught her easily. "Whoa. What happened?"

Stacey looked down, slipped her right foot out and picked up her shoe. Half of the heel was still embedded in a crack between the concrete blocks that made up the steps.

"It broke," she said, holding up the shoe.

"Can you fix it?"

"You don't *fix* heels. Look, I'll just take the other one off and do the last dance barefoot." She slipped the ruined shoe into Matt's tux pocket. She stepped slowly out of her remaining shoe. Matt watched as she wriggled her toes on the cool cement. He bent to pick up the shoe, slowly straightening. Their eyes met. Stacey smiled.

"Here." He offered the shoe to her.

She stepped forward to take it but kept going—into his arms.

"Your shoe."

"Forget about the shoe." Leaning forward she went up on tiptoes and kissed his chin. He hesitated, then wrapped his arms around her. Moonlight reflected off the swimming pool undulating silver-blue as they kissed. The strains of a slow dance surrounded them. As the music ended, the crowd in the ballroom erupted in applause and cries for "More."

Matt broke the kiss and held Stacey at arm's length. A shy smile played at his lips as his eyes devoured her. "They'll be playing the last dance next." He said handing her the shoe. He took a step back from her, one hand still out. "Watch for broken glass. I wouldn't want to ruin your nylons."

Stacey laughed. "You wouldn't?"

He took another step back, drawing her with him. "I mean I wouldn't want glass to ruin your nylons." He smiled. "Come on, I'll lead the way and watch out for glass."

"My Prince Charming."

"Prince Charming? Nah, I think of myself as more of a Zorro type. Swashbuckling, sword fighter for—

"Matt! Behind you!"

There was nothing but air under Matt's right foot. His right hand wheeled urgently trying to find balance. He let go of Stacey's hand as gravity exerted itself. Matt landed, calf-deep, in the wading pool. Helplessly he looked up at Stacey.

Her hands covered her mouth as she tried to suppress a laugh.

"Great. Some Prince Charming I turned out to be."

"Zorro." She put down her shoe, then straightened. She stepped to the side of the pool then gracefully stepped in. Putting her hands on his shoulder she beamed at him.

"I've ruined everything haven't I?

"The last dance has started." She whispered, snuggling up to his chest.

"You want to dance here?"

"Yes." She nuzzled against him as they began to sway to the music. "I hope it's a long dance."

"Me, too."

Cheek to cheek they danced the last dance slowly and languidly, not stopping when the music ended.

Chapter Thirty-One

Her head was leaning against his shoulder as the Studebaker coasted to a stop before Stacey's house. Matt stepped on the brake, his shoes still soggy. He turned off the car and pulled the hand brake, glancing at the well-lit house. Reaching up, he unlatched the convertible roof and folded it down, then settled back into his seat. "Every light is on," he said.

"Oh, yeah, that's my dad."

"You think he's up?"

"Absolutely."

"Is he watching?'

"I have no doubt."

Matt looked up and down the block. Moonlight filtered through sycamore leaves, creating a patchwork of light and dark puddles. The lights from the Moores' house splashed long shadows across the yard.

"If he's watching, that puts a crimp on the goodnight kiss, doesn't it?" he asked, turning to Stacey.

Stacey scooted closer. "Absolutely not." She leaned closer still.

"You sure he's not going to come running out with a shotgun or something?"

"Dad's a little more realistic than that," she murmured. Reaching out, she snuggled closer, lips puckering. "Now kiss me, you fool."

Matt leaned toward her. Lips met, welcoming, soft, questing. The touch of their lips drove all other sounds, all other sensations, away.

"Don't make me repeat myself. Step out of the car," a strange voice said. Red lights strobed across the car, reflecting off of darkened houses.

"What?"

"You heard the sarge, kid. Get out of the car."

"Officer, we weren't doing anything wrong," Matt said, both hands on the steering wheel.

"Her parents might have something to say about this."

"Did Mr. Moore call the police because I kissed his daughter? You guys got here really fast."

"My father wouldn't do anything like that," Stacey said, looking toward the house.

"I need to see some ID," Sarge said.

Matt reached around and pulled out his wallet. "My name is Matt Connors. I live around the corner from here. I don't get it. What is this all about?"

"This is just a student ID, son. You have a driver's license?"

"Well . . ." He handed a card to the sergeant.

The officer scanned it with his flashlight. "This is a farm permit."

"Yes, sir."

"That's not a tractor, son."

"What's going on here?" came another voice from the darkened street.

"Daddy!"

"What's this about, Stace?"

"No idea. They just showed up after . . ."

Her father smiled. "He kissed you."

"And you are?" Sarge asked.

"I'm Kevin Moore. I'm this girl's father. And I am still wondering what this is all about."

"We're trying to determine the identity of this young man and whether he has a valid driver's license." Sarge turned back to Matt. "As I said, this isn't a tractor."

"Sir, the license is for farm vehicles. This is, or was, a farm vehicle. My grandfather used it all the time on his ranch. It has a similar engine as most tractors. Clutch. Prime the pump. A PTO and most important, a hitch. He used this to pull trailers of hay and feed and do all sorts of farm work."

"It's pretty impressive," the other officer said, examining the interior of the car by flashlight.

"Thank you, Rossi," the sergeant said. "Matthew. Even if this *is* a farm vehicle, this is not a proper—"

"I also have this." Matt handed over a carefully folded piece of paper.

"This is a learner permit. You need an adult in the car when you drive for this to be valid."

"I—"

"He had an adult in the car when he was driving," Mr. Moore volunteered.

"You weren't in the car when we got here."

"Really, officer, how could the kids say a proper good bye with me sitting in the back seat? I planned on giving them a few minutes alone. Then I was going to flick the porch light on and off to let them know it was time."

"So, you were with them the whole time?"

"Every dance needs chaperones."

Sarge handed back Matt his papers.

"Now," Mr. Moore said, "what is this really about? Certainly not over some smooching in the front seat of a car after a dance."

"We have a report that this car is stolen."

"Stolen!" Matt cried. "No way."

"The call came about an hour ago."

"From who? Don't answer that, it was my mother, wasn't it?"

"Do we have a name for who reported this, Rossi?"

Rossi thumbed through his notebook. "It's a Mrs. Connors, Yolanda Connors."

"My mother."

"Is the car stolen, Matt?" Mr. Moore asked.

"Of course not, Mr. Moore. I would never take Stacey out in a stolen car." Matt turned toward his date. "Stacey, can you look in the glove compartment and pull out the two envelopes there please. Is that okay, officer?"

"Go ahead, young lady." Sarge pointed the flashlight beam at the glove box. Stacey pulled out two envelopes and handed them over to the officer.

"What am I looking at?"

"The first envelope contains the title for the car. It shows that is a vintage collector car and it shows that my father and I are co-owners. So technically, it's partially my car and I can't steal what is already mine."

"Hmmm. And the other?"

"It's a letter signed by my father giving me permission to drive the car."

"That makes things kind of confusing doesn't it, Sarge?" Rossi asked.

Stacey stepped out of the car and joined her father.

"Yes. We have a report that this is car is a stolen vehicle and yet it seems that you have paperwork that indicates that it's not."

"We can clear this up. I live around the corner. We can go and talk to my mom," Matt said.

"Can you drive this, Rossi?"

"I've driven a clutch before, Sarge. But I've never had any car where you gotta prime the pump or with a manual choke."

"Then you'll need to drive it, son. We will follow."

"Don't I need an adult with me?"

"Quite right. Rossi, you'll ride with him."

"Sure thing."

"Can I say good bye to my . . . girlfriend?"

"I owe you one, kid. Say goodbye."

After reaching into the backseat, Matt walked over to Stacey and her father.

"Thank you, Mr. Moore," he said quietly.

"No problem, Matt. Sorry your evening had to end this way."

"Yeah, Mom's a peach."

Handing Stacey's broken shoes over to Mr. Moore, Matt turned to Stacey. "It was an amazing evening. Hope you enjoyed it."

"Every minute."

They kissed chastely under the watching eyes of parent and police. "Are we still biking to Alum Rock Park tomorrow?" Matt asked.

"Absolutely, but not real early." Stacey yawned.

"See you then."

Turning Matt headed for the car and got in. He looked at Rossi. Rossi turned and waited until the Sarge got into the car.

"Show me how this beauty works."

Matt started the car with Rossi watching intently. Headlights blazed on as he released the hand brake. Matt turned to Rossi. "It gets a little windy. You might want to hold onto your hat." With a slight jerk, he eased off the clutch and they were off.

Matt pulled into the driveway and pulled the hand brake. Sarge pulled up in the driveway behind them and got out of the police car. "This your house? No lights?"

"I don't know why she turned them all off." Getting out of the car, Matt walked over to the garage and tried to turn the latch. "She locked the garage, too." Matt turned to the policemen. "There are light switches just inside the courtyard."

"I'll follow you, Matthew. Rossi, stay here with the car."

Matt open the courtyard gate and stepped to the side door of the garage. He flipped on the lights. "She locked the side door too."

"And that's out of character for your mother?"

"It's hard to say what's out of character with my mother, sir."

"I see."

Sarge knocked on the front door. "Mrs. Connors? This is Sergeant Liotti. I need you to open up, ma'am." The house remained silent. "Mrs. Connors, San Jose Police Department. I need you to open the door." He turned to Matt. "Do you have a key?"

"No, she hid the keys. And the key chain for the Studebaker didn't have a house key on it."

"She hid the keys?"

"My mom can be a little . . . possessive."

"Hmmm." He rang the bell and knocked again. "Mrs. Connors, we need to clear up a police report. Please answer the door."

The lights in the courtyard flared to life as his mother opened the door a crack.

"Thank you. Mrs. Connors?"

Matt's mother nodded silently.

"I'm Police Sergeant Enzo Liotti and I am following up on a report we got on a stolen car."

Again she nodded.

"Mrs. Connors, is this your son?"

She opened the door slightly farther and looked at her son a moment. "Yes."

"Then I guess I'm a little confused here, ma'am."

"He took the car without permission. That's stealing, isn't it?"

"That is how we usually define stealing, but there are some complications. It seems that his father made him part-owner of the car, so taking it wasn't really stealing. He also seems to have permission, in writing, from his father to drive the car."

"When did that happen, Matty?"

"About a week ago, Mom."

"I didn't know."

"So you see, ma'am, we really don't have a stolen vehicle, if you can confirm for me that—" he glanced at the letters in his hands, "Douglas Connors is your husband and legal owner of the vehicle."

She said nothing.

"Come on, Mom."

"Yes, Douglas Connors is my *husband*."

"Does he own the car, the Studebaker?"

"Yes." She clipped the word like a broken bone.

"Then I guess we are done here. There is no stolen car."

"Thanks, Sergeant Liotti," Matt said.

"So you're not going to do anything?" his mother asked.

"Well, ma'am, if his father gave him permission to drive a car he is co-owner of, I don't see that a crime has been committed."

"He doesn't have a valid license."

"A Mr. Moore, the girl's father, says he drove with them to the dance and back, so his permit was all within the letter of the law. Again, ma'am, there is no crime here, except—it is a crime to knowingly file a false report. It wastes time we can be using to investigate real criminal activity." He looked at Yolanda through the narrow gap of the door. "So I'd like to chalk this up as a misunderstanding and close the book on it. Agreed?"

"It's all right with me, Sergeant Liotti," Matt said.

"And you, Mrs. Connors?"

Matt's mom looked from the officer to her son. "Fine." She slammed the door and the courtyard lights were gone.

"That went well." Liotti said, flicking his flashlight back on. "I don't envy you going in there."

"She'll calm down—in a week or two." Together they walked down the driveway and to the cars. Matt fished for his keys. "Thanks again, sergeant."

"Good luck with the dragon-lady—" The policemen stepped into their cruiser and backed down the driveway.

Matt waved and headed for the garage door. Grasping the handle, he jerked. Nothing.

"I forgot." He patted the car on the hood. "I suppose you'll be okay out here for one night." He headed for the courtyard and to the front door and jiggled the knob. Locked.

"Mom. Hey, Mom. Let me in?"

He rang the doorbell and pounded on the door.

"Mom, come on. Enough is enough. Let me in."

His pounding echoed in the silent house. Matt walked over to the St. Francis statue that hung on a wall of the courtyard. He lifted the statue and felt under it. No key.

"Crap. Mom, come on, let me in."

He started walking around the house checking windows and the back door.

"This isn't funny, Mom. Let me in." Nothing. "Son of a bitch, this is so stupid. Let me in."

Matt waited, but there was nothing. He checked under St. Francis again, still no key.

"Fine. Just stinking peachy." He headed to the car and jumped in, gunned the engine and backed out of the driveway. He glanced at Gianinni's house and back in the direction of the Moores' home. Shaking his head, he turned and headed off.

Chapter Thirty-Two

Matt stirred just as Sister Tomas pushed through the large wooden doors from the foyer of the church into the nave. Morning sunlight poured through the eastern bank of stained-glass windows, splashing the interior of the church with an artist's palette of vivid colors. The red flame of the sanctuary lamp danced over its station above the altar. Matt watched as Sister Tomas stepped to a table at the back of the rows of pews and straightened a pile of holy cards.

Shielding her eyes from the bright color pouring in, she turned a brass latch and tilted the stained-glass window outward. A cool breeze crept in, tugging at the veil of her habit. She crossed herself and paused, looking around the church as if uncertain.

"Hello?" Her voice echoed in the solemn vastness of the nave. "Father? Is anyone there?"

Sister canted open the third window and moved to the fourth. Glorious shades of brilliant gold and brown poured through the image of the Sacred Heart, patchworking colors onto her white wimple, tattooing the rich red heart crowned with thorns there. She crossed herself, kissing her fingers after saying amen and gazed at the ruby heart of Jesus imprisoned within the glass art. Again she turned, walking from the windows between two pews, raising a kneeler as she went. She stepped into the center of the church, searching the shadows. "Hello?"

She reached the first pew and stopped. "Matt? Matthew Connors, what are you doing here?"

Matt yawned. "Good morning, Sister." He lifted his head from the pile of cassocks it had been pillowed in and rubbed his eyes. "What are you doing here?"

"Matthew Connors, you are sleeping in church. How did you get in here, Matt?"

He nodded toward the sanctuary window. "The latch in there hasn't been fixed in years. We've told Father about it. I stepped on a box and boosted myself through. These pews are really hard."

"Why are you here, Matthew? You went to the dance last night, didn't you?"

Matt nodded. "Yes. It was a wonderful night."

"And it ended here? Is Stacey sleeping on some other pew?"

"No! I left her off at her house last night. That's when things went really wrong—and before you ask, nothing happened between Stacey and me. Oh, well, other than dancing the last dance in a swimming pool."

"Matt, were you drinking? I heard there was alcohol at the dance last night."

"No, Sister. I didn't drink anything last night. How did you hear about the beer?"

"Ada's father called pretty upset about the behavior of some of the young men at the dance."

Matt said, "There was beer. But I didn't know anything about it until I saw a bunch of broken beer bottles in the pool area. I didn't have anything to drink and neither did Stacey."

"Do you know who did?"

Matt sat up straighter, pulling the unbuttoned tux around him. "I don't know who brought the beer. The only person I saw with a beer was Carlotti."

"Carlotti. Nobody else? So, Matthew, tell me what happened."

He did.

"So you weren't charged by the police?"

"I think meeting my mother helped them believe me."

"I'm sorry that happened. What was she thinking?"

"I think she was trying to do anything to ruin the night. But, you know what? It didn't. It was a glorious night. The best night of my life."

"Pool and all?"

"Yes, Sister. Pool and all. And when I got home, the garage was still locked and Mom had taken the outside key. It was almost two in the morning. I couldn't go to Aunt Rose's. She'd never let me in that late." Matt looked straight into her eyes. "Where else could I go?"

Chapter Thirty-Four

Matt pulled into his driveway, pulling up the parking brake on the Studebaker. He hopped out of the car and tried the garage latch.

"Still locked." He stepped over to the car and pulled out his suit coat, pulling it on as he walked through the courtyard, He opened the door and stepped in.

"Where's your tie?" his mother barked.

"In my pocket."

"Good. I'm not into paying for a lost tie."

"It's in my pocket and what are you talking about? You're not paying for anything. I rented this tuxedo with my own money. You wouldn't even take me to the store."

"Where were you all last night?"

"Does it matter?"

"Of course it matters. Where the hell did you spend the night?"

"Why?"

"Why?" She repeated the question, outraged.

"Yeah, why? You locked me out of the house. You locked me out of the garage. It was the middle of the night. Where did you expect me to go? Why'd you lock me out?"

"You embarrassed me in front of the police."

"I embarrassed you? The police arrested me in front of my girlfriend's house while we were saying goodbye. In front of Mr. Morgan."

"I was concerned about your safety."

"That's a lie. I'm a good driver. In fact, you know I'm a great driver. Even your sister trusts me to drive your mother around."

"I was concerned."

"Then why did you wait until ten thirty to call the police? If you were so concerned, why didn't you drive us to the dance? You could have done a lot of things besides call the police."

"I—"

"I don't want to hear it, Mom. This had nothing to do with safety. Nothing."

"I still demand to know where you were last night. Did you sleep with that little *puttana*?"

"No."

"I don't believe you. Where did you go?"

"Do you really want to know? I went to church. I snuck through the sanctuary window and slept on a pew."

"You expect me to believe that?"

"I don't really care, Mom. But if you don't believe me there was a witness."

"That girl. You slept in the church with that girl."

"Jesus. Mom, you are so willing to believe the worst. No, I didn't sleep with the *puttana* on a pew of the church."

"Don't use words like that."

"Whatever. The witness was Sister Tomas. She found me on the first pew of the church this morning. Since you don't believe me, ask her." Matt stepped past his mother heading for his room. "You called the cops on me, Mom."

"Where are you going?'

"To my room to change. I'm taking that girl to Alum Rock Park. We're going to swim in the hot pools."

"No, you're not. You've got chores."

"They can wait."

"I said no, Matty."

"Why?"

"Because I said so."

Matt paused and turned. "That would have worked, once."

"Don't you *dare* walk away from me." She snatched up a wooden spoon and swung.

"Ouch. Mom, come on. Knock it off." Matt backed into a corner between the refrigerator and the cabinets as his mother hit him with the spoon. He began to laugh.

Matt smiled at his mother as the spoon bounced off his shoulder. "I just realized," he said, intercepting the spoon, "That this doesn't really hurt . . . You can't hurt me anymore."

He plucked the spoon from his mother and easily broke it in two. He tossed the pieces onto the kitchen counter. Yolanda swung impotently with her fists. He grabbed both her hands and held them.

"*You will never hit me again*," he said forcefully, face to face. "Do you understand me? You will *never* do this to me again. *Ever.*"

"Are you going to hit me, too?"

"I am not my father." He released her and stepped out of the corner. "I'm going to change and leave."

"What about my car? The battery is still out."

"Shouldn't you have thought of that before you sabotaged the car?"

"Matty—Matt, I need the car."

"I'll take care of it." Matt stepped into the bedroom. Minutes later he stepped out in cutoffs and a t-shirt.

"Matt. Really? Cut-offs?"

"Yes, Mom. Cut-offs. We're going swimming. Where is the battery?"

"In the fireplace."

Matt laughed. "I'll give you credit. That's one place I wouldn't have looked."

Five minutes later, the family car roared to life. Yolanda stepped into the courtyard. Matt emerged from the garage with his bike. "It's ready."

"Thanks."

"I'll be back sometime after dinner."

"Matt?"

He swung his leg up over the bike and turned toward his mother.

"On your way home, pick up some eggs."

About the Author

Mark has been an Italian all his life. Half-Italian really, there was a glitch in the family tree. I addition to being a writer, an actor, and a singer he has also been an accomplished teacher for about thirty years now. He currently reside in the Pacific Northwest.